EMERALD

Jeff Lovell

TotalRecall Publications, Inc.

TotalRecall Publications, Inc.
1103 Middlecreek
Friendswood, Texas 77546
281-992-3131 281-482-5390 Fax
www.totalrecallpress.com

ISBN: 978-1-59095-081-4
UPC: 6-43977-40810-5
Library of Congress Control Number: 2014945593

Printed in the United States of America with simultaneous printings in Australia, Canada, and United Kingdom.

FIRST EDITION
1 2 3 4 5 6 7 8 9 10

This is a work of fiction. The characters, names, events, views, and subject matter of this book are either the author's imagination or are used fictitiously. Any similarity or resemblance to any real people, real situations or actual events is purely coincidental and not intended to portray any person, place, or event in a false, disparaging or negative light.

To Laurie Rossi of Fairview, New Mexico, a colleague for many years and the editor of all my books. No one knows grammar and syntax better than she and she's been invaluable to me as a friend and expert.

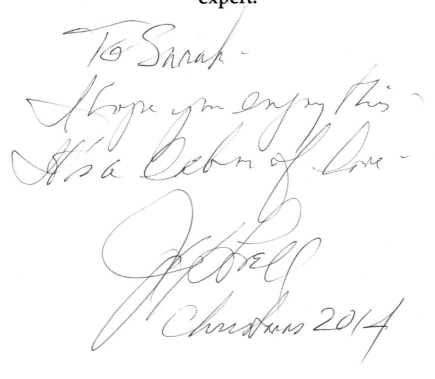

To Sarah —
I hope you enjoy this —
It's a labor of love —

Christmas 2014

Award Winning Author Jeff Lovell

 is a native Chicagoan, with 3 degrees from the University of Illinois and an earned doctorate from Vanderbilt University. Jeff taught high school writing and literature for thirty three years and sponsored the school paper, Student Council and several other activities. He ran the drama program at two high schools, teaching and directing and designing sets, lighting and costumes. His specialty in his career focused on Shakespeare. Since he retired from education, Jeff has served as a theatre and film critic for a television station and appears frequently to review theatre and literature.

Part 1

MONSTER

1715

CHAPTER ONE
The Atlantic Ocean,
off the coast of Ocracoke,
North Carolina

All conversation, whistling, joking, and even movement stopped as if *Emerald* had been encased in ice. Even the creaking of the rigging on the two-masted bark seemed to have ceased.

Josiah Fixx, eighteen years old, looked up from the carpenter's chest he had been struggling to repair. *What could have scared everyone?* he wondered.

He yelled at a cabin boy as the youngster ran along the deck. "Willem," he said. "What happened?" Willem, a ten-year-old orphan, stopped and turned to his friend.

"Oh, Josiah. Captain sent me to look for you."

Josiah groaned. Greyson always sent him aloft when trouble arose. He often told the crew that his young carpenter's mate had quick wits and the sharpest eyes of anyone aboard.

While pleased that the captain thought well of him, heights terrified the young carpenter's mate. He resisted going aloft as much as he could.

Josiah hurried to the deck and snapped to attention in front of Greyson, the captain and owner of *Emerald*. "Sir."

"Fixx," growled the stout little man, whose twitching side whiskers betrayed his nervousness. "Go aloft, if you please. Take the glass. See what you make of that ship yonder."

"Sir," said Josiah. As he climbed to the crow's nest, he kept his eyes on the top of the mast, not daring to look down.

Willing himself to be calm, he trained the glass on the

horizon. He made out a large three-masted ship, armed with many cannon. *Emerald* would have no chance in a fight against this monster. "Sir," he yelled.

"Aye," replied the captain.

"French Guineaman by her lines, sir. I count forty-nine cannons. She's heading toward us."

No one answered, but Fixx knew what the officers were thinking. A French warship this close to Carolina? Strange, indeed.

"Colors?" bellowed Greyson.

"None as yet, sir."

"Stay sharp. Watch her."

"Sir."

Josiah kept the glass fixed on the ship as it continued on an intercept course. In what seemed mere moments, it had closed to within a half mile. "Gun ports just opened, sir!"

"Run the guns out, Mr. Stallings," Greyson barked. "Beat to quarters, if you please." Josiah heard the drum begin and saw the gun crews rushing to ready their weapons.

Fixx wondered. Why would a French ship attack a British ship this close to the Carolina shore? What could the French captain be thinking?

He watched the flagless mainmast of the huge ship, expecting to see the French colors any minute. He saw a banner raised on the quarterdeck. As it unfurled Fixx almost dropped the glass.

The center of the black flag displayed a spectral, silver-white figure with four horns. The demon held a cup in its bony right hand. A spear in the left hand pointed toward a heart. Three enormous drops of blood fell from a wound in the heart.

He recovered enough to scream, "Pirate!"

Josiah saw puffs of smoke from the guns. The thunder of cannon fire from the gun decks of the enormous French ship drowned out Greyson's orders. *Emerald* rocked as three cannonballs slammed into her side. The mainmast quivered and Josiah clutched at the mast in terror.

The pirate cannons lashed out again with extraordinary swiftness. The enemy ship boasted a disciplined crew.

The chase began. Josiah shouted down over the confusion on the deck to describe the pirate ship's course. For more than an hour, Greyson tried to tack toward shore in hopes of finding a cove in which to retreat.

The pirate ship closed on *Emerald*. Its cannons thundered again and again. Captain Greyson ordered the cannons on *Emerald* to fire, but the tiny eight-pounders proved useless against the mighty enemy.

The smoke of the gunpowder and the deafening blasts of the cannon made communications impossible. Josiah, nauseous with vertigo and terror, tightened his grip on the mainmast. He felt trapped in the tiny basket. The stench of exploded gunpowder, the whistling of the pirate cannonballs and the rough sandpaper scratch of the ship's lines in his hands registered but diminished in the fear he felt.

The huge pirate closed to within a hundred yards. The sound of the pirate's fusilade now changed. Its cannons began to fire lengths of chain at the sails. Within moments the mainsail of *Emerald* hung limp, cut to rags.

Josiah heard a different sound as the port side of *Emerald* reverberated. The pirate had changed to firing grape shot.

Josiah peered down at the deck of *Emerald*. Several men lay dead, their bodies in grotesque positions, their blood staining *Emerald's* deck. Many had been hit with shrapnel or grape shot or lethal nails or spikes. Screams of terror rose up to him.

A sudden jolt wrested Josiah's grip off the mast. He regained his balance and peered out of the basket. The mainmast had been hit. It began to lean to the starboard side.

Josiah, head swimming with vertigo mixed with terror, wrapped himself around the mast as best he could.

Emerald slammed to a halt with a crunch, forced onto a sand bar. Men, cannons, ropes, and gear all jumbled together.

The mainmast whipped forward and snapped. Josiah's white-knuckled grip on the shattered spar wrenched loose. He pinwheeled through the air toward the sand bar. The ocean zoomed up toward him. He drew a deep breath, ducked his head and wrapped his arms around his knees.

Josiah hit the ocean hard, feet first. He kept his wits somehow as he plummeted downward. His feet hit the sandy bottom in some ten feet of water. He pushed off, leaving his shoes behind. He fought his way to the surface, trying to hold his breath, his eyes stinging, choking on the profound saltiness.

To his shock, he saw a gnarled hand in the water, stretching toward him. A whispery voice in his mind said, "Take my hand. And hide when you reach the ship. You must be safe."

Baffled, Josiah reached out and clutched at the hand. He discovered that he hadn't seized a hand after all. Rather, he'd grabbed a rope dangling in the water. He clung with both hands.

To his relief, it held tight. Josiah pulled himself up hand-over-hand. He broke the surface, gasping for air.

He found that he had grabbed onto a line from the shattered main mast of *Emerald*. He pulled himself back to the crippled ship. Reaching the side, he grasped the edge of a hole made by a cannonball as it blasted through the small vessel. He climbed the rope to the deck and peeked over the top, careful to remain out of sight.

Holding onto the rope, Josiah found a foothold that allowed him to remain off the side of the ship but hidden from sight. He surveyed the damage, the stench of blood filling his nostrils. His heart wrenched at the sight of the mangled bodies of his shipmates.

The pirate ship, which had not run aground, had dropped anchor off the stern of *Emerald*. The ship's boats came alongside and pirates swarmed aboard.

A gigantic man, naked to the waist, leaped to the main deck of *Emerald*, brandishing a cutlass and a pistol. Josiah thought at first that the pirate had set his hat on fire. As he looked closer, Josiah saw that the smoke came from burning bits of slowmatch which the pirate had twisted into his hair and flowing beard.

The pirate stood at least six and a half feet tall with broad shoulders and long arms. His bare chest was taut and muscular. A sash of scarlet silk wrapped twice around his waist and then draped over one shoulder.

Three pistols hung in the sash and he'd shoved another into the belt. As he advanced he tucked the pistol into the sash at his waist. He clenched a knife between his teeth and slid a cutlass into a scabbard next to his right hand.

Perhaps two dozen of his men followed him, guns drawn and cutlasses ready. The outmanned and outgunned *Emerald* had fought with courage against his assault, but now the surviving crew stood with their hands raised. The monstrous leader appeared dismayed at the lack of resistance.

Greyson's first mate, a tall, thin man with a prominent Adam's apple, stood next to the chubby little captain. As quick as thought, the monster whipped the knife out of his mouth and threw it into the first mate's chest.

Fixx, too shocked to move, watched the giant stroll forward. He heard the creak of the deck planking and realized that the huge villain weighed perhaps double what he did. The pirate yanked his knife from the dead man's chest. After wiping the blade on the man's shirt, he stood to face Greyson. The captain of *Emerald* stood dumbstruck and trembling, his face gray with horror.

"By my soul, Captain," rumbled the monster. "'Twas a hot bit of scrimmage, indeed. Faith, let us drink to the ladies. Bring 'em up on deck, lads." He sounded as cheerful as if he had come to pay a social call.

Some of the giant's crew herded the passengers up onto the main deck while others began transferring *Emerald's* cargo to his vessel.   Fixx saw the pirates lifting liquor and packages and bolts of cloth from the hold.

"Such a day."   The pirate captain laughed.   "Our rum is all out, my company quite sober.   Damned confusion.   Mutinous talk, sir," he said, clapping the pudgy little captain of *Emerald* on his back.   "So I looked sharp for a prize, and we spied your valiant ship."

He broke off.   Fixx saw his eye fall on a beautiful red-headed woman.   Tall and statuesque, she stood with an imperial tilt to her head.   He seized her and kissed her, pawing her body.   Then he grasped her neck.

Fixx thought the pirate intended to strangle her.   Instead the monster unclasped a necklace and held it up.   Emeralds in a white gold setting glittered in the sunlight.   "Very beautiful." He turned as if to go.

The woman, defiance in her eyes, spoke in a deep, resonant, commanding voice.   Her emerald green eyes flashed, framed by the curtain of deep red hair.   "Nehushtan."   The giant turned back to her in amazement.   "Yes, I know you, Snake."   She sneered, taunting the pirate without fear.   "You will never profit from this day.   That which you pillage here will bring death and agony to you and to all who would prosper from it."

In the horrified silence that ensued, the woman's words hung in the air.   The pirate chief stood still, his face twisting into a vicious scowl.   In one fluid motion, he drew his cutlass and slashed at the woman.

The pirate's sword would have beheaded the woman in an instant.

But the woman no longer stood there.   Josiah had to choke back a scream.   She vanished as the flame vanishes when blown out from a candle.

Everything stopped.   People stared at the place where the

woman had stood. "What in the name. . ."gasped the captain, who had almost fallen to the deck when his swipe with the sword failed to connect.

In a moment, the giant recovered. He forced a laugh and barked orders.

Josiah retched, twisting his eyes from the scene. When he looked back, he saw several men continuing to remove the cargo. Other pirates came up on deck with personal belongings from the cabins of the passengers. They took rings, money, jewels and anything else of value.

A crewman hauled a fearful passenger before the huge pirate. The crewman yanked the chubby little man's left hand up to show his chieftain a beautiful ruby-and-gold ring. The crewman sneered that the passenger could not remove the ring. The pirate laid the man's hand on a hatch cover as the passenger pleaded and begged for mercy.

The giant's cutlass flashed. The man screamed in terror and pain as the pirate's sword severed his fingers from his hand. The sailor pushed the man's torso onto the hatch. Again the pirate slashed with the cutlass. The severed head rolled toward Josiah, who saw the look of horror frozen on the murdered man's face. The pirates pitched the dead passenger's head and body over the side.

Fixx stayed hidden, and glanced at the pirate ship. He saw a beautiful girl with copper-colored hair, perhaps fifteen or sixteen years old, standing by the ship's wheel.

What could she be doing aboard that nightmare ship? She must be a prisoner.

Her gaze, roaming over the scene, locked onto Josiah. Her eyes widened as if in recognition. He gasped as their eyes locked. *I think I know her. How could that be possible?*

He smiled and pressed a finger to his lips. Fixx released the rope and dropped back into the ocean.

Josiah swam the short distance to the pirate ship and pulled himself up on a trailing rope. He found himself next to the ship's wheel. The girl, unguarded, stood by the wheel, looking toward the opposite side of the ship, where she had last seen him. He hissed.

The girl turned and beamed when she saw the young man. He vaulted the railing and crossed to her. Kneeling beside her, he hid as best he could.

"Gareth," she whispered, smiling and joyful. "I knew you would come."

When he heard her voice, he knew for sure who she was. He'd known her all his life. "Viviane? How can this..."

Her face fell. "They'll kill you," she hissed at him. "You can't stay."

"Viviane. What ship is this?"

"*Queen Anne's Revenge,* Captain Teach."

"What is your real name?" he asked.

"Prudence Lutrelle. From Charleston."

"I'm Josiah Fixx. What are you doing here?"

"Captain Teach is my husband."

"What!" Josiah's mouth dropped.

She nodded. "He bought me from my mother."

Josiah's head swam. He stammered, "Your mother *sold* you to that fiend?"

"My father died of the fever," she told him, her chin trembling. "He left us without much money. Teach offered her cash for me. I fought the marriage as best I could. Captain Teach's face will have four long scars on it forever." She showed him her long fingernails.

"Come with me. We can swim to shore." He pointed to the sandy beach of Okracoke Island.

"You can swim?" she asked in some surprise.

"Yes," he said. "I grew up in Virginia, not far from the ocean. I learned to swim before I could walk, I think." He peered at her. "Can you swim?"

"Yes, but I cannot get away." She held up her arms to reveal the chains that fettered her to the ship's wheel. "Please, Josiah. Don't let them see you. You cannot help me."

He jerked at the chains. They wouldn't budge.

"Josiah," she said, tears running on her cheeks, her voice trembling. He had the sense that she was memorizing his face. "I can protect myself in ways you cannot imagine. I plan to escape at my first opportunity. I shall try to find you. But then we'll have to hide. I'll be implicated in his crimes."

He nodded, tears of hopelessness rising.

She took his hand and looked into his eyes. Josiah felt the eyes look through his as if searching for his soul. Something happened in his mind. They held hands and fell together through a vortex of colors and light. Then—

They stood together in a graveyard, not on a ship. They had known each other all their lives. But they had only seen one another in dreams until this moment.

"Viviane. Please. We have to get you away."

"I knew I'd meet you some day. I prayed for the moment," she said. **"Now, here I am trapped, unable to escape."**

"I have to help you. Please."

"No. You must get away. Let me help you."

She looked through his eyes into his mind. He felt a strange sensation, as if small sparks were igniting in his mind.

He felt an inexplicable peace, a gentleness, and compassion. His anger slowed and his fear disappeared.

In the next instant they stood again on the quarterdeck of a pirate ship. "What—" he stammered.

"Gareth," she said. "Please help me. Here. Take this and keep it safe." She worked a ring off her finger and slid the ring onto his little finger. The ring fit him as if made for him. "You hold a great treasure. My grandmother gave it to me."

"No," he said. "Prudence. I can find a tool and pry the lock..."

"No. You can't. They shall return at any moment. You have to get away while you can."

"But—"

"Please. Pledge to me that you'll protect the ring. We will see each other again, I promise. You will give it back to me then."

He nodded, staring at the ring. A wide solid gold band, it had a large diamond and two radiant emeralds flanking the diamond. He saw what looked like letters inscribed around the stone.

"No," she said in response to his silent question, "I don't know what it says. Promise to keep it safe. Look for me. I'll find you, I promise."

He agreed. He bent and embraced her. She pressed herself against him. He kissed her on the lips. She returned the kiss, as if it were the most natural thing to do in these horrid circumstances. "Viviane," he said, emotions running high.

Hearing a shout, he turned his head and saw three pirates running toward him. Josiah heard a pistol shot and felt a ball whistle close to his head. With a last smile at Prudence, he ran to the side of the ship and plunged into the ocean. He swam back to *Emerald*, staying close to the keel of the ships to avoid being seen.

He watched as the pirate crew returned to *Queen Anne's Revenge*. Josiah hid until the evil ship raised anchor, hoisted sail, and departed. Then he climbed aboard *Emerald* again.

Bodies littered the deck. The captain, the first mate, the crew, and all the passengers had been stabbed, shot, butchered, or maimed. The pirates had looted the stranded ship and massacred everyone. Blood covered the deck.

Josiah saw one person moving on the quarterdeck. He found Willem the cabin boy lying wounded with a deep, bleeding gash across his chest. *They kill children?* thought Josiah. Willem looked up at Josiah with dull, unfocused eyes and gasped, "Papa?"

Fixx cradled the boy in his arms. He said, "No. It's me, Josiah. Be brave, Willem. You're going to be all right."

"Don't worry about me, Papa," Willem said with difficulty. "I'm not scared."

Josiah choked. "Of course you aren't, Willem." He hugged the orphan boy and stroked his hair, trying to hold the boy's life inside of him.

Willem, sighing, went limp. His head lolled to the right. He gave a final gasp and his terrified young soul found freedom to join his parents and run free among the stars.

Fixx carried the boy to a bloody hatch cover and wrapped him in scraps of canvas. Murmuring a prayer, he dropped the little body over the side.

Fixx looked off toward the eastern horizon. The evil ship had almost vanished at the horizon. He strained his eyes to catch one more glimpse of the green-eyed girl.

The rest of that day, Josiah wrapped the mangled and broken bodies. He pushed them over the side and said prayers for them, horror overwhelming him. He refused to think of the dreadfulness of what he was doing. Instead he focused on accomplishing the chore.

When he finished the funerals, he set about mopping up the blood, trying to stay busy and wear himself out. He ate a sparse meal of biscuit and hardtack that had been overlooked in the hold. At last exhausted by his labors, he fell into a haunted sleep on the quarterdeck, plagued with hideous nightmares.

In the morning, Fixx saw a sail on the southeast horizon. He loaded a charge into one of the cannon and set it off, trying to signal the ship. To his relief, the vessel turned toward him.

The crew of H. M. S. *Excalibur* pulled alongside *Emerald*. At high tide, the crew of the British ship rigged a towline. The warship pulled the derelict off the sandbar and took *Emerald* in tow.

A crewman escorted Fixx to the warship. Josiah saluted the ship's colors, then the captain, a tall, handsome man with a kind face. "Fixx, sir. Carpenter's mate of *Emerald*."

"I am Captain Gordon," said the man, shaking Josiah's hand. "What happened, Fixx?"

Josiah whispered one word. "Blackbeard."

Gordon shook his head, a grim look of fury on his face. "He ran the ship aground, did he?" Josiah nodded. "Yes," said Gordon. "He knows the waters off the American coast as well as anyone ever has."

Josiah related the story of the attack, the man with the ruby ring, and the theft of *Emerald's* goods. He told the story of the beautiful woman and the emerald and white gold necklace.

"After they looted the ship, they killed everyone," Fixx concluded. Someone pressed a dram of rum into his hand. He nodded thanks and drank a little. He explained how he'd managed to hide from the attack.

"You tell an all too common story," Gordon shrugged. "Do you know anything about Teach?"

"Somewhat," returned Josiah. Captain Greyson had told him the story of the pirate.

Captain Benjamin Hornigold, the leader of the pirate fleet operating off the American Atlantic coast, captured the former French slave ship named *Concorde* a few years ago. He then gave the ship to his chief lieutenant Edward Teach, who renamed it *Queen Anne's Revenge.* The world knew its brutal captain as Blackbeard.

The captain of *Excalibur* nodded. "I've been trying to run him to ground for a year," Gordon said, taking Fixx's arm and drawing the young man up to the quarterdeck. "He was born in England and baptized Edward Drummond. However, he changed his name to Teach once he came of age in the New World."

He explained that though *Revenge* was a common name for a

pirate ship, Blackbeard's huge vessel couldn't be called typical. Teach had refitted the huge ship with extra cannon and sail.

Josiah's eyes shifted to the horizon, where he had last seen the nightmare ship. He thought about Prudence. He looked at Captain Gordon and tried to speak.

To his shame, he began to cry in front of the captain. Tears ran down the young man's cheeks and he fell to his knees, overwhelmed with the terror of the last twenty-four hours.

Gordon knelt next to Josiah. The captain placed an arm around the young man's shoulders as Josiah covered his face with his hands.

Excalibur towed *Emerald* to a shipyard in Charleston, where Josiah found employment as a shipwright. His first job was to help refurbish the crippled *Emerald*.

Josiah discovered that Greyson, captain and owner of *Emerald*, had no heirs in the New World. Therefore the crippled ship belonged to him, by the laws of salvage.

With Gordon's recommendations, Josiah found investors who helped him finance the rebuilding of the small ship. Then he put *Emerald* into service as a merchant vessel.

* * * * *

In November, Josiah learned that one of Blackbeard's lieutenants, Stede Bonnet, had been captured and condemned to hang at White Point, near Charleston Harbor. Fixx obtained permission to speak to the pirate in his cell two days before his execution.

Stede Bonnet became a pirate to get away from his tortuous marriage to a nagging, horrid woman. He'd reached the rank of major in the British Army. Though he knew nothing about sailing, he bought a small vessel and hired a crew. He fell in with Blackbeard, who seems to have been amused by the pudgy little delinquent.

After a brief but bloody career, Bonnet fell into the hands of the British Navy. He escaped from jail but the constables recaptured him. The court in Charleston condemned him to hang for crimes of piracy.

Never renowned for his courage, he disintegrated further and became a craven, cringing coward, overwhelmed with terror and dread. He wrote simpering, whining letters to every official he could think of, begging for pardons, even offering to allow himself to be dismembered. His pleading to save his life fell on uninterested ears.

Rather to Josiah's surprise, he found Major Bonnet short, pudgy, and unimpressive. He trembled with such violence that Josiah thought he might have a palsy. His voice shook and his bloodshot eyes stared at Josiah. He hadn't slept for days. Josiah had never seen such terror.

When Josiah identified himself as a survivor of the attack on *Emerald*, Bonnet expressed surprise that anyone had survived. Josiah interrupted him. "What happened to Prudence Lutrelle?" Josiah asked. "I have known her all my life. I spoke to her during the attack."

"How could you have done such a thing?" asked Bonnet.

Josiah told him the story. At last, the little pirate nodded. "I'm sorry, lad," he said. "Blackbeard threw her overboard one night in the Pamlico Sound, not far from Bath."

Unable to speak, Josiah rose to leave. Bonnet called him back. "Could you. . ." he stammered. "Could you speak to the jailer for me? Perhaps, if you say something, about how I cooperated with you—"

Josiah heard no more. He left the jail. Two days later, he made his way to White Point to watch Bonnet die. He arrived about one-half hour early.

Josiah made his way around the crowd to the jailer to ask if Bonnet had given any more information. The jailer shook his head. He told Josiah what had transpired since the evening that Josiah had visited the fat little pirate in his cell.

"If he'd known anything, he would have said it, young man," said the jailer.

"What do you mean?" asked Josiah.

"Last night, the night before his hanging, Bonnet told me why he so feared to die."

"Yes?" asked Josiah.

"I'll tell you what he told me," said the warden.

* * * * *

"*Queen Anne's Revenge*," Bonnet related, "had been at sea for two weeks. We had no contact with any other vessel during that time. Then a stranger dressed in immaculate red silk appeared on board, walking around the vessel as if appraising the crew. When he smiled, we saw sharp white teeth behind red lips. He spoke to the captain in familiar terms. He stayed on board for a week or more.

"One afternoon, we saw the stranger in the crosstrees of the ship, looking toward some dark cloud, making motions we didn't understand. A violent wind came up in a few moments.

"A few days later the stranger vanished off the ship. None of us ever saw him again."

* * * * *

"What a story. You believed him sincere?" asked Josiah.

"Oh yes," said the jailer and turned his attention to the cart bearing Bonnet as it rolled up to the gallows at White Point. Josiah had thought that he had seen terror in the man's face on the night he visited Bonnet in the cell. Now, he realized that the man had been reduced to little more than putty.

Never had Josiah seen such devastation. The warden read the charges. Three men lifted Bonnet to his feet in the cart and struggled to hold the fat little man upright. Bonnet's legs wouldn't support him.

The hangman tightened the noose at the back of Bonnet's neck. An assistant tied Bonnet's hands in front of him and he clutched a farewell bouquet of posies.

The men stepped back and Bonnet's knees collapsed. The hangman whipped the horses drawing the cart and Bonnet slid from the cart.

His legs kicked and flailed in spasms of muscle tension. Still, he'd grown too weak to last long and he succumbed, bearing on his hands the blood of perhaps hundreds of innocent people who had died under his direction.

A half hour later, the hangman cut his body down and it collapsed into the cart. The jailers dumped Bonnet's body on the sand at White Point at low tide.

Josiah made an effort to find Prudence's family in Charleston. He found a cousin named Elizabeth who wept when Josiah told the story of how Prudence perished in the Pamlico Sound.

Elizabeth told Josiah that Prudence's mother had left Charleston. She had taken passage to England with the money she'd received for Prudence and intended to remain there.

Elizabeth's eyes flashed with fury as she related Prudence's story.

"What happened?" Josiah asked. "How could her mother have allowed that creature to marry her daughter?"

Elizabeth frowned. She related what she knew of the unhappy story.

Captain Edward Teach—Blackbeard, the merciless pirate— enjoyed no little reputation as a ladies' man. Whenever he came ashore, he would shave off his famous whiskers and put on respectable clothes. His reckless spending and his witty tales of the sea captivated women.

Blackbeard liked to get married when he came ashore. Some people believed he married and then killed or abandoned at least sixteen women.

On one occasion, in Charleston, South Carolina, he picked out a pretty sixteen-year-old girl named Prudence Lutrelle, the daughter of a widow. Blackbeard found the girl attractive because of her long copper-colored hair, her captivating emerald eyes, and her lithe figure. Blackbeard charmed and bribed her mother into giving him Prudence's hand in marriage.

However, the girl didn't share her mother's enthusiasm for the wedding. She feared the notorious pirate. Prudence pleaded that she wanted to marry for love, not for money.

Her mother scoffed, dismissing her begging as that of a frivolous young virgin with normal consternation about the wedding bed. In a year, her mother asserted, all her fears would seem absurd.

An unannounced visit from the massive villain himself interrupted her pleading to her mother. Prudence tried to flee into the next room. Blackbeard intercepted her and used his monstrous strength to overpower her. He kissed and pawed her.

To Prudence's horror, she saw that Blackbeard brought several of his henchmen with him and the governor of the North Carolina colony. Governor Eden offered to perform the wedding ceremony on the spot. All but Prudence applauded the idea.

Prudence refused to recite the vows. The governor, unabashed, said them for her. When Eden pronounced them husband and wife, the hideous pirate tried to kiss her. Prudence tore at his face with her fingernails. He roared with pain and slapped her hard enough to knock her unconscious. Blackbeard's men dragged her through the streets to his mighty ship, *Queen Anne's Revenge*.

* * * * *

Elizabeth, however, knew nothing of what had happened to Prudence after that. The story passed down through many generations of her family but only could go to that point.

Prudence, aboard the mighty warship, entered into the

worst period of her life. The sailors consumed an enormous bridal cake and copious amounts of cheap rum in her honor. Prudence however didn't share in the celebration. She languished below decks, chained to a bed in a tiny, dark cabin. She remained there, except for brief periods on deck, for the next thirteen months. Blackbeard raped her again and again. On numerous occasions he allowed some of his favored men to have her as well.

A few weeks into the voyage, he allowed Prudence on deck to watch him and his henchmen plunder *Emerald*, a small merchant vessel. She saw Blackbeard steal a glorious emerald necklace from a beautiful woman, whom he then executed. He gave the necklace to Prudence as a wedding gift.

One clear summer night not far from Bath, North Carolina, four of Blackbeard's men burst into her cabin. They unshackled her from the bed.

The captain had brought aboard a new wife, a Spanish beauty with flashing black eyes. Blackbeard needed to rid himself of Prudence.

"Hands," said one of the men, "shall we leave the chains on her arms and legs?"

Israel Hands leered into Prudence's eyes. Then, he froze, his eyes widening in apparent fear. For a long moment, he couldn't speak. "No," Hands said, in a hollow voice. "Take off her chains." The men shrugged and removed her fetters.

They dragged her on deck. Prudence saw the entire crew assembled on deck to watch him execute his young wife. Blackbeard took advantage of the situation to impart terror to the crew.

Blackbeard paced the quarterdeck in a demonic rage, bellowing that he was the master of the ship and that he would be obeyed. Yellowish smoke encircled his head. The smoke came from burning bits of slowmatch—hemp twine dipped in saltpeter and limewater—which the monster had twisted into his hair and ignited.

He grew tired of shouting and cued the ship's drummer. The tension grew as he walked toward Prudence. He drew a pistol, and put it against Prudence's temple. Grinning, he looked into her eyes.

Then he froze, unable to speak. After a few seconds, he dropped his eyes and called to Israel Hands, who came forward with trepidation. Blackbeard turned the gun and fired the pistol ball through Hands' knee. Some crewmen dragged the unfortunate man away screaming and protesting, blind with pain.

"If I don't shoot one of you from time to time, you'll never obey me," growled Blackbeard.

Prudence's captors were a gang of murderous criminals, yet they stood thunderstruck, appalled by the scene. She took one step backward, then two more. No one noticed. She sprinted to the railing and flung herself overboard.

Blackbeard flogged his men for taking off her chains and for failing to take away the emerald necklace.

Everyone on *Queen Anne's Revenge* presumed that Prudence drowned in the Pamlico Sound.

But she survived.

* * * * *

Prudence smacked the water hard, all but stunned by the impact. She managed somehow to call out with her mind, using the legendary gift of the Cymreig. A powerful hand seized her wrist and pulled her to the surface.

She gasped for breath and turned to her rescuer. She almost screamed in her surprise to see her father, dead for many years, swimming next to her. He pulled her to him.

"Papa," she said, "I thought you were dead."

"Be at peace, Beloved," he said, in the loving, soothing voice she hadn't heard for so many years. "I've come to save you."

They tread water while he helped her strip to her underclothing in the midsummer blood warm water of the Pamlico Sound.

"Now, Beloved," her father said, "you have to swim."

"Where, Papa?"

He pointed. She saw an island framed in the moonlight about a mile away. She turned and spied *Queen Anne's Revenge* which had sailed far off in the opposite direction. "Come, Beloved," said her father, with a light tug on her arm. "I'll stay right here with you. You need fear that creature no longer."

He swam next to her, comforting her. Whenever she faltered, he spoke courage to her. At last near exhaustion, she found herself near St. Margaret's Island. He steered her toward a deserted beach. She struggled out of the water onto the sand.

"Go up to the rocks and hide for now, Beloved. Try to rest." He pointed. She staggered to the rocks he indicated. She found a stretch of sand and fell to her knees, offering devout prayers of thanksgiving for her deliverance from the demonic ship and its depraved master. When she turned to thank her father, he had vanished. She never saw him again.

* * * * *

William Oakley discovered Prudence, huddled and shivering, just before dawn on the rocky beach of St. Margaret's Island. Rushing to her, he stripped off his jacket and put it around her shoulders. He hurried to find some dry driftwood and used his tinder box to light a fire.

Prudence told him about her escape from the hellish ship and her swim to the island. Then she asked him why he had come to the beach so early.

He related that he had been a widower for two years and had come to St. Margaret's in agony over the death of his wife. He lived with his children in a small cabin on the island. Just before dawn, he dreamed that a tall man in a brown monk's robe stood next to his bed. This man insisted that Oakley hurry to the beach.

Will awoke with a jerk. So vivid had been the dream that he obeyed.

When her teeth stopped chattering, Prudence told him the hideous story of her marriage to Blackbeard. They sat together on the sandy beach of St. Margaret's Island until she could walk.

Will Oakley helped Prudence to her feet and she leaned on him. The imprisonment and the long swim had exhausted her and left her too weak to go far, so he carried her to his cabin. With help and nourishment from the man and his two young children, she recovered her strength in no time.

Prudence married Oakley and lived a happy, if Spartan, life with him. Still, she never felt safe until November 22, 1718.

Two small ships of the British Navy, *Dane* and *Ranger*, led by Lieutenant Robert Maynard, accosted Blackbeard's ship *Adventure* off the Ocracoke Inlet, North Carolina. They carried a warrant signed by the governor of the colony of Virginia. The ships joined battle off Ocracoke Island after Maynard's hot pursuit of the pirate in the Atlantic Ocean.

After exchanging heavy cannon and small-arms fire with *Adventure*, *Ranger* came alongside. Maynard's men lashed their smaller ship to *Adventure*. Blackbeard, bellowing profanity, leapt to *Ranger*. Brandishing a cutlass, he began one of his famous charges down the deck, making for the sloop's commander.

Maynard staggered him with a pistol shot in the chest. Then Maynard stepped forward and slashed Blackbeard with his cutlass. The blade cut him just below the hairline.

Blackbeard, his blood running into his eyes, knocked the cutlass from Maynard's hand. One of Maynard's men leapt on the monster's back and slashed Blackbeard's neck from ear to ear.

Even that didn't stop the brute. He leveled a pistol at Maynard. But he coughed, spat blood, and fell forward lifeless. When Blackbeard collapsed, Maynard's crew had wounded him with five pistol balls and at least twenty cuts and stab wounds.

Maynard's sword flashed. He severed Blackbeard's head from his body. He hung the trophy, tongue lolling, at the front of the ship.

Legend says that when Maynard's triumphant men threw Blackbeard's body overboard, it continued to swim in search of its head. At last, however, exhaustion claimed the body, and it sank beneath the waves.

His death took the fight out of his men. They surrendered, begging for mercy. Maynard hanged several of the worst at once, including Richards, the demonic first officer. The rest of them shared the fate of their shipmates sometime later on the scaffold. Only Israel Hands, who came ashore to inform on the man who shot him through the knee, and young Samuel Odell, whom Blackbeard pressed into the crew by force the night before the battle, managed to escape the gallows.

The news of the slaying of the infamous pirate spread throughout the Carolina and Virginia colonies, even to St. Margaret's Island. Prudence spent the night in prayers of thanksgiving that she at last could consider herself safe. At dawn, she walked back to the cabin and picked up the beautiful emerald necklace.

She walked to her favorite spot on the island, overlooking the Pamlico Sound. She drew back her arm to throw the lovely, delicate necklace into the ocean. Then, she changed her mind.

She decided to make it a memorial of her deliverance. Her heirs would look at it and see it as a symbol of how she escaped from hell.

* * * * *

Josiah, convinced that Prudence had drowned in the Pamlico

Sound, assuaged his grief with hard work. Captain Gordon of *Excalibur* heard that the people of Charleston regarded young Josiah as bright, hard working with a fine head for business. Within a year of Blackbeard's death, Gordon resigned from the British Navy and joined his young friend as a business partner. Together, they built an exemplary merchant shipping business in Charleston. Josiah became a pillar of his community.

Josiah seemed to know how to strike a fair, competitive bargain with the merchants with whom he dealt. People saw a strange habit develop in Fixx. When striking a business arrangement, he would shut his eyes, bow his head a bit and mutter to himself.

People assumed that he was praying in those moments and respected him for it. Josiah never told anyone the truth. Despite his love for his wife and family, Josiah often thought about Prudence and their kiss. For the rest of his life, he remembered that moment of sunshine on the hell ship known as *Queen Ann's Revenge.* Whenever he became angry or scared, or felt stripped of confidence and in despair, the memory of those gentle emerald eyes would loom up before him. Then, as if a switch had been engaged in his mind, peace and joy would surround him. His mind would clarify, he would see the truth of the situation and know how to strike the best bargain.

Josiah never again went to sea. Three years after Bonnet died, Josiah married a girl from Charleston, with whom he had several children, and they presented him with many grandchildren.

* * * * *

When he was an old man, he buried his wife in the church cemetery in Charleston. Grieving, he took his oldest son Gareth for a walk to White Point, where he had seen Bonnet strangled at the end of a disgraceful rope. He slid a ring from his finger, the first time it had left his hand since he was eighteen. "Keep this," Josiah said, "until the girl who owns it comes for it. Keep passing it down through the generations. Someday, she'll come."

He watched Gareth slide the ring on. His son, bewildered by the command, nonetheless had enough respect for his father to agree. He managed a smile and whispered, "I promise."

Josiah looked out over the Atlantic, his eyes searching for the spot where he'd last seen the girl with green eyes. His eyes filled again.

He whispered, "Prudence." His son didn't ask what he meant. Instead, he wrapped an arm around his father's shoulders and embraced him.

"Gareth," said the old man. "I have a story to tell you."

Part 11:
Affair

CHAPTER TWO

Near Washington, North Carolina

"**W**here are we?"

Eight-year-old Anna O'Neill turned to the voice. A blond-haired boy with striking sapphire blue eyes stood next to her. Perhaps an inch taller than she, he seemed to be her age. He held her hand, their fingers laced together.

Anna looked around. To her surprise they stood in her family's cemetery on the edge of a pit, perhaps five feet deep and ten feet across.

She hadn't been there five seconds ago.

But the cemetery had changed. She'd never seen a pit here before. Nor had she ever seen oak trees marking the entrance to the graveyard.

"We're on St. Margaret's Island," Anna whispered, and heard her voice trembling. "What am I doing here?"

The boy squeezed her hand. "I'm pretty sure we're having the same dream. This isn't the first time."

"How can that be?" she asked, puzzled. From somewhere on the island, she heard a shout. They couldn't hear the words, but the tone was angry and sarcastic. Her eyes widened. "What's that?"

"I know you're scared. I am too. But we have to move. We can't let it catch us."

"What do we do?" she asked.

"Come on," the boy said. "We have to hide." She followed him to a small stand of pines fifty yards away. The boy hid behind a tree and pulled her down next to him.

Lightning flashed from a dark, ominous cloud in the gray winter sky. She looked at the boy's clothing. The suit , fashioned from coarse wool, had breeches fastened below the knee, white socks of a strange material, and shoes with large metal buckles. The deep emerald green color of his suit struck her.

She'd seen clothing like this in pictures and museums. But those garments were old and faded. The boy's clothes looked almost new.

"Why are you dressed like that?" she asked.

He looked down, surprised. "I don't know. I've never had clothes like this. Look at you, too."

She did. She found herself wearing a long, deep blue wool dress with petticoats, a high-collared white blouse, and a long white apron. "What's happened to me?" she asked, perplexed.

"I can't. . ." he began, but the voice called out again. It seemed to be closer. Anna shivered as the fear settled back in.

"Where is St. Margaret's?" asked the boy in a whisper.

"Not far from Bath."

"Where?"

"Bath, North Carolina, near the Atlantic Ocean. That's the Pamlico River," she said, pointing.

He gave a nod, then signaled with his head. They began creeping toward the beach. The wind ruffled her long red hair. She felt chilled despite the woolen dress.

They stopped in a grove of trees to get out of the wind. Again she heard a shout. Anna shuddered.

"Do I know you?" she asked the boy. He seemed familiar somehow.

"I'm called Gareth."

"Like Sir Gareth with King Arthur and the Round Table?"

"Yeah." The boy's face lit up. "Have you read those stories?"

"Sure," she said. "I read all the time—" the voice yelled

again, but seemed farther away.

"Do you know me?" the girl asked, when her heart slowed a little.

"Of course. You're Viviane. But I've always called you Annie," said the boy, stuttering a little.

She wondered why he called her those names. Everyone called her Anna, even her parents. "Where do you live?" she asked.

"I don't know," he said after a moment. "I can't remember when I'm with you. I recall some things about my life, and what happens to me, but I can't remember my real name, or where I live, or anything about my parents. . ."

"How did you get here then?"

He began to answer, but then stopped. His face took on a quizzical look. "I guess I don't know that either," he admitted. "I go places in my dreams."

"Oh," she said, and remembered that she was dreaming. "How can we both have the same dreams?" Her dreams were intense, dramatic and colorful, but she couldn't remember one so real, so vivid. She could hear the boy, see him, and feel the comforting touch of his hand. Though she was afraid, the fear eased when she held his hand.

They looked up and down the beach, but couldn't see a boat. "We have to get away before it catches up to us."

She raised her eyebrows. "It?"

"The monster. Nehushtan. I only know about him when we're together."

"What is he?"

He hesitated, framing his words. "Nehushtan is everything we're afraid of. He's anger, cruelty. He's when you feel sad or afraid. Or lonely. We fight him when we're together. We feel stronger together. We help each other. But he's strong."

She took his hand again. They hurried back into the woods, hiding behind a tree. In the distance, she heard the voice.

Calling. Mocking. Vicious. Now Anna could make out the words.

"Where are you, children?" it hissed. "Come out and play!"

Anna felt sick to her stomach. She didn't think she'd fought a monster before. She couldn't even stand to watch the horror movies her stepsisters enjoyed.

She looked at the boy. She felt better when she heard his voice. "So we're friends?" she asked.

"Best friends."

"That's funny."

"Funny?"

"Well, yeah, kinda," she shrugged. "Most people don't like me."

"I know what you mean. Kids don't much like me either."

She looked into his compelling blue eyes. "Why?"

His head lowered in embarrassment. He took a deep breath. "I'm. . ." He paused, as if looking for a word. ". . .afraid of them, and they can tell."

"Afraid?"

The boy swallowed. "That's not quite the right word. I'm real shy around other kids. My mom and dad say I'm introverted."

She'd heard the word, but didn't know what it meant.

"You make me feel brave," he said. "You're nice to me, and kind. But I only see you in my dreams."

She nodded. "I'm shy, too. But people are scared of me because of my eyes."

He looked at her, his mouth open. "I think they're beautiful."

"Thank you," she said, pleased that this boy thought her eyes were beautiful. "But people get scared of what I can do with my eyes."

"What do you do?"

"I can see what other people are thinking and I can

sometimes change their thoughts, make them feel different."

"For real?" He said, eyes wide.

"My Grandpa Daniel can do it too. The Cymreig—Grandpa calls what we do the Cymreig—runs in our family. But we don't tell anyone about it," Anna said, wondering why she was telling him. "Most of my family doesn't have it. Or even know about it. When we change someone's thoughts, he calls it a Paik. It's an old word."

"That's pretty cool."

They stood and began to walk toward the woods.

"Viviane?" The monster's voice was closer. She clutched the boy's arm. "Gareth? I'll find you. You're making this harder on yourselves, children."

They stood. He took her hand, and they burst from the trees and onto the rocks of the eastern beach.

"Still no boat," said Gareth.

"Could we swim to shore?"

"It's too far and too cold."

"Let's hide over there," she said. They ran to a large pile of enormous rocks and crouched. He put an arm around her shoulders and drew her close. She felt the warmth of his body.

"I don't remember seeing you before," she said.

"You have, but you can't ever remember me when you're awake. I think because you haven't needed me till now. I'm different. I can't ever remember what happens in the dreams but I can remember you. I pretend I can talk to you when I'm awake too."

She turned to him and smiled. Their eyes met.

He gave her his shy little smile. He stuttered when he said, "I'm not afraid after I talk to you. You make me feel brave. I know we've done lots of things together. But I don't think we've ever fought the Snake."

"I'll try my best to remember you this time," she promised. She regretted that she couldn't remember seeing him before.

"Do you know why we're here?"

He looked out over the Pamlico Sound, and drew something in the sand with his foot. She thought he was searching for the right way to tell her. "Nehushtan knows about you. He hates you, and wants to hurt you, maybe even kill you."

The chill wind felt colder. "Why does he hate me?"

He smoothed the sand with his foot. "I think because of your eyes."

"Huh?"

"Did you Paik someone today?"

She chewed briefly on a thumbnail. "I was sitting and reading on the steps of our porch this afternoon when Billy Phipps and a bunch of kids came by. He called me Horse-face."

Gareth's face reddened with anger. "Did you use your eyes?" he asked.

She nodded. "So I Paiked him," she smiled. "He ran off like something was chasing him. His yucky friends laughed at him." She thought. "I know I shouldn't have done that. I don't think I've ever Paiked someone for. . .well, to be mean."

"I bet he's one of Nehushtan's helpers. Anyone who says mean things like that works for Nehushtan."

In a flash of clarity, she understood. "You came to protect me, didn't you?"

"Uh-huh. Someone sent me."

"Who?"

"I don't know. But I think we have to face Nehushtan together."

Anna looked around, half expecting to see a monster swooping down from the sky on them. The ugly name Nehushtan frightened her and scared Gareth too. She could see his hands shaking. But she sensed he wouldn't hesitate to face this creature with her.

She heard the voice calling again and clutched at his arm, her mouth trembling. "Let's go back to the graveyard," she said. They peeked out from their hiding place and saw no one. Finding a path, they followed it back to the cemetery in the center of the island. She pointed and they hid behind a pillar, trying to catch their breath.

When she didn't hear the voice of Nehushtan, she took Gareth's arm. "This graveyard belongs to my family. Look," she said, pointing to an ancient white tombstone. They could just make out the writing on the stone. "My great-great-something-grandmother, Prudence Lutrelle, lies here. She married a pirate."

"You mean it?"

"Blackbeard himself," she nodded. "The British Navy beheaded him over there, just off Ocracoke." She pointed east toward the Atlantic Ocean.

"You're related to Blackbeard?"

"No," she assured him. "Prudence didn't have any children until she escaped from Blackbeard and married my great-great-grandfather. She buried him there." She pointed to a grave marker next to Prudence's. They could just make out the name, William Oakley, carved into the ancient tombstone.

"Blackbeard used this well to fill his water casks for his ships," she said. "His treasure might be buried here on the island somewhere."

They heard a twig snap behind them. They turned. A gigantic snake slithered between the two giant oak trees that marked the entrance of the cemetery. "Viviane and Gareth," The snake said. "The game's over." A fat greasy man, with matted gray hair and beard, waddled a little behind the snake, holding a pistol.

Anna shrank back against Gareth. He put his arm around her. "Don't let him see you scared," he said. His voice had changed. She turned. Gareth looked much older, like Daddy's age, and bigger, now. Tall and handsome with an athletic build, he wore a grim, angry expression on his face.

The snake reared up. It appeared to have been cast from bronze, and she could see her reflection in its metallic skin. She didn't like the reflection. She looked twisted, distorted, all wrong somehow.

In the next moment, though, the Snake transformed into the figure of a tall man, well-muscled and strong. Anna saw a black flowing beard and reptilian eyes. Smoke surrounded his head and obscured his features. He started strolling toward them, insolent and arrogant.

"Is that Nehushtan?" Anna whispered to Gareth. Her voice sounded funny. Now she realized that she didn't seem to be eight years old. She looked down and saw that she had become a woman, with a beautiful woman's body, like her mother's.

He squeezed her arm. "Don't worry," he snarled, baring his teeth in challenge to the man. "I won't let him hurt you. I'll take care of you. You're my friend." She felt Gareth trembling, but sensed fear hadn't caused it. He was angry, ready for a fight.

The man turned into a snake again and lashed out, biting Anna on the leg just above the knee. The fangs plunged through the heavy woolen skirt into her leg. She cried out as it started to wrap itself around her.

Gareth seized the snake behind the head. Choking, it curled around his body. Gareth yelled horrible things in a language Anna didn't understand.

The Snake's choking turned to gasps. Its hold on Gareth loosened.

The fat man started for her friend. Anna screamed a warning and tried to run to help him, but someone held her back. She lashed out in frustration and pain.

CHAPTER THREE

Anna, honey," said a warm, kind voice. "Wake up." Someone was shaking her.

She opened her eyes and saw her Daddy. "Where am I?" she asked.

"You're on the porch swing, silly," he said, hugging her.

"Daddy. Watch out for Nehushtan. The snake. It came right in here after me." She sat trembling, her eyes wide, with tears on her cheeks.

Daddy looked into her eyes. "You had a nightmare. No snake could get in here. Calm down."

Anna looked down and saw that she'd become an eight-year-old girl again. She again wore her long summer nightgown, not the heavy woolen dress with the white apron.

She pulled up the hem of her nightgown and saw no bite marks on her leg. *I had a dream,* she told herself. *Just a dream.*

Her heart began to slow. Safe on the front porch swing in her sleeping bag, she hugged her daddy.

To her delight, she realized that she remembered Gareth, the blond boy who'd been so brave and kind. She remembered his joy in being with her.

"Come on, sweetheart," Daddy smiled. We have to leave soon."

Then Anna remembered. *We're going to the beach. It's summertime. Not winter, like in the dream.*

Most people who met her agreed that Anna possessed a strange gift. But despite the child's great compassion and tenderness, they felt uneasy around her.

Anna didn't care. She had always been content with a few friends as long as Mom and Daddy loved her, read to her, and told her stories. *But now I know Gareth, too,* she thought. *I can see him every night when I sleep.*

Anna's mom had fixed blueberry pancakes, her absolute favorite. Anna poured syrup over the stack in front of her but picked at the breakfast, too excited to waste time on mere food.

At last they piled into the car. Anna and her family—Patrick O'Neill, his wife Meg, and Anna's two stepsisters—headed the rusty Chevy Impala station wagon toward Duck, the picturesque beach town on North Carolina's Outer Banks. Anna's aunt and uncle owned a house on the beach there.

For a special treat, Anna's parents let her sit between them in the front seat of the car. She trembled with excitement as she watched for deer and black bears and birds.

Beside the excitement of this trip to the beach, the new bathing suit mom had bought for her a couple of days ago delighted her. She'd outgrown last year's suit. Now, she wore the new one under a t-shirt and cut-off blue jeans so that she wouldn't have to waste any time changing when they got to Duck.

Anna hoped her new two-piece suit made her resemble her mother, who looked so beautiful in her own new bikini. Anna thought about how Mom had giggled when Daddy stared at his young wife when she'd modeled the new suit for him. Mom reddened when Daddy whispered something in her ear, and whacked him, saying, "Later." Then, they kissed. Daddy had again whispered. This time, Mom nodded.

"Anna, I have to change," she said, her face flushed. She went into the bedroom. Daddy followed her. They shut the door. They didn't come out for some time.

Someday, I want someone to look at me like that, Anna thought. And kiss me like Daddy does Mom.

She liked the color of the swim suit. Her mother had giggled at her when she picked out the color, a deep blue. "That's become your favorite color," observed Mom, as she paid for the two swim suits.

"Don't you like it?" Anna asked.

"Of course. You look adorable."

Anna had blushed at the observation, but she thought about her mom's comment. The blue had indeed been her favorite color for some time.

Now, as she sat between her parents in the old car, she understood why.

Her best friend had eyes this color. She hadn't realized until that moment why she liked it so much. She grinned.

"Mom?" she said.

"Honey?" said Mom, smiling and hugging her daughter.

"I have a new friend," she said.

"Really? Where did you meet her?"

"Not a girl, mom," said the little girl, exasperated.

"A boy?" said Daddy, also grinning.

"Yeah. He's named Gareth." The reaction of her parents surprised her. Daddy chuckled and nodded. Mom, however, looked very surprised, and even turned a little pale. Almost like she'd heard the name before. Anna went on, "He and I do lots of things together."

Mom cleared her throat. "Why haven't you brought him over to meet us?" asked Mom.

She had to think. "I don't think I can. But he's fun and brave too. He likes to read, like I do, and. . ."

A loud snort interrupted her. Her two stepsisters, sixteen-year-old Della and fourteen-year-old Lurene, sulked in the back seat. They wanted to stay home with their friends. The stepsisters both scoffed at the idea of Anna having a friend.

Their complaining annoyed Anna. She wished she could use her gift to help them. She shrugged and decided she wouldn't let the stepsisters ruin her day.

She felt sorry for Della and Lurene. They missed their mom. They hadn't heard from her since she left them and their father ten years ago. The two teenagers hated Anna and their stepmother Meg, whom Patrick had married a year before Anna was born.

Last week, she sat on the porch swing, reading as usual. She heard a commotion at the back of the house. She came into the kitchen and found Mom sitting at the table, holding a soggy tissue.

"Mom?"

Mom looked up and tried a weak smile. "Hi, Honey."

"What happened?"

"Oh, nothing, Honey. Don't be upset." Anna, near tears herself, took her mom's hand, looked into her eyes and Paiked her.

She saw the scene that had occurred just before she came in. Della and Lurene had been rude, insolent, and defiant. They'd shouted at their stepmother for making some little request of them. "You can't talk to us like our real mother," Della sneered.

The nasty comment hurt Mom's feelings. She'd grown weary of dealing with their nastiness.

Anna released the Paik, put her arms around her mother's neck and hugged her. Mom started to cry again. "They just don't like me," she said. "Why can't they ever just give me a chance?"

Anna didn't answer. She just held onto her mom, comforting and loving her, while Mom wept. Mom hugged her back, letting her child share her pain.

Della and Lurene had dull brown eyes that saw no magic anywhere. They told everyone they were putting in time in school, impatient for it to be over so they could begin their lives.

Anna couldn't understand why the stepsisters didn't want her to help them. She knew she could.

She also didn't comprehend their attitude about school and learning. They seemed to enjoy being ignorant.

Anna wanted to learn as much as the world could give away. Her mother, an elementary school teacher, had taught her to read by the time Anna had reached the age of five. Anna spent hours on the porch swing poring over library books filled with pictures of exotic locations or unusual animals, or wonderful people who dressed and looked and talked and believed unlike anyone she knew.

Anna loved nature. She enjoyed talking to the chickadees that she'd trained to eat sunflower seeds from her hand and at the bird feeders on the back porch, which she maintained. Sometimes her parents caught her listening to faraway melodies and voices that only she could hear. When they asked her what she heard, she would smile. "Don't you hear the voices?"

"What voices?" Meg O'Neill asked.

"The voices in the wind, the animals, and the sea voices." That she was the only one who could hear them always amazed her.

At the beach house she greeted and hugged her Aunt Marion and Uncle Claude. Beside herself with impatience, she excused herself and ran to the beach, giggling with joy. She yanked off the t-shirt and shorts and hurried into the ocean as soon as Daddy's head appeared at the top of the dune.

Father and daughter played together in the ocean, diving into waves, bodysurfing, and leaping over the surf hand in hand. Anna laughed the whole time. Before Daddy went up on shore to help his wife set out the picnic lunch, he warned Anna. "You be careful," he said. "You can stay in the water if you promise to stay close to the shore."

"I promise," she said.

When he reached shore, Anna looked beyond the placid waves and saw two porpoises swimming parallel to the shore. The sight of her favorite animals thrilled her. It was the first time she'd never been so close to porpoises swimming in the open ocean. If she swam out a little bit, she could listen to them singing their gentle songs. Forgetting her promise, she began swimming toward them, farther than she had ever gone before.

CHAPTER FOUR

Patrick O'Neill, up on shore, laughed at something his wife said. He looked at his two older daughters, who sat sulking on a blanket some ten yards away. He worried about how they were turning out.

His brother Claude walked over to him. "You've got quite a kid in that little squirt, don't you?" he grinned.

"Yeah," said Patrick, unwrapping a big plate covered with deviled eggs. "She's the light of our lives."

"I know," said his brother.

"I wish she could get along with other kids better," Patrick said. "She told us today that she made a new friend, a boy named Gareth. The news delighted us."

"Ah, don't worry about that shyness. She'll get over it when she gets some self-confidence," his brother assured him.

Patrick beamed, and turned to the ocean to check on Anna. He turned pale when he saw how far Anna had gone from the shore. He saw a huge wave coming. "Oh God, no!" He dropped the plate of deviled eggs. He and Claude sprinted.

"Anna!" Patrick yelled. "Look out!" Running into the water until it reached just below his waist, Patrick dived. He began swimming, frantic to reach his daughter. His brother dove in right behind him.

* * * * *

Anna heard her father yell. She looked back toward shore and was alarmed at how far she'd swum. She started back, but a powerful wave, much larger than the others, hit her hard. It lifted her high and slammed her down. The wave boiled around her, white and terrifying. At first it pushed her toward shore. Then the undertow caught her and pulled her out to sea.

Anna struggled against the current, holding her breath and panicky. Daddy would never be able to reach her. She screamed in her mind with the Cymreig: "Gareth!"

A hand seized her wrist. She opened her eyes. In front of her swam Gareth, the blond boy from her dream. She calmed down when she saw gentleness and confidence in his deep blue eyes. His voice was clear, even though they were under water.

"Don't be afraid, Annie. I've got you. Your Grandpa sent me. We'll get you out of this. Swim with the current. Slide to the side. Good. Now, come on up with me and get some air. You're fine, Annie."

She surfaced and breathed. She treaded water, coughing and gagging. As Gareth held her hand, her confidence returned. Not even the depth of the water way out here frightened her.

Gareth talked to her as they swam back toward shore. After some minutes Anna looked down, saw the sandy bottom and stood up. Then she looked around for the boy.

He'd vanished.

Anna stared around, dumbfounded. Where could he have gone? He'd been right there—

Then Daddy was there. He picked her up and hugged her. His face betrayed his terror but she could see pride in his eyes too. "Good girl," he managed to say. "You handled that undertow like a real professional." Trembling, he carried her ashore.

Mom met them at the water's edge. Weeping with fright, she hugged Anna. She took her daughter's face in her hands. "Honey, why did you take such a chance? You could have drowned."

"Anna," said her father, now grim, "I'm relieved that you're all right and I'm proud of how you handled the wave and the undertow. But I'm angry at you for breaking your promise. We don't break promises in this family. Don't you ever do that again."

"But you didn't need to worry," she protested. "Grandpa sent the boy to help me."

"What boy?" asked Mom with a glance at her husband.

"Grandpa is miles away, at home," said Daddy.

"Gareth came and helped me." Her parents looked at each other.

"Your new friend?" asked Mom.

"Yeah," said Anna, happy. "He told me what to do. He can talk under water."

Anna's stepsisters, sitting on the blanket five yards away, laughed. "You shoulda left the little freak drown," Della sneered, and Lurene laughed louder.

Anna's face contorted with anger. She thought about her stepsisters' rudeness to mom. Their nasty comments. The way they hated her and her mom.

Anna locked onto Della's eyes and Paiked her.

Della, a poor swimmer on her best days, found herself dog-paddling in the ocean. A huge wave hit her in the face and knocked her backward. She didn't have time to take a breath. She felt herself rocketing toward the shore, tumbling in the murderous power of the wave.

The wave then pulled her away from the shore. Her head broke the surface. She tried to inhale but the white water plunged her under the surface and she gulped water.

She began to choke and aspirate sea water. Della clutched for something, anything that would slow down her headlong rush into eternity.

A small hand grasped her wrist. She turned and saw Anna next to her, green eyes ablaze. Anna's voice sounded in her head. "So you wanted me to drown. Do you like it?"

Della started to scream in fear.

Then she sat again on the shore, staring into the smoldering eyes of her stepsister. She stood up, astonished to find herself breathing, not drowning. But she remained terrified, the sense of helplessness and choking still strong.

Her stepmother took four or five quick steps and slapped Della's cheek so hard the stepsister staggered backward and sat down hard on the sand. "Don't you *ever* speak to your sister or to anyone else like that again," Meg snarled. Then the expression of profound fear in Della's eyes puzzled Meg.

* * * * *

Several hundred miles away, a boy with blond hair and sapphire blue eyes woke up from a little nap and found himself lying on his bed. He remembered in a few seconds that he'd shut his door to hide away from the party that his parents were hosting downstairs. He heard laughing and loud conversation.

He'd dozed while reading a Hardy Boys book, *The Secret of Pirate's Hill*, and he'd dreamed of the girl named Viviane. He smiled, thinking about his best friend and her gentle green eyes. It had been a superhero dream, he'd been like Green Lantern, or. . .

But as always, he couldn't remember what had happened. A wave? A beach? The dream faded. He got up and walked downstairs to rejoin the party.

* * * * *

That night, Anna ran down the block to see her grandfather Daniel. She hugged her grandmother and took her grandfather's hand.

With a wink to his wife, Daniel Oakley followed his granddaughter out on the porch. She related the dream of the island and the snake. She told him about the ocean. "The boy you sent, Gareth, came to help me." His eyes widened at the mention of the name Gareth. Then, he nodded. "And I fixed Della," she went on, and related how she had Paiked the fat stepsister for being so nasty.

Grandpa Daniel hugged her. "Honey, I have some things to

teach you," he said. She looked up.

"I didn't send Gareth," he said. "But I know who did. I also know who sent the wave. I'll show you." The two looked into each other's eyes and Daniel Paiked his Beloved granddaughter.

CHAPTER FIVE
Northern Suburbs of Chicago
Westwood High School
August

Anna took her bachelor's degree at the University of Wisconsin and moved to the northern suburbs of Chicago where she completed a master's degree at Northwestern University in Evanston.

After graduation and a whirlwind courtship, she married an older man named Alan DiBiasi. Two years into a marriage with severe problems, Anna accepted a teaching job at Westwood, a large suburban high school.

Her first official day began early on the last Monday in August, though the students weren't in attendance. The school administration gave the day over to orientation activities for new faculty members, and for general faculty meetings. Then the teachers received time to work at setting up their classrooms.

She'd done some work in the classroom the previous week, but she relished the time to put up posters and arrange the desks so that the students would find the room fun and offbeat.

Though not her first teaching experience--she'd taught as a substitute for a couple of years—she'd never had her own classroom. However, her day hadn't been going well as she struggled along in a dreadful mood.

She reflected on what had happened that weekend. Saturday night had been a typical backyard barbecue party with Alan's friends, with one notable exception. Her husband's friend Lou tried to kiss her.

Once the wedding and the thrill of the chase concluded, Alan settled back his life as it had been before he'd met her.

Alan traveled out of town a great deal and worked long hours. He exhibited little interest in her, except for frequent and one-sided sex.

On Saturday night, she'd been standing alone in the family room at the home of one of his friends, observing the party in the backyard through the bay window. She watched her husband standing in a group of his friends, laughing and drinking beer.

"Hey, pretty lady," rasped a voice next to her.

She turned to the voice. Lou Sydney, a business owner and client of Alan's, stood a few feet away.

"Hello, Mr. Sydney."

"Please. Call me Lou."

"Yes?"

"Look, I—uh--been wanting to talk to you for some time."

"And your big chance has come at last, huh?" she asked, sarcastic. She had seen him staring at her.

"Well, I been seen the way Alan treats you. You know, gone all the time, deserting you at parties like this. . ."

"Excuse me. You don't need to concern yourself with that, Mr. Sydney—"

"I know what you're thinking but that ain't it. Alls I'm saying is, well, see, I got some marriage problems myself."

"And *that* doesn't interest or concern me in the slightest. . ."

"No, now that's where I think you could be wrong. I just want to be friends, that's all. I mean, I know you get lonely. I'm lonely myself, lots of the time. . ."

"Please excuse me." He stood between her and the door. She tried to push past him and he took her arm. She stopped and looked at his hand. He didn't let go.

"Let go of my arm. This instant."

"Alls I want you to do is think about it."

"I assure you of one thing. I have given you all the thought I intend to. Now. Let go of my arm."

He gave her a leering smile and bent to kiss her. She averted her face. "Let go of my arm." He didn't.

She again looked up into his eyes. In the next moment, he clutched his stomach as a severe cramp doubled him over. He let go of Anna's arm and fell to one knee. The cramp vanished.

His face reddened and he wiped tears of pain from his face. "I have no interest whatever in you," she stated. He couldn't meet her eyes. "Please stay as far away from me as you can."

She pushed past him into the hall. She walked into the yard and found her husband.

"We have to leave," she said. "Right now."

"Don't be ridiculous," said Alan, in his condescending voice. "This party hasn't even gotten going."

"Take me home, this minute."

"We haven't even had dessert."

"Do you intend to make me call a cab?"

He drew himself up. "Now look. These people here can do me a lot of good. I—" But he never finished the sentence. Anna turned and walked back to the house.

Ten minutes later a cab arrived and Anna left the party. She'd fallen asleep by the time he came home.

On Sunday, Alan had dismissed her allegation about Lou Sydney making a pass and trying to kiss her. "Don't be silly," he said. "I've known Lou for years. He wouldn't do that."

His refusal to credit her stunned her. "Do I understand," she said, "that you are defending him? After he tried to pick me up? Then kiss me?" She struggled not to cry with the hurt.

"I don't have to defend him. You just misunderstood."

"I didn't misunderstand."

"Sure you did. Of course you did. But, look: if it'll make you happy, I'll talk to him, see what he says."

"Of course. So you can take *his* word for what happened."

"Aw come on. Look, why do you have to be so negative?" And so on.

CHAPTER SIX

Anna continued to putter in his classroom. She'd fought with Alan that morning again, and the bout had been a classic. The alarm clock didn't go off and Alan made a hurtful remark. "For Chrissakes, you can't even handle a simple radio alarm?" That crack had prompted a nasty argument.

The fight, a typical one, had become a motif of her marriage.

As she stood on a chair, straightening a poster, a large man in a Banlon shirt knocked at her classroom door.

"Hey," he said.

"Hello," she said, climbing down off the chair. He leered at her legs as the skirt rose above her knees. She felt her face turning red.

"Welcome to the school. I'm Jerry. Gladda meecha."

"How do you do," she sighed, without enthusiasm. "Anna O'Neill."

"Listen, I know my way around here. If you need any help, just lemme know."

"Thank you."

"Say, look, I got an offer for you."

"Yes?"

"Listen, after the day, how about you and me get a beer? You know, talk things over, like that--"

"Thank you," she interrupted, clenching her teeth, "but I don't think my husband would like to hear that I'd gone on a date with another man."

"Oh," he said. He turned and walked away.

She'd brushed him off, but she resented having to deal with a flirtation on her first day. In the meantime, her miserable mood had gotten worse.

Also, this job scared her. *Stop it*, she thought. *This is what you've wanted for years.* But she couldn't quite stop the ache in her stomach and the trembling.

* * * * *

A few moments later, she hadn't lost her feeling of annoyance. A tall, handsome man with wild blond hair knocked at the door and entered her classroom.

For a moment, their eyes locked and his mouth dropped open, as if he recognized her. He began to speak but stopped as if thinking better of what he'd been about to say. When he walked forward, he banged into a student desk and knocked a stack of papers off of it. He apologized, knelt and picked the papers up. He stood and gave her a weak smile, murmuring apologies.

Oh, no, she groaned to herself. *Not another jerk.*

She'd seen this guy sitting by himself in the English Department meeting earlier that morning. Most of the staff avoided him.

Anna noticed that she felt a strange sense of gratitude toward him, as if he'd helped her with something, had done something nice for her, and protected her from something awful.

But that was silly. She couldn't have seen him before that morning. She hardened her attitude toward him.

"Hi," he managed.

When she didn't speak, he raised his head so that his sapphire eyes locked onto hers again. Then he broke eye contact and glanced back down.

"I just wanted to welcome you to the school."

"Thank you." She checked her watch. She made sure he saw her do it. "Now will that be all?"

"I wanted to introduce myself, too. I'm Casey Fixx," He blurted.

"Thank you. Now, will you please tell how I can help you,

Mr. Fixx? I do have other duties this morning."

"Oh, well, see, I wanted to offer to get together with you, when it's convenient—"

"Right," she interrupted, drawing the word out, sarcastic and rude. She thought of the lout who'd tried to pick her up earlier. "I know what you're offering."

He looked up. "You do?" He appeared baffled.

"Yes. I'm not stupid."

Casey Fixx continued to look at her in surprise. "I. . ." he began, stuttering. Then he appeared to think of something and nodded. "So he talked to you?"

"Yes," she said, "He talked to me." She clenched her teeth, thinking about how the lout named Jerry leered at her legs.

"So you know why I'm here?"

"I do indeed."

"Okay, then," he said. "Do you think we could we get together later today? I don't mean to rush you, but see, I direct the drama department here at the school. I start in with the plays right away--"

"I will not be getting together with you at all," she interrupted. "I'm insulted and angry that you think I would."

The blond man's mouth fell open, his lips trembling. "Just a second," he said. "I didn't mean—"

"Good day, Mr. Fixx." Her intonation said, "Get out and don't come back."

He looked at her for a moment, and to her surprise, she saw his eyes fill with tears. He turned away. "I'm sorry," he stuttered. He left, brushing his face with the back of his hand.

CHAPTER SEVEN

Anna immersed herself in work the rest of the morning, putting up posters and bulletin boards and setting out the texts for the classes. By lunchtime she felt organized.

She couldn't get over thinking about the second man who'd come into her room, that Casey Fixx. Anna knew that she'd been cruel to him. Seeing his eyes tear had given her a momentary sense of triumph, maybe, but that passed.

She sat in one of the student desks and stared out the window. Anna, for many years since her parents died, had been—well, lonely. She couldn't think of another word. She didn't make friends well, she knew it.

Grace Malkin, a fellow teacher, strolled in. The two young women sat together at the faculty meetings. "Come on," Grace said. "The school's parent group put together a nice luncheon for us."

Anna perked up. "Sounds good," she said. She stood and crossed to her desk for her purse, straightening a few things. "What's the story on that Fixx guy?" she asked, trying to sound casual, as they walked into the corridor.

Grace squinted as they strolled down the hall. "What do you mean?"

"He came into my room this morning," Anna said. "I had to brush him off."

Grace laughed. "Casey Fixx came on to you?"

Anna nodded. "Why does that amuse you?"

"He has to be the most bashful person I've ever known," Grace said. "I'm surprised he could even talk to you. He never comes to department get-togethers, doesn't hang around in the work area, and avoids most of the other teachers. He does well with the students but most of the teachers regard him as snobbish. I like him okay, though. We date when his schedule allows—well, most of the time, I have to ask him out." She giggled.

Anna's stomach began to feel queasy. *Did I misunderstand what he was saying?*

At that moment Dr. McAllister, the chairman of the English Department, walked up to them. "Excuse me, Grace," he smiled. "I need to talk to Ms. O'Neill for a moment."

Grace gave him a cheerful nod. "I'll save you a seat," she said to Anna as she walked away.

"How did your morning go?" McAllister asked.

"Fine," she said. "Why?"

"What happened between you and Casey Fixx?"

Anna felt angry and defensive at once. "What did he tell you?"

"Just that he offended you," said her new boss, "though he claimed he didn't know how. I'd like to know what happened. If Mr. Fixx insulted you, I need to deal with him." He sounded a little impatient.

She paused, trying to recall Fixx's words.

"I must take some of the blame," Dr. McAllister said. "He's taught all the subjects you're assigned this semester. I thought he could give you some help with your classes. He's a pack rat with papers and tests, so he squirrels everything away. I sent him over to speak to you."

Anna's head shot up. "You asked him to talk to me?"

"Yes. I'm sure he wouldn't have otherwise."

Anna reddened, feeling like an idiot. Fixx hadn't been trying to pick her up. He had been offering to help her.

She recovered enough to stammer, "Dr. McAllister, I made a terrible mistake. I misunderstood Mr. Fixx."

McAllister's expression became stony. "I see."

"I have to apologize to him. Do you know where I can find him?"

"Room 149," he frowned. His face hardened. Anna, sensing the annoyance of her new boss, felt her face redden even more. She excused herself and hurried down the hall to Fixx's classroom.

*   *   *   *   *

After botching his first meeting with Anna O'Neill, Casey Fixx crossed the hallway to his classroom and shut the door. He collapsed into his desk chair, humiliated.

He was weary from overwork. Despite the summer break, Casey hadn't taken a vacation. He'd spent his summer at the University of Illinois, where he was closing in on a Ph.D. in theatre. He'd just gotten home from Champaign the night before.

Later that morning, while the rest of the faculty was at lunch, Casey ate a sandwich in his classroom. Some of his drama students had come in to visit him and talk about the school year. He loved them as if they were his own kids. Now they stood around, sharing anecdotes about jobs, summer romances, vacations and other facets of teenage life.

Casey spent most of his time in room 149 and in the school theatre. During the school year, those two areas seemed more like his home than the little house he lived in.

He tried hard not to think about Anna O'Neill. His stomach hurt as he remembered the way she'd talked to him and how his eyes filled with tears. *What an idiot she must think I am.*

Anna knocked at the open door and peered in. Casey rose, surprised, at once on the defensive. All the students turned to look.

"Mr. Fixx?" Anna's voice trembled.

Casey almost told her to get out and not come back. He had no interest in being insulted in front of his students.

But something in her face made him hesitate. Her green eyes looked frightened and her lower lip quivered. "I'm sorry,"

she said. "I didn't know you were busy. I can come back—"
She started to turn away.

"Wait a minute, please," Casey said. He decided to risk
seeing what she wanted. "Why don't you come on in?"

"Could I please see you in the hall?" Anna asked. The
students hooted.

"We can talk here," he said. He introduced the six students
to her, then shooed them off. "Come on, you guys, hit the
road," he said. The kids hooted again.

A girl with curly blond hair stopped in the doorway next to
Anna. "See you later, Doofus," she said with a sneer.

"That would be Mister Doofus to you," said Casey. "By St.
Loy, I'm going to be treated with some respect around here this
year." The kid stuck her tongue out at him.

"Why, you miserable, disrespectful—" Fixx snarled as he
leapt to his feet and sprinted toward the door.

The girl gave a little scream and took off running, giggling
all the way down the hall, with Fixx pounding in hot pursuit.
The other kids, laughing, waved good-bye and departed.

* * * * *

Anna looked around the classroom. It contained no student
desks, but a horseshoe arrangement of four or five long tables
with chairs. The plaster head of a unicorn and another of a
cartoon bear hung on either side of the blackboard. A plastic
frog hung above the teacher's desk. Bulletin boards displayed
pictures of students.

The eccentric room seemed to suit Fixx, who wore sandals,
jeans and a t- shirt.

"Cute kids," she said as he came back in, puffing.

"Yeah," he grinned. "I chase Emily down the hall a couple
of times a week."

"Why?" she asked.

His face took on a pained expression. "Her father died last

year. She needs a dad at times. I fill in when I can."

"Cool," she said. Anna wished that someone like Fixx had taken an interest in her when her mother died.

"I know it looks pretty undignified but she's worth it."

Anna giggled. "By St. Loy?"

"Oh, that's a quote from Chaucer."

"I know. The Prioress. The prologue to *Canterbury Tales.*"

"Right," he said. The two of them smiled. Then, as if someone had thrown a blanket over him, he fell back into the persona she'd seen earlier. He shuffled his feet and stared at the floor. After a few false starts he stuttered, "I'm glad you came. I should have come to your room to apologize."

"Why?"

"I behaved like a complete idiot. I didn't mean to knock those papers off your desk. I'm sorry."

Anna now felt worse. He'd interpreted her rudeness to him as a reaction to an accident. "No, Mr. Fixx. Please don't apologize. You came to see me to be helpful and gracious, and I couldn't have been more rude and nasty. I'm the one who needs to apologize."

"But, uh—"

"Could we start this friendship over?" She extended her hand. "How do you do? I'm Anna O'Neill." He smiled and took her hand. She looked into his eyes.

Gentle warmth covered Casey like a soft light. His embarrassment and fear eased. A unicorn, graceful and silver-white, stood before him. The unicorn touched him with its horn.

But Anna had a different vision. The night she accepted Alan DiBiasi's proposal, she had a vivid dream of an old man in a spectacular crystal cave. He wore a monk's hood, but she could see the worry on his drawn face. "Viviane, Beloved," he said. "Don't marry him. Your heart will be broken. He doesn't love you."

"I love him, Master," she said. Then the old man transformed into her friend Gareth and the crystal cave became a football field with goal posts and bleachers.

"Please. You can't marry him, Viviane," Gareth pleaded, distraught. She'd seen her friend angry, happy, but never grief-stricken.

"I love him, Gareth."

"You love his money, his house, his Mercedes, his powerful friends at the country club. You love that he gave you a Lincoln Continental, paid off the college loans. It's like a slave auctio."

For the first time ever, she got mad at him. "Look," she said to her dream friend. "I know what I'm doing. I want to marry him. I'm tired of being poor. I'm tired of cheap food, and used clothes, and bills. I can have some happiness in life, can't I?"

"I've never wanted anything other than that for you," he said, and a tear ran down his cheek.

"Well, what am I supposed to do? Wait for you? I don't even know if you're even alive!"

"Of course I'm alive. I just can't ever remember where I live, or who I am—"

Then he couldn't go on. Her friend turned and ran to an old car. He tried to open the car door, but dropped his keys and couldn't pick them up. He stood there, heartbroken. Anna ran toward him, screaming.

In the next instant Anna and Casey stood again in his classroom. But Casey's nervousness and self-doubt had vanished.

She peered into his eyes. "It is you," she whispered. He stared back, bewildered. "I mean—er—I shouldn't have treated you like I did. I had some fights this morning, but that's no excuse for being rude."

"Fights?" he asked.

"I started the morning arguing with my husband. I walked out without saying goodbye." She didn't mention that this sort of fight had become a motif of her marriage.

"Ouch," said Casey.

"I hit disastrous traffic. Road construction blocked the only route I knew to the school and the detours got me lost."

The corners of his mouth twitched. "Welcome to Chicago," he said. "Around here, we say that we only have two seasons: winter and road construction." She smiled and began to relax.

"I stopped at a gas station to ask for directions. I got confused and asked the jerk behind the counter to explain them again. He asked me if I'd ever driven before."

Fixx grinned.

"The other customers in line laughed when he said that. I felt like an idiot." She'd resisted the temptation to Paik the attendant. Revenge wasn't worth a dream visit from Nehushtan.

"Anyhow, getting lost made me late getting here. I had to park way out in the back of the faculty lot and then run to the first meeting in my high heels. At least I didn't break my leg."

Casey chuckled. Anna did too.

"Then some jerk from the phys. ed. department tried to pick me up."

"Jerry Flanders. He told me. I figured he'd tried something like that."

"What an oaf," she shuddered.

"I agree," he nodded. "Then you had to endure those meetings."

"Ugh." She rolled her eyes. "How boring can you get?"

"Sorry, but most of them are a lot worse. Those meetings today ranked as laugh riots compared with some of the drivel we have to sit through." They giggled together.

"I'm glad you got to meet my drama kids," he said.

"Are most of the students like them?"

"What do you mean?"

"Friendly, polite, nice."

"Oh, yeah. We've got a terrific bunch of kids at this school. Some jerks, sure--maybe five percent in a bad year."

"Mr. Fixx," she began, but he held up a hand.

"Please," he said, "call me Casey. 'Mr. Fixx' makes me sound like the mascot for a chain of hardware stores."

"How about if I call you Doofus?" She smiled.

"That's appropriate too," he chuckled. "But you ought to call me Mr. Doofus in front of the kids."

Anna giggled. "Dr. McAllister said you might help me plan the remedial skills course for juniors and seniors. He said you've taught that class."

"Last year."

"Do you have notes or a syllabus that you could share with me?"

He pulled a folder out of his desk, took out papers, and set them before her. "You don't have to use this just because I do," he said. "Of course, you'd be an imbecile if you didn't."

She snickered.

"Use what you want and toss the rest. Once you get rolling you'll want to make up your own stuff."

He grabbed a calendar and a legal pad and pointed to a couple of chairs at one of his tables. For the next half hour, the two plotted out a semester class and organized the writing materials. Then he talked about her other classes.

When she got up to leave, she almost kissed him as she used to do with Gareth in the dreams but realized how inappropriate that would be. She extended her hand and said, "Thanks so much, Casey." When he took her hand, she decided to give him a present. She looked through the blue eyes again. She used the Cymreig to find a certain dream of his, a precious little place. She gave him a Paik. The classroom swirled around them and disappeared —

Gareth found himself sitting up in a queen-sized bed that folded out from a sofa. He faced a fireplace where several logs were burning. They'd turned all the other lights out.

He looked around the room. Through a picture window next to the fireplace, he saw snow falling on the ski slope. Four pairs of ski boots sat by the door, including one tiny pair.

He felt the best he'd ever felt. Happy. Content. Peaceful. Comfortable. Gareth sighed, relaxing after skiing all day with his wife and children. The family enjoyed a dinner in the ski lodge's dining room. Then the kids had gone off to bed.

He looked at the woman next to him. His right arm embraced her shoulders. They each held a glass of red wine. They both wore heavy terry-cloth robes that the lodge provided in the suite.

He ran his fingers through Viviane's lovely copper hair, which she wore somewhat shorter than when they first met. Her head rested on his chest. She turned to him, and in her haunting emerald eyes, he saw the devotion of a life partner. But he also saw concern.

"Do you feel okay?" she asked. "You look upset."

"Of course I'm okay. What could be wrong?"

She snuggled back against him. They talked about the day and how their five-year-old son tried so hard on his little skis. Their beautiful daughter, Mickey, had been the object of attention of most of the young men in the dining room.

At last Viviane set her wineglass on the end table. She took his glass and put it next to hers. She wrapped her arms around his neck and they kissed. He slid his hand up along her thigh. She trembled at his intimate touch. His hand moved to caress her left breast. The kisses deepened.

The ski lodge vanished. Casey found himself back in his classroom, shaking hands with Anna O'Neill. He staggered a step or two and shook his head.

* * * * *

Anna shivered, surprised the Paik had worked so well. They'd shared a vivid episode, like one of her snake dreams. Unlike the terror of the nightmares, this had been enjoyable, sweet, and delicate.

The depth of feelings they had for one another in the dream also surprised her. She felt flattered to be included in his fondest dream. She had broken the Cymreig connection as they settled together to make love. She couldn't have sex with him, even in a vision generated by the Cymreig. After all, she was married.

"Do you plan to work in here this afternoon?" Anna asked. He nodded. "Could I work in here, too, in case I have any questions about my classes?"

"I'd be delighted for your company," Casey said, pleased.

"I'll be right back," she said, and walked to her classroom to get her books and notes.

Nothing would come of the attraction they felt for each other, she told herself.

She also knew, in her heart, that she was lying to herself.

CHAPTER EIGHT

Anna's jitters returned that night. Tomorrow she would meet her students for the first time. She slept little.

Her husband didn't help. He said at dinner, "I called Lou Sydney today."

She looked up.

"Just as I figured," he said. "You just misunderstood his attempt to be nice to you."

She narrowed her eyes and fixed him with a stare. He lowered his eyes to his plate.

"I misunderstood a vulgar pass and clumsy attempt to kiss me?" she asked.

"Yeah," he said, not meeting her eyes. "You didn't let him finish. He and Marcia want you to come to dinner some time when I'm out of town." He forked a piece of potato into his mouth.

"I see," she said.

"And he didn't try to kiss you. He was shocked when I told him you thought that was what he was doing. He grabbed your arm to try to keep you from leaving the room without giving him a chance to explain. He planned to call tonight to apologize for the misunderstanding."

"Oh, I'll bet."

"So you see. It's what I said."

"It is, huh."

"Yeah. In fact, I'd appreciate it if you'd apologize to him. The way you walked out of the room hurt his feelings."

She put her fork down. "I don't care what he said or what you want to believe," she said in a flat voice, struggling not to scream at him. "That lout propositioned me. He tried to kiss me. He restrained me from leaving the room. He bruised my arm." She showed him.

"Now listen. Don't go off crazy about this. I've known him for years. He meant no harm."

"Fine. I don't ever want to be alone with him again."

"Don't be silly. Lou's a great guy—" But his wife stood and fixed him with a cold, angry stare. Then she turned and left the room.

* * * * *

The fight with her husband continued when she dressed the next morning. He again asked her to apologize to Lou Sydney. His request led to another miserable fight.

She drove to the school, rehearsing the things she would say to the students and reviewing her lesson plans for the day. She tried not to think about the argument with Alan that morning or the previous night. *Be professional. Look professional,* she told herself. But the anger continued to simmer.

Once in her classroom, she made a few adjustments to the decorations she'd put up the day before. She stared out the window at the busses unloading the students. She pressed her fingertips together and touched her index fingers to her chin.

She sensed someone standing behind her and turned. Casey grinned at her, and wished her luck on her first day with the students. She could see that he cared about her and wanted her to succeed. He gave her hand a gentle squeeze. Her stage fright and anger began to ebb.

"What if they don't like me?" she said in a small voice.

He put his hand on her shoulder. "Just be yourself. Use your sense of humor. They're going to love you."

"Thanks," she said, and covered his hand with hers.

"Most of these kids are their parents' most valuable possession. I try to take care of them like they were mine."

The kindness in his voice touched her. The pain in her chest and stomach dissipated.

The students surged into her classroom, laughing and shooting glances of appraisal at the new teacher. She greeted them and caught some names. When the bell rang, she told them they could sit where they wished for the day. After a few moments of nervousness, she started to have fun with the students. She taught them to play a silly name game she'd learned in fifth grade.

At first, the students protested and called the game stupid. But she insisted they try it. When they got going, they began to have some fun.

When she had a free period, she headed toward the faculty lounge to find a cup of coffee.

As she walked past Casey's classroom, she heard talking and giggling. She looked in and saw his students listening to Casey introduce the class. She paused in the hall to listen.

"Whaddya hafta do to get good grades?" a kid asked him.

Casey rubbed his chin as if considering, then looked from side to side as if he were imparting a state secret. "There are two ways to get good grades in this class. First, make sure I like you. I mean, let's be honest, okay? Kids I like get good grades. Kids I don't like get terrible grades."

Anna saw some students look up, and exchange nervous glances.

"That's what you've always suspected with teachers, isn't it?" Fixx went on. "Only teachers' pets get the good grades, isn't that true?"

"What's the other way?" asked a kid who sat bolt upright, eyes wide.

"Bribery," said Fixx with a sly smile and a wink. "I have a regular scale of payment: Seventy-five bucks for an 'A'. A 'B' costs sixty dollars."

Several kids began to smile. Others sat with mouths open.

"I make a pile of money. You guys get good grades. We both win, right?" Several more kids were now grinning.

"No witnesses, and cash only, no checks," Fixx resumed. "Small unmarked bills, of course. Slip it to me in a plain envelope any time before grades come out." He walked to the other side of the room, winking like a con man. "Of course you guys know. You don't look stupid. No one ever earns a good grade through hard work and dedication—"

A bushy-haired girl wearing tight jeans and a revealing top thrust a hand into the air. Fixx nodded at her. She took a wad of pink gum the size of a golf ball out of her mouth. She said, "Are you serious?"

A few kids chuckled. "What?" the girl with the gum said. "He can't do that!" Now the laughter spread as the rest of the kids grasped the absurdity of the speech. Fixx began to smile, then chuckle. Anna hurried away so the students wouldn't hear her giggling.

At lunchtime, Anna joined Casey in his classroom. "How'd it go?" he asked.

She told him about the games she'd played with the kids, and their response to her. "How about you?"

His face shone with mischief. "I spent the morning teasing adolescents. Great way to make a living."

"I heard the bribery speech during third hour," she said.

He grinned. "With most classes, I get further along than that before some kid asks if I'm joking."

* * * * *

At the end of the second week, the English department had a potluck lunch. Anna prepared a southern casserole of ham and cheddar cheese grits. Alan hated the dish and refused to eat it. The English faculty, however, raved about it. She received several flattering requests for the recipe.

At the luncheon, she sat next to Grace. The two had begun running and exercising together after school and had become good friends.

"Where's Casey?" she asked Grace.

"In his room, I guess," her friend said. "He never comes to these things."

"Doesn't he like the other teachers?"

"He just doesn't do well in groups."

"But he works so well with the kids. I've seen him."

Grace considered for a moment. "I think he uses a persona for the classroom."

"You mean he performs?"

"When he works in front of a class, his hands have a slight tremble. His movements are jerky, like he's playing the part of a teacher."

"That must be hard."

Grace gave a little shrug. "A day of teaching wears most of us out. It's worse for him though. Teaching exhausts him. Also, when he senses rejection, he works harder."

"Why does he do that?"

"He believes people can't really like him, so he just finds it easier not to put himself in social situations." The conversation stalled as one of the other teachers sat down with them and started to chat.

Anna waited a moment or two. She excused herself and grabbed her purse as if she were going to the washroom. Instead she went to Casey's classroom. She found him eating a sandwich at his desk.

"Hi," she said.

He looked up. "Hi, Anna. What's up?"

"Would you come with me to the luncheon?"

"Thanks," he said. "I've got a ton of paperwork to do."

She wandered over to him and sat down. "What made you so afraid of other people?"

"Afraid?" he repeated, as if ridiculing the idea. "Why would you think that?"

She took his hand, looked into his eyes, and Paiked. The

memories Anna saw appalled her. A frightened little boy hid in his bedroom during family parties. Sat by himself at lunchtime in grade school. Ate alone during high school lunch periods and then worked out alone in the weight room. Endured evil vicious teasing by older kids. Lived in silence with terrifying violence and bullying.

The hand of Nehushtan.

She saw him struggling with speech pathologists, trying to overcome his stuttering. In one memory, some older children bullied him but he didn't tell anyone about it. The little boy thought he deserved the cruelty and he felt ashamed of himself.

As he grew older, the reticent child became coinced that no one could like him. He kept more and more to himself.

Using the Cymreig on her friend, Anna eased the pain of the memories. The bitter edges of fear and self-doubt began to fade.

She released the Paik, but continued to hold his hand. His eyes welled with tears and the tears ran down his cheeks. He brushed at them with his knuckles, embarrassed.

"I'm sorry," he said, staring at his hands. "My eyes tear sometimes."

"I know," she said. "Do you want to come with me to the luncheon now?"

"I can't, Anna. I'm—" He glanced at her and gave a little sigh. She waited. At last he looked at her. In a small voice, he said, "I just don't do well in social settings."

"It's going to get better, now. I guarantee it. Wait here."

She left the room and returned with a paper plate full of ham and cheese grits. "I want you to try this."

He raved about the dish. They sat and talked until the end of the lunch hour.

After that day, she started to drag him to get-togethers. She encouraged him to work in the English office and visit with other teachers. He began to relax, and even seemed to enjoy the other teachers.

CHAPTER NINE

After classes ended for the day on the first Wednesday of October, Anna glanced into Casey's classroom and saw him looking out at the parking lot. She stood next to him and gave his shoulder a gentle punch of greeting. "Don't you have rehearsal tonight?"

"Yeah. I just need to pause and shift gears sometimes."

They chatted a bit about the day, looking out the open window at the students leaving.

To her surprise she began to hear the voices in the wind, for the first time in years. She looked at Casey, and realized he was listening.

"Do you hear them too?" she asked.

"The wind voices. Sure. I don't tell people. They think I'm crazy, so I never say anything."

"I wouldn't call you crazy," she said, with an impish grin. "Maybe a little weird, though." They chuckled and listened. A cardinal and a couple of finches sang outside the window. She saw a chickadee, her favorites when she was a little girl. The tiny creature seemed to sense her presence. She chuckled at its song and its perfect black head with the white mask. Stealing a glance at Casey, she saw he also was grinning.

They stood shoulder to shoulder. It took a while for her to realize that their fingers were laced together.

She released his hand, alarmed that she'd been holding hands with someone other than her husband.

* * * * *

On the first Friday night in November, Anna sat in her classroom after school, reading student essays. They were awful and she had to struggle not to throw them all in the garbage.

Grace walked in. "Hi, Anna. Want to run?"

"Might as well." Anna sighed, capping her pen and grabbing her gym bag.

The two friends left the parking lot and jogged down the sidewalk toward a local park. Anna remained silent.

"Something wrong?" Grace asked.

They jogged in place as they waited for traffic to clear. "My husband and I have been trying to get pregnant," Anna said. "No luck at all."

"How long have you been working at it?"

"About seven months." They turned onto an asphalt path that led into the park. Both women enjoyed the cool air.

"Sometimes it takes a while," said Grace, not without sympathy.

Anna shortened her stride to run up a little hill. They didn't speak again until they started down the other side.

"Did you plan to see Casey's play?" Grace asked.

"I thought I'd go tonight. Alan's out of town until Tuesday."

"He travels a lot, doesn't he?"

"All the time. He thinks he needs to, for his business. Money's the most important thing to him."

"Not to you?"

"Not like him, for sure. He came from a pretty miserable family. His alcoholic father abused him and his mother. He never had much until he started his business after college. Then he made a small fortune."

"So we'd call you—er—rich?"

"Oh, we have enough, for sure, but he lives in fear of the money running out." They approached an intersection and sprinted across the street. "He always seems to think the next big deal will be the real big one. I've told him I don't care about being rich. I'd settle for much less to have him around more."

"What did he say to that?"

"That I'm ungrateful."

"Ow." They ran single file down a narrow cinder path. When they were again side by side, Grace asked, "Why don't we go to the mall and have a bite there, and then go to the play together?"

"That sounds like fun."

"Casey and I plan to go out to Luigi's after the show. You'd be welcome to come with us."

"Oh, I couldn't—"

"It's not a date. The directors and their spouses always go out after the Friday night show for beer and drinks and pizza. We'll be a big group."

Anna agreed. The two women finished their run and showered in the women's locker room. Then they drove in Grace's car to the mall.

* * * * *

Anna felt a little amused jealousy of Grace once in a while. Her friend liked to show off her superb legs with skirts much shorter than Anna's. Anna sometimes wondered how the young men in Grace's classes managed to get anything done.

In one store Grace handed a denim miniskirt and sweater to Anna and urged her to "just try them on."

After some token protesting, Anna changed into the outfit. She came out of the dressing room, shy, but knowing that she looked pretty good. Grace grinned, and gave her a thumbs up gesture. Anna stared at herself in the mirror.

The outfit didn't match her usual style. Anna dressed in far more conservative outfits even though Alan had often told her that he'd prefer to see her in tight sweaters and short skirts. She'd resisted, thinking of the leers of his friends.

She liked the way the skirt shaped around her body and how it accented her hips and legs. Now she began flirting with the idea of seeing what would happen if she wore the outfit to the play that night. The thought made her tingle.

She pirouetted in front of the mirror, trying to decide if she wanted to draw the attention that the outfit would. She cleared her throat. "Alan would like this."

"Most men would," Grace grinned, looking over Anna's shoulder into the mirror.

Anna thought about Casey. She let Grace talk her into wearing the outfit.

During the ride back to the school, she reached up and let down her luxuriant red hair, which she wore in a harsh twist on top of her head for school. She brushed her hair out over her shoulders. Grace gave her a wink and a nod of approval.

The first play of the year was a dramatized version of *Dr. Jekyll and Mr. Hyde.* Anna marveled at the level of professionalism she saw in the young actors. They were exact in their movements; their lines were clear and well enunciated. The scenes of transformation from Jekyll to Hyde made the hairs on her arm prickle.

After the show Anna watched Casey shaking hands with parents and audience members. When he saw her and Grace standing together, he came over. "Wow. You look terrific," he said, eyeing her new outfit.

"Told you," Grace whispered to Anna.

"Thanks, both of you," she said, feeling a blush rising.

"I invited Anna to come with us for pizza," said Grace.

Casey brightened. "Super. Let me run the kids off and we can go."

At the restaurant Casey introduced her to the other directors and their husbands and wives. The group welcomed her, smiling and laughing. "Thanks for coming, Anna," said Thom Kapheim, the technical director.

"Yes," said Rebecca Sanchez, who handled the tickets and publicity for the play. "It means a lot to the kids when their teachers show up for their activities."

"Means a lot to us, too," laughed Casey. "We appreciate the faculty support as much as they do." He gave her hand a squeeze. She grinned to herself, pleased to realize that he had to struggle not to stare at her crossed legs in the miniskirt. The gracious attention of the group made her feel warm and welcome.

After the waitress took the orders, the directors shop-talked, reviewing the production. The technical director talked about problems with the set; the ticket and publicity manager explained what was happening with sales for the next night; the costume and lighting people had ideas for changes. The intensity each person brought to the conversation amazed Anna.

As the conversation went on, Anna came to understand that Grace and Casey planned to sleep together that night. The thought made her feel jealous of Grace. *Mind your own business,* she told herself.

As the shop talk ended, Casey turned to Anna and Grace. "I apologize," Casey said. "Theatre types do this after every performance. I'm sure you found that a grinding bore."

"No, I enjoyed listening," Anna said. "But I am a little surprised at the extent of your involvement."

He shrugged. "The students take it to heart even more than we do. The plays mean as much to the theatre kids as football means to the football team, or dance means to the girls in Orchesis, or a concert to the band and choir kids."

"They were terrific," she said. "I found the show professional and entertaining."

Casey grinned at the compliment. "I hoped your husband would come," Casey said. "I've been wanting to meet him. I'm sure he's a great guy. . ."

"Oh, he went out of town. Business trip. Besides, he would never come to a play."

He averted his eyes but Anna had seen a brief flash of hurt. "I understand," he said, trying to look cheerful. "A lot of people don't think high school kids can do drama." In that moment, she understood the pride he took in his job.

"I didn't mean that," she said. "Alan wouldn't go to anything at the school with me. He never goes anywhere except with his friends." She took a sip of the red wine.

"Doesn't sound like you enjoy his friends," Grace put in.

Anna shrugged. "They don't like me much. Most of their parties, I end up sitting off by myself."

"I'm sorry," said Casey. The waitress began distributing the pizzas. She set a large cheese, sausage and green pepper pizza in front of Anna. Casey held up his soda glass and asked for a refill. He poured Grace and Anna some Chianti from a carafe.

He took a big bite of pizza and waved his hand in front of his mouth. "Yow. Hot."

Anna resumed the conversation. "His friends think I'm either a trophy for Alan or a gold-digger, only after his money." Anna took a tiny bite of her pizza. She inhaled, seized Casey's soda, and took a large sip.

"He's doesn't socialize with any of your friends?" Casey asked.

"That, and he resents me teaching. He doesn't like being bound to a school calendar. So he associates the school with depriving him of me. Not that he's home all that much anyhow. Still, he'd like to go away for cruises, golf, skiing, gambling junkets."

"Gambling?" said Grace.

"Yes," said Anna. "It worries me on occasion, but he swears he doesn't have a problem. I'd rather. . ." she let her voice trail away.

"Sounds like he's gone a lot of the time, huh?" said Grace.

Casey took another slice and caught a huge drip of cheese as it slid off the side. "Wait until you have kids of your own in school. Between little league and soccer—"

Grace shot him a look and rushed to change the subject. She said, "Anna, that's an exquisite necklace. It looks like an heirloom."

Anna smiled, flattered. She unclasped it and handed it to Grace, who admired it with Casey. At least a dozen large emeralds sparkled in a white gold setting.

"I know it's too formal for this outfit," said Anna. "I wore it today with my school clothes."

"If I owned it, I'm not sure I'd ever take it off," Grace said.

"It's beautiful," said Casey, in a voice of awe.

"Quite a story goes with it, if you'd be interested."

Casey and Grace urged her to tell the story. The rest of the group at the large table turned to her.

Anna related the story of her ancestor, Prudence Lutrelle, her marriage to Blackbeard, her daring escape. Then she told the tradition of handing down the necklace from mother to daughter, and how Prudence intended it to be a memorial to freedom.

"That's how I got the necklace," said Anna. She looked up and blushed to realize that the whole group at the table had been listening with rapt attention.

CHAPTER TEN

Just before Christmas break Anna found herself a little depressed at the idea of being away from the school for two weeks. She knew she'd miss the students, Grace, and the other teachers. In particular, she'd miss Casey, who had become her closest friend and confidante.

On Friday, the English faculty had their Christmas party during the lunch period. Casey didn't come.

Anna stormed to his room and found him sitting at his desk with a sandwich. "You're missing the party."

"I had some paper work to finish," he mumbled, eyes downcast.

Anna snorted, took his hand and dragged him to the party. He seemed to have a good time.

Later, as Anna waited for her last class of the day to come in, she looked up to see Grace enter the room.

"I can't run tonight," Grace apologized. "I've got to leave right after school to try to get a jump on traffic." Anna shrugged, trying not to look too disappointed. Grace asked, "Any plans for this break?"

Anna shook her head. "Alan went to Las Vegas for some convention. He'll be home late tonight. We're planning a quiet Christmas morning together. Then, we'll go to dinner at the home of one of his friends." She sighed, unenthusiastic about the prospect. "How about you?"

"Yeah, I'm off to Colorado," Grace said, excited. "My mom and dad own a condo in Steamboat Springs. We have a big family with lots of little kids. We'll all get together Christmas morning."

"Sounds marvelous." A student came in and greeted Grace, who chatted with the girl for a moment or two.

Anna felt a pang of longing as she thought about how much fun Christmas would be with children opening presents around the tree. She and Casey would watch, sitting on the couch, holding hands—

Wait a minute. No. She and *Alan* would watch. Not Casey.

"Here," Grace said, interrupting her thoughts. "I have something for you." She held up a small gift-wrapped box.

"Oh Grace, you didn't have to—"

Grace waved it off. "It's nothing."

Anna tore the package open and found a coffee cup with a smiling Santa. The card read, "Merry Christmas to my running buddy. Love, Grace."

Anna hugged her friend, feeling terrible that she hadn't thought to buy her a gift. Having friends who valued her came as a revelation for her. A tear ran down her cheek.

Grace chuckled. "Good grief," she said. "Don't make such a big deal of it."

"I love it," said Anna. "You can't imagine how much this means to me." They said good-bye and Grace left as the bell rang for Anna's last class.

At the end of the school day Anna walked over to Casey's classroom to say good-bye. She saw him talking to the little blonde girl he'd chased the first day. The girl struggled not to cry. When Casey saw Anna, he winked and waved her in.

"Emily," he said, "you know your father didn't die to spite you. I know he hated to leave. But he'd want you to move ahead with your life. Your mom has to, also."

The girl stood on her tiptoes to put her arms around his neck for a quick hug. The affection the girl felt for her teacher and friend touched Anna again. As Emily left the room she smiled at Anna. "Merry Christmas, Ms. O'Neill."

"Thank you, Emily," said Anna, with a sympathetic smile. "You, too." The girl left, waving to Casey.

"What happened to Emily?" asked Anna.

"Remember I told you her dad died last spring?" Casey asked. Anna nodded. "Well, Emily's mom has met a man. Emily's struggling with the possibility of her mom re-marrying. She's not looking forward to her first Christmas without her father."

Anna clucked her tongue. "Poor kid. I know how she feels."

"So do I. My first Christmas without Mom and Dad hurt a lot." Casey opened a drawer in his desk and pulled out a package. "Merry Christmas."

Choking up at the sweet consideration, Anna stared at the gift.

"Would you please open it now?" Casey asked.

She tore away the wrapping and stared in disbelief at a first edition of T. H. White's *The Sword in the Stone*, the story of King Arthur's boyhood.

"You don't have it, do you?" he sounded a bit anxious.

"Oh, I have a paperback of *The Once and Future King*, but—"

"Do you like it?"

She flipped it open. "Yes, I do. Would you inscribe it for me?" She handed the book to him.

He took a pen and wrote, *Merry Christmas to a great friend. Read this to your children. Casey Fixx, 1984.*

She stared at the inscription, and then put her arms around his neck for what was supposed to be a thank-you hug. He returned it. It wound up being tender. They lingered in the warm, comfortable embrace.

A small voice in her head began to tell her that in another moment, they'd start kissing. She realized that if they did, they might not be able to stop. She forced herself to pull away.

"What a treasure," Anna said. "How did you find it?"

"I know a good used book store. The owner ordered it for me. It took a few weeks, but if you like it, it's worth the effort."

Then disappointment—even some guilt—took over. She bit

her lip. "I don't have anything to give you."

"Forget it. My pleasure."

"But it must be worth—"

"Aw, cut it out. I don't have many people to give gifts to anyhow." She heard a small catch in his voice. "My two little sisters went to Europe with my aunt and uncle for this year and next. My older sister Karen lives in California. Grace and I exchanged little gifts. And I got some things from the kids." He pointed to a shopping bag with gifts stacked in it.

"So you're going to be alone at Christmas?" she asked.

"'Fraid so. But that's okay. I've got a lot of stuff to do."

"Maybe you and I could go for a bite of supper tonight. Consider it my Christmas present to you."

"I'd love to," he said. "But I can't. I've got to leave as soon as I can and drive to Champaign tonight."

"Champaign?"

"My advisor at the University of Illinois, Brian Wilkie, is leaving as soon as I get there to drive to Florida with his wife and kids. I'm going to house sit for him. I have a bunch of work to do at the library."

"By yourself? No, that's terrible."

"Anna, I appreciate your concern but I don't mind. Believe me, I'll stay busy. I'd make a terrific monk. Besides it's only a couple of weeks."

He stood just a foot or so away from her. If she took one step, she could be back in his arms, sharing the tender hug again. No one would see or know. They could pick up the hug right where they left off. They'd start to kiss in the next moment. He'd hold her and they'd—

No. She rejected the thought.

"Thanks for being a friend," he said, his voice husky. "You can't imagine what your friendship has meant to me."

She squeezed his arm. "Okay. I'll see you in two weeks."

CHAPTER ELEVEN

On Saturday, inspired by the gifts her friends had given her, Anna went shopping for Alan's presents. She ransacked several stores and found a muted red tie with a tasteful floral pattern. She thought the tie would make him look younger, and even lighten him up a little. His wardrobe bordered on the moribund.

Then she found a dress shirt with French cuffs. After a search of several jewelry stores, she located the perfect cufflinks: black onyx, in a gold setting, with a small diamond in the center of each.

She bought him a couple of golf shirts, and a dozen of his favorite golf balls. She picked up several stocking stuffers too.

The shopping left her feeling weary but happy. When she got home, she found Alan napping, so she took her time wrapping each gift.

Then, she put up a small Christmas tree. She decorated it with ornaments and lights. As she draped the tinsel, Alan came downstairs from his nap.

"Do you like it?" she beamed.

"Yeah," he said, yawning. "Great. What's up for dinner?"

* * * * *

To Alan, Christmas just meant a day that he had to close the business. Though Anna brimmed with impatience for him to get up and open his presents, he slept until just before 10 A.M.

He opened her gifts. "Well. These are quite—ah—interesting," he managed. His tone left no doubt that he didn't like them.

She said, disappointed, "I saved the receipts."

"Good," he said. "Here." He handed her an envelope and

went to the kitchen.   Inside the envelope she found a gift certificate to a department store. She stared at the certificate, and at the presents she'd picked out for him. Sighing, she went to the kitchen to thank him for the money.

He didn't hear the irony in her voice. "No problem," he grunted into his coffee cup.

That afternoon, they went to a Christmas party at the home of his doctor friend, Jim O'Donnell. Alan wore the necktie, but left the shirt and cufflinks.

After an hour of being excluded from conversations, Anna walked into the kitchen. "Let me help," she said to Ellen O'Donnell.

The hostess looked up and almost frowned, but caught herself. Instead, she gave Anna a smile that suggested that the younger woman might be insane.

"Oh, how sweet of you—uh—Anne."

"Anna."

"Yes of course. I'm sorry," said her hostess, not sounding even a little sorry. "No, I've nothing for you to do, dear. Just go back and enjoy the men."

Anna looked at her in surprise. The intonation implied that Anna had a vast record as a homewrecker and that Anna would be as welcome in the kitchen as massive infestation of e coli bacteria.

"Excuse me?"   said Anna, annoyed.   "I don't quite understand what you mean."

"Never mind, dear." Now the woman spoke as if telling a five-year-old that she didn't need an extra portion of dessert.

Anna gritted her teeth, fighting down a powerful impulse to kick her hostess in the shin. She started to return to the living room, but stopped out of sight when she overheard Lou Sydney saying, "What's with the tie?"

"You like it?" Alan laughed, and a group of men standing around laughed with him.

"Are you nuts?" Lou sneered. Anna again heard laughter from several men.

"I'm wearing it to be nice," he said. "Anna bought it for me."

"I wouldn't wear it to wash the car," said Lou. "Might use it to wash the car, though." The men laughed again.

"I feel like I ought to be wearing a big red nose and a squirting flower in my lapel," chuckled Alan. "Yeah, you're right."

"Well, at least if the lights go out, we can see by the glow of the tie," said Lou, and general laughter ensued.

"It goes back tomorrow, don't worry," said Alan. "As soon as the stores open." More laughter.

"Geez," said Lou, "what did you give her to deserve that?"

"Same as last year. My secretary went out on her lunch hour and got her a gift certificate."

"Well," said Lou, "no wonder. I imagine this thing"—he fingered the tie—"is her form of revenge." Now the group bellowed with laughter. The group broke up.

Burning with humiliation, Anna waited a few moments before she entered the room. She watched Alan remove the tie, fold it and put it on the side table. He walked off into the family room downstairs.

Her face flushed with anger and mortification, she picked up the tie and then went to the guest bedroom, where she retrieved her coat and purse. She carried them downstairs and laid them on a chair by the front door.

She came up behind Lou Sydney and took his elbow. He turned and gave her a patronizing, annoyed nod. He started to turn back to a conversation with someone else, but stopped when she extended her hand. Looking bewildered, he took it. She looked into his eyes.

"Lou," said his hostess, Ellen O'Donnell, "two men just came in. They want to see you."

The room grew silent as two huge men walked toward Lou. "That's him," said a young voice. The men walked over. One of them said, "Lou Sydney?"

"Who wants to know?" he sneered.

"Lake Forest police," said one of the men, holding out a badge. "Are you Mr. Sydney?"

"Yeah, I am," he said.

"Please put your hands behind you."

Sydney didn't cooperate at first. He sneered and crossed his arms in front of him.

Before he knew what had happened, one of the detectives spun him around and shoved him, hard, against the wall. He put out his hands to break his fall. The two burly detectives jerked his arms behind him and snapped on the cuffs.

"What the hell do you think you're doing?" he snapped, enraged. Then he looked to the door. Susan Willis, their sixteen-year-old baby-sitter, stood there. Next to her stood a florid-faced man who looked ready to kill him.

"Sir, you're under arrest for taking indecent liberties with a minor. Mr. Willis here intends to press charges. You have the right..." While the detective read the Miranda declaration from a small card, the other detective held his wrists behind him and pushed him toward the door. Lou winced in pain.

Lou Sydney had driven the girl home two nights ago. She had been baby-sitting their three young children. He hadn't had sex with the girl. But he'd done other things.

She'd promised she wouldn't say anything. Particularly after he'd given her the crisp $50 bill.

"Do you understand the rights I've explained to you?" the policeman said.

"Marcia," he said to his wife, choking with the bile that surged into his throat. "Find a lawyer." She couldn't look at him as she wept with mortification and rage.

The detectives hauled him to the door. Mr. Willis stepped

forward and slugged Lou hard in the stomach. Then he clouted him on the jaw, knocking loose several teeth. The punch stunned him and left his mouth bleeding. "You miserable—" said Willis, but Lou Sydney missed the rest.

The two detectives, holding Sydney under his arms, frog-marched him down the long driveway to a squad car. As they pushed his head down and shoved him into the back seat, he saw the party guests gathering and standing on the porch.

"Angry?" said a voice next to him. He spun and stared in amazement. Anna, Alan's wife, sat next to him in the back seat of the cruiser.

She crossed one lovely leg over the other, pulled her skirt down, and sat back against the seat. He started to demand an explanation, but found he couldn't speak or move. Blood dripped from his lip onto his white shirt.

"Mr. Sydney, you seem to be an uneducated boor, lacking in sensitivity, kindness and social skills. You embarrassed and ridiculed me to a large group of people. I found your comments and jokes not only unkind but hurtful and humiliating. So I'm going to give you a few lessons in etiquette and kindness. This fantasy—" she indicated the squad car "—didn't happen. Lucky for you. Come with me."

The squad car dissolved, and the air swirled. In the next moment, Lou Sydney, still handcuffed, found himself standing atop a cliff, looking at the ocean. Anna stood next to him. "You're looking at the seacoast of Ireland, Mr. Sydney. The land of my ancestors."

She inspected a fingernail for a moment. "Lesson number one. Before the invasion of England in 1066, some of the people who lived there had extraordinary abilities. They appeared to be human, but they could invade people's minds and take them captive, making them slaves. They were called Faerae, the Old Ones. Not Fairies like Tinker Bell. The very name of these creatures terrified the ancient people of England, Wales, and

Ireland."

"They still exist. And they continue to be very dangerous.
You never know when one might be near, and may take offense
at something you say. That Faerae could take you prisoner."

Lou Sydney stared at her in angry bewilderment. He tried
to say something but his voice still didn't seem to work. "I'm
sorry you don't approve of my taste in neckties," she said.
"You ridiculed the tie I selected with care and affection as a gift.
That brings us to lesson number two: keep your nasty opinions
to yourself in the future."

Now the seacoast disappeared and Lou Sydney stood in a
cemetery. Anna stood ten feet away from him, leaning against a
gigantic, gnarled oak tree. Lou heard a roaring fire and felt
chilled with horror. He turned and saw that he stood on the
edge of a pit of green fire. He felt his stomach drop. "Now
you've come to St. Margaret's Island in the Pamlico Sound of
North Carolina, Mr. Sydney. Few people ever come here anymore. I'm tempted to leave you, but I have a better idea."

He still couldn't speak. Anna said, "I think Christmas just
ended for you, Mr. Sydney. Now, here's what I think. I want
you to apologize to me in front of the people. Then, you're
going to have a headache and you'll be in terrible, nauseating
pain for the rest of the night. When you wake up tomorrow,
you will be all right again. However: if you ever touch that girl
again or even think about assaulting her as you did last night,
the headaches and nausea will return at once. Please believe me
when I say that you'll be worse than tonight. You may not
recover at all. Understand?"

He didn't answer. He sneered at her, teeth gritted in fury.

She flipped her head. A violent spasm of pain ripped
through his brain and he all but screamed. "I said,
understand?" she asked.

He managed to nod, his teeth now clenched against the pain.
The pain eased. Then, she stood in front of him and shoved.

Lou Sydney lost his balance and fell backward into the hideous green fire...

Lou stood in the living room of his friends, Jim and Ellen O'Donnell, staring at Alan's wife. Though he thought several minutes had elapsed, he saw to his astonishment that no time at all seemed to have elapsed.

"Anna," he heard himself saying, "I'm glad you came over. I spoke out of turn a bit ago. I insulted you and the gift you gave to the man you love. In fact, I've been callous and unkind to you since I've known you. I've underestimated you and belittled you. Will you please accept my apology?" He watched himself extend his hand, bewildered by what he was doing and saying.

Lou heard faint gasps. The mouths of the people in the group dropped open and their eyes widened in surprise. The group stared at him, stunned.

Anna O'Neill took his hand, smiled at him and said, "Thank you, Mr. Sydney. I accept your apology and I appreciate your kindness and consideration." She leaned up as if to kiss his cheek. Instead, she whispered in his ear: "Never speak to me again."

She turned and strode away. Lou, still angry and dumbfounded, realized that the Lake Forest detectives hadn't really arrested him. Nor had he gone to Ireland. Nor North Carolina. Nor had he fallen into a pit of green fire. Somehow, it hadn't really happened. But he would remember.

When Alan's wife reached the archway to the family room, she turned and looked at him. She mouthed, "Pain."

Lou Sydney became nauseated at once. Holding his mouth against a rising gorge of sickness, he fled the living room, ran into the powder room and slammed the door.

* * * * *

Anna found her husband in the family room, laughing with

a group of people.

"Alan," she said. He didn't respond. "Alan!" she shouted. The group grew silent and turned toward her.

"What?" he demanded.

"I need to see you on the front porch."

"You what?" but his wife didn't hear. She returned to the living room and put on her coat. She opened the door and went out onto the porch.

Alan came out behind her. "What the hell. . ." he began, but Anna interrupted.

"I'm going home," she said, drawing out her set of car keys. "I'd like you to come with me. We have something to discuss. I'll wait thirty seconds for you to get your coat."

"Are you nuts? I can't go now. We haven't had dinner."

"Twenty seconds."

"Besides, look at where we're parked. We're blocked in. People would have to move their cars."

"Ten seconds."

"Don't be ridiculous."

"Very well. You can call a cab or get a ride from one of your weasel friends."

"You can't—"

"Oh yes I can. Watch me." She turned to go, but he caught her arm. She pivoted back and hit him in the jaw with her fist, hard enough to draw tears.

He staggered back, holding his hand to his face.

Anna strode to the Mercedes, unlocked the door, and slid in. She started the engine and turned the wheel to the left. She drove through a small hedge, across the lawn to the street, and headed home.

At home, Anna worked off some fury by running two miles, and then she stretched and did some abdominal exercises. She began to feel better.

After a shower, she heated some water in the Santa coffee

mug and made some tea. She re-wrapped the presents she'd given to Alan and slid them into her school bag.

She lit the fireplace, sat in a large overstuffed chair, and sipped the tea. Then she opened the book Casey had given her. She looked at the inscription and ran her hand over the writing. She smiled and turned to the first page.

An hour later, the anger began to simmer again. Alan had seen how hurt and angry she was, but he chose to stay with his friends.

Fine.

She thought about Casey. They had shared such a sweet hug that last Friday before Christmas break, full of real affection and warmth.

Anna decided to take a chance even though Nehushtan would haunt her dreams and terrify her.

She realized she didn't care.

She thought about the University of Illinois library. Now, she reached out with the Cymreig.

Anna stood in the area just outside the stacks. She found it all but deserted on Christmas afternoon. No one paid attention to her as she walked between the rows. *Let's see. Theatre stuff would be in 800s.* She climbed to the sixth floor and walked up and down the aisles.

At last, she spotted him sitting at a study carrel.

"Hi," she said. Casey Fixx looked up and turned to her.

"Hey," he grinned. "Let me get you a chair." He walked to a nearby cubicle, found a chair, and brought it back.

She sat opposite him. "Why are you here? It's Christmas."

"I felt lonely. If I work, I feel better. I'm glad you're here."

"I'm not really here, you know," she said.

"I know I'm just imagining this. It feels like I'm awake, though."

"How's your work going?" she asked.

They talked for almost an hour about school, his studies, and the house he was staying in, and when he'd come home. At last she said, "I've got to go, Gareth."

His face fell. "Okay. I had fun talking to you. A nice Christmas present. Thanks."

"I think I'm going to dream of Nehushtan tonight."

"We'll face him together."

She took his hand and looked into his eyes. "Go to sleep for five minutes," she said. "When you wake up, you'll remember this as a dream." He turned to his cubicle, put his head down on the obscure volume he'd been reading, and went to sleep.

She breathed deep, smiled, and released the Cymreig.

Alan stood over her. "Thank goodness. I've been shaking you for ages."

She stood and looked him in the eye. "What do you want?"

"Lou Sydney left right after you did, sick with the worst migraine headache I've ever seen. His wife was going to take him to the hospital."

"Good. I hope he's sick all night."

"Anna, you're being mean," he said. Her eyes widened, and she laughed in his face. His face reddened. "My friends didn't intend to hurt you."

"Oh yes they did. You and that buffoon Lou and your dreadful friends took hilarious pleasure in mortifying and ridiculing me."

"Now, hang on. No one—"

She interrupted. "I spent hours searching for the tie I wanted you to have. You paid me back by humiliating me and having a good laugh at my expense. Instead of telling off that lout, you insulted the tie I gave you."

"Well, I'm sorry, but I couldn't wear something that garish," he said. Tears came to Anna's eyes. "Besides, you ruined Jim and Elaine's hedge and probably their lawn. I'm going to have to pay—"

"Don't worry." She handed him an envelope. "Take your

oh so thoughtful gift certificate. Be sure you tell your secretary thank you for extending herself." He took it, flushing with embarrassment. "Buy yourself whatever you want and use what's left to compensate those insufferable, snobbish friends of yours. I don't care. I'll never see any of those people again. And I haven't the least intention of accepting a gift from you this Christmas."

"Now just a minute. I came to try to make things right and you're acting like a spoiled child." He put out his arms to hug her. She smacked them away.

"You can't make things right now. I'm way too mad to accept an apology. Good night. I'll sleep out here."

"Stop acting so silly. Come on to bed." He walked toward her and she shoved him back.

"No. We'll talk tomorrow."

"I don't—"

"You don't care about me or about how you hurt me. Not in the slightest. You're scared that you'll have to skip sex tonight. Nothing in the world could interest me less."

Now he lost his temper. "Don't you ever talk back to me like that." He drew back his hand to slap her across the face.

But he found he couldn't move. He stood on the edge of a pit, which had opened in the middle of his den. Green fire lashed up and he heard ghastly sounds of pain and terror.

From the other side of the pit his wife looked into his eyes, furious. "Never lift your hand to me, Alan. Never. I'm showing you a little sample of what would happen. You'll never recover from what I'll do to you," he heard her say.

Then he could move and finished the slap. But his young wife didn't stand where he thought she was. She stood behind him, somehow. He couldn't remember how she got there. He lost his balance, staggering across the room and falling to his knees.

He stood, flustered and shaken, the vision of emerald fire

still not faded. He turned to find her scrutinizing him, cold as an iceberg with fury. "Don't forget what I said. Ever." She pointed to the doorway. "Get out."

Humiliated and still scared, he walked out of the room.

As she imagined, she had fiery dreams filled with visions of Nehushtan. But Gareth came to be with her. It felt so good to see him that she didn't care about the terror.

CHAPTER TWELVE

When school resumed after winter break, Anna walked into Casey's classroom at the end of the day. She found him standing by the window, staring out. He turned and grinned when he saw her. She shut the door and motioned him to a table.

"I brought you a Christmas present," she said.

"You what? Aw, Anna, you didn't have to do that. . ."

"Sit down and shut up," she smiled.

He sat down at the table, and she opened her school bag. First, she pulled out the shirt package and watched his fingers tremble as he opened it. Then, she gave him the tie, which he laid atop the shirt. His mouth dropped open and his eyes filled as he looked at the elegant cufflinks.

He still hadn't said a word, mouth open in amazement. He took the tie and stroked the silk with fingers that couldn't quite be still. Then he put the cufflinks next to the shirt. He placed his fingertips together and pressed them to his lips. *Why didn't Alan react like this?* she thought.

At last he found his voice. "What a beautiful gift, Anna. I've never had such—"

"Do you really like them?"

"I don't know what to say. Thank you so much."

"Serves you right."

"Huh?"

"Now you know how I felt when you gave me the book." They laughed together.

Anna had a brief vision of them in bed, thanking each other by sharing a gift more valuable than any that could be purchased. She shrugged the vision away and they chatted until he had to leave for a meeting about the winter play.

Anna resumed her routine of meetings and conversations at lunch and free periods with Casey and Grace. She often joined him at his hall duty, just to talk and share a laugh.

* * * * *

Anna began to feel lonely again in the middle of February. Casey became involved with another play. Grace, the varsity girls' softball coach, didn't have time now to go running with her.

One day at lunch, Grace told Anna, "I met a guy named Rudy. It's starting to look good."

"That's terrific," said Anna. "Did you tell Casey?"

Grace looked puzzled. "Well, yes. Why?"

"I thought you two were pretty tight."

"I love Casey to pieces. But he's just my friend."

Anna felt a strange sense of relief. When she returned to the English wing, she saw Casey outside his classroom and waved. He grinned back at her.

As she entered her room, she thought about how her affection for this shy man had affected her life. He'd become a friend who believed in her, encouraged her, and enjoyed being with her. He took pride in his friendship with her. She liked the feeling.

Then, she almost murdered him.

CHAPTER THIRTEEN

One Friday afternoon in late April, Anna walked into the faculty lounge. To her delight she found Casey sitting and talking with a group of counselors and teachers. She waved at him. They hadn't been able to spend much time together all week.

"I should have known I'd find you loafing here," she said.

The group laughed.

"Could you talk to one of my students?" she asked. Casey rose from the couch and joined her in the corridor. Anna introduced him to Will Wallace, who clutched a camera and a notepad.

Casey shook hands with the young man.

"Will writes for the school paper," she told him. "He wants to interview you about your plans to go to the University next year."

Casey grinned and agreed. Will asked if he could take a picture of the two of them. She took Casey's arm as Will flashed a couple of snapshots.

Anna went into the lounge while Casey answered Will's questions. She sat down with the other teachers. Relaxing and joking with friends felt terrific.

She'd finished teaching for the week, though she planned to stay at the school for the rest of the day and catch up on some paperwork.

Casey returned as the rest of the group left. They chatted, resting their feet on the old coffee table.

"So, what's going on with you tonight?" he asked, after a few moments.

"Alan had to go out of town until Sunday morning. I'm thinking of driving up to Wisconsin to see my aunt and uncle."

"Would you like to do something around here?" he blurted.

She crossed her arms on her chest, amused. "What do you have in mind?"

"Do you know how to get to Whizzer's? The bar and restaurant?"

"Sure."

"I guess you know, a bunch of teachers meet there on Friday afternoons," he said.

"So I've heard."

"Yeah, the place has a band, and Friday afternoon Happy Hour with an Oyster Bar, stuff like that. So—er--if you're not firm in those other plans, maybe—er—" He looked like a seventh grader asking a girl to dance with him at a school party.

She resisted the temptation to tease him. "I'd love to come, but don't you have rehearsal tonight?" she asked. The spring musical, *Camelot*, which would open under his direction in a couple of weeks.

"No. I gave the cast the night off."

"This close to production? Doesn't that scare you?"

"Yeah, sure, but the tech staff needs the theatre. Thom and his kids have to set lights, work set changes, set the stage up."

"Oh, I see. So he wants you—"

"Out of the way, right." They chuckled. "I've been going full bore for weeks now. I sure could use an evening of fun myself, too."

When the final bell of the school day rang, Anna and Casey walked to his rundown Chevy Impala. She giggled at the styrofoam coffee cups, fast food wrappers and bags, and mouthwash. Red-faced, he apologized, seized a gym bag from the back seat and began jamming the clutter into it. He tossed the bag into the back seat, muttering excuses.

He took a deep breath and held the driver's side door open for her. "Sorry," he mumbled. "The latch on the passenger side broke and I haven't had time to get it fixed." He continued to blush as she snickered at him.

They talked and laughed as they pulled out of the parking lot, but when they got close to the tavern Casey began to stutter.

She understood and felt touched. Even though her best friend still feared crowds, he'd brought her to this place to be nice to her and give her a pleasant afternoon.

Flattered and delighted, she reached over and hugged his arm. He smiled and gave her a puzzled grin. "What's that for?" he asked.

"Just for being such a good friend," she whispered.

Casey's hand slipped on the door handle as they got out. He wiped his palm on his jacket. He breathed deep and opened his door. He gave her his hand as she slid across the seat and climbed out. She took his arm and felt him trembling. "Casey," she said, "we're going to have a great time."

He gave her a weak smile as they walked to the tavern. When they reached the door, she stopped him. She touched his elbow, looked through his eyes and Paiked. He relaxed.

A large and noisy Friday afternoon crowd jammed the smoky bar. Casey led Anna to the Westwood table, where the teachers greeted her with enthusiasm. Casey introduced her to a couple of people she hadn't met.

"Why haven't you ever come with us?" said Jane Fletcher, one of the counselors.

"No one ever asked me," she said, as if her feelings were hurt. The group laughed, and she blushed with pleasure. One of the guys drew up a chair for her and the group shifted to make room for them. Casey pulled a chair in next to Anna.

The conversation resumed. The group made a point of including her and listening when she spoke. She tried in vain to buy a round of drinks. Several said she should consider herself a guest this time.

Casey, rather to her surprise, drank cola. "I have what Shakespeare calls 'poor brains for drinking,'" he explained, blushing a little.

The band turned out to be terrific. Anna and Casey danced, and then she danced with several other teachers, happier than she had been in ages.

Casey turned out to be a good dancer. "Years of doing choreography in plays," he told her. The band performed an old Jerry Butler ballad, *Make It Easy on Yourself.* She pressed her cheek to his, her hand on the back of his neck. "Beautiful song," she said in his ear.

"Not as beautiful as the girl I'm dancing with," he whispered.

"Thank you," she murmured. She felt a little weak. Without thinking, she put both arms around his neck and hugged him. The vocalist sang, "'Cause breakin' up is so very hard to do."

When the song ended, she didn't release him at once, but gave him a hug and said, "Thanks so much for bringing me today." Casey smiled and nodded.

For Anna, sitting and talking with a group of people close to her own age, and dancing and listening to her favorite music, came as a welcome and fun change. Alan would have felt uncomfortable with the place, the music, and the conversation.

The people at the table began telling war stories of teaching debacles. Everyone laughed.

When Casey excused himself to the washroom, one of the young counselors, Kim Saunders, whispered into Anna's ear, "What's going on between you and Casey?"

Anna smiled back. "Oh, nothing. We just drove over here together."

"Well," Kim said behind her hand, "he's crazy about you."

"Oh come on," Anna said.

"He never takes his eyes off you. Believe me, he's nuts about you." Something distracted Kim and she turned away. Anna sat, stunned.

When Casey returned, he put his hand over Anna's and gave a little squeeze. She saw the look Kim mentioned. She had a sudden flash of memory. Her father used to look at her mother like that.

Now Anna became alarmed. She looked into Casey's eyes and gave him a Paik.

Viviane and Gareth stood together on the quarterdeck of a sailing vessel. "I can't get away," Viviane said, holding up her arms to reveal the chains that fettered her to the ship's wheel. "Please, Josiah. Don't let them see you. You can't help me."

He jerked at the chains. They wouldn't budge.

Then the picture changed and she saw the two of them sleeping together in a sleeping bag, outdoors, naked and enfolded in one another's arms. They were older, perhaps mid-forties, and they'd just made love.

Once again the scene shifted and she saw herself telling him she was pregnant. Both of them were overjoyed.

She released the Paik in a panic. She leapt out of his mind without closing the link, something she'd never done.

The exit from the Paik left Casey stunned. He shook his head and clutched at his temples. He leaned back, groaning with pain.

The truth hit her hard. She'd been fighting the thoughts, but now they loomed up, inescapable as a prison cell.

Everyone at the table had seen her out on a date with a man other than her husband. She stood, and rushed out the door, panicky.

She paced around the parking lot, trying to fight down her alarm. What would the gossip mill at the school make of this? What if it got back to Alan?

Casey hurried out and stood in front of her, holding her coat. She slipped it on.

"What happened? Did you get sick?" He put his hand to his temple, still in pain, his face pale and drawn.

"I'm fine," she said, waving him off. "I just needed a bit of air."

He stared at her, puzzled by the sudden shift in her attitude toward him. Then he blinked and squinted his eyes. He wiped at moisture on his cheeks.

Tears of pain.

The tears startled her for a moment. Then, she figured it out. He hadn't thrown off the effects of the Paik yet. He'd feel okay in a few minutes. For sure.

"What happened? I didn't—" his voice trailed off. His eyes watered with the headache.

She glanced at her watch. Seven o'clock. More than three hours had sped away at the bar. She interrupted his apology. "You don't need to concern yourself. I have to go," she said. "Would you drive me back to Westwood to retrieve my car? I could call a cab if that would make things easier."

His face fell and he stammered, "Well—well—" Then he made a visible effort to gain control. "Sure. I'll take you. Let me get my coat."

He went into the bar and came out in a few moments. They drove back to Westwood, saying nothing. He pulled up next to her car.

He turned to her. "Look, you're angry with me. Please let me apologize. I didn't mean to—"

She cut him off again, her tone artificial and formal. "I'm not angry with you. Now please. Let me out."

"But something happened. I—"

"Thank you for a pleasant afternoon. Good night."

He climbed out of the car, then extended his hand to help her out. She ignored his hand, slid out, and strode away without another look at him.

He followed her. She unlocked the Lincoln and slid in. "Anna, please," he pleaded. "At least tell me how I offended you—"

She slammed the door, cutting off the rest of his question. She drove off, forcing herself not to look back.

CHAPTER FOURTEEN

That weekend, Anna thought about little except what had happened at the bar. On Sunday afternoon, Alan packed his suitcase to go out of town again, this time for a week. She decided to take a long walk. The day had turned raw and cold, so she tugged on some old jeans and a hooded sweatshirt. She found her favorite baseball hat, an old one in the powder blue of the University of North Carolina, with an NC emblem.

She put on her old navy blue pea jacket, and yelled to Alan. He didn't respond.

She walked down to Lake Michigan. A chill wind blew off the lake, and the waves were high. The sky sputtered a cold drizzle, the threat of a huge storm hovering in the air.

She couldn't let herself think about the wounded look on Casey's face when she turned away from his rusty Chevy to climb into the light blue leather upholstery of her Lincoln. She knew that she had been cruel to him and she felt ashamed of herself.

His pain had been temporary, of course. She felt sure he felt okay an hour after she left him. Just a temporary headache.

She remembered that on her eighteenth birthday, she had walked along the Pamlico River with her father. He knew that he'd contracted terminal cancer. He had to use a cane.

"Why did she leave you, Daddy?" she asked.

Her father understood that she meant Janice, his first wife. He nodded. "Over the years I've come to regard her as nothing more than human trash, Anna. I've tried not to speak ill of her for the sake of your sisters, but you ought to know. . ." A fit of coughing took him for a moment, and they sat together on a bench.

At last he resumed. "I married her because I only looked at

how gorgeous she appeared. I think she was, too, at the time."

"Pretty as Mom?" asked Anna.

"Your mom, when we got married, had much more than just a physical beauty. She had an exquisite peace and gentleness about her."

"I know, Daddy."

"The vows we took meant nothing to Janice. We'd been married about five years when I learned that she'd been carrying on an affair with some man out of town a couple of times a month. I confronted her. She packed and left. I learned that she worked her way through several other lovers as well."

"Oh Daddy," she said, tears rising. "That must have been terrible for you."

"Oh, at the time, yes. After a few months, I began to realize I enjoyed living outside of a lie."

"What do you mean?"

"She never intended to keep the promises we made, Honey. So, when I met your mom, and our friendship became serious, we decided that we would make telling the truth one of the central values of our whole marriage. Keeping promises. Doing what you say. Following through to others."

"You've always said those things, Daddy," she said, hugging his elbow.

They stood, and walked to the water's edge. A fish leapt as they gazed across the river to St. Margaret's Island, just visible in the distance.

"Honey, please don't marry until you feel you can keep the promise to be faithful, to stay with your husband, to love and honor. . ." A fit of coughing overtook him.

A week later, he entered the hospital. He never came out.

Anna walked along the beach, hands in her coat pockets. She wondered if Alan honored his marriage vows.

She knew he'd been far from celibate before they married. She remembered how much it had bothered her to learn that he'd been intimate with many women. He came to their marriage regarding sex as a recreational activity. What would she do if she discovered that he'd continued to sleep with other women even now?

Anna kicked at the sand of the beach, and looked out at the huge steel gray waves that crashed not far from where she stood.

How much of what he said was the truth?

Well, I've never caught him in a lie.

She resisted the inevitable conclusion. She just couldn't see any other solution short of leaving Alan.

She had to end her friendship with Casey.

She thought again about her father. Anna had been raised to honor and keep promises. What promise was more important than a marriage vow?

Anna regarded every minute she spent with Casey as a treasure, precious when they happened and priceless in her memory later.

Nevertheless, she knew what would happen if she kept seeing him. They'd start to go places together when Alan traveled out of town. Casey would take her to dinner. They'd wind up in bed. *Well, I'd have to proposition him.*

I'd do it.

But she knew an affair with Casey would make her crummy marriage even worse. She'd destroy it and damage Alan.

The idea of a lifetime with Casey appealed to her a great deal, to be sure. She remembered the vision she had experienced with him when they first met. She recalled the vision of the two of them in a romantic ski lodge, kissing one another on the pullout sofa bed, his gentle hands caressing her, their kids asleep in the bedroom. The memory of the image still felt wonderful.

But then she thought about the Christmas gifts she'd given him. The expensive shirt and tie, the lavish cufflinks: of course he'd interpreted them as a flirtation. *What could I have been thinking?*

When she met Alan at an exercise class at the local YMCA, he'd treated her like a princess. He'd rescued her from debt, from living in a tiny rented room in someone else's house. She'd had no prospects, no friends, no future.

When she met Alan, he paid her extensive college debts. He gave her the Lincoln she drove now. She stopped buying clothes in second-hand stores. Now, she ate real food, fresh vegetables and fruit, and enjoyed financial security.

But I'm so lonely. He goes away all the time. I don't like living alone.

She looked down the beach at a man and woman playing with their dog. The dog, a lovely golden retriever, had fun chasing and bringing back a stick, with a huge goofy grin on its face. The couple looked at one another. Even from her distance, she could see how much the man and woman loved each other.

Okay, she thought. *Let's say I want to divorce him.*

On what grounds?

Alan hadn't harmed her. He'd been loyal. Faithful, as far as she knew. He didn't lie to her.

She thought again of her own father, Patrick O'Neill. No one had ever loved someone like Patrick did his wife, Meg. But he'd been devastated for years when his first wife left him, Anna knew it.

Alan didn't deserve to be abandoned and turned into an emotional wreck. That's what would happen if she left him for another man.

She picked up a flat stone. She curled her index finger around the edge and skimmed it over the waves. It hit and skipped several times before it sank.

Her daddy had taught her to skip stones, she remembered with affection. She missed her dad every day.

True, she hated Alan's friends. She hated that he expected her to like them. She hated the fact that he wanted her to spend time with them and became angry with her when she resisted. The men leered at her and the wives patronized her. She regarded them as snobs, nasty, rude and snide with her.

But the friends weren't him.

Were they?

She picked up some beach glass, chips and shards from broken bottles, rounded and scarred by the waves. Pretty brown, some blue, a piece of red glass. She had a big jar of it in her bedroom. Alan had asked her what she was going to do with that stuff. Just keep it, she told him. He shook his head, saddened by what he regarded as an aberration in his wife.

And what had she done to make their lives better?

She walked across the beach back to the sidewalk and started home.

When he gets home, she told herself, *we're going to make some changes in this marriage.*

She hadn't insisted on alternatives to the way their lives went. She hadn't suggested counseling. She hadn't invited her own friends over. Or joined a church.

She'd been married for less than three years.

But she'd started to fall in love with another man.

Anna paused at a crossroads and waited for traffic to clear.

No. That wasn't true. She loved Casey. She had loved him since the moment she saw him. She understood that her nasty treatment of him when they first met had been fear. Fear also caused the unspeakable way she'd treated him Friday.

She started across the street.

Now, she thought again of what her parents had always taught her. When you make a promise, you keep it.

She had stood before a judge and promised to love Alan, under all conditions.

She reached the other curb and started walking past the

huge houses. She admired the beautiful landscaping of one of the mansions.

Maybe, things would get better once they had children. Maybe Alan would do okay as a dad. He'd be good to the kids. He'd start to stay home more, and take care of them with her. And they would have every advantage. Alan had wealth, influence, and he treated everyone with generosity. The children would lack for nothing.

Casey, while not impoverished, couldn't provide for her and children in the same way as Alan. With Casey, the children would just have a daddy like hers, a daddy who loved kids, who treat them with gentle love and kindness, who would be a partner with her in raising the precious little lives, who—

I'm not married to Casey, she thought. *I'm married to Alan. Stop it.*

Anna couldn't betray Alan. No. The friendship with Casey had to come to an end right now. She'd explain. Of course he'd understand. He'd get over it. He'd have to.

She found herself at the foot of their driveway, staring up at the large house.

It occurred to her that she could turn, walk into town, call Casey, have him come and get her, walk away from this marriage. Alan wouldn't even know she was gone.

Or give a damn. She tried hard to deny that.

She watched smoke rise from the furnace flue and dissipate in the air. *That's my love for Casey. Right there. It's chimney smoke. It'll go away. It'll dissipate like smoke in the wind.*

I just have to stay away from him. I'll try to explain. He'll understand.

Besides, why would he want me? What do I have to offer Casey?

She looked down the street. It wouldn't be hard to walk to town. She could be there in no time. In an hour, she could start her life down a new bright path with Casey, someone who'd cherish and protect and love her, who'd be faithful to her for the rest of their lives.

Anna O'Neill drew a deep breath.

She walked up the driveway back into the cold, joyless mansion. She took off all the winter gear, and put it in the closet.

Alan had finished packing and sat now watching a baseball game on TV. "What's the matter with you? You been crying?"

"No, just the cold air," she said.

CHAPTER FIFTEEN

On Monday, near the end of the day, the principal made an announcement over the public address. Rehearsals for the musical would have to be postponed for a couple of days.

When the dismissal bell rang, Anna, her stomach a lump of lead, walked to Casey's classroom to tell him he had to stay away from her. But she didn't find him there. She met Dave Dunbar, a math teacher, turning out lights and closing the door.

"Where'd Casey go?" she asked.

"I don't know. I think he got sick. I took his last class."

Casey didn't come to school for the next few days. She saw him on Friday, talking to drama kids. A student teacher ran the rehearsals.

The next week, Anna avoided Casey whenever she could, not seeing him at lunch and in the hall. When they met, she remained courteous but cool toward him. The pain and hurt in his eyes bothered her, of course, but she felt she had no choice.

He took another few days off. He came in to run rehearsals, but not for classes. Anna thought that seemed strange. Casey never missed work. But she began to find it easy just to hide and not to talk to him.

One afternoon, as she was getting ready to leave for the day, she looked up. It startled her to see him standing in the doorway.

"Anna," he said. "I need to talk to you."

Caught off guard, she almost gave him the smile that had always welcomed him to her life. She realized that she couldn't tell him right then. Steeling herself, she said, "I'm sorry. I have an appointment and I need to rush off. Please excuse me."

She strode down the hall.

He followed her for a few steps. She ignored him as he said,

"Anna, please. I just want to talk for a moment. Something has gone wrong. I . . ." Then she pushed through the hallway doors and went outside. He didn't follow.

So he didn't see the tears on her face.

After picking at her dinner and sleeping in short, troubled bursts that night, Anna decided that she had to talk to Casey. She rehearsed it several times.

She'd be polite, but firm. They couldn't continue to be intimate friends. His friendship made her life far too complicated. *Please*, she'd say, *let's continue to be courteous, but let's be realistic.*

She rehearsed all morning and at lunch. Then, she went to find him on his hall duty post.

She saw him sitting in the hall. He had some papers spread on a table in front of him. She watched him from a distance, out of his sight, while he spoke to passing students, tried to focus on the papers, leaned back, and tried again. He propped his elbows on the table and rested his head in his hands.

She stopped behind him. She rallied for a few moments before she said, "Excuse me."

He jumped. Blinking, he turned to look at her. He rose. She realized that he had fallen asleep for a few moments.

He peered at her in some confusion. "May I sit for a moment?" she asked.

His eyes focused. Now Anna turned numb, scared to her soul. "Well, well," he said, his voice cold and harsh. "The North Shore Princess. Do you deign to visit one of your humble subjects, Princess? Sure, go ahead and sit. I'm honored."

The eyes that stared back at her bore no resemblance to Casey's eyes. These eyes terrified her, hard, cruel, and indifferent to her. The stare became icy and implacable.

He indicated the chair across the table from him and resumed his chair. He hadn't spoken.

She sat, and glanced up and down the empty corridor. The

silence lengthened. After several moments, he picked up his pen and adjusted a student essay in front of him. He began to read, ignoring her.

"I need to say something to you," she said.

He looked up, and lifted an eyebrow. The sapphire eyes reflected ice. He put down his pen, leaned back and folded his arms across his chest. "Well?" he sneered.

"I feel I have to return this to you." She pulled the book he'd given her from her book bag and held it out. He made no effort to take it from her. She laid it on the table.

"I want to make sure you understand," she said. "I know where things would go between us. I can't let that happen. I like you a lot, of course. We've been good friends. But that has to stop."

He didn't say anything, just stared at her, stony. At last he said, "I intended the book as a gift. I went to some trouble to get it for you. I don't want it back."

"I can't accept a gift this inappropriate. I know you meant it to be kind. . ."

"Inappropriate? I gave you a book, not lingerie or jewelry. We both teach English. What do you find inappropriate about it?"

"We never should have exchanged gifts that had such value."

"Why not?"

"Because—because these gifts suggest that we have something more than friendship. . ."

"A child's book about King Arthur implies romance?"

"Well—"

"Look. You seem to think I'm a snake. You have that right. And I may be no good at all. But despite what you think: I *never* tried to break up your marriage," he said, his voice hard and cruel. "I've made no effort to seduce you. I've tried—though you make it obvious that I've failed—to be appropriate and a good friend."

"But the point is, I'm married. I can't afford the appearance of impropriety with a man. Please understand," she pleaded.

"Oh yes," he said. "I understand. I understand that the Anna I cared for as my best friend wants nothing to do with me. And she intends to give me no idea what I did to alienate her."

"Surely you see that I can't—"

"Oh yeah, I know a brush-off when I see it," he sneered, sarcastic. "But you present me a problem. I'm afraid that I won't be able to return the things you gave me. My sister Karen flew into town for a few nights. I wore the shirt and tie to dinner with her. I'm sure no store would accept them back now."

"I don't mind. I don't think. . ."

"No, I want to make it right. I insist," he said, mock politeness searing her. "I forgot my checkbook today. Would you be kind enough to give me a statement of how much I owe you? I'd prefer to see the receipts if you still have them."

"Okay." She spoke in a tiny voice. The mean, nasty person who sat across from her shocked her. She'd never seen him rude, or sarcastic.

"Would you accept a check, or should I get cash?" he asked. "If cash, I'll of course need a receipt."

"Oh, Casey—" She looked down and shut her eyes.

"He belongs to me now, Viviane," hissed a cruel, sibilant voice.

She looked up. Then she stood and backed away, terrified.

Casey had disappeared. A huge snake reared up like a cobra across the table from her. The tongue flicked in and out. "I'm coming, Viviane," it hissed. It slid over the table toward her. Anna, too scared to speak, couldn't even run in her fear.

Anna backed away down the corridor, terrified, looking side to side for help down the empty hall. The snake reared to strike. "Please," she said, and shut her eyes.

"Something wrong?" said Casey's voice. The tone sounded bored, disinterested. Not concerned, as the Casey she knew would have been.

She opened her eyes. She hadn't gotten up and backed away. She still sat across from Casey at the hallway table. The snake had vanished. Casey sat at the table, pen poised above a paper he'd been reading. He looked at her, curious and cold. Now, three feet away from him, she saw his face, lined with strain, tears in his eyes. One word occurred to her.

Pain.

"Anything else you need to say?" he asked, face blank. "I've got work to do. You interrupted me," he sneered.

"No. I just—" she felt nauseated with fear. She couldn't look at his eyes again.

"Please—and I know I have no right to ask--do me one minor favor," he said, and pushed the book she'd returned to him toward her. "Take this book and put it in a garbage can. I'd rather not see it again."

"But—"

"Damn it, I don't want it," he snapped. "I don't like having memories of failed friendships around the house. I've got a ton of those memories without adding to the total." His voice cracked. He cleared his throat. "And I'm an English teacher. We don't throw away books. Nor can I hope to re-sell it since I wrote in it, as you asked."

She didn't look at him as she put the book into her bag.

"Now, if you have nothing else to say, I fear I must ask you to please excuse me," he said, formal. "I have papers I have to finish." He looked down, dismissing her.

"I'm sorry," she said. "I don't. . ." Then she turned and fled down the hall. At the doorway to the next hall, she stopped and looked back. Casey sat at the table, not looking up. He'd cradled his head in his hands again.

Her stomach felt like lead, still reeling with the terror of the

Snake vision. She walked into the faculty lounge.

She found a garbage can and dropped the book in. The bile rose.

Anna crossed to the women's washroom. She knelt in front of a bowl and vomited.

She stood when the spasm at last seemed to have ended. She flushed the toilet and took a long drink from the fountain in the washroom. Then, she lay down on the couch. Grace came in, glasses perched on top of her head. "Anna," she said, her face drawn with concern.

"Hi, Grace," Anna murmured, weak.

"I saw you cross the room. You looked wretched. What—"

"I felt nauseous for a second. I just laid down. I'll be okay in a moment."

Grace sat on the couch next to her and laid a hand on her forehead. "My gosh," she exclaimed. "You're cold as ice."

"I just need a second or two. I'll be okay." She closed her eyes and tried to relax.

The bell for the next class rang, startling her. She realized that she'd fallen asleep. Grace looked up from a stack of papers she'd been grading. "Good," said Grace. "You've got some color back. You've been napping for fifteen minutes."

"I didn't sleep much last night," said Anna. She didn't say why. She knew she wouldn't sleep much that night, either.

That night, she unpacked her book bag. To her astonishment, she found the book nestled in among the papers. She stared at it and felt a shiver of—what? Fear? Surprise?

Alan looked up from the TV, and saw her face. He asked, "What's that? Jeez, you look like you'd seen a ghost."

She said, "No, just an old book. I thought I'd gotten rid of it."

A couple of days later, Alan had gone out of town to San Francisco. Anna realized that she still felt nauseous. She hadn't gotten her period for—

How long had it been? She tried to remember. She pulled out her school planning book and reviewed it.

Anna recalled. It had been six weeks ago.

She stood, and walked over to look at herself in the mirror. A smile crossed her face, for the first time in a long time.

She walked downstairs and made a phone call.

"Yes," said Alan, when the switchboard at the hotel connected her to his suite in San Francisco.

"Hi, it's me," she said. He didn't respond for a few seconds.

"Your wife?" she added.

"Of course. What do you need?"

"Great news."

"Good. So?"

She told him. A dead silence greeted the news.

"Alan?" she asked.

"Yes. Well, that's what you wanted, right?"

"What I wanted?" she said, amazed at his tone.

"Look, I'm busy here. I'll call later." He hung up. He didn't call later.

A few days later, he came home. Anna met him at the door as the airport limo drove away.

"Bad news," she said, a tear forming.

"What?"

"Oh, I'm so disappointed. My period showed up late yesterday. I'm not pregnant."

"I see," he said. "Are we having dinner in or out?"

She looked at him, unable to respond. She fled from the room, sobbing. He didn't follow.

She heard him making a phone call. Then, he went out for a few hours in the Mercedes.

The next morning, Anna found him sitting at the kitchen table. Before she could speak, Alan put up his hand. "I took some tests last week at Jim's clinic," he announced. "I hadn't been feeling well for a little while. I just got the results yesterday. It looks like I'm sterile and my prostate needs some work."

"What?" she pulled out a chair and sat opposite him at the table.

"I have to have surgery." She stared for a moment, then took his hand. "Jim told me a week or so ago. He confirmed it yesterday when I went to see him." Anna's stomach fell. Alan gave her a few more details, like time, date, and clinic.

CHAPTER SIXTEEN

A few days later, Anna stood waiting outside the surgery suite at a private clinic at five o'clock in the evening. Alan had been in surgery for three hours. What if her husband had cancer? What if the cancer had spread through his whole system?

The surgeon, Alan's friend Jim O'Donnell, came out looking grim. He pointed Anna to a chair and sat next to her. He took her hand. "I'm sorry," he said, his faint accent revealing his Cajun roots. "Alan had cancer, as we feared. We had to remove Alan's prostate."

Anna looked down at her hands. She felt as if everything were collapsing around her.

"I do have good news, though," said Jim. "We caught it in time, before it spread. No need for chemotherapy or radiation. Alan will lead a normal life. Except for one thing."

She looked up at the doctor. He told her, "Alan will be sterile for life. He also will be impotent for a little while, but after that, your sex life should be unaffected."

Anna shut her eyes, trying to grasp the notion that she would never be a mother.

Jim took her to Alan's hospital room. She was surprised to find him awake and alert, sitting up. "Honey, I'm so sorry." He didn't meet her eyes.

"The important thing is that you'll be okay," she managed. She kissed his cheek. Then she turned to the window to cry.

She looked out over the dark parking lot. In the reflection of the window, she thought she saw Alan and the doctor exchange a smile. She turned back. No, she must have been mistaken. Their faces reflected serious concern for her.

The hospital released Alan the morning after the surgery.

He showed few signs of discomfort and went back to work later in the morning.

* * * * *

Casey's musical, *Camelot*, would open later that week, three weeks before the end of school. Casey seemed to be so busy with the musical and his classes that he didn't have any free time. Anna had never seen him so absorbed.

She caught brief glimpses of him in the halls and at lunch, but he always seemed to be attending to last minute things like tickets, publicity, costumes, and other production problems. He looked frazzled and tired most of the time.

Not talking to her best friend still caused her deep pain. She longed to tell him about her husband's surgery and her depression about not having children.

But every time she saw him, she remembered the Snake vision. He all but sneered when he saw her.

His eyes still scared her. When she looked at him, fear shot through her. Something about him now terrified her.

On Friday, Anna sat at lunch with Grace. They chatted about the excitement around the school about the musical, which had opened the previous night.

Casey ran into the faculty cafeteria, eating a sandwich. When he saw Anna, he stopped. He stammered as he said hi. She nodded a cool greeting, then averted her eyes as pain—was it rage?--twisted his face. He turned and began to hurry off. "Casey, wait," Grace said. She rose and ran to him.

Anna watched Grace talking to Casey, holding his arms at the elbows and looking into his eyes. He shook his head as Grace pleaded with him. At last she sighed, embraced him for a moment, and came back to the table as he left the lunchroom.

"He's working himself into exhaustion," Grace said. "Someone must've been nasty to him."

"What do you mean?"

"When he doesn't want to deal with something, he overworks," Grace said. "Don't you know what's been going on with him?"

"We agreed to stop being friends." Grace's eyebrows shot up. "We haven't talked for a while."

"Anna," Grace said, taking Anna's arm. "He's dying."

Anna stared at Grace. Part of her wanted to rush to him and try to help. The other part said, *you can't. Stay away.* "I'm—ah--very sorry to hear that," she said.

She chewed a bite of her sandwich in silence until she looked up and saw Grace still staring at her. "What?"

"What happened between you and Casey?"

Anna let a bit of annoyance creep into her voice. "I really don't think—"

"I know, I know. It's none of my business. But a lot of people here at the school are worried about Casey."

Grace's glass of ice water had left a circle of water on the table. She traced her finger through the little puddle. She started to speak. She stopped. At last she said, "A couple of weeks ago, Casey stopped by my room. He told me you and he planned to go to Whizzer's that afternoon. He looked so thrilled I thought he might explode. He assured me he didn't consider it a date, and I believed him."

"We did not go out on a date," Anna asserted, her voice a bit sharper than she intended. Grace didn't seem to notice.

"I saw you two together many times. Lunch, hall duty, the plays. I've never seen him so happy. He'd fallen in love with you."

"I'm married," Anna said. "You and he both know I won't and couldn't pursue a romance with him."

"He promised me he wouldn't do anything to embarrass you or put you in an awkward position. But ever since he took you to Whizzer's he's been ill. He's gotten worse every day."

"Yes?" said Anna, putting her sandwich down, trying to

look as neutral as possible.

"Last week, on Monday, they canceled rehearsals because I drove him over to the emergency room at Northwest Hospital. The doctor admitted him."

"What?" Anna asked, putting a hand to her mouth.

"Yes. I spent the night there. I went in and taught the next day, and spent the night in his room again. And on Wednesday, too. He'd become so sick I thought he might die."

"I'm sorry. I didn't know—"

"Not many people do. He didn't want anyone to know."

"Why not?" asked Anna.

"He doesn't want people to worry about him. In fact, I'm betraying his confidence here. But I'm so scared."

"What happened?" Anna twisted a napkin in her fingers below the table. She made a concerted effort not to let her panic show.

Grace shrugged. "They ran a bunch of tests. They saw no evidence of a stroke, no cancer, lesions, nothing that they could detect."

"So where do things stand with him now?" Anna whispered. She thought, *This can't be from the Paik I gave him. The effects of a Paik never last more than a few hours, or a day at the most.*

"The only thing they can figure is migraine headaches," Grace continued, near tears. "They tried injections. That allowed him to sleep a little, but he kept waking up with pain after a few hours. The doctors gave him some pills but they didn't help. They upped the dosage. Still no relief. Every time I see him, he looks worse. I'm about ready to call his aunt and sisters and tell them to come home."

Grace took a deep breath. "The two of you went together to Whizzer's, dancing, talking, and laughing."

Oh, brother, thought Anna. *The rumor mill. Just as I thought.*

"Then you ran out. He gave a little scream of pain, and sat

there for a few moments, holding his head, in a daze. They said his face turned as white as a picket fence. Several people tried to help him. When he came around, he grabbed your coat and ran out after you. A few minutes later, he came in and got his coat. A couple of the guys offered to drive him home. He refused."

"I asked him to drive me back to the school," Anna said. "He did. That's all."

Grace's eyes searched Anna's face, her expression cool. "Did he try something inappropriate?"

"No. He brought me back here. I picked up my car and went home."

Grace sipped at a carton of milk and grew silent. Anna rushed to change the subject. "What have you been doing, Grace?" she asked. "We haven't talked for days."

Grace looked up with a weak smile. "I've been out all week," she said. "Oh, this has been great the last few weeks."

"Don't tell me you've been sick too," Anna cried.

"Not me," said Grace. "My dad. I had to go to Colorado. I just got home last night."

"Serious?"

"My dad had prostate surgery last Friday. He came home yesterday, just before I left."

Boy, Anna thought, *he had to stay in a long time. Alan came home the next day.*

"If Dad hadn't gotten an exam, he might not have survived." Grace's voice faltered, and she pressed a paper napkin to her eyes. "He'll have a big scar, I guess."

Anna spread mayonnaise from a packet on a slice of bread. *Alan doesn't have a scar. Not even stitch marks. That's strange.* She took a bite of the sandwich. Anna felt terrible for Grace's mother, knowing how the woman felt.

"I feel bad for my mom, having to give up sex," finished Grace.

Anna stopped chewing her cheese sandwich and stared at Grace.

"I'm sorry. I shouldn't have gotten so personal. I embarrassed you."

"No," said Anna. "Please go on. What do you mean, give up sex?"

"During prostate surgery, the doctors sever a nerve. The surgery leaves the patient impotent for good."

Anna went numb. "Always?" she stammered.

"I think so."

Anna swallowed the bite of sandwich with some difficulty. She pushed the rest of her lunch away.

CHAPTER SEVENTEEN

Anna struggled through her last class. Her thoughts kept whirling out of control. She told Dr. McAllister she didn't feel well and went home early that night, her head buzzing.

The situation with Alan bewildered her.

She ran through the scene at the clinic. *His doctor told me he'd be okay. They'd removed all the cancer. Alan would be sterile, but not impotent.*

A doctor doesn't lie to the wife of a patient. I just took for granted that he told me the truth.

Could they really be that mean? That—

--Evil?

Am I that stupid?

When she got home, she called her gynecologist, Joel Goodnough. He confirmed what Grace had told her about the sterility that came with the operation. "But don't give up hope. Of course we can still extract sperm from Alan and cause pregnancy."

Anna struggled for words. She managed to say "What?"

"Sure," said Joel. "Didn't his urologist didn't tell you?"

"No, he didn't," whispered Anna.

"Hmm. Strange," said Joel. "Anyhow, it would be complicated but not impossible."

She hung up, her ears burning with humiliation. Fury began to build.

They tricked me. The whole thing. Nothing but a scam.

She drove to Jim O'Donnell's clinic. The receptionist, a striking woman whose desk nameplate identified her as Lucia, became rude and patronizing when Anna identified herself. She said that the doctor's appointment calendar precluded any unscheduled visit.

Anna, puzzled by the receptionist's boorish attitude toward her, forced a smile and told her that she hadn't come about a medical issue. She just needed a quick word with the doctor.

The receptionist, making it clear that she was doing Anna a big favor, walked into the suite of offices. She came out smiling. "The doctor would be delighted to see you." She showed Anna into Jim's office. She could see a private washroom with a shower and lavish appliances.

Jim came in between appointments. "Well, my favorite southern belle," beamed O'Donnell. "I have a couple of minutes. What's up, Anna?" He extended his hand. She took it and gave him a Paik.

She saw Alan with his golfing buddies on the thirteenth tee waiting for a slow foursome ahead of them to clear the green. Alan told the group about a date with Anna.

"Just a couple more days till the wedding, huh?" Jim asked Alan.

"I invited her over for dinner last night," said Alan. He didn't look happy. "You know, steaks on the grill, some wine, sex afterward."

"Sounds great," said one of the men. "Yeah, well," said Alan. "She started talking about having kids."

One of the men, a divorce lawyer named Bill Kidd, laughed. "Well, when people marry, children do tend to come along, you know."

"I sure as hell don't want any kids," said Alan.

"Have you told her that?" the lawyer asked.

"Hell, no," Alan asserted. "She'd go nuts."

"Maybe you could change her mind," Jim shrugged. "Explain that if you didn't have children, you could spend your lives snorkeling in the Caymans, golfing in Scotland, cruising the Mediterranean, skiing the Alps."

"I wish we'd never had kids," said Lou Sydney. "I'm up at that stupid school four or five times a year with conferences.

The damn kids use drugs, get into fights, flunk subjects, cut classes."

Jim told them about the nightmare his three kids had become. He couldn't believe how much time he wasted on them, to say nothing of the phenomenal expense.

The divorce lawyer told a couple more horror stories about raising his kids.

"You know what I think?" Jim said. "You ought to come in next week for a vasectomy."

Alan considered for a moment. "I don't know," he said, shaking his head. "That's pretty permanent. I imagine she'll get over it once she sees how good she has it." The men laughed.

"So," said Lou Sydney, "What happened in the sack last night?"

Alan and the other guys laughed. Alan looked at the group that lingered on the green. He winked and began to narrate the details of his intimacy with Anna the previous night.

* * * * *

Anna didn't want to hear anymore. Cold fury surged through her.

She became livid as she thought about her husband discussing their sex relationship with friends. No wonder those men leered at her all the time.

Then she thought about how she'd bought the lie. She hadn't even asked questions about the operation. The operation had been an act, a monstrous, evil deception. She'd just accepted the doctor at his word.

How stupid I've been. What an idiot they think I am! She moved in Jim's mind. A glowing hot spot indicated the center of his deepest fear.

* * * * *

Jim O'Donnell ran through the Bayou not far from the

prison. The guard on the chain gang had turned his back as Jim wandered toward the Louisiana swamp. Jim had slipped away.

Now night had fallen, black as tar, and he knew he had to trudge some twenty miles through the swamp. But that presented no problem. He'd kept himself in good condition and he'd grown up not far from here. He knew the bayou like he knew his prison cell.

The plan couldn't fail. Tomorrow, on the coast, he'd steal a boat and head to Texas. He'd swipe some clothes and hitchhike to Mexico. In two days he'd be free and safe.

Then he heard the dogs. Looking over his shoulder, he saw the flashlights of the deputies. Panicked, he abandoned caution and sprinted down the path deeper into the swamp. He missed a step and fell face down in a puddle.

To his dread he began to sink. He couldn't stand, couldn't feel bottom. The bog gripped him and began to pull him down.

He almost vomited. Since he'd been a boy, quicksand had been his greatest fear.

The bloodhounds stood on the bank of the pond, baying at him as he clutched for tree roots. He'd sunk down to his neck by the time the posse showed up.

"Well, lookee here. Ole Jim done saved us the trouble of a neck-stretchin'," crowed the fat underwarden. The others bellowed with laughter.

"Please," Jim screamed. "Help me."

To his horror the guards transformed before his eyes. They no longer looked human, but rather as twisted, vile distortions of flesh. Their eyes glowed red as they danced with delight at his terror. Their laughter echoed through the swamp, cruel, wicked, and sarcastic.

Jim's bowels and bladder released in his revulsion and dread. "Well, g'bye, Jim, you no good sumbitch," the fat leader laughed. "We be waitin' on the other side for you. Aw, we gonna have a good ole time. Well, you sure as hell ain't." The others howled with laughter. Then the muck covered his ears, then his nose. He couldn't breathe. . .

Jim staggered as Anna released the Paik. He careened back and hit the bookshelf, knocking several books to the floor. He sat down hard.

He watched her stride over to him and speak into his face. "Are you all right?" she asked.

"I'm fine," he stammered. "I just felt weak for a second." He realized he'd fouled his two-thousand-dollar suit. Humiliated, he struggled in getting to his feet.

Anna slammed a hand into his face and he sat down hard in his own filth.

"You sick, disgusting degenerate," she snarled. "In case you're wondering: yes, if I were you, I'd be very worried about Alan's stupid trophy wife contacting the state medical association." She dropped the note in his lap and stalked out of the office without another word or glance, slamming the door. He opened the note. It had one word written on it. "Liar!"

Chapter Eighteen

Alan started for home at eleven that night. He'd enjoyed a great dinner with a client at Eli's, one of Chicago's premier steak houses on the Near North Side.

He'd thought about trying to pick up that little tart at the bar who'd been giving him the eye. The Drake Hotel waited only a few steps away. But she left before he could make his move. Oh, well. He had Anna waiting at home.

Of course she'd be asleep but he could wake her up. He enjoyed her when she woke up, fuzzy with sleep. The way he felt now, he wouldn't need much time. His hands tightened on the steering wheel in anticipation.

Sex had improved so much for him now. He didn't have to worry about getting her pregnant. Yeah, she'd been a little disappointed, but she'd get over it. Maybe he could schedule a cruise. Yeah, they could sail right after school ended. She'd see it as a little treat.

He pulled into the long driveway, and saw to his annoyance that Anna had left the trunk of her car open. Now he saw that most of the lights on the first floor were on. Damn it, what a waste of money.

He found Anna in the living room, sitting perched at the front of a three thousand dollar leather wing chair, staring at him. A small suitcase sat on the floor next to her.

"Hey," he began, "what's with leaving the trunk of the Lincoln open? Didn't you see it's raining? And what's with all the lights on?"

She didn't return his greeting. Then he noticed she'd been crying. "What happened? Has someone died?"

She rose. "I'm leaving, Alan," she said, her voice flat and calm. "I've instituted divorce proceedings. I stopped at a lawyer's office and made an appointment for next week." She handed him a business card. "I presume you'll want Mr. Kidd to represent you. Please have him call this woman. She'll be my attorney." He took the business card, numb, unable to speak.

"I've rented a room from Mrs. Merlini, where I used to live, if some emergency arises. Be sure to ask someone else to call me," she said, a bit more hostile. "I don't want to hear from you or see you under any circumstances."

Alan stood, looking at the lawyer's card, trying to process the idea that his wife was leaving him. He had some trouble hearing her over a roaring sound in his ears.

She maintained her poise with an effort. "Do you plan to work tomorrow?"

"Uh. . .uh, yes, I have to take care of—" he began, struggling to speak.

"Fine," she interrupted. "I need to come back tomorrow for a few more things. I can leave the key then. Please don't call the police," she bit off the sarcasm.

"Stop being absurd," he said. "What on earth. . ."

"I know about the operation, Alan. You miserable snake. You know that I watched my own father die of cancer. You frightened me."

"I. . .uh—" he stammered.

"Our whole marriage has turned into a colossal lie," she told him. "Not only that, you patronize me. You insult me. You let your disgusting buddies leer at me and excuse them when they abuse me and make passes at me. You brag to them about our most intimate moments. No wonder their wives have insulted and ignored me the whole time we've been married."

"Now just a minute," he managed. "You can't talk to me like—"

"Don't say anything." Now she all but shouted right into his face. "Your time to talk to me has ended. You just listen. You knew how much I wanted children. You figured I'd never see through this operation scam. Well, you won't lie to me again."

"Don't be ridiculous," he scoffed, making an effort to regain some dignity. He felt dazed, blindsided. "How do you think you plan to survive? You don't have any employable skills." He crossed to the bar and helped himself to a couple of fingers of Glenfiddich. His hands trembled as he poured the scotch.

"I don't, huh," she snarled. "Maybe I am as stupid as you think. In any case I'd rather forage for food in the streets than live with you." She threw her wedding ring in his direction. She turned and stalked to the door.

He tried to laugh. "You'll be back. Once you see how good you've got it here."

Anna ignored him and opened the door. The truth hit him. This situation had gone beyond his control.

Alan stumbled across the living room and caught her arm. "We can talk this over. Tell me what you want. I'll—" Bile rose in his throat, almost choking him.

"We have nothing to discuss."

He tried to take her in his arms. She shoved him away. "Please close the door," he begged.

"Take your hands off me," she warned. "You have no idea what you're about to unleash."

He tightened his hands on her arms. "I'll be damned before you just walk out on me." He raised his hands.

She looked into his eyes. "Okay, if that's what you want. . ." she said, but Alan heard no more.

Alan no longer stood in his front foyer. A judge, a golfing buddy, stood ready to marry him to Anna O'Neill. She held the arm of her elderly grandfather as he escorted her down the aisle toward him.

She'd wanted to hold the wedding in her little church. Alan, with no interest in church whatever, had persuaded her to hold it here, in the ball room of his lavish North Shore country club.

The lovely decorations had transformed the room. The guests smiled as she walked by them.

Then Anna, a stunning bride, stood in front of him, radiant and joyful at marrying him. Her grandfather extended his hand toward him. He took the hand, and looked at the grandfather's eyes---

And then he couldn't move.

Alan staggered in a swirling vortex of color, wind, and screeching noise.

Then he found himself in a graveyard before a hideous pit of emerald green fire. Not even in his worst nightmares had he ever visualized such hellish surroundings: Cold, harsh, unrelenting terror.

He heard agonized screams and smelled vile odors of sulfur and excrement. Roaring fire leapt out of the pit. His flesh crawled with horror, and he could taste the fear slithering over him.

A spectral creature rose from the pit, emerald fire licking around, and came to Alan, towering over him. Under the creature's black hood, Alan saw a face set with glowing green eyes.

Now the Chimera gripped his hand with a claw that yearned to tear his existence from his body and spoke to his mind: "I regard you, sir, as nothing more than a no-good, vile son-of-a-bitch. I'm nauseated that she wants to marry you. Let me warn you to be careful. If you ever hurt her or betray her, I'll know. Then you shall never recover from what I'll do to you."

The creature compressed Alan's right hand. He opened his mouth to scream with the pain but nothing came out. The creature reached forward and put its left claw against his chest.

Alan watched in horror as the creature's claw sank into his chest. He felt the hand close around his heart.

Alan's chest began to hurt as if a red-hot rail spike had been driven into it. He couldn't breathe. An unbearable pain radiated from his shoulder down his left arm.

The monster let go of his hand, smiling with grim satisfaction. It withdrew its claw from Alan's chest. . .

Alan found himself back in his front foyer of his lavish Lake Forest mansion. The monster had vanished. He released his wife's arms.

His chest, though, continue to blaze with pain. In hideous agony and terror, he collapsed and crawled to a phone. The ambulance. The attempt at emergency resuscitation. Electric paddles. The resigned, sad look on the doctor's face. The white sheet over his head. The church ceremony. Anna stood in front of the casket, holding the hand of a tall blond guy —

Alan again found himself back in the foyer of his house. He lost his balance and careened backward, crashing into the steps to the second floor. He gasped as the vision faded.

Anna opened the door and walked out. She slammed the door behind her.

Alan staggered to his feet. He wrenched open the door and stumbled onto the front porch, his hands trembling. He watched the taillights of her car vanish as the rain soaked his expensive suit. Still terrified, he sank to his knees, vomiting his steak dinner into the landscaping.

He wouldn't sleep much for the next several nights. Bad nightmares, he told his doctor.

CHAPTER NINETEEN

Anna went back to the house late Saturday morning. She made sure Alan had left and then finished removing her personal possessions. It didn't take too long. She dropped the house key in the middle of the white wool carpet in the living room.

She returned to Mrs. Merlini's and stayed busy hanging pictures and posters in the little room. Alan telephoned several times, but she refused to talk to him. She managed a two-hour nap about three o'clock in the afternoon.

When she awoke, her mind cleared a little more. She knew she had to see Gareth.

Anna showered and went shopping. She found a miniskirt outfit she knew that Casey would like.

After a failed attempt to eat, she changed into the outfit. Scared and nervous, she drove to the school for the final performance of Casey's production of *Camelot*. She stood at the back of the theatre for the performance.

She enjoyed the passionate energy of the teenage cast and crew. The re-telling of the love affair between the greatest knight and the king's wife left her teary-eyed.

Casey walked through the theatre lobby after the show, greeting parents and faculty, thanking the cast. She stood off to the side in the shadows where she could watch him.

His appearance horrified her.

He looked exhausted, thin and gaunt, as if he hadn't eaten or slept. He wore the shirt and tie and cufflinks she'd given him. The shirt had fit well when he'd worn it for her just after the winter break, beaming with pride and gratitude. Now, it hung on him.

He'd lost weight. Lots of it. Dark circles disfigured his face beneath his hollow eyes. His skin suggested the pallor of the grave.

In a flash of horror, she realized the truth. He hadn't recovered from the Paik she'd given him at the bar. The Paik had ripped something loose and something vile had come after him. Her best friend faced imminent death in hideous, constant pain.

And she'd done it. Because of her carelessness and self-absorption, the best friend she'd ever had faced a tortuous death.

When everyone left, Casey went back into the theatre and turned out the lights. As he walked out, he noticed Anna standing across the hall from the entrance, waiting for him.

"Nice shirt," she said. "Very nice tie."

For several moments, he stared at her. At last he asked, "My goodness gracious. A princess stands outside my humble theatre. How can I serve you, Princess?" His voice dripped with sarcasm.

"I'm so proud of you," she said.

"Oh. You're proud of me," he said with that sarcastic smile.

"Of course."

"I hate to disillusion you, Princess. I just tell the kids where to walk and stand."

"You took some high school kids and made them professionals," she said.

"Your kindness leaves me weak with gratitude," he sneered. "Thank you for this incredible condescension, Princess. . ." He broke off. He uttered a soft groan, shut his eyes and clutched at his head. He pulled out a vial of tablets, unscrewed the top, extracted a pill, and popped it into his mouth.

"I'm sorry," he said. "I've been eating these damn things like candy. Sometimes the pain gets so—" He stopped. Apologized again. Pulled out a ring of keys and locked the theatre door.

He turned back to her. "May I know what you want?"

She walked across the hall to him. "What happened to you?" she asked. She'd never seen anyone respond to a Paik like this.

"What the hell do you care?" he sneered.

"Please, Casey," she pleaded. "Please tell me."

He shrugged. "Okay. The doctors tell me I'm having migraine headaches," he said, with his back to her. "I'd never had one in my life until—"

She knew he was going to say, "Until I met you."

She came close to him. She almost put her hand on his shoulder, but stopped herself. He cleared his throat. "I work until I'm exhausted so I can sleep. When I sleep, it doesn't hurt."

"How—" she tried.

"I'm not afraid to die," he shrugged. "I'm pretty sure that's where this is heading. I keep dreaming about it, anyhow. At this point, I'd welcome it."

"No," she said. "Please. Don't talk like that."

"Oh, well," he shrugged. "Now that the play is over, maybe I'll recover. I doubt it. If I die, perhaps I won't be afraid all the time."

"What are you afraid of?"

He paused, then shrugged. "I can't begin to guess why you'd give a rip about it," he said. "But I suppose I can tell you. I keep having this terrifying dream. You and I have been taken prisoner, I think, on an old style sailing ship in the ocean. The scene shifts and we find ourselves in a sleeping bag. You tell me you're pregnant, and I feel happy. But then you turn into a snake and attack me. You slide into my brain through my eyes and tear at my brain."

Horrified, Anna remembered the Paik. She'd let the Snake into his mind. It was devouring his soul.

"At that point, I always jerk awake with my head pounding

in pain." He turned to her. "And the pain grows and becomes so intense I can't go back to sleep. Then there's the nausea, the vomiting. It's just wonderful." She stood only three or four feet away, but he couldn't look up at her.

"How often does this happen?" asked Anna. She stared at his back, desperate to embrace him, but scared that he would shove her away.

"Every time I go to sleep. So I try not to sleep. But I'm worn out and tired all the time. Maybe you recall, *Princess*," he said with a sneer, "that I came to see you one afternoon. I tried to tell you about this then. Perhaps you remember that you brushed me off like an insect."

"I'm sorry," she mumbled. She felt nauseous herself at what she'd done.

"Yeah, sure," he sneered. "Okay, this talk is over. Tell me what you want, then beat it. I've got to close up and I'm worn out and I need to go home."

She couldn't speak. She pressed a Kleenex against her eyes.

Now, he looked up at her with those dark, hostile eyes. He nodded. "Oh, okay," he sneered. "I get it now. You want your money. No problem. I've got my checkbook tonight. I hope that's okay. It's a bit hard to get any cash at this hour. But the check will go through, I promise." He pulled the checkbook out and opened it. "How much do you want?"

"I don't know," she said, her voice cracking. "I don't want money."

He stared at her, puzzled. "Then what in the hell do you want, *Princess*?" Again the sneer.

"Would you please not call me that?"

"Hey, Princess, you're in my theatre. I live here. I'll call you what I want. Answer the question or beat it."

"I know you're tired," she stumbled, flustered. "But could we please go someplace private to talk? Maybe a restaurant? You need to eat."

"Why on earth would a rich spoiled North Shore Princess want to talk to me, a simple, humble court jester?" His voice dripped with antagonism.

"Well, I just thought—" she choked.

"A princess who couldn't deign to *look* at me for days, and now she wants to talk?"

Casey looked at her for a long moment. Then he raised his left wrist and studied his watch. She remembered doing the same thing to him when she first met him. "I can stay awake for twenty more minutes. You can have one of them. Let's say for old times' sake. Ready? Talk."

"I know I've been unkind," she stumbled. His eyebrows shot up. "But I didn't know what to do."

"Please tell me what you want. I do have other duties," he mocked.

"When we were together at Whizzer's, I realized that our friendship had turned in a direction I couldn't go."

He considered for a couple of seconds. Then he laughed, sarcastic, nasty. "Thank you. How very generous. You've been a *big* help. But if you meant that as an apology, I think I might have missed it."

"Do you want an apology?"

"I want to go home and go to bed. So, *Princess*," he sneered. "Your minute just expired. I've tried dropping hints. Now let me try to make myself clear: I don't want to go anywhere with you. I want to go home and I don't want to talk to you again. I want you to go away. Right now. This minute. Don't look back. Good night. Clear?"

"Casey. Let me help." Sobbing, she stepped forward and grabbed his arm. He started to push her away, but she looked into his eyes and froze him. She took his face in her hands and probed into his mind.

* * * * *

Viviane stood in a graveyard, next to a pit of green fire. Gareth struggling lay on the brink of the pit, tormented and helpless. The Snake had wrapped itself around him, inching him closer to the pit. Gareth's armor afforded him little protection. One of the great serpent's coils was wrapped around his head, while other coils were crushing his body.

To her horror, she saw that Nehushtan had wriggled into Gareth's mind through his eyes.

"Nehushtan!" she screamed, sickened by the vision.

The snake withdrew from Gareth's head and turned to regard her. It had grown since the first time she'd seen it in the graveyard when she was a child.

The Snake hissed in triumph. "Viviane. Excellent. I shall finish the knight. Then I shall come for you."

"No," said Viviane. "Come for me now, Demon! It's me you want anyway."

A large tombstone stood next to her, with a statue of the Archangel Michael on top of it. She saw that the figure of the angel held a deft Sword, double-edged and razor sharp. She seized the Sword's hilt and pulled.

The Sword was not carved from stone. It was bright mirrored steel, light and double handled. It came away from the stone and fit her hands as if made for her.

She walked to the Snake and slashed a deep cut into its side. "Get away from him, Snake. Come for me!"

The snake hissed in fear and began to uncoil from around Gareth. As it did, it began to undulate away from her, weaving, bobbing.

The Sword terrified the Snake. She advanced, menacing, the Sword in front of her.

At last The Snake freed Gareth. He sat up, groaned and held his head.

The Snake rose up before Viviane. It weaved, ducked, and feinted, looking for a way to strike at her. She held the Sword before her, unafraid. "You can't hurt us both, Demon," she taunted it. "You have no power over us when we fight you together."

"You wounded him and you know it. Then you deserted him, Viviane," hissed the snake. "He needed you, and you didn't come to him. Now he belongs to me. I shall destroy you and then come back for him. He can't fight with you. I have what I need."

It drew back and struck at Viviane. Gareth seized it just below the neck. The snake choked as Gareth raised its head high. In the same instant, Viviane struck at the snake.

The Sword sang a high pitched whine. "Pow!" A sound like an electrical explosion echoed as the Sword dissevered the serpent just above Gareth's hands. Sparks flew around them and Nehustan's scream of rage stopped. Both parts of the Snake writhed, then lay still.

Gareth, covered with blood, threw the serpent's body away. It fell to the ground. He kicked it aside. Stepping toward Viviane, he collapsed to his knees. She knelt to help him up and he embraced her.

The Snake dissolved into a puddle of stinking, fetid mud, tinged with red. The blood on Gareth's armor turned to steam and blew back to the puddle. The two parts flowed back together and the Snake became whole again.

It reared up. Gareth and Viviane stood together, unafraid. Gareth drew his sword.

"You can't kill me, Viviane. But you will betray Gareth yet again. I will be back when you have his child—" The last words of the snake faded as it turned to a mist. Then a powerful wind blew, and the mist evaporated.

Viviane turned back to Gareth. Smiling at her best friend, she slipped away.

* * * * *

"What—" Casey murmured as the Westwood High School hallway again appeared. He put his hands to his temples for a moment. He sank to his knees on the carpet, stunned. She knelt and embraced him. She held his face with her hands, looked into his mind, and Paiked him again.

She searched for the tear in his soul. She saw first an old ship. A sleeping bag. Good news. Excitement. Nehushtan. There, she found the rip. She repaired the pain center. Then she closed the link and eased away.

He looked around, dazed. "Annie?"

"Yes," she said, tears of strain and terror on her cheek.

"Where did the Snake go?"

"It vanished. For now."

"We beat him, didn't we."

"Yes, we did. You're free again."

He shook his head. She saw reality return to his eyes. "We're at Westwood. How did we get here?" his voice quavered. "I remember coming back from the washroom at Whizzer's." He looked terrified. "Annie? What's going on?"

"It's the middle of May. You just closed the musical."

He looked around, dazed. "Right. I've been working. And I've had headaches." His face fell. "And you hate me. I remember that."

"No. Never hate. Never."

"I seem to feel better."

"Yes. You'll be okay now."

"My life has been a nightmare for—"

"Several weeks," she prompted him.

"I glad you're here with me."

He helped her to her feet, but continued to embrace her. "Can I—" he choked in a small voice. "Can I please just hold onto you for a few more minutes? I'm sorry. I'm kind of dizzy…"

"Of course."

After a minute or two, he drew back a little. "Thanks," he said. "Did you say something about getting a bite?" She nodded. "You want to go somewhere for a drink, a sandwich?"

"I look wretched."

"You look sensational," he said. "That outfit would stun the ordinary man."

She smiled, gratified. "Thank you," she said. "No, I mean I've been crying, my face looks awful. . ."

"We could go to my house," he suggested. "I'll make us a couple of my special Manhattans. We can order in a pizza—"

She started to refuse. Then she reconsidered. *He's vulnerable, worn out, spent. Maybe we could bolster one another. Good friends do that sort of thing.*

Besides, a pizza does sound good.

"That sounds fine, but let me drive. We can get your car another time, okay?"

"Right."

As they sat in the car, Anna gave him a Paik to get directions to his house and to help him sleep. He dropped off in a moment, lost in a deep and dreamless sleep of peace. She used the electronic control to tilt his seat back.

Anna saw another car start up as she pulled out of the parking lot. She didn't pay much attention.

CHAPTER TWENTY

Casey's house charmed Anna. It reminded her of a honeymoon cottage in a movie with its quaint antiques and comfortable furniture. Anna thought she wouldn't mind staying forever in this precious house.

The brief nap had invigorated him. His eyes had brightened and become alert. He'd chatted with her, cheerful and laughing. He seemed to be revitalized.

Casey ordered a cheese-and-sausage pizza. She told him to order onions and green peppers as well. He grinned and added them on.

Casey showed her around the little house. Understated wallpaper complemented tasteful color schemes throughout the home. Books lined the walls everywhere. She saw a Grand piano, a guitar and a music stand, and several other musical instruments, including a very old violin above the fireplace mantlepiece. Framed artwork, including original oil paintings and water colors, hung on the walls.

"This can't be your house, can it?" she asked.

"No, I'm just living here for a little while," said Casey, chuckling at the teasing. "It belongs to my Aunt Victoria and Uncle Steve. He works as an importer."

"How lovely," she murmured, looking around at the treasures.

"They got a lot of this artwork and sculpture from his trips to Europe and South America. These—" he pointed to a wooden mask and a few small wooden carvings—"came from Africa."

"How beautiful," she murmured, finding herself in love with the house and its furnishings.

"Vic and Steve moved to Switzerland for this year and next.

They took my two kid sisters with them. I plan to buy a house when I get back from the university next year so the girls can come live with me."

"You miss your sisters a lot, don't you?"

"All the time," he nodded, beaming with pride. "Every minute. Cinnamon just turned thirteen and Cheyenne had her eighth birthday a couple of months ago. I've been raising them since Mom and Dad died. Victoria and Steve have been helping me out while I've been working on my doctorate. At Christmas they took the girls to Italy."

"What a terrific experience for them."

"They call me every two weeks. The girls are having a smashing time."

He went into the kitchen and fixed a batch of Manhattans, adding cherries as garnish.

They walked into the living room and sat on a blue leather couch. She sipped her drink. "Yow!" she said, coughing a little.

"Let the ice melt a bit." He sat next to her on the couch and leaned back. "So?" He lifted an eyebrow.

She took a deep breath. "I left my husband. I'm filing for divorce next week."

His mouth dropped and he raised his eyebrows. "I'm sorry. You must be crazy with hurt."

"I moved into a room last night, the place I lived in before I got married. I spent most of the day fixing it up. When I wasn't crying."

He shut his eyes. Then he stared at the floor. "Does this have anything to do with me?"

She took his hands in hers. "You're part of it," she said. "I'm not sure I can tell you why. Knowing you gave me the courage to walk out."

He shook his head, perplexed. "What happened?"

"Alan told me one of the most vicious lies I've ever heard." She described her husband's deception. His mouth hung open for most of the story.

"That's terrible. You must've been furious."

"You're right," she concluded. "The worst part is the way he humiliated me."

"I can't believe he'd treat you like that." He took her in his arms.

They talked until the pizza arrived. Anna's first experience with deep-dish Chicago-style pizza overwhelmed her.

"That was marvelous," she said. "But I really should go. It's late." She felt a deep excitement, nervousness in the pit of her stomach. Would he let her walk out?

"Okay," he said.

He walked her to the door and opened it.

"Thanks for being such a good friend," she said. She put her arms around him for their first hug in some time. She started to kiss his cheek, but he turned. Their lips came together for the first time outside of a dream.

Anna lost track of time, place, beliefs, promises, and right and wrong. She realized she stood right where she'd always wanted to be, where she was supposed to be, in the arms of the man she loved.

She drew back and put a finger on his lips. "Just a moment," she said. "I don't think I want to go anywhere tonight." She reached behind her and shut the door.

His smile made her feel weak. The kiss began again.

A few moments later, she realized that he'd taken off almost all her clothes, which now lay on the floor around her. She'd also removed most of Casey's clothes at the same time, even though they hadn't stopped kissing. In a few minutes, he drew back and looked into her eyes. She understood the question. She grinned and nodded. Casey picked her up and started down the hallway.

Everyone always remembers the first time that he or she entered into the passionate communication of sex with a specific individual. The most intense form of communication possible between two people changed Casey and Anna forever. Joining together would alter the way each of them saw the world.

Anna used the sex to drive away all the disappointment, the anger, the hurt and the embarrassment of the last few days. The lovely feel of her body pressed against Casey ignited passions she'd never experienced.

The sex cleansed her of all the negative emotions and disappointment.   Casey responded with an intensity she'd never experienced.

Anna felt strange during the sex.   To her surprise, she experienced not the slightest twinge of guilt nor did she feel afraid. As they embraced, she had a gradual epiphany.

Casey loved her. He didn't care about technique, about past experience, about anyone else. He used this encounter to express the love he felt for her. She felt him waiting for her and when she did achieve climax, he helped and encouraged her through it.

They lay together afterward, talking in whispers, as if anyone could hear.   The caressing of one another's body continued in the dim light of the bedroom. In a few moments, to her surprise, she realized that they were about to make love again. After a few moments, they joined together again.

She looked into his mind. She locked on to a place she hadn't visited in months and gave him a Paik.

* * * * *

Gareth and Viviane lay together in the fold-out bed in front of the fireplace in the ski lodge. He had always loved her, all his life, since they were children. Each time they made love they fell deeper in love.

They were snuggled together when Viviane said, "Uh, oh." She got up and drew on a black negligee, his favorite, which she saved for special occasions. She had laid it at the foot of the bed. Then the terry cloth robe she'd worn earlier. She threw him his tee shirt and a pair of shorts. "Put these on," she ordered and hurried into a bedroom.

She came back carrying a little boy. In the firelight Gareth could see the child's copper hair and green eyes and knew that his wife held their son. He felt some surprise that Viviane heard the boy crying but he hadn't.

Viviane laid the little boy in the bed between them. She talked to the boy in a calm, gentle whisper.

She smiled at her husband and said, "He got scared with a bad dream, Daddy."

The little boy said, "A Snake came into the bedroom and chased me. It said mean things."

"Nightmares on vacation?" smiled Gareth. He stroked the little boy's hair. "What's the matter with you, Timmy? You're supposed to be having fun. Besides snakes always sleep through the winter." The boy smiled and laughed with his parents a little bit. The tears subsided, his fears driven out by his parents' love for him.

"Dad?" The voice sounded concerned, even worried. "Is Timmy okay?" Gareth saw a beautiful girl, about twenty years old, who looked worried. The girl had inherited Viviane's red hair but his blue eyes.

He nodded and his daughter relaxed. "Yes, Mickey, he's fine," said Gareth. The private name Mickey reflected the deep affection and pride that he and Viviane felt for their daughter. "He just woke up and couldn't remember where he was. Go back to bed. We have a lot of skiing to do tomorrow." The girl waved goodnight and went back into her bedroom.

The little boy, secure between his parents, fell asleep again in two minutes. "I'll take him, Annie," said Gareth.

He picked up his son and took him back to the bedroom. He came back to the living room. He drew back the covers and found his wife naked except for a lovely emerald necklace.

"Uh," he said.

"Something wrong?"

"Jeez, Annie, twice in the same evening? I mean we aren't twenty-five years old anymore."

"Coward. You used to rise to a challenge." She giggled at her own wit.

"Great. The Viviane Fixx Cliché Festival," he groaned. But he pulled off the shorts and tee shirt and slid into the bed.

They pressed their bodies together and resumed kissing. He remembered something and drew back a quarter of an inch. He said, "How did you hear Tim, Honey?"

"I don't know. Didn't you hear him?" she asked.

"No. I guess that you must me the best mommy of all time."

"See?" she said, encouraging him.

"It's being with you."

"Shut up," she said.

"Okay," he said and gave a gentle push.

"Oh!" she said, and clutched her husband.

* * * * *

Anna released the Paik, smiling at the compliment about being a great mother. They shifted from the ski chalet back to the house. They were making love for the second time, just like in the Knack vision.

The second time they made love that night went along with less intensity yet more passion even than the first time. However, something happened at the height of the encounter. Anna felt it. She didn't know what it meant at the time, though in the next few months it would become very clear.

Somehow, the Cymreig worked to bond her together with the man she loved. She would never be free of the love she had for him. He wrapped his right arm around her and cupped her left breast. She again covered his hand with hers and pulled herself closer to him.

She heard a car outside start up and drive away. It occurred to her that it seemed pretty late for someone to go out for a drive. They dozed off, lying on their left sides with her back pressed against his chest.

CHAPTER TWENTY-ONE

Casey sneaked out of the house before Anna woke. He borrowed her Lincoln and drove to a shop in town. He purchased a couple of bagels, which he served with coffee and the Sunday paper in bed.

They spent the day together watching television, talking, and taking a walk in a nearby forest preserve. They went to the grocery together and retrieved his car from the Westwood parking lot. He slept for two hours, snuggled up to her on the couch. After a large salad for lunch, he grilled a prime rib roast for dinner.

After supper, Casey and Anna sat on the couch sipping wine, their fingers entwined. He'd lighted the fireplace, which provided the only light in the room. Anna couldn't remember ever being so contented and peaceful. Except in a dream.

At 7:00 P.M. she told him, with considerable effort, "Casey. This has been one of the nicest days I've ever had, but I have to go. I need to get some stuff ready to teach tomorrow." She put her arms around his neck. "Would you please stay home and sleep tomorrow? You really need the rest."

He resisted at first, but then agreed to stay home the next day. He called Mr. McAllister to request a substitute.

"Okay," he said.

"Thank you," she said. "I have to go. . ."

"Wait a second," he said. "Not so fast."

"What do you mean?"

"That call came with a price, you know," he leered.

"What? A price. . ." She got the picture. She grinned and began to peel off her sweater.

An hour or so later, as she left, she gave him a Paik to help him sleep.

Arriving at her little rented room, Anna found that Mrs. Merlini had taped several messages from Alan to her door. She wadded up the notes and threw them away as she entered.

* * * * *

On Tuesday Anna, still feeling a pleasant soreness and enjoying true happiness for the first time in years, walked over to Casey's classroom after school dismissed for the day. He looked rested and cheerful. She shut the door and they talked about the weekend. He had boxes lying around the room as he tried to get packed for the summer and the next year.

"Casey, we can't make love again," she said.

His face fell. "Never?"

"I'm filing for divorce. I don't want a big fight with Alan. If he found out about us—"

"It would be bad, wouldn't it?"

"Let's be friends again for a while."

"It won't be easy. But I'll try. However, in the meantime, since we're alone—" He took her in his arms. They kissed.

The resolve about love-making ended at his house a little while later.

Chapter Twenty-Two

Three weeks later, at nine o'clock in the evening, Anna sat in her room reading some exams. She heard a car stop on the quiet street outside the house. Moments later, someone rang the doorbell of the house.

In a few moments, someone rapped at her door. The knock sounded again as Anna crossed the room. She attached the safety chain and opened the door an inch.

Alan stood in the hallway, unshaved, hair mussed, wearing a bedraggled suit, tie askew. Mrs. Merlini stood behind him, looking annoyed. "Can I come in?" he asked.

"What do you want?"

"I have to talk to you."

"Call my lawyer."

"Anna, please, I need to talk to you."

Several other people lived in the house, so he wouldn't try something. Afraid he'd make a scene in the hallway, she unlatched the chain and stood aside. She nodded to Mrs. Merlini, who frowned and walked downstairs.

He put out his arms to embrace her, then dropped them to his sides when she backed away. He walked to the window and looked out. She left the door open and sat on the bed.

He took a deep breath. "I'm miserable without you," he said.

"Oh, Alan, for heaven's sake."

He took a deep breath, trying to control himself. "I miss you. I can't work, I can't sleep, I can't eat. My life has gone to hell since you've been gone."

"What am I supposed to do about that?"

"I want you to come home."

"No. Now, if you've nothing else to. . ."

He began to cry. "Please, Anna. I think about you all the time. I made a terrible mistake."

"No, you didn't. A person makes a mistake when he adds seven and nine and gets fifteen. You choreographed a careful, deliberate plan with your sleazy doctor pal to humiliate and deceive me."

"But—"

"Our marriage has ended. Deal with it. Then start your life over with someone who can live with your duplicity. Now, will you please leave?"

"Who's the guy you've been dating?" he asked, his face red, his fists knotted.

She unclenched her jaw with an effort. "Alan, my life no longer includes you. You needn't consider what I do or who I spend time with as any of your concern. I won't discuss my friends with you."

His face contorted with pain. He strode to the door and pushed it shut. "Okay. I think I can get past this one affair."

"How generous of you," she said, voice dripping with sarcasm. She stared, furious that he'd been stalking her. Now, she remembered the car following her to Casey's house, and leaving as she fell asleep in Casey's arms.

"We're still married. I'm offering to put your infidelity behind us."

Anna stopped him with a slashing movement of her left hand. "But I can't put what you did behind us. Even if I could get past your hideous lies, I want children. You and I can't have a family."

"Yes, we can. I came to tell you. I went to an urologist the week after you left, a doctor in Chicago named Dr. Asbury. He performed a reversal on the vasectomy."

"What?"

"Honest. Let me show you the receipt." He pulled a pink sheet of paper from his pocket. She walked to the window and stared out at the rain. Lightning flashed over the lake.

Alan had made a major concession. But he'd done it too late. She'd fallen in love with Casey now. She wanted to marry and have children with him.

"I've changed. I swear it," Alan said. "I'm going to cut back on the traveling. I won't go on any more junkets. Just come back."

She turned back. "I'm sorry. I'll never be able to forget what you did. Now please get out."

He sighed, thinking. Then he nodded. "If you say the word I'll sell the business."

Anna had been ready to blister him with a retort. She hesitated at this concession. She folded her arms across her chest. In a moment or two she said, "How could I ever believe anything you say?"

His face contorted with pain. He looked at the floor. "I won't lie again. I promise."

"That's nice to hear, and easy to say. But you made a lot of promises when we got married. You've been very casual about keeping them. I can't let myself be hurt like that again, Alan."

"I'm ashamed of how I treated you. But we made vows. I know you can't break a promise. You've never been able to do that."

That stung. She'd been breaking her marital vows for months. Anna had allowed herself to fall in love with another man. She'd been planning a life with Casey while married to Alan.

"Anna," he said, taking her arms. She didn't draw back. "I've never told you everything about my family. You know I grew up with a drunk for a father. He beat my mother and my brother and me." He dropped his hands and sat in a straight chair.

"I haven't told you everything, though," he said in a soft voice. "My mother passed away just before I started college.

Before she died, she gave me instructions about what she wanted for the funeral." He turned back, his face twisted with the pain of the memory. "I had to organize the funeral by myself." Anna closed the door.

"My father showed up at the funeral home, plastered as usual. I refused to let him in. I accused him of killing Mom with his drinking, cruelty, and selfishness. I kicked him out and haven't heard from him since." He ran his fingers through his hair, his face wreathed with anguish at the memory.

"When you and I started planning to get married, I got scared about having kids," he continued. "I didn't want to create the same kind of family I grew up in."

Anna now saw a different side of her husband. The story moved her to her soul with sorrow. She remembered how she felt when her parents died.

After a few moments, she asked, "Why didn't you explain this to me before?"

"I figured you wouldn't marry me."

"And you're telling me now because---?"

"I thought you'd forget about being a parent when you saw how our lives went on without children. I was wrong."

"And now you'd be okay with having children?"

"Yes," he said. "If it means you'll come back."

Anna remembered Casey's joy at being with her. His gentle, sweet nature.

But she had married Alan. He had made an effort. He promised to change.

She looked at him, aware that she faced the biggest decision of her life. Even bigger than marrying him. She couldn't draw back or change her mind.

She'd made a promise.

She nodded. "Okay."

His look of apprehension changed to an expression of disbelief. "You'll come home?" She nodded. He started to smile and tried to hug her. She put up her arms and wouldn't permit it.

He said, "I'll have all your things moved back tomorrow."

She shrugged. She packed up some clothes and some toiletries. Then, she climbed into the Lincoln and followed him.

As she walked into the big, cold, joyless house, she felt a little nauseous. She thought about Casey's warm little house.

She tried not to think about Casey as she unpacked. She shook herself and came back downstairs.

He had poured them a little champagne. They sat and talked about what had happened since she had left.

At last, they went to the bedroom. When she came out of the bathroom, she found him in the bed naked. "I think we should make love," he said.

"I'm a long way from that. But I'll try sleeping in your bed." She saw the disappointment and hurt on his face. He put on some pajamas, and she climbed in next to him. They didn't embrace.

In the morning, she found him naked again. "What about now?" he said. She thought for a moment, and relented. *Why do I need to wait now?*

She let him pull off her nightgown. For the first time he made a real effort to please her.

CHAPTER TWENTY-THREE

Anna avoided Casey the next day. She knew she had to tell him, but she couldn't bring herself to do so that day. Or the next.

Friday morning arrived, the last day of finals. She put on the short denim skirt that she'd worn to Casey's production of *Dr. Jekyll and Mr. Hyde* that first night. She wanted Casey's last memories of her to be special. She didn't have any idea how she'd tell him.

When Alan saw her in the outfit, he came to her and kissed her. He suggested a return to the bedroom. She promised she'd wear the outfit later that night. Despite the promise, she almost didn't make it out the door.

When classes ended, Casey entered her classroom. He had a strange look on his face, but when he saw her in the denim skirt, his face lit up. "Wow," he said, and kissed her cheek.

She opened her mouth to tell him that she had to end things between them. But the pain that washed over her wouldn't let her. "Wow yourself," she said with a laugh.

He wore the shirt and tie and cufflinks she's given him, with dress slacks and dress shoes. He looked like his old self: eyes clear, skin healthy, his normal weight. "Have you finished with grades?" she asked.

"Yeah," Casey said. He picked up a pencil on her desk and studied it. "I've got all my stuff crated up. I loaded it into my car and said all my goodbyes. I just have one more thing to do."

He cleared his throat in the way he did when they first met, timid and reticent. Still staring at the pencil, he managed, "Would you come for a little walk with me?"

She nodded, not trusting herself to talk.

When they walked out of the building Casey took Anna's

hand. She didn't pull away.

They crossed the parking lot together on a beautiful day, warm and sunny with a gentle breeze. He took her to a bench on the football field.

He put an arm around her. She leaned her head against his shoulder. "I have to apologize," he said in a soft voice.

"For what?"

"You must've noticed I've been avoiding you the last couple of days." He'd been avoiding her? She started to speak, but he held up a hand. "I've been hiding from you. I didn't think about what that would do to you."

"Why?" she asked.

"I'm not sure how to tell you what I have to say," he said, running his hand through his hair. "I keep rehearsing, trying things out. . ."

Relief flooded over her. He planned to break things off with her. That was why he appeared so nervous, so timid, even scared.

He pulled out a package from a pocket. "I want you to have this, even though I know you could buy yourself something much better."

She stared at the package, trying to memorize how the wrapping looked. He'd done it himself.

"You can open it," he said, sounding anxious.

She tore away the awkward wrapping and opened the package. Inside a long box she found a delicate wristwatch. An inscription on the back of the watch read, *To A.O. Love C.F.* She held her right hand to her mouth as he showed her how to use the unusual clasp.

She knew he couldn't afford such a present. Looking at the pride on his face, she realized he'd given her far and away the most expensive present he'd ever bought for anyone.

She understood. Of course. How like him to do that.

He'd bought it to soften the blow of breaking up.

"Oh, Casey, what a lovely gift. Thank you." She hugged him. Then she reached into her purse and pulled out a little gift for him. Will, the student who wrote for the newspaper, had printed up a couple of copies of the candid picture of the two of them posed outside the faculty lounge, smiling and happy.

He laughed and thanked her, not showing any sign of disappointment that she hadn't reciprocated with an elaborate gift. He took out a pen and signed one of the prints. "You realize, of course, that some day this picture and signature will be worth a fortune."

She smiled and put the photo in her purse. He slid the duplicate into his pocket.

She wiped away tears with the back of her hand.

He looked at his hands, which were trembling. "I have to tell you something. I've thought about this a lot," he said, not looking at her. "I've thought about almost nothing else for days."

Anna stared at a goal post, unable to meet his eyes.

He took a couple of deep breaths. "I think about you all the time. Being with you that weekend and every time since will always stand out to me as the greatest things that ever happened to me. I admire and respect you. I think you're beautiful and brilliant."

"Thank you," she said, touched by the loving praise.

He paused, studying the back of his hands.

Here it comes, she thought. She smiled to herself, composing an appropriate response. *Yes, Casey, I imagine you're right. Long-distance love affairs never work out.*

"I want you to come to Champaign with me," he blurted.

Her mouth dropped. He slid off the bench and dropped to one knee in the grass.

Pulling a ring off his little finger, he took her left hand. His hand trembling, he slipped the ring onto her third finger.

The little ring slid onto her finger without effort and fit as if it had been made for her by magic.

* * * * *

Anna stared at the ring, which was beyond doubt a family heirloom. It had a small but brilliant diamond embedded in its wide gold band. On either side of the diamond two emeralds glistened in the bright sun. The band had curious letters engraved on it.

She stared at the ring, then at him, then back at the ring, stunned.

"Annie," he said after a few false starts, "as soon as you finalize the divorce, I want you to marry me. I can't bear the thought of letting you out of my life. Hell, I can't even bear to let you out of my sight.

"We'll have to live in furnished married student housing the first year, but I promise it won't be bad. The apartments are pretty nice.

"Then, when I finish the degree, we can find a house around here. I have to teach at Westwood for at least one more year after I come back anyhow. I've saved money for a down payment." He went on and on.

She sat with her hand covering her mouth, unable to speak.

His face, drawn and tense, looked terrified. His sapphire eyes watered. "We can have a judge marry us or we can have a big wedding with family, friends, even the major press and media if you want." Now a tear started down his cheek.

Oh, no, she thought. How can I tell him now?

He held her hand and gave it a squeeze. He rose from his knees and sat next to her. He took a deep breath and continued.

"My sisters come home from Switzerland in a year and I'd like them to live with us. I imagine an instant family doesn't sound real appealing, but my sisters are going to love you. You're so good with kids, too. And I promise you that I'll take care of you and them and our own kids."

Now he stood, and paced back and forth, talking, but Anna didn't hear what he was saying.

Anna continued to stare at the ring, lost in a daydream. She could picture the two of them in the little house with his two sisters and their own children running in their back yard. Not for the first time she thought about what a wonderful daddy Casey would be.

She imagined little people waking them up and jumping into bed with them on cold mornings or snuggling with them to be comforted after a bad dream. She and Casey would take the kids to the zoo and museums.

At Christmas, they would dress them up in little suits and dresses, and ride the train downtown to see Santa Claus at one of the department stores. She and Casey would hold hands while the children opened presents under the Christmas tree.

She thought about a lifetime of making love to Casey. She saw them growing old together and welcoming grandchildren.

She would change her name this time, not like with Alan—

Alan. She shook herself out of the daydream. She'd just taken him back. Alan had promised to make an effort. He'd undergone painful surgery for her. How could she toss him out?

Casey continued to pace back and forth a few times. Then he knelt again, took her hand and brought it to his lips, "Annie, I don't have a lot of money. I can't imagine how I could begin to take care of you the way you deserve. But I'll make it up to you. I'll never make you cry. I'll love you as long as I live. That's a promise."

She couldn't leave Alan. She owed him everything. She was out of debt because of him. She had fine clothes, a beautiful car, a gorgeous home. She couldn't repay his generosity by divorcing him.

Besides, she'd made a promise. A vow.

She could hear Alan laughing, sneering at the little ring and the watch Casey had given her.

"Annie?" he whispered, jolting her out of her reverie. "Er. . .look, if you don't like the ring, we can pick out a different one."

"I love the ring," she murmured. "I've seen such a beautiful ring."

He smiled. "I'm relieved to hear that. It's been in my family for generations. A legend goes with it. Just before Mom died, she sold it to me."

She looked up in amazement. "Sold it to you?" He laughed, and she got the joke. She managed a smile.

"By tradition it goes to our oldest son," he said. *Oh heaven. He's planned on children and everything.* "I hope that's okay. I wish you could have known my mom and dad." His voice choked up. "They'd have been thrilled to have you as their new daughter."

When she didn't say anything, he stood and walked away a few steps, staring at something on the other side of the field. He clenched and unclenched his hands, then kneaded the back of his neck.

He turned back to her. "Okay. You need more time. I took you by surprise. I know it'd be a major shift in your life. Look, you can think it over. I'm not leaving for Champaign until next week."

She looked into his eyes, and choked in a small voice, "I can't marry you."

* * * * *

Casey's smile faded. She took a last look at the precious little ring on her finger. Then she slipped it off and put the ring into his hand. She pulled his fingers to her lips and kissed them.

"But," he said in a small, hurt voice, "I love you."

"I know," she said. She pressed his hand against her face. "I love you too." The words leapt out before she could think.

It shocked her to realize that she'd never told him that before. "You have to forget about me."

Now the anger. He yanked his hand away and stood. "Well, I've made a complete fool of myself. I misunderstood what happened between us the last three weeks. The last year, too," he said, voice trembling.

She stood and took his hand again. "Please don't be hurt."

"Don't be hurt, huh," he snapped. "Tell me, Ms. *Princess*, how in hell am I supposed to manage that?" Tears glistened in his eyes.

"I don't want you to hate me," she stammered. "But I can't see you anymore. Ever. Please don't try to contact me. Just forget about me."

"Forget about you?" he said.

"I just can't—" She hugged his hand and began to sob.

He pulled away and grabbed her shoulders. He looked in her eyes. "This doesn't make any sense. What's going on here?"

"I went back to Alan a couple of nights ago," she blurted.

A moment or two of stunned silence ensued. He dropped his hands. He stammered, "But you can't be serious—"

She nodded.

His reaction exceeded her worst fears.

Casey clutched his stomach as if he might retch. "Why on earth would you go back to him? After the way he treated you? After those atrocious lies? And why didn't you tell me sooner? Why did you let me go on like this, making an idiot of myself—" he broke off.

"Stop, Casey, please. I had to make a decision." She choked, appalled at the devastation in her friend.

He stood there, breathing hard, trying to gain some composure. "Okay, then." His mouth became a grim line. "Forgive me, *Princess*, if I don't walk you to your car," he said, bitter and sarcastic. "I hope you enjoy your life with the lying bastard rich guy." He turned and took a couple of paces. Then he ran, without looking back.

Anna started to run after him. Stepping in a sprinkler hole, she broke a heel, giving her ankle a twist. She pulled her shoes off and hobbled to the edge of the parking lot.

He reached into his pocket, fumbled with his keys, and dropped them. He knelt but couldn't seem to pick them up.

He looked up at her. Their eyes met as she limped toward the car.

"Casey, wait a moment," she blurted.

He climbed into his car.

"Casey," she said. "Let's not say goodbye like this."

He slammed the door and drove away, tires squealing.

She watched the taillights vanish. "Casey," she murmured. She reached into her purse for a tissue. Her fingers closed on the picture he'd signed. She read the inscription: *To Annie, all my love, always. Casey Fixx, June 7, 1985.*

She drew herself up, wiped her eyes and blew her nose. She went back into the school and into a washroom, where she repaired her makeup. Then she strode to Dr. McAllister's office. She thanked him for his kindness but said she wouldn't be returning. She knew she couldn't stand coming into the school where she'd met Casey. The memories would be too painful. Then she exchanged tearful good-byes with Grace and the other teachers.

She and Alan went to bed early that night. He told her he couldn't wait. He'd been thinking about her in the jeans skirt all day, he told her.

The sex with Alan bordered on violent in its intensity that night. She responded with the fervor of emotion that had stirred her heart all day.

Afterward, he lay back, happy and satisfied. She wept to herself. In a few moments, he took her again.

She went in to the school a few days later and turned in a

letter of resignation. She cleaned her room out. She packed up all her materials and turned in her keys to the office.

Sometime later, she realized that she had missed her period that month, due, she felt sure, to the stress, pain and loneliness. She considered that if Casey had died, she couldn't have felt worse.

When she missed again the next month, and began to feel sickness and nausea, she went in for a pregnancy test.

Weeping, she told Alan that they were going to be parents. The smile he gave her didn't reach to his eyes as he pretended to be happy.

And the terror in her dreams started again. This time, Gareth didn't come to protect her.

CHAPTER TWENTY-FOUR

Anna asked Alan to turn off the air conditioner one cool summer evening. They opened the windows to enjoy a soothing and gentle breeze off Lake Michigan. Anna lay in her bed next to her husband, her middle just beginning to bulge with the pregnancy.

She saw the door to the bedroom open. Her face contorted with fear as she saw a huge snake enter the room and slither to the side of the bed. She tried to wake Alan but found that she couldn't move or talk.

A strange unnatural light illuminated The Snake's fangs and its red anthracite eyes. *Where could Gareth be now?*

In a terrifying flash, she understood. Gareth wasn't coming. He would never come again.

The Snake reared up like a cobra before a charmer and transformed into a tall man who stood at the side of the bed. She couldn't see all of the demon's face, as usual. Through a cloud of yellowish smoke encircling his head, she saw a long, flowing beard.

She saw the demon's lips draw back in a hideous grin, revealing pointed teeth. He stroked her face with insolent hands. "So here we are at last, as I promised, Annie," he said in his sibilant hiss, using the little name that only Casey had ever called her. "And you've betrayed him, just as I said. I have something to show you, Sorcerer's Daughter."

She reached for the Cymreig but the demon made a swatting motion as if swiping at a gnat. "The Cymreig," he sneered. "I have no time for that nonsense."

He pointed to the open bedroom window which transformed into a movie screen. She heard a film projector start up behind her. "Watch," the man commanded. She had no choice. She couldn't turn her head.

The film showed her assassinating Casey Fixx. The movie showed the kissing. The beautiful little house. The skirt she'd bought with the full intention of seducing him. The bed. The warm June day when Casey proposed. The rusty old Chevrolet speeding out of the parking lot.

In the film she saw him walk into the little house she loved. He slumped to the floor, weeping, all alone in his misery. She struggled to rise and go to him but of course she couldn't move. She tried to protest that she didn't mean to destroy him.

The film ended. Then it played again. And again. And again. Over and over.

She wept with self-loathing. She had wounded his soul, torn his heart, and crushed his shy nature.

When the film ended at last, the stranger towered above her. The malevolent voice hissed, "I've come for you, Viviane. And the baby, too." He climbed onto the bed, and she realized that the stranger had stripped off his clothing. He shoved her legs apart. She screamed with terror and pain.

* * * * *

Anna heard Alan saying, "Anna. Wake up." She opened her eyes and saw the early morning sun shining through the window. Alan shook her shoulders, looking annoyed.

"You all right?" he said.

She looked around. The dream man had vanished. "I'm sorry," she said. "I had a nightmare." She lay huddled, still shivering with terror.

Alan rolled over. "You woke me up," he said in a nasty, unsympathetic voice.

The Snake visited Anna every night. Sometimes the dreams would end with her wrapped around Alan in terror. She couldn't recall the entire dream once she woke but she remembered the terror.

"This is ridiculous," Alan said, after a week. He sat next to her in their bed, looking down at her as she struggled awake from yet another nightmare. "Maybe you should go to the doctor for some help."

No doctor has a cure for my problem, she thought. "I imagine the pregnancy caused the dreams. If they continue after the baby's born I'll do something then."

"I can't keep having my sleep disturbed," he said.

She bristled at his annoyed tone. "I'm not doing this on purpose," she said. "The dreams scare me so much I'm afraid to go to sleep."

"I need my rest so I can function at work." He moved down the hall to another bedroom, telling her she needed to cope with the dreams by herself.

The next week, they sat at dinner. "I have something to tell you," he said. "I have to go out of town to a conference."

"But you made a promise," she reminded him, bitter. "You said you weren't going out of town anymore."

"I know, but I have responsibilities. Besides, I have to deal with an emergency."

Then he had to go Las Vegas for a business meeting. Then he had another meeting in Atlantic City. Then he needed to entertain some clients at the Riviera Country Club in South Florida and was gone a week.

She didn't deal well with his absence. She managed only fitful sleep in the big house. She lay awake listening to the creaking noises. She lived in fear at night.

One morning she came downstairs, angry at Alan. He planned to be out of town for ten more days.

The phone sat next to the couch. She remembered Casey's number. Without thinking, she reached for the phone and started to dial.

When it began to ring, she realized what she was doing. Anna hung up.

Only then did she remember that she couldn't call Casey at the little home she loved. He wasn't there. He'd gone to Champaign.

No, I can't do that, she thought. *I can't ever call him. If I do, I have to leave Alan.*

Besides, Casey hates me, now.

She turned on the television. She watched a soap opera. The silly love story made her cry.

CHAPTER TWENTY-FIVE

About two months before her baby's due date Anna registered for Lamaze classes. Alan refused to go to the classes with her. "Have you gone nuts?" he said. "I don't have six Tuesday nights to devote to some damn fool classes. And I'm not going into any labor room, much less a delivery room. Just have them knock you out."

"It doesn't work that way. Besides, I don't want anesthesia," she said. "Please reconsider." She didn't tell him that she lived in terror that if the Snake found her asleep, he might take her. And the baby.

"Not a chance," he asserted.

"I'm having your baby, Alan."

"You're the one who insisted on this kid. I'll pay for it. That'll be my contribution," he chuckled.

Casey wouldn't do this to her, she thought. He'd want to be there.

Anna's labor began about noon on a cold February day almost a month early. She called Alan at work. He said he couldn't get away. He called a cab for her.

* * * * *

Two hours later, Alan's secretary buzzed him. His wife had telephoned, telling him that she'd arrived at the hospital, having his child, and why hadn't he come?

He frowned. She had interrupted an important business call and he had a difficult time even being civil with her. "I'm busy," he told her. "I haven't got time to chat. Good luck." He clicked back to the business call on the other line, apologizing to the client.

He drove to the hospital about seven. Anna still languished

in labor. He'd been hoping it would be over by the time he got there. He asked a nurse to let his wife know he'd remain in the waiting room.

The nurse returned and told him that Anna still had several hours to go before delivery. He left the hospital and went to a restaurant for dinner. After lingering over coffee and dessert, he returned to the hospital at 9:30. Nothing new with Anna. He worked a crossword puzzle and read part of a novel, bored senseless and irritated. He dozed off about eleven.

The nurse woke Alan at midnight and told him that they had moved Anna into the delivery room. He made a phone call and slipped out of the hospital.

*****

The delivery room became a medieval chamber of horrors for Anna. She screamed in pain as the contractions came faster and harder.

Though the pain debilitated her, the fear was worse. It tore at her like a rusty knife. The Snake waited for her and for her baby. She could almost hear his sneering laugh and feel his vulgar pawing at the height of each contraction. *"I'm coming, Viviane,"* his voice hissed.

Anna accepted a little Demerol to help her relax, but the pain kept increasing. The Lamaze teachers had explained how to breathe and relax, and she had been faithful with practice. But in the midst of the grinding, demoralizing pain and distress, she couldn't remember a thing.

I'm coming, Viviane.

The doctors and nurses strapped her legs into the stirrups and draped her middle.

She felt a spasm of fear and felt the blinding terror of the night steal over her. She knew what it meant.

She turned her eyes to the side. Nehushtan stood there, lounging against the wall of the delivery room.

Nehushtan couldn't be here. He only came to her when she slept. Yet there he stood. He grinned at her, showing pointed teeth, and ran his tongue over his upper lip. He picked up a scalpel and tested the edge with a finger.

Pleading and afraid, she whispered, "Casey."

Casey walked into the labor room.

He stood next to her and took her hand. He wore the white shirt and tie and slacks and shoes he'd worn the last time she'd seen him. "Well," he smiled, "You've really done it this time. Look at you, another fine mess."

He bent and kissed her. Nothing in her life had ever felt so good. She felt the fear ease. She looked for Nehushtan.

"He's gone," said Casey. "Don't be afraid."

She'd called out to Casey but she hadn't used the Cymreig. That must mean he was really there.

But this couldn't be happening. Casey lived in Champaign now. Two hundred miles away.

"How did you get here?" she whispered.

"You invited me."

"Do you still hate me?" Tears of loneliness, despair, and longing ran down her face.

He stroked her face. "Don't be ridiculous," he said, gentle and loving. "I could never hate you. We've loved each other for centuries."

She felt a contraction start. Her face twisted with the pain.

Casey took her face in his hands and smiled. "No, no. Don't be afraid. The Snake lives in our fear. Put him away." He stroked her face. "Focus on my eyes. I've got you. Listen to me."

He demonstrated the panting breaths. "Remember?"

She nodded and breathed, her eyes holding his. The pain became manageable. The fear vanished as she gripped his hand and gazed at his familiar smile. It didn't matter that it was absurd for him to know the Lamaze training. She'd work all that out later. Now she had to focus on the baby.

The contraction eased and Anna exhaled a cleansing breath as she'd been taught. He patted her shoulder. "Good job, honey." She managed to return Casey's smile.

As Anna rested between contractions, the doctor asked, "Anna, would you introduce this man to me?" His eyes sparkled above his surgical mask.

Anna introduced the doctor to Casey and they exchanged waves and smiles.

"The baby is breach," the doctor said in a few minutes. "If we do a vaginal delivery, the pain could be extreme. Do you want to go Caesarean?"

Casey looked in her eyes. She knew he'd support whatever she wanted to do.

"No," she said. "We can do it."

Anna worked hard for several minutes, breathing and pushing as Casey and the doctor directed.

At last the doctor said, "We're almost there. Just a couple more pushes."

In the mirror the nurse had set up for her, Anna saw the doctor work free one tiny leg. Then the other. A few moments later Anna gave birth to a little girl. Laughing and crying and clutching each other's hands, Casey and Anna watched their newborn sputter and take her first breath. The doctor held her up for Anna to see, and then placed the baby on her stomach.

"You two talk a minute while I do the embroidery here," the doctor chuckled. He delivered the afterbirth and stitched the episeotomy.

"What a beautiful baby, honey," Casey told her. He wiped his tears, then hers. "I told you we could do it."

"You did not," she corrected him with a giggle. "I told *you* we could do it."

He chuckled. "Okay. I'm so proud of you."

Anna clutched his hand. "Thank you," she said. "Thank

you for everything."

They embraced and kissed for the first time in months.

"I didn't bring a gift for her, not even a card," he said. "I'm sorry."

She smiled. "I've never received a better gift than the one you just gave me."

Casey stroked the baby's head. "She's gorgeous. Just like her mother. My lady Dulcinea."

The doctor put the baby in Anna's arms. Anna let go of Casey's hand to hug their baby.

"Who are you talking to, Anna?" The doctor said.

"I told you," she said. "I'm talking to Casey, my best friend." She reached out her hand to Casey. Her hand touched nothing. She turned to look. Casey had vanished.

A chill spread through her body. "Where did he go?"

"Anna," the doctor said, "you were dreaming. It worked, though. You calmed down and began to breathe. Who's this Casey?"

She saw the same question on the nurse's face. Anna couldn't believe it. No one remembered Casey being there.

Anna thought fast. "Oh, I had an imaginary friend named Casey when I was a child."

"Amazing what the mind can do," said the doctor. "So do you have a name for your little girl?"

"McKenna," said Anna. She'd decided to give the baby her grandmother's maiden name.

"How do you do, McKenna?" said the doctor, poking the baby's palm. McKenna wrapped her tiny hand around his index finger. Everyone laughed with delight.

Anna asked the doctor, "Joel—Is the baby okay?"

The doctor knew what she meant and smiled. "Ten fingers, ten toes, red hair, blue eyes. She's perfect."

McKenna began to cry, a soft, healthy whimper. "See?" said the doctor. "She has perfect lungs."

CHAPTER TWENTY-SIX

A second before, Casey Fixx had been standing next to Anna in a hospital delivery room. Now he found himself in an ethereal cave, radiant with refracted light, stunning color and strange music. Delicious smells surrounded him.

An old man lying on a cedar bed raised himself on one elbow and grinned at Casey. "Thank you, Gareth," he said. "Nehushtan would have killed her and the baby."

Casey sat at the old man's side. "The little girl. I'm her father?"

"Yes," said the old man.

Casey began to cry from the loneliness and anguish that had been hanging over his soul for months.

The old man put a hand on Casey's shoulder. "Viviane loves you," he said. "Try not to hate her for her decision to go back to her husband. She will suffer because of it."

"I could never hate her. But—"

"Yes?"

"Who will help her now? Her husband? He doesn't love her—"

"The baby will be her great joy and comfort. She will devote herself to protecting and caring for the child."

Casey looked at the man's face. "Why do I know you?"

"You've known me for centuries, Gareth."

All at once, Casey's mind cleared. He knew this man. Of course. "Myrthynne," he said. "Master."

"Tell me of your work at the University."

Casey sat on the ground next to the cedar bed and discussed the problems he'd been experiencing with his dissertation. He described his pain and frustration that he couldn't see the direction for the book.

"Let me help you," said the old man. He gazed again into Casey's mind.

Casey again felt as he sometimes did when Anna looked into his eyes, as if someone were throwing switches in his mind.

Tears came to Casey's eyes again. "Master," he said.

"Yes, son."

"Will I ever see Anna again?"

The huge sorcerer paused, as if looking into the distance. "I cannot answer that. I know she broke your heart. You will forget the visit and the baby." Again the eyes locked onto his. "Be at peace, Beloved Gareth."

* * * * *

Casey woke up. He looked at his watch. 2:30 A.M. He had dozed off in his cubicle at the University of Illinois library.

He remembered having a dream about Anna having his baby. Then something about a cave and—

He couldn't quite remember.

Casey steeled himself. He needed to get over her. The dreams and the memories had to stop.

He picked up the obscure tome before him and sneered. He'd become convinced that the publishers used chloroform in the book's ink. He forced his mind back into reading.

To Casey's surprise, the words in the book began to make perfect sense. He grabbed a legal pad and begin to write. To his amazement, he saw the entire plan, structure, and direction of the dissertation. To jot down his impressions took the rest of the night, but he knew it was right on track.

Six weeks later, Casey defended the dissertation before his committee. He received his degree at graduation ceremonies the first week in May. No one celebrated with him. No one applauded as the professors put his doctoral hood over his head.

CHAPTER TWENTY-SEVEN

The doctor, Joel, gave little McKenna her first medical exam. Then the nurses cleaned up the baby and helped Anna with her first breast-feeding. After a few moments, the baby drifted off to sleep next to her mother.

Anna wept, kissing and hugging the baby. She couldn't see Alan in the child's face but she didn't really see herself either. She saw the features of Casey Fixx.

The baby hadn't come early. McKenna was Casey's baby.

Alan still hadn't come in to see her or the baby.

Anna longed to show Casey the baby. She tried to rationalize. *He hates me. He wouldn't care about seeing her.*

In her heart, she knew she was telling herself a lie.

McKenna slept well that night, but her mother slept in fitful bursts. Alan still hadn't come in. The nurses said they couldn't find him in the waiting room.

Alan woke her the next morning when he stopped in on the way to work. He didn't show much interest in seeing the baby. "I'll see her soon enough. No rush. We'll have plenty of time."

"Where were you?" Anna couldn't understand where he had been during the delivery. He hadn't come to see her after she was moved from recovery to her hospital room.

"I ran out to get a bite to eat," he said, well-rehearsed. "Then I realized how tired I felt, so I went home to bed. After all, you can relax today, but I have to go to work." He reached for her hand, smiling as if speaking to an imbecile for whom things had to be spelled out in words of few syllables.

Anna grew furious. She sensed him lying about something.

That night she'd walked out on him, she had whacked him with a Cymreig jolt, but she had resisted using the Cymreig to check his veracity. Anna gripped his fingers, gazed through his eyes, and gave him a Paik.

She saw the truth. Alan had gone to visit a woman named Lucia while Anna struggled to give birth. She was his buddy Jim O'Donnell's receptionist, the woman who'd been so rude to Anna. Alan dated her before he met Anna and continued to see her on a regular basis since. He'd come home from trips a day or two early to sleep with her.

In the last few weeks, when the doctors advised against sex with Anna, Alan had sneaked out to sleep with Lucia several times. He spent last night with her while Anna struggled to give birth to the baby. He planned to see Lucia several times while Anna recovered.

She probed further and found that he had other lovers, not just Lucia. He'd slept with lots of women since he'd married Anna.

Anna remembered Alan's words at Mrs. Merlini's: "I can get past this one affair." She gritted her teeth, livid and humiliated.

Now she went even deeper into his mind.

She saw a man behind a desk, waving a pencil over a legal pad. She recognized him: William Kidd, one of Alan's cronies and a divorce attorney by profession. The attorney, tall and distinguished, wore a fabulous suit and sat in a lavish office.

Kidd's handsome face betrayed concern. "Who did you say Anna has retained?"

"Here's her card," said Alan, leaning forward and tossing it across the desk.

Kidd looked at the card and frowned. "Oh, boy," he muttered. "This woman is a real wildcat. She is a terrific lawyer who can tear your throat out."

"Ah, I don't think Anna wants anything," Alan said. "Let's just get it over with."

"This lady," said Kidd, waving the lawyer's card, "will want a cut of the settlement. She's going to go after everything you've got: the house, the business, the stock portfolio. And you're going to have to disclose every penny you have."

"Can we fight it?"

"I'll do everything I can. But your fake operation, the lying, the refusal to give her children—that's not going to play real well. Have you been seeing other women?"

"Sure," said Alan. "But Anna doesn't know."

"Don't count on it. She figured out the operation scam."

"How bad can this divorce get?"

"Well, she could get the house, a big cut of both the business and the portfolio."

Alan sat in stunned silence as his friend went on, painting a bleak portrait of what would happen.

He took a stab. "She's seeing this guy," he said.

Kidd shrugged. "We could maybe go after him for alienation of affection. Does he have a lot of money?"

"I doubt it. He teaches at a high school."

"So he makes, what, probably twenty-some thou a year." Kidd stood and walked to the window, staring out at the parking lot. "Okay, look. Do you see any possibility of a reconciliation?"

"I doubt it. She's pretty steamed."

"Could you do something to make it up to her?"

"Like what?"

"How about getting the vasectomy reversed?"

"Ow."

"No kidding. But if you get her back, you can go on with your life. Look, give her a kid. What the hell, you know?"

"But—"

Kidd turned back to Alan. His face had a grim set. "Alan, you know me. We've been friends for years," he asserted. "I'll fight tooth and nail and hammer and tongs. But believe me, this isn't going to go well, or nor is it going to be easy."

"What do I have to do?"

The lawyer said, "Well, start by seeing a urologist. Schedule a reversal. Then you'll need a speech. . ."

Anna released the Paik and returned to the hospital room.

Alan blinked as he regained his senses. "How long will it take for you to get your figure back?"

She fixed him with a stare as cold as the North Atlantic.

He averted his eyes. "Well, I'd better be off. I've got a big day."

"You'd better sit down, Alan," Anna said in a chilling voice. "Sit down if you value your sanity."

He stared at her in shock. "What did you say?"

"You aren't going to work until we have a talk."

He sat down.

She told him she knew about the deception he'd used to persuade her to come home. The women. The gambling. He listened, dazed, without saying anything.

She blasted him for several minutes. "Here's the deal. No more women. No more patronizing me. No more leaving me alone for extended vacations. You're going to help me take care of McKenna. You're going to come home at night at reasonable times. The nights out with the boys are going to be cut way back. We're also going to seek out a different circle of friends. We're going to start attending church. And you're going to be a great father. Not good, great."

At last he said, "Okay."

"You can go to work after you see McKenna," she said. "Come back by noon. We have plans to make."

The nurse brought McKenna to Anna for a feeding. As Anna brought the baby to her breast, Alan stood up to leave. He said, "I don't think I can watch that. I'll just wait in the hall."

"Sit down," she told him, teeth clenched. He started to say something, but shut his mouth and sat in the chair. She fed McKenna in the silence. Then she handed the baby to her husband. "Let me introduce you to your daughter McKenna.

Burp her." She told him how. He did so.

"No more dates, Alan," she said. "Ever. I'll know and I swear I'll divorce you on the spot. No questions, no second chances. I'll take everything."

"I promise," he said. Still holding the baby, he called his office. "I'm not coming in today. Re-schedule my appointments. My wife and I just had a baby."

* * * * *

Anna agreed to resume sex about six weeks after McKenna's birth. She insisted that he wear a condom. "God knows what you might have contracted from your other women."

She found they could have sex, but she couldn't make love to him. She didn't love him.

Instead, she pretended that Alan was someone else; that she was in a soft, cozy bed in a snug little house; that she was surrounded by artwork, musical instruments, books. And joy. And love.

The dream of the Snake went away for a time after the baby's birth, but returned when Anna started having sex with Alan. Alan moved into the guest room again. He made the move permanent.

Anna insisted on implementing major changes in their marriage, and thought he was making an effort. She also became a different person in her marriage. She thought about Casey often, but it gave her little pleasure. She felt pain, guilt and sorrow. And grief.

One night, as Alan was leaving for his bedroom, he said, "Goodnight, Anna."

After he left, she whispered, "My name is Annie."

Part III:

Nehushtan

CHAPTER TWENTY-EIGHT
Shoal Creek, Wisconsin
January

"Oh, nuts," said Wendell Witkay, as he swiped his napkin at the mess on the table.

Lucille, his wife of fifty years, looked up from her menu. "What happened?"

"I spilled some of my martini."

"Call the waitress over."

"No, she's busy. I'll just grab a couple of napkins from the bar. I'll be right back."

Wendell walked up to the bar and stopped next to a fat man with greasy gray hair. "Excuse me," said Wendell with a nervous smile.

The man turned toward him. He looked Wendell up and down and snarled, "Da hell you want?"

"Sorry to disturb you," said Wendell. "But would you please pass me a couple of those cocktail napkins? I spilled a little of my drink—"

"Beat it." The fat man turned back to his beer.

"Excuse me," Wendell stammered. "I just—"

The fat man again fixed him with a scowl. He grabbed the lapel of Wendell's jacket and jerked him forward. "I told you to beat it. You want your ass kicked?"

"Cut it out, Nick." Both men turned to see the immense bartender standing behind the bar. The man named Nick released Wendell's lapel.

"Please take these napkins, sir." The bartender handed him a small stack of napkins. "I do apologize."

Wendell looked back and forth between the two men. He hurried back to his table.

"What happened?" asked his wife.

"See that man at the bar? Long gray hair? Beard? He threatened me. Grabbed my coat."

Lucille's jaw dropped. "What did you say to him?"

"Nothing. Just asked him to pass me a couple of napkins."

The waitress appeared next to them. "Here," she said, placing two fresh drinks in front of them. "Mini sent these over." She gestured to the bartender. "On the house. He says sorry."

"Why did that man talk to me like that?" asked Wendell.

"Oh, who knows," said the waitress. "Nick's a little nuts, you know? But Mini can handle him. Nick's afraid of Mini."

"I can see why," said Wendell, regaining his composure. The bartender appeared to be the size of an Aerostar.

"He won't bother you again," the waitress said. "Mini will toss him out if he so much as looks in your direction."

Nick leaned his head to the side and gave it a little jolt, as if trying to knock water out of his ear.

"What's wrong with him?" said Wendell.

She shrugged. "No one knows. He's been to doctors, psychiatrists, hypnotists, everything. Something happened to him during college. Maybe bad drugs." She took out her order pad. "What can I get you?"

* * * * *

Nick Wolfe looked up. Mini leaned toward him, both hands on the bar. "Something wrong tonight?"

Nick grunted. "Nah. My old lady made me slap her around before I came."

The bartender stared for a moment. Then he walked away without a word. Nick mouthed a profanity that he never would have said to Mini's face.

Nick saw himself in the mirror behind the bar. He knew that he'd let himself go since college: long filthy hair. Scraggly beard. Crooked teeth. Huge gut. He looked like a wino.

Still, he had to grin when he thought about the way he'd handled the old man who interrupted him asking for napkins. He'd sure told that geezer where to get off. The violence reminded him of the scene at home earlier.

He sat at the table watching his wife Nora clearing up after dinner. Her two worthless kids had gone out somewhere. "I'm going up to Romano's for a couple of pops," Nick announced.

She paused, her mouth moving as if rehearsing. Nervous. Scared. "Be careful," she said.

"Da Hell's zat supposed to mean?" he shot back.

"If you get caught driving drunk again, they might put you in jail. We can't afford for you to lose your job."

Some job. Sweeping out the science classrooms at the local high school. Cleaning up hallways and laboratories after a bunch of spoiled kids.

The shift pusher had assigned him to clean up after the basketball game Saturday, so he'd been given the night off. "Ah, would you leave me alone?" he gnashed at his wife. "I can handle it."

"Please don't drink too much. You could—"

"Stop nagging!" He jumped up, crashed back his chair and charged her. He slammed her up against the wall hard enough to knock down a picture. Pinning her to the wall with one hand, he slapped her silly. Backhand. Forehand. Again. She screamed, terrified, and begged him to stop. Nick, bellowing profanity, continued slapping her until he got tired. She wept with pain and humiliation.

He liked the humiliation part best.

Nick stared at his glass of cheap beer. It tasted like weasel spit.

He'd just slapped her. She'd be sore, but not like if he'd punched her. She'll get over it, he sneered to himself. She always did.

Nick took a swallow of beer and thought about his rotten marriage. He had knocked up Nora, a local Shoal Creek woman, after he quit college. What a loser she'd turned out to be. And what an idiot he'd made of himself by marrying her.

He should've skipped town, gone to the West Coast, Florida maybe. Instead he'd married her.

Now he found himself stuck in this crummy town with no prospects, no future, nothing.

Might as well be in prison.

Oh, no one would think her unattractive. A tiny woman, maybe 5'-2", she had never gained any weight, like a lot of the fat sows in Shoal Creek. But her stupidity embarrassed him.

She'd given him two boys, both of them jerks. The oldest, Dale, nineteen, found himself in trouble all the time at school or with the law. Nick couldn't say much more about the younger one, either.

After the second kid, he made her get her tubes tied.

A picture of Anna O'Neill slipped into his mind. Violent situations often made him think of her. He jostled his head again, as if he were pushing the reset button.

He remembered, too. He couldn't forget the six months he'd spent in love with Anna O'Neill. He rehearsed the events again.

* * * * *

Shoal Creek, Wisconsin
The Fourth of July.

"Nick," his mother said, drawing him aside at the picnic in their backyard, "how much beer have you had?"

Nick Wolfe snorted and swigged at the bottle he held. "Give me a break. I'm twenty-one years old. I just got off work. Besides, this is my first today."

His mother's eyes clouded with concern. "Okay then. But I am getting concerned. You change when you drink. You become almost vicious."

"I'm a linebacker, Mom. We're mean by nature."

"Well, you know we don't need another episode."

"Geez, do you hafta nag all afternoon? That's been over for weeks. Today's a holiday."

"Come with me," she said. "I want you to meet Anna."

She steered him to the lake, which lay at the back of their large backyard. Nick saw a tall young woman with radiant red hair standing on the boat dock and looking out over the lake at the family's speedboat. She turned when she heard them approach.

The late afternoon sun shone in her copper hair, which framed her face. Nick thought he'd never seen such a beautiful girl.

He took her hand. "Hello, Anna." The summer outfit she wore flattered a lovely athletic figure. The sleeveless green top accentuated her striking emerald eyes. The white shorts revealed exquisite legs. On closer inspection, he noticed the threadbare and frayed condition of her clothes.

She spoke with a gentle Southern accent. "I'm glad to meet you, Nick." He muttered something that might have been a greeting.

"What a grand boat," she said, releasing his hand and indicating the motorboat tied to the pier.

Nick, dazzled, had difficulty framing a reply. "Yeah. You're looking at a twenty-one foot Chris Craft Capri. My dad got it in 1957, but it still has a good motor. A Chrysler Hemi. Two hundred horsepower."

She nodded. "It must be fast."

"We use it for skiing here on the lake. Do you ski?"

"I love it, though I'm not very good," she said, and again gave him the shy grin.

Seeing her athletic build, he doubted that she wasn't adept at the sport. Or anything, for that matter. "You're from the south," he said, as his mother drifted away.

"Yes," the girl said, sipping her iced tea. "A town called Washington in coastal North Carolina. My parents died a little while ago." Nick expressed condolences. She smiled her thanks. "I moved here to live with my aunt and uncle until I finish college," she added, and pointed to a couple chatting with Nick's parents.

"Oh, sure, Claude and Marian. They're good friends of my parents." He took her down the pier and showed her the Hobie Cat catamaran sailboat.

"Where did you go to school?" asked Nick.

"The University of North Carolina at Chapel Hill."

Nick, impressed, knew that she referred to one of the top universities in the country. He realized that Anna had to be a brilliant young woman. He held up his can of beer. "Can I get you a drink?"

"Thanks, no, I'll stick with iced tea. I may have a little wine with dinner."

He shrugged. "So, can you tell me your plans?"

"I'm transferring to The University of Wisconsin at Madison."

"That's where I go," he said. "I used to play football there. I tore up my right knee last season." He talked about his knee injuries. The pain. The operation. Rehabilitation. The amount of work he'd put in.

"The orthopedist said I can't play football any more," he said, taking a swig of his beer, finding a bit of solace in the cold foam.

"I'm sorry," she said. "That must have been difficult for you." She put a gentle hand on his and looked into his eyes.

Nick felt like a switch had been turned on in his mind. A warm glow came over him. Then it faded and he found himself again staring into beautiful green eyes. He returned her smile.

After the late-night fireworks in the public park, Nick walked Anna home. He asked her to go to dinner with him the next night. She agreed, delighted.

As the summer progressed Nick brought her flowers, gifts, and cards, and showered her with attention. He took her water skiing, and Anna loved sailing on the Hobie Cat.

In August, Nick and Anna each took a day off work to go to the Wisconsin State Fair, just outside Milwaukee. They ate bratwurst, sweet corn, and several cream puffs. Anna drank lemonade. Nick had several beers, but stopped short of getting drunk when Anna began to get nervous. She drove home, also.

She told him one night, "Nick, I'm worried about you."

He bristled. "What do you mean?"

"You change when you drink. You turn aggressive, even rude, sometimes downright abusive to others."

"I do not."

"Other people have noticed it, too."

He started to respond, but breathed deep and shrugged. "Okay, I'll watch it."

* * * * *

Nick worked hard to continue the summer romance into the fall. He took Anna to his fraternity, to dances, movies, and football games. They studied together. Though Nick earned good grades, Anna distinguished herself as a brilliant student.

Anna's employment limited their time together, however. During the day, she worked as a lifeguard at a campus pool. She waited tables in a fine dining restaurant on weekends.

Nick had plenty of girls he could date and have sex with when Anna went to work. He made sure she didn't know.

A week after the Thanksgiving holiday, Nick escorted Anna to the winter formal at his fraternity house. Anna wore a floor-length sapphire blue strapless gown with a provocative slit that went halfway up her thigh. As Nick helped her on with her wrap, he leaned forward to kiss her shoulders.

They double-dated with Nick's roommate Marty and his

date. Nick drove them to a classy steak house. Nick saw the eyes of every man in the room turn toward his exquisite girlfriend. Never in his life had Nick felt so proud.

At the fraternity house, Nick and Anna danced, but he couldn't stop thinking about the surprise he had planned for her that night. He and Marty had reserved a room at a local motel. The room had two queen sized beds, one for Marty and his girlfriend, and the other for Nick and Anna. Marty and Nick had stocked the room with champagne, hors d'oeuvres, and dessert candies.

He intended to dispense with her virginity that night. He almost drooled at the thought.

Between songs, Nick helped himself to beer from a half-barrel. After the fifth glass, Anna took him aside.

"Nick," she said. "You're scaring me. You're slurring your words, staggering, laughing too loud. You're getting drunk. Stop or you'll ruin our evening."

He barely restrained a snarl and said in a hostile whisper, "Look, we came here for a good time. Relax, will you?"

Her expression now became stony. She narrowed her eyes and said, "I'm not feeling well. Please take me home, now."

"What do you mean?" he belched. He heard his voice getting louder, felt his face reddening. "The dance won't be over for an hour."

"All right, then. I'll go by myself." She turned and went to the closet for her wrap. Then she strode toward the door. He put down his beer and ran after her.

A diminutive freshman pledge was just coming in the front door with his date. He stumbled over the doorstep. Anna caught him and helped him up, laughing as the boy apologized.

Nick's anger blazed. He seized the pledge by his jacket lapels, jerked him off the ground and rammed him against the door. Nick slapped him hard, first forehand, then backhand. He bawled vulgarities.

"What's the matter with you?" Nick barked, an inch from the freshman's face. The room became dead quiet.

"I didn't mean anything," stammered the pledge, tears in his eyes, humiliated. "I tripped on the step."

Nick enjoyed the mortified terror on his face for a few moments. Then he set him down, released his lapels and seized the younger man's necktie. "Apologize. Right now."

The pledge looked around. "Who should I apologize to?"

Nick turned to point to his girlfriend, but couldn't spot Anna anywhere. His stomach fell. He ran to the sidewalk and looked up and down the street. He asked people standing around where she'd gone. Someone said she'd gotten a ride home.

Frantic, Nick sprinted to her dormitory. He arrived in time to see her step into the elevator. He ran to a bank of phones on the far wall. Her roommate answered.

"Rita, let me talk to Anna."

He heard Rita cover the mouthpiece and say something. Several moments passed until Rita came back on. "Anna doesn't want to talk to you." The line went dead.

She wouldn't talk to him the next day either. Or the next. After a week of staking out her dorm, he caught her going in. "Look, I'm sorry," he began.

Her eyes blazed. "That's not good enough. You disgraced yourself and me, and embarrassed everyone standing there. What you did was unnecessary and uncalled for."

"He almost knocked you down. I got mad."

"He stumbled. And you humiliated and degraded him. No one deserves to be treated the way you treated him."

He swallowed hard. He had never seen her like this. She was ready to dump him. He tried his best to reconcile, offering apologies, promising to apologize to the freshman. He said, "Look, I know it bothers you. I'm going to swear off the booze."

"All right," she said at last. "As long as you follow through with these promises." He agreed. Now she gave him an ultimatum. "Your drinking has been getting worse and worse. I don't care if you have a drink once in a while. But if you lose control again, we're done."

Nick knew she was wrong. He didn't have a problem with alcohol. The promise caused him no concern.

* * * * *

Nick and Anna studied together the night before his physics final. "I'm struggling with this," he told her.

"What's wrong?" she asked.

"I don't know. It's like this physics stuff fried my brain."

She took his hand and looked into his eyes. Again he got a strange feeling. "What did you do?" he asked.

"I just took your hand and smiled at you." She looked amused. He chuckled and went back to work.

To his surprise, the difficult concepts began to make sense. The effect this girl had on him amazed Nick.

The weather, cold and overcast with swirling flakes of snow in the air, didn't diminish his good feelings the next day. He walked into the physics exam infused with self-assurance. He killed the test.

Anna had tests all afternoon. They'd made plans to go out and celebrate with dinner and a movie. He couldn't wait to tell her how well he'd done. She'd be proud. The thought of pleasing her made him smile.

In a splendid mood, he went to lunch at the fraternity house. A couple of the guys offered him a cold beer.

"No, thanks," he said. "I'm seeing Anna tonight. She gets mad if I've been drinking."

Ned Horcher, a loudmouthed bumpkin from a farm up north, unleashed a violent belch that rattled the Venetian blinds. "Let me get this straight," he sneered, wiping his mouth. "You're gonna let some girl tell you when you can have a beer?"

Nick hesitated. Then he thought: *Ah, nuts, one or two won't hurt.* He popped open a can, laughing it up with the guys. He washed down the brew with a shot of White Lightning. Then he drank another beer. And took another shot. Again. By the time he picked up Anna he'd damn near become plastered.

When she saw him in the lobby of her dorm, she stopped several feet away. "I'm not going out with you." She started to turn back to the elevators.

He caught her arm. "Why not?"

She looked at his hand, then into his face. Her green eyes turned stone cold. He let go.

"I've told you," Anna said. "I don't like being with you when you're drunk."

"I'm fine," he assured her. "I drank one or two beers with the guys, that's all."

She looked down, her resolution wavering. "Look, we've been planning to go out all week," he wheedled. "Come on. I'm okay." She gave in, skeptical. She put on her coat and they walked to the restaurant.

Nick washed down a triple cheeseburger with a couple of beers, despite Anna's objections. Then they took in a movie, which Nick hated. She wanted to go dancing afterward but he said, "Let's go back to my apartment."

At the apartment he popped open another beer. "That's it," she said. "I'm going home."

He caught her at the door. "Like hell."

He dragged her to the couch, kissing her and pawing her. He threw her down and pinned her to the couch.

She struggled to breathe. Begged him to stop. Nick yanked her sweatshirt up, and had her bra unhooked in a few seconds. He seized her breasts and kissed them, then started on her jeans.

Anna kept trying to push him away. Nick overpowered her and laughed, enjoying her terror. He told her to relax. Holding her down with his knee in her chest, he pulled her jeans down and extracted a prophylactic from his pocket. After unzipping and lowering his jeans, he tore the prophylactic wrapper open with his teeth and rolled the rubber on.

Anna fought. Pleaded. Cried. "Nick. I'm not ready for this. Please, stop. Nick, no." Her green eyes bored into his.

Nick felt the eyes bore into his mind. He shivered in a moment of fear. He shook it off and tried to pry her legs apart. He let go of one of her hands to position himself for the thrust.

Anna wrenched her other hand free and slapped his face. He laughed.

She seized his face with both hands and looked into his eyes.

* * * * *

Someone grabbed Nick's hair and yanked him off of Anna. He crashed hard to the floor and rolled to his back. His opponent dropped a knee into his stomach. Nick's breath left him in a Rush.

He saw a tall athletic man standing over him. The man glowered at Nick with fury in his arresting sapphire eyes. His long blond hair looked tousled as if it hadn't been combed for a while. "Get away from her," the man snapped. "Now."

Nick rolled away from the couch, gasping for air. He rose. As he bent to pull up his jeans, the blond man gave Nick a terrific kick in the rear that propelled him across the room, knocking the wind out of him again.

"Who are you?" Nick wheezed, climbing to his feet.

"I'm her best friend. And I'm going to take her home." He turned to Anna. "Come on, Viviane. Get dressed. You don't have to be scared now."

He helped Anna to her feet, giving her a gentle, loving smile.

"Thank you, Gareth," she whispered.

Gareth? Thought Nick. *What kind of name is that?*

"Did he...I mean..." he heard the blond man ask.

"No, he didn't really hurt me. I think I'll have a few bruises, that's all."

"You mean he didn't rape you?"

"No. You came just in time. Thank you."

"I warned you about this loser."

"You're right," she said.

Gareth stood between Anna and Nick, keeping his fists raised and his eyes fixed on Nick. She pulled up her jeans, snapped her bra together, and adjusted her sweatshirt.

When Nick at last got his breath, he lurched to his feet and started for Gareth. . .

He fell into a swirling vortex of light, sound, and wind. When things stopped spinning, Nick stood in an old graveyard next to a sand pit. He heard the ocean, felt the sea breeze.

Gareth and Anna stood five feet from him. Anna's expression of fury matched the look on Gareth's face. Nick stood, unable to move with surprise. "How did I get here?" he spluttered.

Gareth threw a handful of sand into Nick's face, blinding him. Nick choked and pawed at his eyes.

Now the blond man grabbed Nick's hair and neck. He shoved Nick against an oak tree that stood at the entrance to the cemetery.

Gareth kneed him hard in the groin, then kicked Nick's football knee. Nick screamed, blind with pain. Gareth slugged Nick's face. Again. A third time. Nick's head smacked against the tree each time.

Gareth slammed his knee into Nick's stomach. Then he clouted him on the temple.

Nick, close to blacking out, sank to his hands and knees in the weeds. He retched with the pain and choked for air. Never had he received such a comprehensive beating.

Anna embraced the blond guy from behind and pulled him away. She spoke to him in a voice Nick couldn't hear. The man stopped punching Nick. Gareth turned and put his arms around her.

"I saw it. Nehushtan wrapped around his heart," Anna told Gareth. "The Snake sneered at me."

"I figured something like that," said Gareth. "What else?"

"Last year, the police in Shoal Creek arrested Nick for assaulting a seventeen-year-old girl."

"No surprise," said Gareth. "Why didn't they toss him in the clink?"

"The girl dropped charges when Nick's father wrote a check for her first two years of college."

"Right," said Gareth.

They embraced, standing before an old grave marker, a statue of Michael the Archangel. Gareth stroked her hair and comforted her as she leaned her head against his shoulder. They spoke to each another in a strange, private language Nick couldn't understand. She kissed his cheek, familiar and gentle.

Nick's fury blazed. Who did this guy think he was, pawing his girl? He'd tackle the guy as soon as the pain in his groin and knee and the ringing in his head faded. He'd- -

Then he found himself back in his apartment. To his astonishment, he felt no pain. The beating he'd taken from the blond man left him shaking, however.

Anna had her coat on. She opened the door and turned back to him. She said, "I don't want to see you again, ever. Don't call and don't come over. If you see me on campus, go the other way."

Nick wanted to call after her. The vision traumatized him too much, though.

Over the next few nights, Nick had the same dream over and over. He'd walk in and find Anna in bed with some familiar-looking blond guy. Nick, all but crazy with jealousy, would watch her make love to him.

In the dream he'd find himself in a graveyard next to a pit. Anna would change into a writhing snake. The snake would begin to bore into his chest.

Nick began to drink a bit more each day. The alcohol eased the pain.

Every day, just getting out of bed and leaving the house became a bigger challenge than the day before.

Semester grades came out. Nick received straight A's. His parents called to congratulate him. They told him they'd mailed him a hefty check so he could take Anna out to a celebration dinner. He wept with agony.

He stopped going to classes. His professors contacted the school's social worker, who came to see him. He refused to talk to her.

One morning, after fighting the Snake dream all night, Nick called his mother. "Come pick me up."

The tone of his voice terrified her. She dropped everything and drove to the university. When she saw him, she said, "Let me take you to the emergency room."

He dismissed the idea. "Just drive me home," he muttered. On the way, Nick didn't say a word, just stared at the dashboard.

Nick continued to deteriorate. His parents hospitalized him as suicidal.

He told the doctors about feeling like a switch had been flipped in his mind. They prescribed drugs. Diet changes. Hypnosis. Total rest. Exercise. No conventional therapy helped in the least degree. The terrifying nightmares wouldn't leave him.

Nick enlisted in the army but they sent him home halfway through boot camp. He tried different jobs and even got married. Nothing helped.

After close to twenty years, the vision of an emerald hell still haunted him.

* * * * *

Nick Wolfe's thoughts dissolved and he took a long swallow

of the cheap draft beer. He stared at his reflection in the mirror behind Romano's bar.

He still couldn't figure out what Anna had done to him that night when they were seniors at Wisconsin. His life had been okay until then. Then everything turned to guano.

She did it to him. He knew it, but he didn't know how she managed it. Couldn't imagine how. Somehow, she threw a switch in his mind. He couldn't turn the switch off.

His hands tightened on the beer glass. He'd make her sorry someday—

"Nick," said a man's voice.

Nick looked up from his beer. A well-dressed and distinguished man stood next to him. He wore a beard.

He also had terrifying eyes. Nick almost shuddered.

He recovered enough to sneer, "Yeah?"

"I'd like you to do a little job for me," said the man. "Terrific pay. Easy work." The man had a strange way of talking, almost hissing some of his words.

Nick tried his bluster routine. "Who the hell are you?"

"Lose the attitude, Nick. Right now," said the man, without raising his voice at all. "I'm called Cray. I can help you a great deal. I need a man with your skills."

Nick wanted to tell the guy to beat it, like he'd done to the old man. Something in the man's peculiar brown eyes stopped him. The red eyes looked almost reptilian.

Nick didn't know what skills the man was talking about. He'd left college a semester short of graduation. His father, his brother, and his brother-in-law all begged him to go back and finish his bachelor's degree. They offered to pay for the tuition, room and board, lab fees, books, whatever. He only needed ten or twelve hours to close it off, but instead, he—

"Come on, Nick," said Cray, with a little more amicable tone. "Doesn't cost anything to listen, right?"

Mr. Cray pulled out a wad of money. He extracted a crisp

new one hundred dollar bill and laid it on the bar. The man signaled Mini. He ordered Nick a bottle of Heineken's and a shot of Jack Daniels.

Mr. Cray winked at Nick. "Keep the hundred. Lots more where that came from."

Nick hesitated just a moment or two. Then, he pocketed the money. He rose from the bar stool and followed Cray to a booth at the back.

The man made Nick a proposition. Nick had to become a pirate for a week, maybe two at the most. Nick thought he was kidding. Cray insisted that Nick regard it as a serious offer.

Cray handed him a picture of a pretty teenage girl, and her mother. Then Cray showed him a picture of a man. Nick froze. He knew that guy: blond hair, tall, named Gareth. Nick had seen him in nightmares for more than twenty years.

How did this Cray know?

As Mr. Cray continued talking, Nick began to smile.

CHAPTER TWENTY-NINE
Two Weeks Later

McKenna DiBiasi, dressed for school in her customary uniform of jeans and sweat shirt, carried her school bag into the kitchen at 7:30 A. M. She made a deliberate effort not to cry.

She saw her mother looking out the window at the little wild birds on the feeders she kept for them. Without turning, her mother said in her North Carolina accent, "Good morning, Darling. What would you like for breakfast?"

"How do you do that?" asked the sixteen-year-old, sullen, slamming her school bag down on the floor.

"Do what?" asked her mother.

"Know when I'm there without looking."

Anna O'Neill turned to look at her daughter. "I don't know. I just do. Do you have to be so nasty?"

"Do you know what happened on this date?" snapped the girl.

"Yes, I do," said her mother, calm. "Your father died two years ago today."

"Right. I'm surprised you got it."

Anna, bewildered at her daughter's uncharacteristic behavior, stared at McKenna. "Why does that make you angry?"

"What time did you come in?" asked McKenna.

"I don't know that either," said Anna. She leaned against the kitchen counter. "Why?"

"I heard Tom drive off," said McKenna, spoiling for a fight. "It seemed like the middle of the night."

"No," said Anna. "We just saw a movie and had a quick supper. Then we came back here."

"Did you screw him?"

Anna's mouth dropped. She floundered for a few seconds before she asked, "Did I what?"

"You heard me." McKenna couldn't meet her mother's stare. She studied the top of the table.

Anna placed her hands on the girl's shoulders. When McKenna glanced up, Anna held her gaze. "Honey, my personal life with Tom doesn't concern you, nor will it ever concern you. Two people do not discuss such private matters with someone outside the relationship."

McKenna gave a shrug. Her mother dropped her hands. "I'd never ask you to share such personal information with me unless I thought you were endangering yourself."

"I wouldn't either," snapped McKenna, every fiber of her body insolent.

Mom paused, considering this answer. "You mean you think I'm in danger?" asked Anna.

"Do you intend to marry Tom?" asked McKenna.

Mother and daughter stared at each another for a moment. "Tom wants me to marry him, yes," Anna said. "In fact he asked me to go to Las Vegas with him today."

"Then you're in danger. I don't trust him."

"McKenna. Don't be unkind. He would be good to both of us."

"You wouldn't really marry that guy, would you? You don't mean to tell me that?"

"No, not today, anyhow. I want you to be able to love him, and that he love you as well."

"Like that would happen," said McKenna, with a roll of the eyes.

Mother made a visible effort to stay calm. "I don't mean you have to love him in the same way you did your daddy. That would be unreasonable."

McKenna looked away, annoyed with herself for the tears

that started in her eyes.

"I just need to see that the potential exists for the two of you to love one another. I don't want to rush into marriage because of loneliness."

McKenna stood and walked to the sink, not looking at her mother. She drew a glass of water and drank. Anna said, "Honey, you have to know that your father didn't die to spite you. I'm sure he hated to leave you. I'm also sure he would want you to move ahead with your life. I have to as well."

McKenna turned back as her mother seemed to choke. To her surprise, her mom's eyes moistened. Mom hadn't mourned much over Dad's death.

A moment or two later, Anna cleared her throat. "I know that watching me becoming serious about Tom hasn't been easy," Anna said. "I'm sorry."

McKenna understood. But her heart was not ready to have her mother marry someone else. "But--" she sniffed. "He isn't Daddy." She began to cry. She grabbed a paper towel and held it to her face as grief, heartache, and pain transformed her crying into sobs.

Mom came to her and took her in her arms, as she had done every day of McKenna's life. "I know, honey. I know. But nothing will ever change, even for an instant, how much I love you."

The crying ended at last. McKenna saw black smudges on her soggy towel and knew she'd smeared her makeup for school. She went to the powder room off the kitchen and fixed her face.

McKenna heard her mother calling her counselor at the high school, telling him that McKenna would be late because of a family emergency.

When she returned to the kitchen, McKenna embraced her mother, then sat at the kitchen table and managed to eat a little fruit and cereal. "Your counselor wants you to stop in to see him this morning when you get there," said Mom.

McKenna nodded, not trusting herself to speak. She stood, averting her eyes. Mom put her arm around McKenna's waist and walked her to the little car she'd bought for McKenna when her daughter turned sixteen. When McKenna opened the car door, Mom hugged her.

Anna said, "I won't let anything—or anyone—come between the two of us. I promise."

McKenna kissed her mom's cheek.

"My little Mickey," Anna said. McKenna hugged her mom and said good-bye, then slid into the car.

A rusty blue minivan tailgated her all the way to school. She wondered if anything could be more obnoxious than a tailgater.

Then a thought struck her. She'd seen this van several times in the last couple of days. Don't be silly, she told herself. Lots of minivans populated the roads on the North Shore.

Annoyed, she checked the rear-view mirror to see the license plate, but the van didn't seem to have one. It kept going when she turned into the student parking lot.

* * * * *

McKenna found her counselor sitting in front of his computer. He turned and smiled at her.

Bernie Nieweem, tall, dressed in casual clothing, served as the school's outreach counselor. His work focused on students with serious problems: behavior disorders, learning disabilities, drug or alcohol dependence, abusive families. McKenna's counselor referred her to him as a freshman when her father died of a heart attack on a golf course in Puerto Rico. McKenna, a well-adjusted kid, had lost one of the anchors of her life. She needed some kindness and personal support from an adult friend.

Bernie motioned for her to sit down. "What's up, McKenna?"

"I had a fight with my mom. I think she's sleeping with her boyfriend."

Bernie stroked at his beard. "What else?"

She composed herself for a moment or two. Then, "My dad died two years ago today."

"Okay," Bernie said, handing her a box of Kleenex. They talked for fifteen minutes. McKenna choked up when she talked about her mom and the fight she'd picked with her mother that morning.

Bernie promised her that he'd talk with the attendance office and excuse her tardiness to school that day. He wrote her a hall pass.

Her day settled into a normal routine. At lunchtime McKenna phoned home. "Mom?"

"Who is this?" said her mother, suspicious.

"Cut it out," McKenna giggled at the old family joke despite herself.

"Yes, honey."

"I'm sorry about this morning."

"I know. Don't think about it."

"Could we go out to dinner tonight?"

"Of course," Anna said. "I had a tentative date but I'll call Tom and cancel."

When the last bell rang McKenna went into the locker room and changed into sweat clothes. Freddie Russell, one of her informal boyfriends, jogged five miles with her, matching her pace so they could chat. Then she went through her stretching routine in the weight room, visiting with her friends and teammates.

At the end of the workout she felt energized. The melancholy washed off in the shower.

She changed back into her jeans and drove Freddie home, gossiping and laughing with him about friends and teachers. He waved as she drove off into the evening.

She decided to stop to rent a video on the way home. Maybe she and Mom could build a fire in the fireplace and watch the film cuddled together on the couch like they used to when she was little.

McKenna pulled into a parking space at the video store. As she climbed out of the car, she noticed that a rusty blue minivan had parked right behind her car, blocking her car in.

A huge fat man rushed forward and pinned her arms behind her. Before she could scream, another man clapped his hand against her face. He held a smelly rag over her nose and mouth. Everything faded away.

CHAPTER THIRTY

McKenna awoke, feeling groggy, thirsty, and dizzy. As her mind cleared, she realized that something dreadful had happened. Apprehension hung on her like a wet garment.

"Beloved."

McKenna jumped, startled at the sound of a gentle, calm voice. She started to scream but the voice stopped her: "Do not speak or move. They will react."

To her surprise, she realized that the voice spoke inside her mind.

"Be still, Beloved," the voice said. "Let me bring you to me."

She felt strange but pleasant warmth. Like someone was moving around in her mind, turning on switches, making little mental connections.

She found herself in a special place. Music and beautiful scents surrounded her. "Now," the voice said. "Look at me, Beloved."

A huge man wearing a brown monk's robe stood before her. His gray hair and beard were streaked with copper. McKenna stood almost six feet tall, but he towered over her.

She felt gentle peace as she looked into his deep emerald eyes. She had seen those eyes every day of her life. They were her mother's eyes.

"Do not speak," he said. "Just think to me. I will hear."

Who are you? she thought.

"Think for a moment," he said. "You know me."

She considered. Then, *You're Myrthynne. Master,* she thought, not sure why she knew him or called him Master. It just seemed natural. He gave her a faint smile and nodded.

McKenna's surroundings came into focus. She found herself in a grotto filled with rose quartz crystals growing like flowers.

Sunlight filtered through the ceiling and struck the crystals, refracting light in exquisite prisms. The crystals vibrated like faint wind chimes, setting up a soothing symphony of sound. Next to her a bubbling hot spring emitted a beautiful scent.

McKenna sank to her knees next to the man, holding his calming hand, the glory of her surroundings overwhelming her.

"Be at peace, Beloved," the big man said. "Time does not progress here as it does in your world. No danger nor evil can touch you here." He raised her to her feet and brought her to the only piece of furniture in the cave, a cedar bed, where they sat together. He put an arm around her shoulders. She leaned into the embrace, feeling safe.

"We haven't much time. When you awake, you will feel nauseated but I will try to help."

Thank you.

"Beloved, two men have stolen you. They intend to hold you prisoner until your mother produces riches for them. They would kill you."

Who are they?

"I do not know their names. One is young, not much older than you but foolish and vain. The older man, the younger's father, hates your mother to the point of murder."

McKenna stared at him in surprise. *Who would hate my mother?*

"I cannot tell you someone else's story. I must let you see who you are. The knowledge will give you courage for what you must do."

Who I am? she asked. She started to speak but caught herself. *Yes, Master.*

Again she felt switches flipping in her mind.

McKenna realized that she witnessed something that happened long ago. She saw the world through the eyes of Myrthynne. She could feel his despair.

French and Viking mercenaries lurked in the woods all

around Myrthynne. Mordred, the king's bastard son, had charged them to hunt down Myrthynne and his apprentice and kill them. The mercenaries, however, lived in terror of him. They yet lacked the courage to attack.

Myrthynne could use the Cymreig to confuse most of them, but Nehushtan could shield a few of them long enough to set upon him.

Nehushtan had won, at least this time. The battle, however, wouldn't cease as long as the Cymreig existed. Viviane and Myrthynne could confuse the mercenaries enough so that she could escape with Gareth, the young Welsh knight, who had come to live with them.

Gareth would defend them to the death. *No*, thought Myrthynne. *Gareth must not be in danger for me.*

Tears of despair and pain welled in Myrthynne's eyes. He looked over at his adopted daughter, realizing he would never see Viviane again.

McKenna started. The young woman known as Viviane looked a great deal like her own mother.

Myrthynne wanted to welcome and enjoy the children who would come when she married Gareth. Myrthynne cherished Viviane like a daughter. The nineteen-year-old had grown into a true beauty, with copper colored hair, emerald eyes, and a lithe figure.

Myrthynne sighed. He knew he'd miss her as much as he'd miss the king, his best friend and former student. At least Myrthynne would see Arthur again, when Time came full circle.

Until that time, Myrthynne had to seal himself in his cave, where time and space weren't quite the same as they were elsewhere. With Viviane's help, he could cast deep doubt in the minds of the mercenaries charged to hunt him down and kill him. She and Gareth could still escape.

Viviane, like Myrthynne, had inherited the Cymreig. Myrthynne, though, would become the most famous as well as the most powerful person ever born with the ability. A form of his name would someday turn out to be synonymous with magic and sorcery.

The legends of Myrthynne would say that a young woman betrayed him. In a moment of weakness he revealed the secret of the Cymreig. The world would remember her as a whore or a witch who enchanted him into a Crystal Cave or an oak tree to live a wretched existence of imprisonment, neither dead nor alive.

But Viviane—whom the legends also know as Nimue, Vivienne, and several other names--didn't betray him. She loved Myrthynne as her father.

Myrthynne first saw Viviane, a terrified ten-year-old orphan, begging food to survive. Myrthynne rode with Arthur into a village that had been devastated by a gang of bandits.

The king and his knights had caught all but a few of the thieves. Bedivere, Bors, Lionel and a few others were still in pursuit of those who had escaped. Those who had been apprehended were dangling from trees outside the village or lying beheaded in a ditch.

The other knights began distributing food and clothing to the desperate villagers. Several would stay to help the villagers rebuild.

Myrthynne first saw her standing by the road at the end of the village. The girl looked up at him. When he saw her emerald eyes peering through disheveled, filthy copper-colored hair, he sensed the Cymreig within the child.

He dismounted and walked to her. She drew back, frightened.

"Don't be afraid, precious one," he said. He took her hand and she relaxed a little. He looked into her green eyes. "Be at peace. Tell me your name."

"Viviane," she murmured.

"Be still, and look in my eyes, Viviane," he told her. She

obeyed.

He Paiked the secret places in her mind. He felt her astonishment to meet someone who had the ability to do what she could do. She Paiked back.

The sorcerer showed her that an unseen enemy known as Nehushtan or the Snake posed a mortal danger. She had sensed the peril all her life. But she knew she faced no danger from Myrthynne.

As they dropped the mental link she managed a weak smile. He knelt before her and took her in his arms.

Her shaky veneer of strength slipped away. She hugged him back. He felt her sobs of grief and terror against his shoulder.

"What happened to your parents?" he asked so only she could hear him.

"Dead," said the child, voice quavering. She pointed to the remains of a small hut. "The bad men killed them last week."

Myrthynne knew why the bandits murdered her parents. Nehushtan.

The child's lip trembled with grief. "No one took you in, Beloved?" Myrthynne asked. "Or fed you?"

"No, sir," said the child through her tears. "They fear me. They call me a witch."

The sorcerer stood, and regarded the villagers who were standing nearby. He struggled not to lash out in fury at the people of the village.

The villagers knew the great sorcerer and feared him. They saw his indignation and shrank back, terrified. He restrained himself by remembering the wretched conditions in which the people had been living for the last several days.

He picked Viviane up and carried her to his horse. The child, still scared, couldn't let go. He had to loosen her hands from around his neck.

He reached into his leather saddle pack for some bread and

handed her his water bottle. She devoured the bread, telling him she couldn't remember the last time she'd eaten. He made her eat all of it. Several knights brought the child more provisions.

"Would you like to come with me?" he asked. He told her that he would protect her, care for her, and love her as a father.

"Yes, Master, please," she said. She raised her arms and he enfolded her as she began to cry again, face buried in the giant sorcerer's robe.

A knight brought her a horse that had belonged to one of the thieves. She rode from the town with the King and Myrthynne, holding the sorcerer's hand whenever she could.

She didn't look back.

That night his attendants bathed and clothed her. The women took great pleasure in brushing the child's lovely hair until it shone with amber glory.

When the attendants brought her to Myrthynne's chambers, her beauty stunned him. Her excitement to be with him in the great king's court touched and pleased him.

She ate a supper of meat, bread, fruits and vegetables. She slept in a real bed in the chamber next to his.

Just before dawn the next day, Myrthynne heard Viviane screaming. He rushed to her chamber and woke her from a terrifying nightmare. She hugged him, weeping, and told him that she had dreamed of Nehushtan.

The next morning Myrthynne began her apprenticeship, teaching her the mysteries of the Cymreig. She also learned to read, write, and do mathematics. He taught her mythology and the history of Faerae. The child proved herself bright, willing, eager and earnest.

The dreams and the horror that came with them continued each night, however. Then, one morning she came to his chamber, beaming. "Master," she said.

"Beloved?" he asked, amused.

"I have a new friend. A dream friend."

"Yes?"

"Yes. I call him Gareth. We fought Nehushtan together last night. We drove him off."

Denied children of his own, he adopted her and she became the pride of his life. She and the great wizard came to love each other as father and daughter.

Myrthynne let go of the precious memories, returning to the clearing where he hid with Viviane and Gareth. "Beloved," said Myrthynne, shaking off his memories. "Help me to the cave, child." He leaned on her and Gareth while they walked.

Gareth, the blond Welsh knight with sapphire eyes, had fallen in love with Viviane. He knew about the Cymreig. He didn't understand it, but he didn't fear it, either. He saw it as part of the girl he loved.

The sorcerer knew he needed to hide. The final battle loomed just ahead, inevitable and fatal.

First, though, Myrthynne had to make sure she understood her danger. She had to keep the Cymreig safe and pass it on to her children. She also had to protect it from Nehushtan.

Myrthynne would remain suspended between life and death, between sleep and consciousness. He would wait, lying on a cedar bed, sealed within the crystal cave. "Viviane," he said. "The Cymreig must not be lost. Take Gareth and this money and go to Ireland. You must escape the bastard Mordred."

"I can't leave you."

"You must. He will kill you. Hide in daylight, travel at night. Avoid main roads."

"I am afraid."

"Gareth will protect you always. Marry and have children. Some of them will have the Cymreig."

The girl agreed, and took Myrthynne's hand for the last time. He looked into her eyes, which filled with tears. She found the right place in his mind and she Paiked.

She would pass the knowledge on to her children who would be born with the ability. The link to Myrthynne would pass to her children and their children.

He felt Viviane's horror as the Cymreig revealed the Snake, waiting, eager to destroy her and her offspring. She could hide from Mordred and his mercenaries in Ireland. But the Snake would always pursue her and her progeny. She moaned with dread.

"I will try to protect you and your children," the wizard thought to her. "One of them will know that the time has come and will wake me when I am needed again."

He removed a ring from his little finger and slipped it onto her ring finger. The ring, a gold band, had two lovely emeralds flanking a magnificent diamond. "Keep this safe, Beloved Viviane. It has a history from antiquity. Now go. Be at peace."

He showed her the plan for escape. They smiled together with anticipation.

She said the words that would put him into the Sleep. Myrthynne closed his eyes.

Myrthynne felt the mind link diminish, though it did not sever. Some of his mind would always remain with her. They would communicate through the Cymreig until the moment she died.

He would, on occasion, reach out with his mind to help Viviane or one of her children. He would link with them and send help. Once in a while he'd work through someone who didn't have the Cymreig. Whenever the Snake would attack, he would intervene. The Snake liked destruction and chaos. If Nehushtan and his minions could defeat and eradicate the Cymreig, pandemonium would reign.

Myrthynne, using the Cymreig, watched Viviane and Gareth laboring to pile stones at the cave's entrance. At night they rode toward the coast. She journeyed on Regulus, Myrthynne's grand war charger, a gift from the king. Gareth rode Bayard, a horse given to him by his older brother Gawaine.

That night, two fugitives walked into the Mercenary camp. The old man and the young woman made no attempt to escape or to free themselves.

The captors brought them before Mordred, who kept a respectful distance. He ordered his men to blindfold the two sorcerers, knowing the power in those green eyes.

He condemned them to death but couldn't resist taunting the old man he feared so much. "The King's tutor. The witch who enchants people with his eyes."

The old man's expression and posture showed neither fear nor dismay.

"Mordred, the traitor." The old man's voice rang through the clearing. "The son who strikes at his father. You will never wear the crown. You will die at the hands of your own father."

The voice terrified the mercenaries. Mordred broke the silence. "You and your whore daughter—once as dangerous as you, they say—will not stand in my way. My father"—he sneered the word—"will die. You haven't the power to stop me. Take the girl," he ordered the Viking soldiers. "Burn her. Let the wizard watch. Then, burn him."

Some men tied the young woman with the blaze of red hair to a stake. They piled brush and kindling and dry brittle straw around her. She stared ahead, calm and fearless. The killers brought the old man forward to watch his apprentice die.

The executioner, his face covered with a black hood, came forward with a flaming brand. He touched the torch to the kindling in thirteen places, as witch-burning tradition dictated. The fire caught and spread. The mercenaries licked their lips in visceral anticipation.

The flames shot up. The young woman didn't scream or yell or twist against the ropes that bound her, rather to the disappointment of the assembled group of hired killers.

The fire surged up to engulf her. The flames blocked her from their vision for some moments. They shielded their faces from the intensity of the blaze.

When the flames died down, they expected to see her charred remains. The stake held the remnants of the ropes from the cross-members. Of the girl they saw not the faintest trace that she had ever existed.

"Where did she go, Sorcerer?" demanded Mordred.

"She went somewhere safe, where you cannot touch her," replied the old man.

"Very well," said Mordred. "We will witness his death. He will not get away."

A soldier with a long handled war ax offered to execute the old man. The mercenaries erected a makeshift platform. A stump of oak served as the chopping block.

The old man ascended the scaffold. The guards positioned him kneeling with his head on the block. The killer swung the ax.

The ax bit into nothing but wood. The old man vanished as fog before a sudden wind. The mercenaries never saw him again.

* * * * *

The real Viviane rode with Gareth to the coast and took passage to Ireland. She married Gareth.

Two of her children were born with the Cymreig but one died in a fearful accident. At least, the people of Viviane's village called it an accident.

But she knew the terrible truth. The Snake would follow her children wherever they went.

CHAPTER THIRTY ONE

In the cave, McKenna stirred as the story and the vision ended. *Did I just see my great-grandmother, Master?*

"Yes, Beloved," he said, "The Cymreig came to your mother through Viviane's blood."

Do I have it?

"You were not given the ability to use it as she does. But your blood carries the charm. Your descendants will inherit it. Some of them will learn to use it as your mother does."

Do you mean these men have taken me because of the Cymreig?

"Yes, beyond doubt, though they unaware of it. Nehushtan wants the Cymreig to cease with you. The men don't know that they have joined in service to the Snake." He put a massive hand on McKenna's shoulder and smiled. Her fear eased under his loving, gentle touch. "I brought you here to bolster you. You have your father's courage, I can feel it."

You know my father?

"Yes, for centuries. His courage will serve you well. I will also try to help you, Beloved. The Cymreig must not be lost."

Can my mother tell where they are taking me?

"No, Beloved. She cannot see that far. She has been under attack for years by Nehushtan. Your grandfather Daniel also has the gift, though illness has fogged his mind now."

McKenna assented. Her great-grandfather Daniel had all but shut down since the stroke two years ago. Like he didn't have anything to live for any more.

"I will try to work through him," the huge sorcerer told her. "He often sees the future as I can, but even he does not know where the men will take you."

McKenna thought about the times that her mother and Grandpa Daniel seemed to know what each other was thinking, when they would speak identical words, when they would nod in unison.

"Beloved, I must send you back to the men now. You are in mortal danger from them but you can overcome them. Conceal your identity. Do not let them see your intelligence." McKenna looked at him, puzzled. "Yes," he said. "As criminals and thus conceited, they believe themselves far wiser than others."

I understand, she thought. She felt scared, but willing to fight.

"Cooperate. Do not antagonize them. Work out a plan. Find a way to escape. I will send help for you."

Will I see you again, Master?

"I cannot say. I think so, someday."

"She's moving, Dad," said a strange voice. A hand removed the hood that covered her face. She found herself in the back seat of the rusty minivan that she had seen tailgating her. Handcuffs bit her wrists.

Her eyes began to adjust. She saw a clock on the dashboard. 8:30. The men had kept her unconscious for at least three hours.

"How do you feel?" the younger man said.

"Groggy. Thirsty."

"We're almost there," the young man said. "Just relax."

In the glare of the headlights, McKenna saw the old truck lumbering down a dirt and gravel road, rutted and rough. No street lamps pierced the black night.

Both men wore dark clothing, with black watch caps and dark leather jackets. They seemed to be large men, overweight, with long unkempt hair. Both needed a shave.

As the time dragged by, McKenna thought about the vision of Myrthynne. She now understood her mother a great deal better than she ever had before. The occasional fear in Mom's eyes. Her dreadful nightmares from which she woke up weeping with terror.

The younger man kept trying to talk to her. McKenna

responded with shrugs and nods, pretending to be lethargic. *Are you there, Master?*

To her relief, an answer came. *Always. Have courage, Beloved.*

McKenna thought of Myrthynne's comments. What could he have meant when he said he'd known her father for centuries? He spoke about her father as if he still lived.

The minivan turned into a long gravel drive from which snow had been cleared. It stopped in front of a metal cyclone fence gate. The younger man jumped out and opened it. The father drove the van through and stopped before a long ranch-style house. McKenna had an impression of fields and a barn or some other type of outside structure.

The sliding door next to her opened and the young man pulled her from the seat. Holding her by the elbow, he took her up on a rickety front porch and opened the front door.

He escorted her down a hallway to a bedroom. He turned on a weak overhead light that illuminated a single bed, a dresser, and a closet. He stood behind her and unlocked the handcuffs.

He took off her coat and her jogging shoes and padded down the hall. She heard a door creak open. He returned in a few moments. "Okay. Welcome to your room," the young man said. "You'll find the bathroom across the hall. Kitchen and living room are down the hallway."

When she didn't respond, he continued, "We ain't holding you in no jail. You can move around if you don't try to get away."

She stared at him in hostile silence, remembering Myrthynne's words: *Don't let them see your intelligence.* She rubbed her wrists, trying to restore feeling.

"We stocked the dresser with some clothes for you. We got medium sizes on everything."

She tried to look defiant.

"You got something to say?" he asked.

"Let me go," she said. "Let me call my mother."

His smile seemed sincere. "You're going to call her in just a few minutes. But let me tell you this. If you try to escape, we'll kill you. The electric fence will get you if we don't. Plus we're miles away from any place and it's too cold outside."

She stared at him, hoping that she looked intractable. *Oh, I'll escape, you jerk,* she thought. *You just wait.* "Do you have a name?" she asked him.

"How about Scott?" he said, after thinking for a few moments.

The father came into the room. McKenna shrank back to the wall.

He appeared to be a mountain of fat, with long gray tangled hair and beard. He leered at her, displaying crooked, mossy teeth.

She'd seen the same look in Mordred's eyes in the vision. She could see the evil radiating from him.

The son didn't realize the stakes involved in this escapade, she could tell. He regarded this kidnapping as an adventure.

"What's going on?" said the fat man.

"She's fine, Dad, but she's scared and mad," said the younger man.

The fat man smiled. *He enjoys this,* McKenna realized. *Enjoys seeing me scared and helpless.*

"Don't worry," sneered the man. "You won't get hurt unless your mother gets stupid."

He's lying, she thought, as he gave her a typewritten sheet of paper.

"Do you have a name?" she asked.

"You just call me 'sir'."

"Okay," she snapped, voice blistering with sarcasm. "As long as it doesn't make you think I respect you."

He stepped forward and slapped her. The pain brought tears to her eyes. She snapped right back and stared at him in defiance. She almost sprang at him to claw at his eyes with her nails. Then the voice spoke in her mind: *No, Beloved. You mustn't provoke them. Hide your intelligence and courage from them.*

"Dad," said Scott. His voice quavered. His father cowed the younger man.

"Read that," said the fat man, pulling a piece of paper from his pocket. "Then you're going to call your mother and read it to her."

McKenna glanced over it. She looked up at their faces, bewildered by what she read. Then she shrugged, took the proffered cell phone and punched in the numbers.

* * * * *

Anna O'Neill sat in her living room in her huge house in Lake Forest with her knees drawn up. She stared at the phone.

In a few minutes it would be nine o'clock. McKenna never came home from school this late.

Something must have happened.

Should I call the police?

McKenna often came home late from a sports practice or a play rehearsal, so Anna didn't start worrying until about seven. Then she called everyone she could think of. One of McKenna's friends, Freddie, said that McKenna had dropped him off at home between four-thirty and five o'clock. The kids set up a call chain. Several went out looking for her. No one found her.

Anna drove the route to the school, then Freddie's house, then back toward home. She spotted McKenna's Toyota parked outside a video store. No one in the store had seen the girl. No one named DiBiasi had rented anything that day.

Anna hurried home, praying her daughter had returned. She hadn't come home still.

Anna remembered how her best friend had come to help her at McKenna's birth. "Casey?" she said, staring at the phone. He didn't come into the room this time. She hadn't seen him in years, not even in nightmares.

She looked at the clock and made up her mind. *Okay,* she told herself. *Five more minutes, then I call the police.* She watched the clock tick away. One minute. Two. Three.

Four.

The phone rang.

CHAPTER THIRTY TWO
The Next Night

McKenna looked at the plate before her. Cheap boxed macaroni and cheese and two overcooked hot dogs. *Yuck.*

"Could I please have some fresh food? Like a salad?"

The father sneered. "If your momma don't do what we say, you ain't gonna need no fresh food."

"I could prepare it. I don't mind. I'm a good cook," she said. "It'd give me something to do."

The father muttered a foul expletive and made a sound McKenna found repulsive.

"Dad, take it easy," said Scott. "McKenna, listen, we'll try to get some stuff in. It's a long way to a grocery store. Meanwhile you see what we got and you hafta eat."

The father snorted. "Damn spoiled rich kid."

McKenna ate some of the macaroni and one hot dog. She couldn't let herself get weak.

She'd been planning her escape. Grandfather Myrthynne believed she could. She continued to develop a plan.

* * * * *

Casey Fixx sat at the restaurant table, staring into his glass of wine, his stomach in a knot of anguish and nervousness.

He reviewed the plan one more time. Sarah would sit down across from him. He'd let her order. Once she had her wine, he'd show her the ring. Then, he'd ask her to marry him.

Right.

He found the diamond ring at a jewelry store in Woodfield, the huge mall not too far from him. He asked the woman behind the counter what ring she'd like to receive. Her choice had been expensive, but what the hell.

The ring would show where he stood. He wanted to move the dating thing to the next level. He loved Sarah. He thought he did, anyhow.

For some reason, he couldn't bring himself to give her the heirloom ring his mother had left him. He kept thinking of it as—

Well, Anna's ring.

He couldn't imagine someone else wearing it.

He shook his head and refocused on Sarah. He thought about how much fun they had.

Misty, Sarah's daughter, was a student of his not too long after his marriage to Grace fell apart. Misty had sought out Casey as an adult confidant and friend.

A year or two before, the girl's father had abandoned the family and headed for parts unknown. Misty introduced Casey to Sarah, her mother. They found each other attractive, and she asked him to dinner. They began to date. Five years ago, he started to plan to marry her.

He had to grin as he thought back to the Christmas party at Sarah's house. Sarah had invited her twenty-four-year old daughter Misty and her husband. When Sarah went into the kitchen, Misty nagged him to get his tush in gear and ask her mother to marry him. Dan, Misty's seventeen-year-old brother, had been vigorous in seconding the motion. *Okay, okay,* he chuckled.

He liked Misty and Dan a great deal. He thought about becoming a father to the two young people. *Well, better late than never. I always did want kids of my own. Those two would be just about as good.*

Then he saw Sarah walk into the restaurant, shaking snow from her coat. The maitre d' walked her over to Casey's table. He stood as Marco seated her.

Sarah, tall as Anna, maybe didn't have quite as good a figure as her, but her lovely legs were as beautiful as Grace's. Sarah, competent and intelligent, had always been a lot of fun. Jealousy and possessiveness had never entered into their friendship.

She hadn't spoken, which seemed uncharacteristic. She stared around the restaurant, taking in the quaint French motif, the impeccable linen, the unimpeachable silver and candles.

He realized she avoided eye contact with him. Strange. She didn't seem angry. Maybe nervous. That would be unusual for her.

"You look weary," she said at last in her smoky voice. "Anything wrong?"

"No, nothing's wrong. But I am tired, I admit."

"From?" she asked.

"From skiing with Joey. The little creep kept yelling at me to keep up," he said. "I had an excuse, though."

Sarah lifted an amused eyebrow in question. "I flew to Los Angeles three days ago and took the red-eye home last night," he smiled. "I managed some sleep last night and took a nap today before I came."

"Los Angeles?"

"Yeah, we did a final cut on one of those soft drink commercials." He sighed. "It's a living."

"Before I met you I had no idea what went into a thirty-second ad."

"We won an award last year."

"Typical Fixx modesty. *You* got the award."

"You were the highlight of the evening," he assured her. "Every man in the auditorium kept staring at you. You looked sensational in that black and silver gown."

"Well, you looked so handsome in your tuxedo. I was so proud of you." She giggled, and grinned as Darla, the waitress, brought her water and a napkin. Casey ordered them a glass of wine, but Sarah said to Darla, "No, thank you. Not for me."

Casey felt even more puzzled.

Sarah's face clouded over again she avoided eye contact again. She took a sip of water and still didn't open the menu.

Okay, he thought. *Here we go. I'm not going to wait for the wine.* He started to launch into his little speech but stopped when she looked up. To his surprise, a tear ran down her left cheek. "Misty is furious at me," said Sarah. "She wants me to marry you."

He paused, confused by the tears. "Well, why don't you?"

"Please don't make me say it." She lowered her head.

Silence. He ran through some possible explanations. Then he looked at her ring finger.

A large diamond ring, one he'd never seen, adorned the finger. With an unpleasant jolt things fell into place. "You're marrying someone else?"

She hesitated, still not looking at him, then nodded.

Darla came to take their food orders. She looked at the two of them and said, "I'll just come back."

"Okay," Casey murmured. He felt as if someone had kicked him in the stomach.

"When?" he managed, as Darla walked away.

"About two weeks. We're going to the court house."

"Am I invited?"

"Please. I couldn't stand to have you there."

"Tell me about the lucky guy," he suggested, trying not to sound as if his heart teetered on the edge of splitting in two.

"You introduced us."

He thought for a moment. "Jimmy Schalk?" She nodded. "But he's way older than you."

"He just turned sixty-five. His wife died three years ago."

"I remember."

"Well, we started dating two years ago," she said. "Sex came along pretty soon after that." Then, noting the wounded look on his face, she told him, "You and I have never had an exclusive arrangement, Casey."

He shrugged a little, and managed to say, "I know."

"You see other women."

"Not many." Zero, to be exact. He decided to try to be gracious. "Ah--congratulations, Sarah."

"Thank you."

"Why didn't you tell me sooner?" he asked.

"We just decided two nights ago."

"When I had to go to Los Angeles."

"Uh, huh."

"So you're dumping me? Just like that?"

"I'm sorry. I know it appears that way." She wiped away a tear and sipped at the water glass. With an obvious effort, she said, "Okay. I'll try to explain. I think I owe it to you. Have you ever figured out the real reason that Grace divorced you?"

"I've told you," he said, surprised at the mention of his ex-wife. "She didn't want kids; I did. She didn't like my work hours."

"And you still believe that?"

He considered. "Shouldn't I?"

She shook her head. "She and I have the same reason. You just don't understand."

"What do you mean?"

"You don't love me, Casey. Not the way I want to be loved. Oh, we get along. We complement each other. The sex never ceased to be tender and sweet. But you don't love me."

"And Jimmy does."

"He's devoted to me and my son and daughter. They like him. Not as much as they like you, but—"

"Do you love him?"

"Not quite. But I can live with liking him since he loves me. I can learn to love him once I'm away from you."

He thought about her theory. He knew little about love. Maybe it could work like that.

"I understand why you can't love me," she said. "You gave

your heart away once. And the person never returned it to you."

"Sarah, when Grace divorced me, it hurt, but—"

"Not Grace. Someone else, someone you never speak about. You bonded with her in a way that changed your life." Her face twisted with pain.

A vision of copper colored hair and emerald eyes rose in his mind. He knew who Sarah meant.

Sarah resumed, "Jimmy has a lot of money and Dan needs a father now. Jimmy can love him and help him."

"And I couldn't?" The comment about wealth stung. Anna had gone back to her wretched husband for the same reason.

"Oh, Casey, you'd be a wonderful father. You were a great teacher. Misty still loves you. So did the other kids you worked with. They love to talk about Dr. Fixx whenever they have their reunions at our house."

"Then why?"

"Dan's going to college in the fall. Jimmy and I plan to travel. I can quit working at the restaurant."

And he's got tons of money, Casey thought.

"Can I use your phone to call Dan? His car's been acting up. I want to make sure he made it home."

"Well, sure," he said, and pulled the cell phone from his pocket. He flipped it open, surprised to find he'd turned it off. A little puzzled, he pushed the power button and handed it to her.

Then he remembered. He'd powered it down as he boarded the plane in LAX last evening.

Casey watched Sarah making the quick call. Her news began to sink in. He'd never see her again, never sleep with her again, never have Christmas at her house. . .

He'd miss her. He began to realize how much.

Sarah ended her call in a moment. "Dan says to say hi," she said. An awkward silence ensued, in which neither could meet the other's eyes. At last, she said, "I have to go. I'm meeting Jimmy."

"Then I guess you're saying goodbye for good," he said.

"I can't see you after I'm married."

"I know," he said. Sarah struggled not to cry.

They stood. She embraced him for the last time. Then he helped her with her coat. She walked to the door and through it, out of his life.

Casey stared at the door, thinking of how he'd miss his dates with Sarah. To be sure, he and Sarah didn't match up well in terms of interests, intellect, experiences or senses of humor. Still, they'd helped each other deal with the humiliating rejection of their spouses.

Darla came over. Casey sat, not looking up, feeling a little stunned. "How about a drink?" she said.

"Good idea."

She sat opposite him. "She said no, huh?"

"How did—"

"Give me a break. You look like you've been beaten with a stick."

He looked up at her and smiled a little. Darla, who had been married for twenty years, befriended him when Grace split with him and he began to come in to the restaurant.

"It'll be okay, Casey."

"Thanks," he said. Vince, the owner, came over. The three chatted for a few moments. Casey's cell phone rang.

He smiled when he saw that the caller was his Aunt Victoria. She, like Casey, had taught English for many years. Their conversations tended to sound like an episode from a P. G. Wodehouse novel, wherein he sustained the role of Bertie Wooster and she Aunt Dahlia. Both loved the game.

Her husband, Uncle Steve, counted his money by the bagful. Casey thought that, except for the little hat and shoes, Steve bore a strong resemblance a lawn gnome.

Casey wiped his eyes and pressed the talk button. "What ho, Much-loved Aunt," he said in a flawless British fop accent.

Darla and Vince rose and edged away. He lifted a hand of thanks to his two friends.

"Well, thank heaven," Victoria thundered in her normal voice. "You've decided to answer the phone at last."

He winced, trying not to laugh. Aunt Vic, though well struck in years, would never be accused of being inhibited.

"Your telephone call comes as would a glass of cold water to a drowning man," Casey said. "To what blissful fortune may I adjudge myself indebted for this pleasure?"

Aunt Vic snorted. "Never mind the banana oil, you scoundrel. A beautiful young woman has been trying to contact you since last night. She called your cell phone scores of times. Why did you refuse to answer your phone?"

"I didn't refuse to answer my phone," he grinned. He explained about returning from Los Angeles last night and skiing all day with his sister Karen's son.

"So why didn't you carry your cell phone, you hound?"

"Skiing? Are you nuts?"

"This young woman," she grumbled, "called your cell phone every few minutes since last night. Never mind that now. How can she find you?"

"I may be found sitting in a very cozy booth at Dino's, sipping a commendable cocktail," he said.

"Excellent," Aunt Vic said. "Hold on." She put her hand over the phone for a few moments. "Very well. She just left. She should arrive in a few moments. Stay there until she arrives."

"Aunt Vic, who did you send to see me?"

"Someone you brought into my home for scandalous comportment," she sniffed.

"When did I do this?"

"Fifteen or sixteen years ago."

"Huh?"

"When Steven and I moved to Switzerland with your sisters and let you run our house, you engaged in behavior that would not have been tolerated in a New Orleans brothel."

"Aunt Vic—"

"You have brought calumniation to the family crest, an emblem that has never before endured derogation. Except your Uncle Roderick, the cad."

He again started to ask the name of the woman she had dispatched to the restaurant, but instead, "What conceivable indictment could you bring against Uncle Roderick?" he inquired, amused.

"A card sharp. His outrageous and unrelenting duplicity at Old Maid and Rummy when we were but striplings remains an evil legend in the family. Furthermore, to this day his swinish table manners continue to give the lie to the notion that humans should be considered the creator's ultimate statement."

"Uncle Roderick?"

"Yes, the same. He reminds one to this day of an anthropoid ingesting his daily allocation of banana."

"Right," said Casey.

"Revolting," concluded his aunt.

"I see," said Casey. "Now how am I like him?"

"In your infamous disregard for the sanctity of the family name, knave. You, no doubt feral with strong drink, brought a callow, blameless young girl here into the home of your ancestors, deflowered her, impregnated her, and then, with merciless vindictiveness, turned her out to wander and beg through the ice-bound, wind-swept streets with her child, penniless and clothed in rags."

Casey sighed at the Dickensian melodrama. "Aunt Vic," he said, "I speak now your last warning. I shall count to three. Then, mark you, I shall bellow with sickening violence. One. Two."

"Never mind. You'll know her when you see her. Call me when you get home." Victoria hung up.

Darla brought his drink. He sipped. Wild Turkey over the rocks, a splash of soda.

"Bad news?" said Darla.

"I don't have any idea. Someone wants to see me. Show her over when she shows up, will you?" Darla nodded. The Wild Turkey tasted like ashes in his mouth.

Casey sat for several minutes. Then he went to the washroom, splashed his face with cold water and dried off. He looked at himself in the mirror. He stared at the gray hair at his temples. He made a half-hearted attempt to smooth the funny looking stuff down. "You're getting old," he told himself. "You don't have a lot to show for your life, partner."

The reflection nodded.

He returned to the table, and buttered a roll. He sipped at the drink.

He grew aware of someone standing next to him. He turned.

He recognized her at once, but it took several seconds to register.

For the first time in seventeen years, he looked into the emerald green eyes of Anna O'Neill.

CHAPTER THIRTY THREE

"Hello, Casey," she said, the voice and the North Carolina accent just as he remembered them.

Casey had wondered many times what would happen if he ever saw Anna again. None of his speculation had prepared him for the impact that seeing her had on him. Anna wore her hair down, somewhat shorter than he remembered. Still, in spite of dark circles under her eyes, she looked as beautiful as ever to him.

His stomach hurt, and he couldn't speak.

For the first time in years, he became aware of the echoes of a headache.

Again he tried to speak but nothing came out. He made a deliberate effort to breathe as he stood. She extended her hand. He took it. Neither let go. He managed to ask, "You were with Aunt Mel?" She nodded.

Anna and Casey looked into each other's eyes. Casey felt again the pain of the warm and breezy June day when she broke his heart.

An awkward moment arose as they tried to decide if they should hug. They wrapped their arms around each other for a moment and stepped back.

"Casey," she said. "Do you—" she swallowed. "Do you hate me?"

"No. Never hate."

Her face twisted. She stepped toward him, arms raised. He enfolded her, remembering just how she used to feel in his arms.

As they lingered in the hug, the years melted away. They remained for several moments. He felt her body trembling.

She leaned back a little bit and kissed his cheek. Without

thinking he kissed her on the lips. She responded.

Some time passed.

They drew back from the kiss at the same time. She gave him a listless smile. He brushed away the tears on her cheeks. She gave him a little smile and leaned her head against his chest.

In a few moments, she lifted her eyes to his. "Oh, Casey, I'm so scared," she said.

"Okay," he said, puzzled. "I'll try to help."

She stepped back and looked him up and down. "A suit? And a tah?" she asked, teasing. The tension eased.

He smiled at her North Carolina accent, thinking how much he'd missed it. He looked in some amusement at her informal clothes. She wore a casual sweater over a simple white blouse, blue jeans, and jogging shoes. Then he shrugged.

"I received the tie as a gift," he said. "I rented the suit, but I had a coupon for half off." She snickered a little. He sat across from her in the booth.

Darla came over and Casey introduced Anna. He ordered her a glass of Chianti. When Darla turned away, he asked, "So—ah—to what am I indebted for the honor?"

She shook her head. "Let me get my wine first."

They made strained, awkward small talk. Yes, Aunt Vic was indeed a character.

Yes, the drive was okay.

No, she didn't have any trouble finding the place.

Yes, the restaurant was very nice.

Yes, she still had the watch, which kept perfect time. And yes, it was cold outside, terribly cold. She was in good health. So was he.

He raised the ante a little. "Does your husband know you're here?"

She took a sip of water and looked at her hands. Then she met his eyes for a moment. "Alan suffered a heart attack and died on a golf course in Puerto Rico," she said. He murmured condolences and she nodded thanks. "He designated our daughter McKenna as the beneficiary of his life insurance policy, though he stipulated that she can't collect on it until she's twenty-one."

"That's strange," Casey blinked. "He didn't provide for you?"

She shrugged. "I'm okay. We had mortgage insurance which paid for the house. With the sale of his company and a summer house in Door County, I'm well enough off. I had good advice in investing the money."

She's still rich, he thought. *I'm still not in her league.* He asked, "Why would he leave you off the policy?"

Anna described some of their marriage problems, which had become acute in the few years before his death. "He began to hate me and resent me. Not that anyone would ever describe our marriage as intimate and loving. I figured we'd always go along like that." Darla brought her the glass of Chianti. They sipped.

"Did anything major change in your life?"

Anna shook her head. "We did sell our one house in Lake Forest and moved into a much bigger one a few years ago. He said we'd receive a big tax advantage. Our old house had always been fine with me. . ."

She paused for a second. "You know, though, the problems began about that time, now that I think about it."

"Any reason?" Casey asked.

She thought for a few seconds. She shook her head. "Well, I did insist on an apartment in the new house for my Grandpa Daniel. Alan may have resented that. It's funny, but something about Grandpa seemed to scare him."

"Scare him," frowned Casey, drawing his chin back.

She shrugged. "I suspected for a while that he might have met another woman. I confronted him, but he denied it. He continued dating and sleeping with women after we were married. We conducted our whole marriage at an arm's length."

"I see," said Casey, taking a sip of wine.

"I put a stop to the running around after the birth of our daughter McKenna. He stayed away from other women for several years but then fell back into the habit five years ago. By then I didn't want to divorce him. I couldn't see how I'd benefit and I knew McKenna would be devastated. In fact she grieved for months when he died."

Casey averted his face and clutched at his stomach. He thought that if he concentrated on inhaling and exhaling, the pain would subside. Even after seventeen years, he couldn't think of Anna making love to someone else without agony.

She didn't seem to notice. Darla came back over, her pad and pen ready. He ordered some dinner for them, though neither felt hungry.

"You didn't marry?" she asked when Darla walked away.

"I'm divorced." Her face twisted with pain and she averted her face. He went on. "I married Grace from Westwood. No kids. It lasted five years. She—" he cleared his throat a little— "She dumped me."

"I'm sorry," she said.

"She remarried," he said. "We remain friends and we see each other often."

"What happened to that guy she went with when I taught there?" she asked. "She seemed crazy about him, I remember."

"The year I went to finish the doctorate at Illinois, Rudy moved to New York to work on Wall Street. They broke up. When I moved back from Champaign, Grace and I started dating and got serious. Then we married."

"I see," she said, taking a sip of wine, studying her napkin.

"About five years later his office transferred Rudy back here. He called her and she left me for him. They had a couple of kids." He gave a weak little smile. "They call me Uncle Casey."

"I'm glad to hear that you're still friends," she said, playing with her fork.

"I'm sure she'd love to see you."

Anna toyed with her wine glass. The salads came and they ate in silence for a while. She said, "Do you ever think about us?"

"Yes I do. I still dream about you."

"I think of you often, too."

He lost patience with the chit-chat. "Okay, you got the wine," he said. "What did you need to see me about?"

She looked down. She sipped the wine. Her mouth worked for a few moments. "Two men kidnapped our daughter yesterday."

"What?" said Casey. Without thinking he took her hand and squeezed.

She nodded. "They stole her yesterday afternoon and she called last night. She's scared but she seems okay." She filled him in on the details.

He listened, and thought for a few moments. "Anna, I'm sorry and I feel terrible for you. But why would you come to me? I don't see what I can do."

She reached in her purse and pulled out a wallet-sized picture of a pretty teenage girl with hair like hers. Except for the hair, the kid looked like his sister Cinnamon.

"Cute girl," he said. Then he looked at her, then the picture again. The light dawned.

Casey stared at her, unable to frame the question. She couldn't meet his eyes. He thought about Aunt Vic's reference to a child. But he thought Vic had been joking. Of course.

"She's—" he stuttered, then stopped, remembering the old techniques. "She's my daughter?"

She nodded and gave him a tentative, wan smile. "McKenna looks just like you. She walks like you. She even has a little stutter when she gets upset. She dresses like you too, in jeans and t-shirts."

He stared again at the picture of his daughter, an altogether charming young woman with long copper hair. His eyes began to fill.

Then rage began to build. He fought it, trying to remain calm, but at last he exploded. "I get it now. Sure took me a long time, didn't it?" He chuckled without humor. "You invented that whole crock about your husband's operation. When you couldn't get pregnant by him, you came to me. Then you dumped me like a sack of garbage and went back to Mr. Wonderful."

Anna's eyes grew wide. Her mouth opened. "I did no such thing--"

He spoke over her voice. "You knew that last day, didn't you, Princess?" She winced at the name of contempt he hadn't used in so long. "You must have suspected at least."

She held up a hand and tried to speak but he waved it off. "I wouldn't believe you now, no matter what you said," he sneered. "To think that I fell in love with you. What an idiot I've been."

"Casey, please." She put a hand on his wrist but he brushed it away.

"How could I have been so stupid?" he marveled. "You never felt anything at all for me, did you?"

"I'm sorry," she said, looking at her hands. "I have been for seventeen years."

"And now, after keeping me away from my daughter for all those years, you have the gall to ask for my help?"

Her head snapped up and her eyes flashed green lasers as she pointed a finger at him.

"You listen to me. You weren't the only one in love. Two of us climbed into that bed and both of us loved what happened. What we did changed my life forever, and I don't mean just with my daughter."

"Yeah, right..." he scoffed, but she interrupted.

"I cried so much my husband wanted to hospitalize me. I kept lying to him, telling him the tears were related to the pregnancy. I missed you and your friendship so much I felt like I'd been widowed. I wanted to tell you about McKenna for years. But I knew you'd want to see her and get to know her, and McKenna would be as hurt and confused as me." She shook her head. "And you and I still wouldn't be together."

"To hell with that. I would have been thrilled to learn that you were pregnant and you know it damn well. I'd have given up everything for you."

He pulled out his wallet, extracted a credit card and looked for the waitress. "No. Please don't go," she begged.

"Good luck with your daughter. Don't ever call me again." He saw Darla and raised his hand to catch her eye.

Anna began to cry. "Casey, please. I need your help. They'll kill her."

Something in her voice made him put his arm down.

"I'm sorry, Casey," she said. "I didn't mean it. But now they've stolen McKenna and she's such a terrific kid and I love her so much. . ." she sobbed, now, pain and horror overwhelming her.

Casey slid out of the seat and came around to sit next to her. He embraced her and murmured, "Okay. Okay. We'll take care of it."

She looked up. In a moment she hugged him. He wiped her tears. "Okay, Annie."

Then they were kissing.

Sometime later, they drew back. He returned to his seat.

"I'm sorry. I'm so sorry," she said, wiping her eyes. "I didn't mean to hurt you. I've always been thrilled that I had your baby. I could keep some of you with me the rest of my life. I've never looked at McKenna without seeing you." She teared again. "And I've never forgotten how you came to help me with the delivery of McKenna."

Casey's jaw dropped. He couldn't speak for a moment. At last, "How I did what?"

"It's the most precious memory of my life. She was born in the middle of February. They took me into the delivery room about 1:00 A. M. I called out to you. You came to be with me and help me. When McKenna showed up, you vanished. The doctor and the nurses didn't remember you. They called it a hallucination. I know better. You were there."

Casey sat agape, mouth trying to form words. His brows knitted.

"You came into the room and kissed me, just as you always did. You held my hand, coached me in the Lamaze breathing, and kissed the baby when she was born. You told me you were proud of me. We joked and laughed. You patted McKenna's head and said she was gorgeous. Then you were gone." She took a sip of wine. "I'll always remember it as the kindest and sweetest thing anyone has ever done for me."

Casey found his voice. "You were dreaming. In February that year, I spent almost every night at the university library."

She took his hand between hers and looked into his eyes. He felt a sensation he hadn't experienced in years. Like switches being thrown in his brain.

He recollected a vivid dream he'd forgotten for years. A chill enveloped him. Anna released his hand. "You remember, don't you?"

"Your doctor wore glasses. He was named Joel."

"Yes. Joel Goodnough."

"She was born breach," he said.

"Right."

"But you didn't need any anesthetic—"

"--because you were helping me."

Casey sat back and stared, trying to comprehend. "I couldn't have."

"I've been haunted by horrible dreams ever since."

The pain in Anna's face made Casey's anger dissolve. He reached out. She took his hands and squeezed hard. "Okay, it's in the past," he murmured after a few moments. "We can't change what happened. I'm sorry for being cruel."

She smiled, and the tension eased. "Tell me about my daughter," he said and choked on the word.

At that moment their dinners arrived. "I'm not hungry," Anna said as the waitress walked away.

"You should eat," he said.

She ate a couple of tiny bites. "My goodness," she said.

"I know. They have an exceptional chef."

"Make you cry right out," she said. He snickered. They both became ravenous. He hadn't realized how hungry he was.

At last, Anna put down her fork. "McKenna does well in school, though not quite as well since Alan died. I know you'll be proud of what a fine athlete she's turned out to be. She's on the girls' track team. A few years ago, she and I began taking karate lessons together. She hasn't quite made black belt but she is superb."

"Good grief. *Crouching Tiger Hidden Dragon*." They chuckled together.

She said, "When she entered high school, she began to take an interest in theatre. She enrolled for some acting classes and she's been in the drama program at school. She played the lead in the last play."

"I wish I could have seen it."

"She stole the show. I saw it four times." They laughed.

Then, he sobered a little. "Have you been holding up?"

"Yes," she shrugged. "But I haven't slept more than a few hours since yesterday afternoon."

"I'm sorry, Annie."

"We just have to get her back."

"Have you called the police? The FBI?"

"No," said Anna. "The kidnappers said if I contacted the police they'd kill her and come after me."

"Do you have any idea who's behind this?" he asked, cutting a piece of veal.

"I can't imagine. But—" she paused, and he looked up "— they insist that you be involved."

Casey stopped a forkful of pasta halfway to his mouth. He started to respond, then couldn't. He stared at her, eyes wide. "Me?" he managed. She nodded. "What for?"

"They want us to find something for them. If you don't help, they'll—" she swallowed hard. She took a sip of wine. "They'll kill McKenna."

He shook his head. "This makes no sense."

Anna said, "Casey. Please help me get McKenna back. You can see her and become part of her life, I promise."

"Sure," he nodded. "Of course I'll help. But who knows that I'm McKenna's father except the two of us?"

"I never told anyone," Anna said. "No, wait. I told Tom, the man I'm seeing now."

Casey winced at the stab of pain that shot through him. "Tell me about the afternoon McKenna vanished," he suggested.

Anna told him about that day. "When she called, she told me two men took her. She read me a prepared statement. They gave me forty-eight hours to contact you. Once I found you they'd give us further instructions." Casey nodded. "They gave me your cell phone number—I don't know how they got it—and I called it every fifteen minutes. When you didn't answer I set out to find you."

"What are we supposed to do, Annie?" He stroked the back of her hand with his thumb..

She took a breath. "They want us to find Blackbeard's treasure."

CHAPTER THIRTY FOUR

Casey stared at Anna. "Anna," he managed. "Don't joke about this."

"I'm serious," she said. "They'll call us on my cell phone tomorrow morning around eight o'clock."

"But Anna," he said. "No one knows where Blackbeard hid his treasure."

Anna looked surprised. "You know about Blackbeard?"

"To call Blackbeard demonic would be an understatement," he said. "He terrorized the East Coast from Maine to the Virgin Islands. St. Thomas dedicated a monument to him called Blackbeard's Tower. God knows why anyone would want to memorialize that monster."

"You seem to know a lot about Blackbeard," said Anna.

"As a boy, I loved to read about pirates," Casey said, with a self-conscious tilt of his head. "But I sure don't know enough to go looking for his treasure. Smarter people than you or me have looked for it for three centuries," he said.

"What do you know about his treasure?"

"Some mythology, I guess," he shrugged, and thought for a moment. He said, "If I recall, legends say he might have buried some in New England, on an island called Smutty Nose in the Isle of Shoals off New Hampshire and Maine. He might have buried some in the British Virgin Islands, on an island called Dead Chest."

"Anywhere else?"

"Some people thought he buried something on Plum Point, near Bath, North Carolina." His eyes widened as a light clicked on. North Carolina. He stared at her. "You mean you know something about that?"

"Uh, huh, I do," she said. "I know who found the treasure

in North Carolina."

"What?"

"Some trappers on the Pamlico River discovered an open vault on Christmas Day, 1928," said Anna. "They found the vault empty but the area around the vault showed that someone had removed a large chest from it."

"What happened to it?" he asked.

Anna unbuttoned the top button of her blouse. She unloosened the clasp of a necklace, which she handed to him.

The necklace was fashioned from at least fifteen enormous emeralds. "The chain and setting are white gold, and the stones are genuine. The craftsman fashioned this necklace at least three centuries ago, but it could be much older. I don't know anything about the original owner, but it's pirate plunder beyond question. My family has owned it for years."

"I've seen this before, haven't I?"

"Yes," she said. "I wore it the night I saw *Dr. Jekyll* and for the weekend of the musical." She gave him a shy smile. "For a considerable portion of the weekend, it was the only thing either one of us were wearing, if you recall."

"I do," he said, enjoying the memory.

A distant picture of a ship and a girl flitted into his mind but dissolved in a moment. He shook his head.

Anna reminded him of the story of Prudence Lutrelle and her escape from *Queen Anne's Revenge*. "The necklace was the only thing she kept."

"It's beautiful," muttered Casey. "How did you get it?"

"I inherited it from my grandmother. I'll give it to McKenna when she gets married. . ." Mentioning her daughter's name reminded her of McKenna's danger. Anna put her hand to her mouth, overwhelmed with grief and horror.

Casey squeezed her free hand and murmured comfort until she could speak again. "What does this have to do with finding the treasure?" he asked.

"Blackbeard told Prudence where he'd hidden the treasure from that year's voyage. Contrary to what most people think, pirates didn't bury much money. They spent it. When they looted ships, they sold the goods. Pirates liked money and fine clothes and gambling. They stole and killed so they could live as they wanted to."

"Yeah, that makes sense," Casey nodded.

"Nonetheless Blackbeard did bury some, at least one chest. He hid the treasure in a vault at Plum Point where he maintained a hideout.

"Blackbeard killed the men who helped construct the vault and threw their bodies overboard when they returned to the ship.

"Only three people—Blackbeard, Stede Bonnet, and Great-grandmother Prudence—knew the hiding place. Bonnet and Blackbeard died with the secret.

"Prudence wanted nothing to do with the treasure. But she did make a map. My great-grandfather found it in an old Bible that had belonged to her. He used the map to dig up the treasure at Plum Point. Then he hid the loot again. He planned to dispose of it once the news on the mainland died down. But. . ."

"Yeah?" asked Casey.

"Casey, he died before he could get rid of it."

"You mean, a sudden death?" said Casey.

"Yes. Terrible things happen to everyone who tries to profit from it. People say the treasure carries a curse."

He drew his chin back and examined her with amused curiosity. "A curse?"

"I know it sounds like superstitious nonsense. But the family legend says the treasure is haunted. Great-grandfather's directions for how to find it are fuzzy. It's supposed to be hidden between two oak trees on St. Margaret's Island."

Casey fiddled with a fork, and took a small bite of potato. "Does anyone else know about this treasure legend?"

She shrugged. "My whole family. I wouldn't call it a secret. I even told Alan about it not long after McKenna was born when we took McKenna to North Carolina to see my grandparents. I've told my friend Tom, also. My cousins and stepsisters have looked for it for years. My grandfather Daniel, who lives in a nursing home in Arlington Heights, might know how to find it. I think he might have helped dig it up. But he had a stroke a few years ago and has a hard time talking. I stopped there tonight. I told him about McKenna and the kidnapping. He's frantic."

He put down his fork and nodded. "Why don't you spend the night at my house?" She protested, but he reminded her, "We need to be together to take McKenna's call in the morning." She smiled and agreed.

Before they left the restaurant, they split a piece of apple pie. They talked about McKenna and tried to form some plans.

At the house Casey introduced Anna to his sister Cheyenne and her husband, who met them at the door. He told the young couple that Anna's daughter had been kidnapped, but avoided mentioning that the girl was his daughter.

Casey led Anna to the guest bedroom next to his room. He gave her one of his bathrobes, a toothbrush, and a towel. Cheyenne loaned her some pajamas.

He put her into the bed and kissed her. They talked until she fell asleep. Casey disentangled his hand from hers and went to his own bed.

* * * * *

The Snake came in from the hallway.

She tried to call Casey, but failed. Her voice never worked in the dreams.

The Snake transformed into a tall man who strutted to her bed, with sulfurous yellow smoke surrounding his head. She could never see all of his face. But the light revealed the two red eyes and sharp, cruel teeth. She realized he had a beard.

"Hello, Annie," he said, reveling in her terror. "Ruining Casey's life once wasn't enough? Watch this, Annie."

He pointed to the door, where a movie began to play. The scenes of sex with Casey tore at her heart. She grieved again as she saw him as a young man, kneeling by his car, unable to pick up his keys, overwhelmed with grief and hurt.

The film changed. She found herself in the film, out in the country, near a farm. She saw McKenna struggling with two men on a path next to a snow-covered field. The men laughed at McKenna's terror.

Beyond them Anna could see an abandoned barn. One of the men told McKenna to start running. He shoved her forward and she started across the field, slogging through the deep snow toward a storm cloud. Lightning flashed from the cloud and a cold wind blew.

She screamed at McKenna, who turned and saw her. Anna realized that her voice worked in this dream.

The barn door opened and the tall man came out. He turned into the monstrous Snake and started after McKenna, slithering with appalling swiftness on top of the snow. Anna saw that the Snake would catch McKenna but she couldn't move. She screamed a warning at her daughter.

McKenna turned and saw the Snake coming. Her face twisted with horror.

The Snake caught up to her daughter. It reared, ready to strike.

Then Gareth—a different, younger, red-haired Gareth—stepped from behind McKenna. Anna knew him at once and screamed his name. He positioned himself between McKenna and the Snake.

Anna struggled through the deep snow to help Gareth. She saw him seize the Snake and twist its neck as it wrapped itself around him. But it had grown over the years. It had become too strong for him. He'd be crushed. . .

She became aware of two strong arms around her. Thinking one of McKenna's captors had grabbed her, she struck out hard.

She heard a voice saying, "Wake up, Annie. I've got you."

Her nightmare receded. She woke and gazed at Casey. He sat next to her on the bed, holding her and stroking her hair. She clutched him as if afraid he would evaporate. "Am I still dreaming?" she asked.

He gave her an encouraging smile. "No, honey, I'm here," he said. "Calm down."

"I'm so sorry I hit you," she stammered. "I thought you were someone in my dream."

"What happened?"

She said, still choking a little, "I dreamed of Nehushtan. He chased McKenna and wanted to crush her."

"What do you mean, Nehushtan?" Casey asked, thinking that the name sounded familiar. Odd.

"Sometimes he's a snake, other times a man. I can never see the man's face. Most of the time, I don't remember much about the dreams except for Nehushtan and the terror."

"I'll stay here with you tonight." He took a tissue from a box on the bedside table and wiped her tears. His tender kindness made the tears flow again.

* * * * *

Casey tried to calm Anna down. He'd never seen anyone so terrified after a nightmare. "I'll be right back," he said, giving her a small pillow to clutch. He ran to the kitchen, where he poured her a small glass of brandy. In the bathroom he wet a washcloth with cool water.

He came back and put an arm around her. She leaned against him and he hugged her. He caressed her face, her neck, and her arms with the cool cloth. She drank the wine in small sips. When she finished the wine she smiled at him. "Thank you. I must look a wreck."

"You look beautiful."

"Flatterer. I bet my hair looks like a hooraw's nest now."

He stared at her, struggling to restrain a wild giggle. "What the hell is a hooraw?"

She thought for a second. "I don't know. But it must have a terrible nest."

He began to laugh. She did too, just a little and her tension eased.

She slid down into the bed while he went to the closet and took out an old quilt. He spread it over the top of her covers and slid under it.

They lay on their right sides and snuggled like two spoons in a drawer. He sensed that she didn't feel afraid anymore. Casey put his arm over her. She pulled his hand to her lips for a gentle kiss of thanks. She laced her fingers with his.

When Casey felt her relax into sleep, he allowed himself to drift off, still holding her. He realized, in his last few moments of consciousness, that he still loved Anna. He'd always loved her. Would always love her. *Oh, brother*, he thought. *Now what have I gotten myself into?*

CHAPTER THIRTY FIVE

McKenna woke up from a dream. She felt better this morning, as if someone had been with her all night, holding her hand, encouraging her.

The sun shone through the filmy curtains in her room. She thought, trying to call back what had happened in the dream. .

.

No, the vision had dissipated, like smoke from a chimney.

She hadn't found anything yet that she might use as a weapon but she'd begun to develop some ideas. She needed somehow to incapacitate the men who were holding her.

She stepped from the shower and dried her hair. Knotting her robe, she returned to the room they'd put her in. The clothes they'd given her didn't fit well but they were clean. The cheap cotton socks wouldn't provide any sort of protection if she tried to run for it. They'd put her Nikes into the padlocked hall closet with her coat.

She composed herself, dropping into the nitwit persona she'd adopted for the men, and went out into the living room. Scott sat there smiling, reading a newspaper. She didn't see the older man.

"Where'd your father go?"

"Into town. He'll be back. Whoa. Your hair looks beautiful this morning."

McKenna reddened at the compliment. She stared at the floor, realizing that this lout had just made a mild pass at her. She felt his eyes on her. She looked out the large picture window at the deep snow. The bitter cold snap continued again today, below zero for sure.

"Scott," she asked, looking him right in the eye. "Do you plan to cut my hand up?"

"Ah," he turned away and waved his hand. "Don't worry about that. We said that just to get them scared. I couldn't hurt you."

The tone of the words surprised her. He spoke in a voice that sounded almost tender. She recovered. "But your father could," she said. "You terrified my mom."

"She'll get over it when we send you home, that's all I can say." McKenna didn't respond. "We're all gonna be rich." She shrugged.

Like I care about a legendary treasure, she thought.

"Want to see a picture of that Fixx guy?" he asked.

She looked up and shrugged. He handed her a glossy print.

Her life changed.

She stared. Fixx appeared to be about Mom's age, handsome but scruffy. He wore a tuxedo but it seemed—what? Almost *inappropriate* for him. Like he belonged in much more casual clothes, say jeans and tee-shirts.

The picture showed him smiling, talking into a microphone and holding some sort of a plaque.

He looked *familiar.* McKenna considered for a moment--and then understood why. Casey Fixx and she *resembled* each other. Anyhow she looked a lot more like him than her father, whom she had never resembled in the slightest.

"Quite a resemblance, huh?" Scott chuckled.

McKenna nodded, baffled. "Can I keep this picture?"

"Sure," he shrugged. "You want to get some air?"

"You took away my shoes and coat," she pointed out.

"No problem." Pulling a key ring from his jeans pocket, Scott walked to a closet and unlocked the door. He took out her jogging shoes and her fur parka. Next he tossed her woolen socks and heavy leather mittens lined with fleece. She took off her slippers and put on the warm clothes.

Pulling on his own coat, Scott undid several locks on the front door and they went outside. The bitter cold took her breath away for a few moments, but she adjusted to it as they walked. He took her down the drive and showed her the electric fence that extended all around the house. He reiterated that if she got out of the house, she couldn't get past the fence.

While he yakked, she thought how he'd complimented her hair. He'd said that he couldn't hurt her. There had to be a way she could use that.

CHAPTER THIRTY SIX

Cheyenne came into the kitchen at 8:00 A. M., dressed for work. She put on some coffee, chewing at her lower lip.

Cheyenne couldn't help feeling both puzzled and curious. She'd seen Anna's haunted eyes and the way her mouth trembled when she came into the house. But she didn't question Anna. Cheyenne figured Casey would tell her the story at the appropriate time.

But that didn't diminish her curiosity. She wanted to understand the relationship between her shy, introverted brother and this Anna woman.

When Cheyenne and Derek went to their apartment in Casey's basement, the young couple discussed what they'd seen going on between Anna and Casey. They looked like they belonged together. They acted like a couple who had been together for years.

Cheyenne knew that if Casey had been dating someone as attractive as Anna, he would have told her. Yet Anna had said she'd been married until two years ago. Cheyenne felt certain her brother wouldn't pursue a married woman. So Anna and Casey couldn't have had a romantic involvement, Cheyenne reasoned.

She sneaked upstairs to see if Anna had awakened. She peeked through the open door of the guest bedroom.

She started with surprise to find her brother sleeping next to Anna, his arm around her. He lay under an old quilt but not under the covers with her.

Anna lay awake, hugging Casey's arm. She smiled when she saw Cheyenne. She put a finger to her lips as she slid out of the bed. Casey didn't stir. Anna slipped on the robe Casey had given her and the two women crept from the room.

In the kitchen Cheyenne begged Anna's pardon for intruding. Anna waved away the apology. "You must've been surprised, seeing us like that," Anna said.

Cheyenne shrugged. "I wouldn't consider it my business."

"Of course what happens to your brother is your business," Anna said. "I'm guessing you want to know if we made love."

Cheyenne went to the refrigerator and poured them each a glass of orange juice. "Do you want to tell me?"

"A nightmare scared me," Anna said. "Casey heard me screaming. He came in to comfort me and we fell asleep together." She gave Cheyenne a little smile. "And we might have made love if he'd asked me."

Cheyenne giggled with her new friend. She sat down opposite Anna. "Must have been a terrible dream."

"Yes," Anna said, sipping at the orange juice. "As always."

Talk about enigmatic, thought Cheyenne. She decided to ask the question that had haunted her. "Let me ask you something," Cheyenne said. Anna looked up and nodded. "I can see how my brother feels about you. Do you love Casey?"

If the abrupt question surprised Anna, she didn't show it. Anna looked Cheyenne in the eye. "I've loved Casey every minute of my life."

Cheyenne poured them each some coffee and toasted a couple of bagels. *Let me get this straight*, she thought. *They love each other. But they haven't seen each other in years. And her daughter has been kidnapped. And that worries Casey as much as it does her. . .*

Anna interrupted her thoughts. "Do you have a big day planned?" she asked, eyeing Cheyenne's trim business suit and heels.

"I try to dress up a bit for a first visit to a client," Cheyenne smiled. "I'm consulting with a nursing home today."

"I see," said Anna. They chatted for a few moments about Cheyenne's job.

Cheyenne eased Anna into talking about the kidnapping. After chatting for a few moments, Cheyenne nodded. "It really sounds like someone you know has to be involved in this."

Anna agreed, but shook her head. "I can't imagine who, though."

"Any bad relationships, even from years ago?" asked Cheyenne.

"I went through one terrible breakup with a guy in college," Anna shrugged. "But that happened twenty years ago."

"What happened?"

Anna told Cheyenne about the conflict with Nick Wolfe. She explained how Nick had tried to rape her, how she'd dumped him and refused to see him. She also related that she'd been run out of the small town of Shoal Creek, Wisconsin. The residents had taken Nick's side.

Cheyenne asked more questions until she had to leave for work. To the surprise of both of them she hugged Anna like a sister. Anna's eyes teared at the gentle kindness.

* * * * *

A few moments before 9:00 A. M., Cheyenne pulled into the parking lot of an extended care facility. Armed with legal pad and a felt-tip marker, she walked around, making notes, meeting and chatting with some of the residents and the staff.

Cheyenne made her living as a business consultant, specializing in finding ways to help organizations run better. Her MBA gave her the credentials she needed to go head-to-head with older businessmen. When they met the bright-eyed young woman in the business suit with the short skirt, they often felt that the consulting company was ripping them off. Then the young woman would show them something that would save them big money or rescue a disastrous situation.

When she turned the corner on the third floor she bumped into a tall man. "Excuse me, sir," she said.

His face lit up. The sluggish look vanished from his striking green eyes. She put his age at about eighty and saw that he had shaved and dressed. "Cinnamon," he said with relief. "Thank God. I didn't know how to reach you."

"Sir?"

"That Nick character took her. Please. You have to go get her," Cheyenne felt a chill as he said the name Nick. "Do I know you, sir?"

"Am I not addressing Cinnamon Fixx, Casey's sister?"

"No," she smiled. "I'm Cheyenne, their sister. Cinnamon and I do resemble one another, but she has blond hair and she's taller than I am. How do you know her?"

"No, that hasn't happened yet," he mumbled. Then he grew silent and his green eyes clouded. He turned and walked into a nearby room and sat down, staring out the window. The name on the door, Mr. Daniel Oakley, didn't register.

Cheyenne shivered a little as she followed him into the room. "How do you know Cinnamon and Casey?" He didn't respond or even look at her.

She left the room and hurried down the hall to the nurses' station.

"Excuse me," she said to one of the women.

"Can I help you?" asked the nurse.

"Yes. What can you tell me about Mr. Oakley, room 326?"

The nurse looked puzzled. "He came here two or three years ago," she shrugged. "He speaks very little. His family lives in the area. They visit him, love him, and take him home for holidays."

"He says he knows my sister and brother."

"I'm sorry I can't help. No, no one named Fixx has ever come to visit." Cheyenne walked away, thinking. Then she shook herself and took a deep breath. The facility paid her by the hour to find ways to help them run better. She needed to focus on what they hired her to do.

CHAPTER THIRTY SEVEN

Casey came downstairs and found Anna sitting at the kitchen table, sipping coffee. With her hair down and the morning sun shining on it, Anna looked radiant. His heart melted again. He drew a deep breath.

She stood and put her arms around his neck. "Do you remember the first time we kissed?"

"Refresh my memory," he said. They lost themselves in the kiss. For a few moments they became once again a young man and woman with their lives before them. Seventeen years of loneliness hadn't intervened since their last kiss.

Sometime later they pulled back. She stroked his face with long, elegant fingers while he caressed her hair.

"Thanks for being so nice last night," she whispered. They kissed again, the familiar kiss of devotion between a husband and wife.

He had to struggle to refrain from suggesting a return to the bedroom. No, he couldn't put her in the position of having to make that decision. She might regret and resent that he'd taken advantage of her.

They sat and held hands, fingers laced together. Anna smiled and sipped her coffee. "Cheyenne left for work a while ago. She needed to get to an early appointment. What an impressive young woman."

"I do have talented and beautiful sisters," he said. "Cinnamon passed the bar a few years ago and works at a high powered legal firm. Karen teaches at a college. A lot smarter than their brother."

"Cheyenne looked very professional this morning," said Anna. "And adorable," she added. Both chuckled.

They fell silent, holding hands.

"How are you this morning?" he asked.

"Not as bad. I did sleep well after you came in."

"I'm glad."

"Something about you," said Anna. "I'm not as scared."

Again a pause. They looked into one another's eyes. "I never expected to see you again," he said.

"I know." She paused. "We have a few moments before McKenna calls," she said, pointing to her cell phone on the table between them. "Can we talk?"

"Sure."

After a brief pause, she spoke again. "You didn't say last night. Are you involved with anyone?"

"No. One woman threw me in the landfill a few moments before I saw you last night, in fact."

"I'm sorry," she said.

"Since the divorce I've dated a few women but they all dumped me. I guess I've never been able to make a real commitment."

Anna scrutinized the rim of her cup. "What happened to your marriage?" she asked, not looking up.

He looked out the window at the birds at his feeders on the back deck. He spoke in a small voice. "My marriage lasted for almost five years. Grace and I married a year after I returned to Westwood from my leave of absence. One day she told me that she gotten fed up with my crazy work hours. I apologized and offered to change. She rejected that and told me she didn't want to have any kids. Irreconcilable differences, the lawyer called it."

Anna took his hand and squeezed it. Casey saw a little junco land on the deck and begin to peck at some seeds that had fallen from the feeder. "What really happened was she fell back in love with Rudy. He works as a commodities broker at the Board of Trade. He deals in Eurodollars and makes a ton of money. So when we met at the lawyer's office," he said, his voice growing thick, "Grace listed her charges while Rudy laughed at me. Well, you know me. I couldn't keep my composure and started to cry. My lawyer asked for a break. Rudy continued to ridicule me."

Casey related the aftermath.

"When we finished I walked into the hall by myself. Rudy sneered that Grace would be with a real man now, and not some dancing faggot." He choked a little to think of it. Anna's eyes flashed with indignation.

"I don't remember the next few moments," Casey continued. "I'm not real proud of what I did. Things went black. When I came to myself, I found myself standing over him, rubbing my knuckles. Rudy lay flat on his back, holding his mouth. I learned later that I'd broken his jaw. Must've been a lucky punch."

"Sounds like he deserved it," muttered Anna.

"Well, anyhow, my lawyer ran out, grabbed me and pulled me away," Casey went on. "Rudy tried to sit up, mumbling that he'd be calling the cops and pressing charges. I ignored him and walked off. Grace cried and tried to apologize to me. I brushed past her and shuffled out of her life."

He decided not to tell Anna what happened when he came home that afternoon. He found the house cleared out, all the furniture gone, her closet empty, and no note of good-bye.

When Cinnamon and Cheyenne came home from school several hours later, they found their brother still sitting by the front door, paralyzed with grief. Frightened, they called Aunt Vic who came right over. For days Casey ate little, slept little, and did little.

"Grace married Rudy a few days after we finalized the divorce. She gave birth to their first baby nine months later."

He wiped his eye with the back of his hand. The pain still hadn't gone away. "I guess that's when I understood. When Grace told me she didn't want to have kids, she meant that she didn't want to have kids with me."

"That must have been horrible for you," she said.

He stared out the window for a moment. A male downy woodpecker jabbed at the suet block. Casey stared for a moment at the perfect little black and white head with the red spot.

His voice remained quiet. "A bit more than a year after the divorce, Grace began to reach out to me. It took a while but I couldn't stay mad and hurt at her. We'd been friends too long. We've gone back to being good friends now, teasing and laughing like we used to."

"I'm sorry, Casey."

"It turned out for the best. Our names didn't work together. Ridiculous. Gracie and Casey. A Vaudeville song and dance act." She smiled at the little joke.

A silence ensued, while the two friends watched two purple finches kicking at some black thistle seed. "Anna, I have to ask. Shouldn't we get the police involved?"

"We can't," she asserted.

"Please reconsider. I'm good friends with a cop here in Palatine. He lives a few houses away. He might be able to help out, you know? I mean, at least he could advise us." A thought struck him. "Hey, listen. I work with a private agency. They provide security on my commercials—"

She shook her head. "McKenna won't be harmed if we do what they want—" Anna's cell phone rang. She tensed and nodded to him. He picked up the phone and pressed the button. "McKenna?"

"Yes," a girl's voice said. "Doctor Fixx?"

"Yes," he said, choking at hearing his daughter's voice for the first time. She even sounded like his sister Cinnamon. "It's him," he heard her say to someone.

"Are you okay?" he asked.

"Yes. Can I speak to my mom?"

"She's right here." He handed the phone to Anna.

"Hi sweetheart," Anna said, struggling to stay in control. "Can we do anything for you?" A few moments later Anna said she loved McKenna and waved Casey over next to her. "She wants to talk to both of us," said Anna. She put the cell phone on speaker-phone. Anna and Casey put their heads together to listen.

"Dr. Fixx, you have a week from today to find Blackbeard's treasure," said the young voice. "If you don't find it, they're going to start hurting me. Every day, they will chop off a piece of my fingers." McKenna started to cry. "Once you find the treasure they want you to post a message on a Web site." She gave him an Internet address, which he wrote down. "Mom?"

"Yes, honey."

"I've seen Myrthynne."

The telephone went dead. Casey hugged Anna, baffled to see her smiling.

CHAPTER THIRTY EIGHT

"Grandpa." Daniel Oakley stirred from a doze in his room's institutional easy chair at the nursing home. A gentle hand lay on his arm.

He looked up to see his most beloved relative standing in front of him. "Hi, Anna. Thank you for coming."

"Grandpa, some people took McKenna," said Anna, kneeling next to him. "They want me to go to St. Margaret's and to find Blackbeard's treasure. I need your help."

Daniel's face twisted with pain and he took his granddaughter's hand. "What can I do?"

"Tell me how to find the gold. They'll kill her if I don't."

He winced and reached for her. She came to his hug.

He gave her a Paik. She Paiked back. The pastel walls of the nursing home room vanished and they stood together on St. Margaret's Island, hundreds of miles away. The day felt wonderful, clear and cool with a gentle ocean breeze. He breathed deep, relishing the salt air. To his surprise, he found that his mind was clear, focused and alert.

They walked together as he pointed out things about the island. Drawing her attention to the swamp, he begged her to be careful there.

At last they stood together before the gate of the cemetery. "Something's important about the graveyard," he said. "I don't know what, though."

As they walked back to the eastern beach, anxiety overwhelmed him. "Honey, that treasure has a curse on it. Don't consider that a legend or a joke. People always suffer or die when they find it or even look for it. Please don't go. We'll get the money some other way."

"Grandpa, they want the treasure."

"All right, then," he said. "Let me go with you. We'll find it together."

"No, Grandpa." She took his hand as tears of affection rose in her eyes. "Thank you, but I have someone who loves me to help me. Anyway the people who took McKenna demanded that he come with me."

"Who? Not that Tom character, I hope."

"No. You've never met this man. He's named Casey Fixx. I've loved him all my life. He protected me from Nehushtan many times. He promised to take care of me."

The old man liked the idea of his granddaughter being with someone she loved. He'd despised that snake Alan.

They looked in one another's eyes and nodded. Grandfather and granddaughter released the Cymreig and came back to his room at the nursing home. He found that his mind had remained clear. For the first time in—what? A couple of years?—he could think straight. He told Anna what he remembered about the lost treasure of Blackbeard.

CHAPTER THIRTY NINE

Derek owned some outdoor cooking equipment and a couple of large and well-insulated sleeping bags. Cheyenne and Derek helped Casey crate it all up. He figured that he and Anna might need to spend several nights on St. Margaret's Island.

Anna had driven back to her house to pick up some clothes for the trip and a couple of items for camping. She'd meet Casey at O'Hare. He'd opened the door to walk out but stopped when his house telephone rang. "Casey?"

He recognized the unusual raspy voice. "Yes. Hi, Jerry." Jerry LaBonte owned a private detective agency and had provided security for him on local commercial shoots around the Chicago area. He'd been a friend for about a year.

"Hey. I wanted to settle the details on that soft-drink shoot we talked about."

"Thanks for calling," said Casey, "but we don't shoot for about a month. Let me give you the dates." He flipped open his calendar and read off some numbers.

"Okay, pal. Everything else okay?"

"Well, no," Casey admitted.

"Something wrong?" Casey heard concern in his friend's voice. "You don't sound so good."

"I feel okay, yes. But. . ."

"Can I do anything to help, pal?"

Casey hesitated. "Listen. Do you ever do missing persons stuff?"

"Sure, of course. All the time."

Casey hesitated, but then said, "Let me tell you what's going on." He started to tell Jerry the story.

"Wait a second, Casey. Let me get this on tape. Okay, go."

Casey told Jerry about Anna, McKenna, and the kidnapping.

"Oh, Jeez, they took your daughter?" said Jerry. "I'm sorry. You gotta be frantic."

"Yeah. They told Anna that if she called the cops they'd kill the girl."

"That's standard with these creeps. Okay. Do you have this Anna's phone numbers?"

"Sure," said Casey and gave them to him.

"I'll get right on this. One of my guys seems to know everything about electronics. I'm pretty sure he can trace the calls. If we find the location, I'll get some guys and go after her."

"That would be great, Jerry," said Casey.

"Look, I gotta tell you, pal," said Jerry. "I bet they intend to kill the girl whether you find the loot or not."

"Don't say that."

"I'm sorry to scare you even more. Let me get going on this. Look, don't tell anyone. The fewer people who know I'm working on this, the better."

"Why?"

"We don't want to take a chance and tip them off. What people don't know keeps the girl safe. You shouldn't even tell Anna." Casey agreed, thanked his friend and they hung up.

* * * * *

Casey's sister Cheyenne and Derek drove him to O'Hare Airport.

As they handed his luggage to the sky caps at the curbside check-in, Cheyenne said, "Oh, I almost forgot. An old man in a nursing home mistook me for Cinnamon today." She related the incident in some detail.

"He knew Cinnamon?" asked Casey, as the sky cap processed his ticket.

"He knew you too," said his sister. "I wrote his name down.

I'll call you with it."

"Don't bother. I imagine he knew Mom and Dad. He saw the family resemblance."

Cheyenne frowned and looked unconvinced. She started to speak, but at that moment Anna hurried out of the terminal. "Sorry to rush you," she said. "We're running late."

Casey and Anna said quick good-byes to Cheyenne and Derek. They hustled through the security check-in and ran to their plane. They boarded with just moments to spare.

After the plane took off, Anna lifted his arm, and put it around her. She dozed on his shoulder. He was pleased that she could sleep.

About thirty minutes into the flight, Anna jerked. She looked at him wide-eyed and trembling. "Casey," she said. "The Snake—" Then she came awake. He embraced her and she began to calm down.

"A nightmare," she said. "Even during a nap."

"It's okay," he said.

She smiled, but then her face became serious. "I got into a big fight with Tom on the phone," she sighed.

"I'm sorry." Casey felt sure she was sleeping with this guy. The pain that the thought produced continued to stun him.

"He thinks I'm crazy to go running off. He got angry when I told him I'm going with you. I expected him to offer to come along. But he didn't."

"Sorry," Casey repeated, aware that he wasn't holding up his end of the conversation. His linguistic skills seemed to have deserted him.

"He's been under a lot of stress for several months with his business at the Board of Trade," Anna sighed. "His business needs a big cash inflow."

"Do you—" He had to swallow before he could ask the question. "—plan to marry this guy?"

She studied his face. "He asked me. But he doesn't seem to

like McKenna. Nor she him. I've been stalling him, hoping they'll learn to get along."

"I see."

"Does that upset you?"

"Should it?" Petulant.

They fell silent, but he noticed the corners of her mouth twitching.

In a moment or two, she shrugged. "I went to the nursing home one more time after I left your place," she said. "I found Grandpa much more lucid this time. He told me what to look for once we get to St. Margaret's."

She reached into her purse and pulled out a small notebook. She flipped a couple of pages and nodded. "We have to find the two oak trees, and then find the initials WO, for William Oakley. He married Prudence. Their children buried them on the island."

"What then?"

"We have to look in the light at ten o'clock. We'll find the treasure below the initials."

"Does that make sense to you?"

"No."

After the plane landed, they rented a car. Anna proposed they stop at the ancient town of Bath, the little village that once served as the headquarters of Captain Edward Teach. She knew a bed and breakfast where they could stay.

She also suggested they go out to Plum Point and see the place where Blackbeard's treasure had been found. They could go to St. Margaret's Island in the morning.

CHAPTER FORTY

McKenna lay on her bed reading a two-year-old magazine. The door slammed open. Scott and his father barged in.

"Tough luck, kid," the father yelled. "Time just ran out for you." When she screamed, he slapped her. They seized her and dragged her to the kitchen.

To her horror she saw a large butcher block in the middle of the table with a cleaver next to it. Scott held her in a hammer lock with one arm twisted behind her back. The father draped a handkerchief over the mouthpiece of a cell phone and poked at the keypad.

"We want to give you a little preview to make sure you take us serious," he growled into the phone. "We're going to chop off your daughter's little finger on her left hand. You get to listen."

He set the phone next to the block and seized the cleaver. He held McKenna's hand on the block and twisted it so her little finger protruded into the middle of the block. McKenna heard her mother pleading with terror.

"You listening?" he yelled, and swung the cleaver.

McKenna screamed.

* * * * *

Anna shrieked "No!" She struggled to find the callback function on the phone. Casey pulled the car off the road. He jumped from the driver's seat and ran to the passenger side. He lifted her out and held her. She continued to scream, near hysteria.

"What happened?" Casey asked, but a long time passed before she could tell him.

* * * * *

Anna, struggling to be coherent, directed him to the Pirate's Den Bed-and-Breakfast, managed by Lesha Brooks, a woman who had gone to high school with her. Lesha poured Anna a little brandy.

Lesha's husband, Roger, gave them directions to Plum Point. Then the couple reviewed the legend of Plum Point with Casey and Anna.

Years before, some trappers found the old vault open. Inside they saw the bones of the vault's engineer. Several tracks led to the water. The trappers mentioned seeing a gigantic snake in the vault.

Casey followed the street out of town and then south to Breezy Shores Road. They parked, and found something like a path to Plum Point through brambles and thorns.

Casey held Anna's hand while they surveyed the Pamlico Sound from the little spit of land. They looked out over Bath Creek where it emptied into the Pamlico River. Behind them lay a swamp where rattlesnakes came out in the summer. *A perfect place to hide treasure*, thought Casey.

Anna squeezed his hand. "Not a pleasant place," she said.

They heard a noise behind them and turned to see a man and a woman trudging through the undergrowth toward them. They wore old-fashioned khakis and boots. The two people smiled and waved as they approached. A cold wind off the river struck Anna and Casey as the people joined them.

They introduced themselves as Cole and Elaine McClelland. The two couples exchanged pleasantries. "What would you two be doing out here?" Casey asked.

"Looking for Blackbeard's treasure," said Cole, with a pronounced New York accent.

"We've searched everywhere with no luck," said Elaine. An attractive woman, she had a glow of health about her and an infectious laugh.

"It might be out there," Casey said, pointing to the Pamlico River. To his surprise, he found that he felt an implicit trust for the couple.

"You mean lost at sea?" cried Cole.

"No," said Anna. "On St. Margaret's island."

"That would make sense," said Cole, after thinking for a moment or two. "Two or three people took the treasure chest away in a boat. We figure they went out to sea and hid it again."

So they've heard the same stuff we heard, thought Casey. "Look," Casey said. "We don't care about the treasure. Some people kidnapped our daughter for ransom." Cole and Elaine looked horrified.

"They're threatening to kill her if we don't find this treasure," Casey continued. "If you want to work with us, we'd appreciate your help." The McClellands agreed without hesitation. "Can you meet us on the island tomorrow?"

"Sure," said Cole. "If we find the treasure, we'll split it with you."

"Thank you," Anna said. "No one knows how much treasure still exists. I'm sure those jerks won't miss your share."

Chapter Forty One

McKenna pulled away from Scott, ran to her room and wept with rage. When he swung the cleaver, the father came as close to her finger as he could. She'd screamed in terror. As he hung up the phone, he laughed.

Her fury blazed at the kidnappers, of course, but also at herself. She'd let her guard down a little. *What could I have been thinking of, reading a magazine? I've got to get ready to escape. These two plan to kill me.*

She needed some weapons. Although she knew she could outrun these thugs, she would be no match for them in a struggle. She had to incapacitate them.

She'd seen the delight in the father's eyes at the horror he'd caused her. The unspeakable charade had terrified her mother.

An hour later, McKenna had worked out a plan. She walked out to the living room. She stood, staring out the picture window at the Siberian-like landscape.

Scott came out of the kitchen and saw her. He came up to her and put his hand on her shoulder. "Look, I want you to know that—"

She lashed out with a karate sidekick that caught him on the side of the knee. She felt ligaments give way as it bent to the side. He fell, shouting as excruciating pain set in.

"Don't you ever touch me again, you miserable worm," she snarled. She stalked back to her room and slammed the door.

Then, she smiled. She had incapacitated one of her captors. Plan under way.

CHAPTER FORTY TWO

Casey drove Anna back to the bed-and-breakfast. In the bedroom, she embraced him as the tears flowed. Casey held her for a long time and let her sob. "Anna," he said at last, "they didn't cut McKenna."

Anna looked up. "What do you mean?"

"Think about it. If they hurt her, we abandon the search. Then we go after them with the police and the Feds and every other tool we can find."

Anna grew silent and wiped her eyes. "You do have a point."

While Anna took a shower and prepared for bed, Casey went out on the back porch. He called Jerry LaBonte and told him about the hideous call. Jerry cursed at the story.

"I think you're right that they were bluffing," said Jerry. "But knowing about the call helps. I'll pass this on to my electronics guy." Casey thanked him and returned to the room.

Anna and Casey kissed before they went to their separate beds. He had a hard time letting her go.

In the morning Casey woke to find her cuddled up to him in his bed. When she woke a moment later, she looked embarrassed. "I'm sorry. I had the nightmare of the snowy field again." He held her and assured her that he didn't mind. They kissed for some time, pressed together.

He had to struggle not to make love to her. He couldn't take advantage of her in this situation.

CHAPTER FORTY THREE

Derek came in from giving Casey's dog her evening walk and found Cheyenne sitting on the edge of their bed. She chewed at her lower lip.

Derek sat next to her and put an arm around her. "Honey, everything's going to work out. Casey will find the treasure."

"Yes, but this whole thing makes no sense," she said, slapping the bed in frustration. "Why would the kidnappers insist that Casey help?"

She stood and paced. "And why make them hunt for a treasure that's been lost for centuries, that may not even exist? Why not force them to knock over a liquor store? Or a bank?"

She reached for the phone and called her sister Cinnamon. Cinnamon started to chat about news and family business, but Cheyenne cut her off after a few moments.

Then Cheyenne filled her sister in on the details about Anna and McKenna, the man at the nursing home, and the devotion their brother exhibited toward Anna, and the search for Blackbeard's treasure.

Cheyenne asked, "Can you think of anyone who would want to hurt Casey?"

Cinnamon thought for a moment. "How about that bozo who married Grace?"

"I know he's jealous of Casey. But I don't know if he hates him enough to hurt him. Besides, how would a cluck like Rudy know a classy woman like Anna?" Cinnamon didn't know.

Cheyenne chewed her lip. She asked, "Did Casey punch out Sarah's ex-husband one time?"

Cinnamon laughed. "That dunce. Casey ran him off when he threatened Sarah. I don't think it came to a fist fight."

"All right. Let's go another way," said Cheyenne. "Do I

remember that you know someone who lives in Shoal Creek?"

"Yeah," said Cinnamon, after thinking for a moment. "Durango's pal Mini tends bar in a restaurant in town. Why?"

"About twenty years ago, Anna went through a hard breakup with a guy named Nick from Shoal Creek. He tried to rape her, but she fought him off. Anyhow, right after that he went off the deep end. The town blamed her and she moved away. Do you think you could get Mini to ask around a little?"

"I can ask. He's lived there most of his life, I think. I imagine he knows everyone."

"The guy who stole McKenna may be named Nick," Cheyenne said, remembering the old man at the nursing home. "Don't make me explain."

"Okay," said her sister. "Let me call Durango."

"Sooner the better," Cheyenne emphasized. "Beside the danger to the girl, I've never seen Casey so frantic."

Cinnamon paused. "Frantic?"

"Yeah. The feelings he has for Anna go way beyond friendship, but I just don't. . ." her voice trailed off. Cinnamon told her she'd get to work on it.

"Good work," said Derek as Cheyenne laid down the phone.

"Thank you," she snapped.

"Er. . ."

"Yes?" she said, fire in her eyes.

"How about making love?"

"Great idea," she asserted.

* * * * *

Cinnamon hung up from talking to Cheyenne and called her boyfriend. She caught him about to leave his job at a small chemical plant in Milwaukee. Durango, a gigantic man, held a doctorate in Chemical Engineering from Wisconsin.

His best friends were also enormous, genial, and talented. All of them held advanced degrees and all rode motorcycles the size of Clydesdales.

Cinnamon told Durango about Cheyenne's phone call. Durango thought for a few moments. Then he told Cinnamon he'd get back to her.

Chapter Forty Four

McKenna woke up from another dream. This time she could remember it. Her dream friend had walked with her to her closet, and opened the door. He'd pointed to the clothes bar.

Awake now, she eyed the clothes bar. She could use it as a club.

If McKenna could incapacitate Scott and his father, she knew she could get over the fence. She'd competed on the track team at the high school the last few years. She could pole vault over that fence if she had to.

She decided that she needed a sharp knife. She gave it some thought.

She heard the minivan chugging down the drive. She walked out to the living room and saw Scott sitting alone on the couch. He looked up. She came into the room, trying to look apologetic.

He wore a pair of shorts. She saw how his right knee had swelled up. She stifled a smile of satisfaction as he gave her a vicious sneer.

"Hello," McKenna said, giving him a look that she'd practiced to appear both seductive and contrite. She swished past him into the kitchen and found a plastic bag. Opening the freezer, she put a few ice cubes in the bag and tied it shut. She grabbed a dish towel.

She slinked over to him. Kneeling, she flashed him a comforting grin. Placing his leg on the coffee table, she put the ice on his knee and tied the bag in place with the towel. He winced as the cold struck him.

"What the..." he managed.

"Your knee swelled up," she said, sounding sweet and

concerned. She used the dishtowel to tie the ice to his knee. "We have to get the swelling down. Now keep that on for fifteen minutes."

She sat next to him on the couch. "I'm sorry I hurt you," she lied. "I shouldn't have been so angry and frustrated with you. You've been so kind to me. I know you didn't mean anything when you put your hand on my shoulder." Apologizing to a creep who held her hostage made her ill. But she had to seem authentic.

McKenna's speech created the desired effect. Scott managed a weak grin. His shoulders relaxed.

"I understand," he said. "I startled you. I apologize." She touched the knee and laid her hand on his bare thigh. She beamed. He returned the smile.

"Let me fix you some lunch. You stay there and relax," she cooed. "Don't move, now."

He nodded with a little smile. Just what she wanted.

Once in the kitchen McKenna rummaged through the clutter in the drawers. She found a sharpening steel and a small whetstone. She tucked the stone into her sock and pulled the elastic cuff of the sweat pants down over it. She took a steak knife from another drawer and hid that in her other sock.

She used the steel to sharpen the other kitchen knives, which wouldn't have cut mashed potatoes. *What a couple of slobs*, she thought.

CHAPTER FORTY FIVE

Casey helped Anna into Roger's boat and they headed for St. Margaret's. "The island runs about a half-mile long," Roger told them over the drone of the outboard motor. "In the center it rises twenty feet above sea level. I can put you ashore on a rocky beach on the eastern side."

"Does anyone live out there?" asked Casey.

Roger shook his head. "A few hardy souls camp out there in the summer. You can bunk and escape the rain in a lean-to shelter. Somebody put up a couple of outhouses and a freshwater pump. The power lines go across the island and there's even an electrical outlet at the shelter, in case you need to charge cell phones or something."

"Should have brought a television," said Casey. Roger chuckled. Anna whacked his arm and gave him a little grin. "What?" he said. "The NCAA tournament is on." She grinned and he put an arm around her and kissed her cheek.

"Most of the island is nothing more than a sandbar covered with beach grass," Roger said.

"Any oak trees?" asked Anna.

"Oak?" Roger rubbed his chin, and then shook his head. "I don't remember any. There's a fair stand of pine and a lot of scrub. I could ask some of the old-timers in town if they remember any oaks from a long time ago."

Anna shrugged and asked him to do so. She wrapped her arms around herself, looking worried. Casey squeezed her shoulder to reassure her.

Roger promised to come over every couple of days to deliver food, or bring them back to the bed-and-breakfast if they needed a night or two indoors.

"With any luck," said Roger, "You'll find the treasure in no time." Casey, who had never been much for camping, said he hoped they wouldn't need more than a few days' supplies.

Roger helped them haul ashore their sleeping bags, tent, tools, and provisions. Anna and Casey bid him goodbye and then hiked toward the wooded area on the western side. "Prudence lived out here?" Casey asked, amazed.

Anna nodded. "I'm sure she saw the island as a good place to hide. If Blackbeard ever found out Prudence had survived, he'd have come to kill her. Even after he died, she wanted to be away from everyone. Not only that, she thought she might be implicated in some of his crimes. " She adjusted the pack on her back and squinted into the morning sun. She took a different grip on the bag of groceries. "When I was a little girl, we came out here often for picnics on nice days."

The two of them stopped in front of an old overgrown cemetery surrounded by a waist-high cast iron fence. Two cement pillars framed the entrance and an elaborate cast-iron archway joined the pillars.

"Prudence, Will, and several of their descendants lie over here," said Anna, directing his attention to a group of ancient stones. "I buried my mom and dad there." She pointed to a couple of more recent headstones. "I think I'd like to be buried here too."

She broke off. A tall man, muscular and handsome, advanced toward them out of the trees. He had the same coppery hair and green eyes as Anna and appeared to be about her age. Casey liked him at once. "Hello," the man smiled. "My goodness, you must be Anna."

Anna held out her hand. "Yes."

"I'd recognize you anywhere. We're relatives. I'm Daniel."

"That's my grandfather's name," smiled Anna. "He lives in a nursing home in Illinois."

Daniel's face fell. "I'm sorry to hear that," he said. Then he recovered his smile. "Casey. Nice to meet you."

Casey returned his handshake, noting the man's good, firm dry grip. Daniel resembled Anna a great deal. His eyes sparkled with good humor and intelligence.

"Come camp with me. I have a fire going. We'll need it tonight. It gets pretty cold out here at night," Daniel said. "Except in the summer. Then we keep warm by slapping mosquitoes."

Anna and Casey chuckled.

They walked to an old shelter, built near the sea. They found two other people sitting by the fire. "I want you to meet my new friends," said Daniel. "Say hello to—"

"We've met," Casey grinned. He felt a chill breeze again as he shook hands with Cole and Elaine McClelland.

Casey appreciated having these people around to comfort Anna with him. Just being with them encouraged him, as well.

So why am I feeling that something's wrong? Casey thought.

Then it occurred to him. Daniel greeted him by name. Casey couldn't remember Anna introducing him. *She must have,* he thought.

CHAPTER FORTY SIX

McKenna spent the afternoon chatting up Scott about music, school, dance clubs, and her drama work. Just before dinner, it grew pitch dark outside. He took her out to see the stars. Having grown up next to the big city, the dramatic star field out in the country impressed her.

He hobbled around the fence perimeter with her, leaning on an old golf club. She tried not to smile.

"Any towns near here?" she asked, trying to sound casual.

He pointed. "You go about ten miles that way and you come to Bridgeton. Not much of a town. Three bars, a grain elevator, and a gas station that sells some groceries, beer, bait and fishing licenses, and like that."

"What's a grain elevator?"

He explained. She nodded and said uh-huh a few times. *Fine,* she thought. *I can run ten miles once I get away from these clods.*

While he yakked, McKenna saw a switch box for the electric fence on the porch and another on the other side of the gate, both padlocked. She looked around, looking for an idea.

Then she saw what she needed.

Next to a woodpile not far from the house lay an old wooden ladder. A couple of the rungs were broken but if she could be careful, she could use it to get over the fence.

When they came back inside, she thanked him "for the lovely walk." Then she stood on her tiptoes and kissed his cheek. He reddened.

Kissing him made her want to shower and immerse her face in Listerine. She struggled not to wipe her mouth in front of him.

As she intended, he misconstrued the purpose of the kiss.

He reddened and his face became tender. "When this thing ends, maybe we can see each other. I think when you see what's going on, you'll understand why we did this. I'll—" his voice had a slight quaver—"have something to offer you then."

Uh, huh. Jabba the Hutt telling Princess Leia, "Soon you will learn to appreciate me." Yech. She had a brief vision of pouring bleach over her face.

She tried to make her smile look coy, but inviting. She wanted him to think he was having an effect on her.

McKenna, working hard to cultivate the image of an air-headed ditz, forced herself to ask inane questions. At dinner the two men began discussing fishing.

"I like to fish that pond on Vanderhye's property for smallmouth bass in the summer," the father grunted, mouth crammed with cheap bread. "He stocks it every couple years."

"I didn't know Vanderhye let you use it," mumbled the son through a mouthful of instant mashed potatoes.

"He doesn't," sneered the father. "But he doesn't go out and count the smallmouth in the pond, either." Both laughed.

Trying not to choke, she asked in her best ditzy voice, "Could one of you tell me the difference between largemouth and smallmouth bass?" They stared at her for a moment. Then they laughed at her.

She gave a splendid look of confusion. Then she said, "Oh, yeah. How silly of me." She pretended to be embarrassed, thinking, *Laugh it up, you morons.*

McKenna waited until the TV was off and the two bedrooms down the hall fell silent. The two men who'd stolen her were confident that they'd sealed her in this compound.

The steak knife she'd swiped from the silverware drawer came from of a set of eight, but she knew these two slobs wouldn't notice. She'd hidden this knife in her socks along with the whetstone.

She'd brought a newspaper to her room and wrapped the

paper around the knife and the whetstone. She put her pillow over everything. The paper and the pillow deadened the scraping sound as she whet the knife. The farmhouse, built to withstand severe winters, had thick well-insulated inner walls. The two men wouldn't hear.

McKenna worked at sharpening the knife for an hour. Then she examined her handiwork and tested the edge with her finger and grinned. She'd turned it into a scalpel.

CHAPTER FORTY SEVEN

The five treasure hunters sat around a campfire in the cool evening air. The McClellands talked about their plans to spend their share.

"Cole and Elaine," Daniel said, "we're glad to have your help but I don't think you want the treasure. It's cursed. People have died over it, been slaughtered, burned, buried alive, and drowned. Blackbeard almost murdered one of my ancestors over it."

"Do you think the treasure is evil?" Anna asked.

He frowned, laying a fresh log on the campfire. "Stede Bonnet told a story just before they hanged him."

He told the story of Stede Bonnet, the army major who became a pirate. Bonnet, Daniel said, died on the gallows in Charleston, South Carolina. Daniel related the tale of the handsome stranger in the red silk.

"Bonnet told his jailer that the crew lived in terror for the two weeks that the stranger stayed on board. The crew of *Queen Anne's Revenge* spoke of this stranger with fear and ashen faces. They believed that they were in the presence of Satan. Blackbeard convinced the men that he had made a pact with the devil and that the settlement included their own immortal souls."

Elaine shivered.

"The secret of Plum Point died with Bonnet," said Daniel. "Except for my ancestor Prudence Lutrelle."

"What a story," said Cole.

"Stede Bonnet believed that he would spend eternity looking into the stranger's red eyes and horrible grin," Daniel said, poking at the fire with a long stick.

Casey, lying on top of his sleeping bag, propped himself up

on one elbow and stared into the fire. He thought the story illustrated what a master showman Blackbeard was. The trouble Teach took in setting up this charade must have been significant. The drama plunged his superstitious sailors into horror.

Next to him, Anna shuddered. Casey looked at her and saw her face drawn with strain. "Nehushtan," she muttered to him.

Anna rose, went to her sleeping bag and picked up her sleepwear. "I keep thinking how many people died for the sake of this treasure," Anna said. "If it weren't for my daughter, I sure wouldn't look for it."

Cole smiled, waving a hand in dismissal. "Anna, gold and jewels can't be good or bad."

Anna walked away toward the outhouse, but turned back. She said, "I hope those creeps who kidnapped McKenna enjoy it as much as the rest of the treasure hunters have."

The group fell silent for some time.

Blackbeard's demonic laugh joined the night voices that echoed in the wind that blew through the pine trees. The night grew colder.

* * * * *

Anna slept little for the first few hours of the night. She woke up when Nehushtan flitted into her dreams again, terrifying her. She dreamt about Blackbeard, too.

She huddled in her sleeping bag, freezing cold despite her sweatshirt, sweat pants, heavy wool sweat socks and the thick sleeping bag. Casey slept in his sleeping bag on the ground beside her. She wanted him to embrace and stroke her in his gentle way, but didn't want to wake him and spoil his night's sleep.

Trying to be gentle, she turned Casey's wrist so she could look at his watch. 1:38. Phooey. She lay back, afraid to go back to sleep.

By the light of some embers glowing in fire pit, she looked at Casey's face. He stirred just a little.

She thought about how terrified her daughter must be. Was she sleeping? Eating? Tears of anxiety ran as she prayed: *Dear God, please help us find this treasure and put things right. Please protect my little Mickey—*

She jumped as a gentle hand touched her shoulder. Casey wiped the tears from her cheeks. "You okay?" he whispered.

"I'm scared," she sniffed. "And freezing."

"Come on in here with me," he offered. He pulled down the zipper on his bag. "There's room for both of us." She considered for about a fifth of a second before she nodded.

He folded back the edge of the sleeping bag. She slid in next to him.

She smiled and hugged him, and the cold eased away.

She drew back and looked into his eyes. She pressed her body against his. Their lips came together.

When Anna kissed him, her fears began to dissolve. Their hands began the familiar caressing of seventeen years ago as the kisses deepened. They helped one another remove most of their clothing. . .

Just before things reached the point of no return she thought about the people they were camping with.

Anna drew back and whispered an apology. "Casey," she said. "Please, we can't. We'll wake the others."

"Are you kidding?" he puffed.

She smiled and stroked his face. "Give me some more time, please."

"Okay," he managed.

She pulled her sweatshirt closed and zipped it up a little. Turning her back to his front, she snuggled against him. His body felt warm and comfortable. Nehushtan couldn't get her while she snuggled with Casey.

She listened to his breathing. In a few moments he'd gone

back to sleep. She snuggled his right arm between her breasts and wrapped her arms around it.

Sometime later Anna woke up. She found Casey's hand inside her sweatshirt, cradling her breast. Though she enjoyed it, his gentle touch distracted her, making sleeping difficult. She took his fingers and began to move the hand.

When he stirred, she stopped. She sighed. *No sense disturbing him anymore,* she decided. She covered his hand with hers and pulled herself closer to him.

For the first time in years, Anna soothed herself by thinking about sex with Casey. She recalled the little house, the pizza, the kissing, and how they had made love with such deep joy. When she fell asleep, Nehushtan didn't return to torment her.

* * * * *

Behind her, Casey grinned to himself and struggled not to think of sex. By now he'd become so desperate to make love to Anna that he kept having visions of himself running shrieking through the island, wild-eyed and hands over his head. Still he knew he couldn't push her. The situation remained too tense to complicate her life further. He sighed, and composed his mind for sleep.

CHAPTER FORTY EIGHT

At dinner the next night, McKenna had to struggle not to show her intense apprehension. She had completed her preparations to escape. The thought scared her.

But didn't alter her determination.

McKenna picked at her food. Her minimal appetite concerned Scott. "C'mon, McKenna. You gotta eat."

"Huh," grunted the father. "She ain't gonna need no food much longer."

"Dad," said the son, his tone a mild rebuke. But the father's statement did frighten her. She knew she didn't have much time.

She thought about that vicious and sadistic leer that came into the father's eyes whenever he spoke to her. When he'd wipe his mouth with the back of his hand, she knew that he was thinking about killing her.

In the last few days the leers and the comments about pain and death had become standard conversation for him. He planned to maim and torture her before he killed her, probably rape her too, whether or not her mom found the treasure. He'd been working himself up to the violence and looking forward to it. He got excited thinking about it.

She forced herself to eat some of the canned beef stew.

Tomorrow.

Chapter Forty Nine

Cinnamon fumbled for her bedside phone at 7:00 A. M. "Hello," she mumbled, trying not to sound resentful at being awakened early on her day off.

"Yo," boomed a deep voice on the other end. "It's Mini."

"Hey, buddy," she drowsed. "What's up?"

"I think I know where they took the girl, yo."

"What!" Cinnamon came alert at once.

"Yo. Durango called me. I spent the last few days investigating. I know this Nick character from the bar. I went to see Anna's aunt and uncle. They gave me Nick's address. I went over there and talked to Nora, his wife."

Cinnamon hurried into the washroom. "Go on," she said, brushing her teeth.

"Well, Nora, she told me Nick went snowmobiling up north with his son, kid named Dale, in trouble all the time here in town. They've been gone for several days. She was puzzled."

Cinnamon spat toothpaste. "Why did that puzzle her?"

"He's never done this before, I mean, take off to go snowmobiling. He doesn't own a snowmobile. He doesn't even have the money to rent one. She says he sometimes goes up to this cabin by himself for a day or two, but never this long. She didn't seem worried, though. I'm guessing she's glad to have the numbskull gone for a while," said Mini. "I know he beats her." He continued his narrative as Cinnamon brushed out her blond hair.

In the midst of his monologue, Cinnamon heard a voice: *Nick. That's him. He's the one.* She turned to look behind her. No one, of course. She shook her head.

Mini went on, explaining about Nick and how he beat his wife, his nasty personality and terrible reputation in the town of

Shoal Creek.

"Did his wife tell you how to get to the farm?" asked Cinnamon.

"Yo," said Mini. "She made me a map. We have to go about two and a half hours north of here. Near the town of Bridgeton, way out in the country."

"So this Nick's never gone snowmobiling for an extended period like this?" asked Cinnamon.

"No," said Mini.

"Call Rush," Cinnamon said. "See if he'll come. I'll grab Durango and we'll meet you." She threw on some warm clothes and sprinted to her car, punching in Durango's number on her cell phone.

"Get dressed," she commanded him, careening down the road.

She found Durango at his apartment and they jumped into his Dodge SUV. They met Mini and his even bigger friend Rush at Mini's apartment in Shoal Creek. Durango, pushing his truck hard, reached the farm in about three hours.

As they pulled into the drive, Cinnamon heard the voice again. *This is it. She's here.* Again she looked around. Again no one was there. She shook her head, bewildered at hearing voices.

"What's wrong?" asked Durango.

"Nothing," she said. "I'm sure we've come to the right place."

"Wait, Durango," said the huge man nicknamed Rush who had a graduate degree in Electrical engineering. "That's an electric fence."

"Around the house?" rumbled Mini. "Who puts an electric fence around a house?"

"No one," shrugged Rush. "Except someone running a jail." Durango nodded.

Rush bailed out of the SUV and ran to the junction box. He

used bolt cutters to snip off the lock on the box and had no trouble shutting off the power to the electric fence. He hollered something about "Amateur Night." He used the bolt cutters to demolish the lock on the gate and threw it open. Durango drove up to the house.

As they climbed the porch steps, the picture window smashed outward with a splintering crash, startling them all as glass flew everywhere. A tall girl stood there, staring at them, looking dazed. Cinnamon scrutinized the girl's features. In that moment, she understood why Casey was so worried.

CHAPTER FIFTY

McKenna awakened early and reviewed the plan. She had to wait for the father to go to town, as he did every day. He'd buy supplies—Slim Jims, potato chips and liquor—and come back breathing cheap beer.

That didn't bother her today. She'd be long gone by the time he rolled home.

Using her knife, she cut her top sheet into strips. She knotted them together.

She thought about the dreams she'd been having the last few nights. Someone had come to take care of her. He had red hair, like hers, and soft, wise green eyes, like her mom's. And like Myrthynne.

She felt pretty sure he had an unusual name, like Gary, but she couldn't remember. She also couldn't recall his face when she was awake, but she knew him at once when she dreamed at night.

McKenna hid the cut-up sheets and her closet clothes pole and the duct tape under her mattress. She tore a few lengths of the tape and stuck a corner of each of the lengths to the back of her door.

Then, she sat on the bed, waiting for the father to leave. She thought of her mom's courage. And her father's courage.

She also knew, now, that the plot involved someone beside the father and Scott. She'd heard the father talking to someone on the cell phone from time to time. Whoever it was had to be the brains of the outfit, she figured.

About 10:00 A. M., she heard the front door slam. In a few moments, the minivan chugged down the driveway.

Forcing herself to be patient, she waited a couple of minutes. She used the time to arrange her hair so it would appear seductive. Scott had complimented her hair often, making it clear that he wanted to get his hands on it.

McKenna put on makeup, overdoing it. She arranged and then tied the bathrobe so it would display her legs when she walked.

McKenna took several deep calming breaths, preparing her mind to play the role of a coquettish ditz. *Here we go.* She oozed into the living room.

Scott sat, looking at a newspaper.

"Why do you bother to read that thing?" she asked in her best naïve voice, as if a newspaper couldn't interest her less.

He laughed. "I like to look at the pictures," he said. She sidled over to him. She bent her left knee, slouching just a little to the side. The robe fell open, affording him an enticing look at her leg. "Where's your dad?" she purred. She ruffled her luxuriant hair a little, hoping she looked sexy.

She struggled not to giggle at the thought of herself as a— what was that old word? A vamp, that had to be it.

He swallowed before answering. "He left for town a few moments ago. He'll be gone awhile. When he gets back we'll call your mother for an update."

She smiled and walked to the window. His breath came in gasps. She put her hands in the robe pockets and pulled the robe tight around her rear. She could feel him staring at her.

She recited the line she'd rehearsed all morning. "I've been thinking about what you said the other day. Maybe later, after this ends—" She turned back, head down. She raised her eyes. "Maybe we could start seeing each other."

She heard him breathing hard now. She went to him and extended her hand. "Come on," she said, motioning with her head. "I know what will make that knee feel a lot better." She gave him the smile her mother used on her father.

He followed her into her bedroom as if in a trance. She put her hands on his shoulders and backed him to the wall next to her closet. She loosened the tie on her robe. It fell open. He put his arms around her waist.

He seemed a trifle disappointed that she wore the sports bra and spandex shorts she had on the day they stole her.

She ran her hands down over his chest, then his stomach, seductive and slow. He kissed her neck.

McKenna tried not to retch as she ran her hands over the front of his jeans. As she hoped, he'd put the keys in his left pocket.

She loosened his belt and undid the button. She lowered the zipper and eased the jeans off his hips. When they dropped to the floor, she looked down, then back up into his eyes, smiling as if in anticipation. "You know what?" she murmured.

"What?" he managed to gasp.

"I know a secret," she whispered. "Here, let me show you a little trick." With a mysterious smile, she used her feet to spread his legs wider. She took his hair in one of her hands and pulled his head back so he looked up at the ceiling. With her other hand she pulled his tee-shirt up over his face. He moaned with pleasure.

She gritted her teeth.

Striking like a cobra, she kneed him in the groin. He expelled his breath in an agonized whoosh. She side-kicked the bad knee. It bent outward at a sickening angle.

Tangled in the t-shirt, he tripped over the jeans. He staggered off balance.

She kicked his groin again. He bent over, now yelling with the nauseating pain. She ducked and spun a vicious whip-kick to his ear. He went down, dazed, curled into a ball of agony.

She stepped back and reached under her mattress to her weapons cache. She extracted the closet clothes bar and swung it as hard as she could into his injured knee. His feral scream echoed through the whole house.

She steeled herself and struck him in the temple with the closet bar. He groaned and collapsed to the floor, now almost unconscious. She grabbed a length of duct tape off the door and pulled his hands behind him. She taped the wrists together. Then she taped his ankles. He lay there, too dazed to resist.

McKenna, moving like lightning but in complete control, reached under her mattress again for the strips that she'd knotted together. She put a foot against Scott's throat, choking him.

She pulled a slip-knot around his wrists, securing them behind him.

She tied his feet to the rags holding his wrists together, leaving him in an inverted C-shape.

McKenna now jammed a rag into his mouth. She duct-taped over the rag so he wouldn't be able to chew the makeshift ropes off. For good measure she reinforced the bonds with more tape.

He stared at her, his eyes watering, groaning.

Reaching into his jean pocket, she pulled out the keys, then kicked and tugged him into her closet. "I'll send the cops back for you, Tubby," she snarled. "I hope you rot in jail forever."

He strained to say something. McKenna ignored him and slammed the closet door. She turned the key in the old-fashioned lock and dropped the key down a heating duct in the floor. Now she pushed her dresser in front of the closet door.

Running into Scott's room, McKenna found two pairs of heavy socks in his dresser. After unlocking the hall closet, she rummaged through the clutter and found her running shoes and her parka.

She pulled on the socks, then her jeans and the Nikes, a tee-shirt and a hooded sweatshirt. Then she slipped into her parka and pulled on the heavy mittens.

She decided not to spend time unlocking the front door. She crashed a kitchen chair through the picture window next to the door. She started to climb out, but screeched in surprise.

Three gigantic men in black leather jackets and a woman stood on the porch, looking amazed.

CHAPTER FIFTY ONE

One of the men recovered enough to smile. "Hello, McKenna," he said.

McKenna backed across the living room to the opposite wall and slid down it to the floor. She pulled out her knife and held it up. She started to cry.

The man stood outside the shattered window and held up his hands. "Wait," he said. "We're the good guys. Casey sent us to get you. Are you McKenna DiBiasi?"

McKenna, too scared to say anything, managed to nod.

The woman climbed through the window and walked over to kneel before McKenna, handing her a business card. "Honey, don't be frightened. You don't have to be afraid any more. I'm Cinnamon Fixx, Casey's sister. I'm an attorney." Cinnamon reached into her purse. She pulled out a picture of her with Casey, and then her driver's license.

McKenna, beginning to relax, examined the photos and identification for a few moments. Cinnamon exchanged glances and nods with the men. They'd seen what she had, also.

"Can you introduce me?" McKenna asked, as Cinnamon helped her to her feet.

Cinnamon introduced Durango, Mini and Rush. McKenna began to relax. She said, "You guys really came to help me?" Cinnamon nodded. McKenna started to sob and held up her arms to be hugged. "Thank you," she said. "They scared me. They were going to—" but she couldn't say it.

Cinnamon embraced McKenna and stroked the beautiful hair. "Don't worry now, McKenna," said Durango, his massive hand on her shoulder. "Anyone wants to hurt you, they have to go through us." The other men murmured agreement.

"Where'd they go?" asked the one called Mini.

"The father left about a half hour ago to drive into town. The son might be unconscious. I left him tied him up in the bedroom closet—"

McKenna stopped talking as she saw her four new friends stare at her for a moment, then at each other. The one named Rush said, "Do you mean to tell us that you beat the hell out of this guy, hogtied him and shoved him in a closet?"

She shrugged. "Well, yeah—"

The new friends bellowed with laughter. When they settled down a bit, she pointed to the bedroom where she'd imprisoned Scott.

"Leave the stupid sumbitch there," said Mini.

"Great," said Cinnamon. She'd called the state police on her cell phone. "Okay," she said. "The state police are on their way. Is the father armed? Do we need to get out of here?"

"No, I don't think so. I've never seen a weapon," said McKenna, and again hugged Cinnamon.

Cinnamon disentangled a hand. "Let's try to call your mom," said Cinnamon, dialing the cell phone again.

CHAPTER FIFTY TWO

The clue of the two oak trees had proved worthless. The treasure hunters hadn't found so much as an oak stump, not even an acorn. Anna stamped her foot in frustration.

The group broke into two parties. Anna, Casey, and Daniel started exploring near the graveyard for the initials, while Cole and Elaine worked the other side of the island.

In a few hours they took a break near the pillars of the gate to the old graveyard. Casey jumped when his cell phone rang. He walked away a little bit as he flipped it open.

"Hi, Casey, it's Cinnamon. Good news."

"Cinnamon?" he said, dumbfounded. "What happened?"

"We found McKenna. She's safe. She wants to talk to her mom."

"Anna's right here," he said, running back and seizing her hand. To Anna he said, "My sister Cinnamon. She found McKenna."

Anna's hand flew to her mouth and she snatched the phone. She spoke to Cinnamon for a moment. She paused while the young lawyer turned the phone over to her daughter. "McKenna, are you all right?" She was almost dancing up and down, her free hand clenching and unclenching in anxiety. She listened and seized Casey's arm. "What about—"she swallowed—"what about your hand?" She squeezed his arm harder and began to cry. "Oh, thank God. Where are you?" She listened, waving her hand and dancing. Tears of relief streamed down her face.

After a few moments, Casey took the phone back and talked to his sister. "Hey, shouldn't you guys get out of there?"

"No, not necessary," said Cinnamon. Casey could hear the smile in her voice. "McKenna handled one of the guys. He's locked in the bedroom closet."

"Huh?"

"Yeah. McKenna crippled him, then beat him senseless with a closet clothes rod and tied him up with duct tape." Both laughed.

Casey said, "Call the state cops, maybe the FBI, right away."

"Already did it," she said. "The troopers are on their way. The father, a guy named Nick—Mini knows the creep—went into town. He won't be back before the police show up. If he does show up, I'll have a struggle to keep Mini from obliterating him."

"How did you get involved in this?" he asked.

"Cheyenne called me. After she talked to Anna, someone told her that this Nick guy had taken McKenna."

"How did the person know?"

"Cheyenne didn't know. But she asked me to check out Shoal Creek." The young lawyer paused. "McKenna wants to talk to you."

"Okay," said Casey. "Put her on."

The girl came on the phone. "Hello, Dr. Fixx."

"Please," he said, "call me Casey."

"Okay, sure. Er. . .am I related to you?"

He took a deep breath and looked at Anna, who had walked away a few feet, chewing at a thumbnail, a typical pose for her when lost in thought. "Yes, McKenna. Your mom and I will talk about it with you when I see you, I promise."

"Okay."

"Look, you're safe now. Those guys will protect you," Casey assured her. "You're going to love them."

"I already do."

"Great. Put Cinnamon back on, okay?"

"Sure. Bye, Casey," she said, with affection. He got a little choked.

When Cinnamon came back on the line, she filled him in on

how they'd found McKenna and what had transpired. "Thanks, Cinnamon. Tell the guys thanks, too."

"Any luck finding the treasure?"

"Not yet. We may come home. I'll call later," he said, and they hung up.

Anna, chewing a different fingernail, stood a few steps away. She turned back to him and said, "I think we still need to find the treasure."

Casey blinked. "You must be kidding. I feel like even if I found the loot I'd want to shove it into a volcano."

"I don't want others risking their lives looking for it."

"Anna," Casey said. "Some guy named Nick stole McKenna. Do you know who that might be?"

She blanched and shuddered, then explained about Nick, their romance, the attempted rape, the breakup, and how she had to leave Shoal Creek. "He's a thug," she concluded. "I haven't talked to him in more than twenty years."

"You mean to tell me," Casey said, "that twenty years later, this guy still blames you because his life didn't go the way he thinks it should have?"

"I'm afraid so," she nodded. "Did they arrest him?"

"No," he said. "They got another guy, this Nick's son, maybe a year or two older than McKenna. He and Nick abducted McKenna. They were holding her at a farm in Wisconsin. McKenna beat the son into mush."

"I think Aunt Marian told me his name is Dale," said Anna, looking sick with worry.

"He told McKenna to call him Scott. But I don't get it. Why would this Nick be after me?" Casey asked.

She shrugged. "Nick didn't plan this train wreck. He may be crazy, but he's not smart enough to come up with this scheme. Someone else has to be involved. Someone who knows about you and the treasure."

Casey considered, and then shrugged. "Should we put a

time limit on the search? I want to see McKenna."

"So do I," Anna said, "but we still have to contend with whoever set this up. If we go home now, they'll try to get at us some other way. We might be able to buy them off with the treasure and put an end to this."

Casey leaned against the graveyard pillar as Anna hugged him. He felt the uneven surface of the pillar and realized that a design had been chiseled into it.

He turned and examined it with the flashlight. He pointed. Anna looked. Their eyes met.

The pillar had the intricate design of an oak tree chiseled into it.

CHAPTER FIFTY THREE

Nick Wolfe drove down the icy country road toward his grandmother's house. When she died, his family kept the house and outbuildings, but rented out the farmland. Nick liked to use the house for private weekends away from his wife and her stupid kids.

He leered, thinking that he'd call Anna and frighten her again. This time, he planned to twist her daughter's arm up behind her back and make the girl scream into the phone.

He had never killed anyone. But that didn't scare him.

Nick smirked, thinking of how he could best take advantage of the situation. Once they found the treasure, he'd kill Anna's daughter.

First, however, he planned to enjoy himself with her. Yeah. She had to be a virgin. After he'd had enough, he'd drag her out to the lower acreage and cut her throat. Then he'd stash her body out in the back lot. No one would find her corpse out there. The soil in the tree line would hide that body forever.

He also planned how he'd kill the green-eyed witch who'd wrecked his life. He'd shoot Anna in the feet, then the knees, the thighs, taking his time, working his way slowly up her body. He'd let her bleed for a while, then tell her what he'd done to her daughter. Then he'd shoot out those green eyes he still saw in nightmares.

That Gareth creep, too. Nick couldn't wait to kill her boyfriend. Nick had always known Anna should have spent her life with him, having his kids. Well, he could get his life together at last.

He'd just needed the right break and some money. The break had come. He'd have plenty of money now.

A siren erupted behind him, startling him so that he all but went through the roof. A state trooper. He looked at his speedometer and calmed down. Well under the limit. He'd had two beers, that's all. No problem.

He pulled off onto the shoulder of the road. The state trooper shot past him.

Nick started to pull out but stopped when he heard a *second* cruiser. This one rocketed past him as well, in the direction of. . .

It hit him.

He pulled out and put the accelerator down. With the old minivan choking and sputtering in protest, he followed the two police cruisers to his grandmother's house, just keeping them in sight.

The electric fence stood wide open and a Dodge SUV sat in the front yard. He saw the shattered picture window. Two enormous biker types stood on the porch talking to one of the cops.

Nick turned the van around and blasted off, the engine of the old minivan sputtering and coughing. He headed back toward Milwaukee and called Mr. Cray.

"Bad news," said Nick, when the man picked up. He told him about the troopers.

Cray cursed. "All right," said the man. "Time for plan B."

"What's plan B?" asked Nick.

"Pull over, Nick, and take some notes."

Nick complied.

"Go to O'Hare Airport. Dump your van in long-term parking and find the American Airlines terminal. I'll leave a ticket for you."

"Where to?" asked Nick.

"North Carolina." The man continued giving his instructions.

CHAPTER FIFTY FOUR

Casey found another oak tree chiseled into the second pillar ten feet away. Near sundown Elaine found the initials W. O. chiseled into a lump of granite not far from the pillars.

"Now what?" Casey said.

"The instructions said to look into the light at ten o'clock," said Daniel.

"What does *that* mean?" Casey asked. Daniel shook his head.

Elaine asked, "Why don't we start digging?"

"We can't start digging. Let's haul our tools in and start in the morning," Casey suggested. In the daylight that remained, the men hauled the tools to the graveyard.

* * * * *

Casey's phone rang as they prepared for sleep.

"Hey, big bro." Cinnamon's voice sounded cheerful. "We've taken McKenna to Anna's aunt and uncle in Shoal Creek. The guys and I plan to stay with her for a couple of days. I'll keep her with me until you get back."

Casey murmured thanks to his sister.

"Casey?" she asked.

"Yeah."

"This kid is my niece, right?"

He hesitated. "Yeah."

"She doesn't know, does she?"

"No."

"Did you know about her?"

"Not until a few days ago. I've never met her, either, just talked for a few moments on the phone."

"Do you plan to tell her?"

"Oh, yes."

"You're going to love her," Cinnamon said. "McKenna's an extraordinary young woman. Are you coming home soon?"

"Not right away," said Casey. "We found a big clue. We think we need to keep looking."

"Could we bring her to you?" asked his sister.

"Let me check." He looked at Anna. "Cinnamon wants to bring McKenna down here."

Anna raised her eyebrows, a big smile blossoming, like the sun breaking through a bunch of clouds. "Do you think it's safe?"

"I think all of us could keep her safe here. What do you say?"

Anna nodded, excited. "Okay. Tell her to bring Durango, too."

* * * * *

Anna and Casey slipped into the sleeping bags they'd zipped together. He'd just about drifted off when Anna whispered, "Casey?"

"What?" he mumbled.

"We're alone."

He sat up, expecting to see Cole and Elaine asleep on the other side of the fire.

They weren't there. He didn't see Daniel, either. Nor did he see sleeping bags, clothes or the other camping gear belonging to the others.

What the hell?

"Where did they go?" he asked. "Why didn't we hear them leave?"

"I can't imagine," she said.

She put an arm around his neck. "You know something?" she asked, in a moment.

"What?"

"I'm tired of not making love to you."

"I can identify with your frustration. How can I make it up to you?"

She smiled. "Do you remember when we made love after the musical?"

"I remember I liked it a lot."

"Me too." She tugged at the zipper on his sweatshirt. "I think we need to try again."

He peeled off the shirt and his sweats while she removed her clothes. They planned to take their time and relish the moment.

The plan didn't last too long.

When their bodies pressed together, all the stress, the heartache and loneliness of their lives began to evaporate.

The sex felt so good, so right, that both people gasped in the middle of their kissing. He remembered how much he'd cherished her so long ago.

The joy continued for some time. They had seventeen years of misery to overcome.

* * * * *

McKenna DiBiasi woke up from a deep and dreamless sleep. For the first time in several nights, she didn't feel scared sick. She felt fine.

She reviewed the arrest and its aftermath. The father hadn't come back, and the police said he'd probably seen their cars in the driveway and abandoned his son to his own devices. Scott still was dazed and almost unable to talk after his imprisonment.

As the state police hauled Scott away, they told McKenna his real name. Dale Wolfe, they said, had quite a reputation with the Shoal Creek police.

The state cops questioned McKenna for some time. "Did someone come here to help you?" asked one of them.

"Cinnamon and the guys," she said, a little mystified.

"No," said the cop, shaking his head. "It's strange. This Dale keeps saying some guy came into the bedroom to help you during the fight. He didn't know how he got in the house. Red hair, tall. . ."

McKenna felt a chill. She knew who that sounded like. How could he. . .

The troopers asked several more questions. They ended by telling her she was a hell of a kid. She grinned at the compliment.

She'd talked to Mom before going to bed and Mom had told her that they were staying in North Carolina for a little while longer. Still, they would soon be reunited.

Mom had told her about Casey. McKenna sensed that Mom's peace, even joy, had to do with being with this Casey. He'd been so sweet to McKenna on the phone, so loving and kind.

Now, McKenna looked at the beautiful young woman sleeping next to her, who looked so much like the picture of Casey that Scott—no, Dale—had given her. Cinnamon had offered to spend the night in the bedroom with her in case she got scared in the night.

In that moment, she grasped who Casey and Cinnamon were. She began to get excited about how her life seemed to be changing. She let herself drift off to sleep again.

* * * * *

Cinnamon dreamed that night of an old man and an exquisite crystal cave. She sat next to him on a cedar bed. The crystals shone prisms of color, the bubbling well gave off a beautiful fragrance and the cave echoed with gentle sound, like that of soft wind chimes.

"Stay and talk to me for a time," the man smiled. His voice sounded familiar.

"You came to help, didn't you?" she asked. He nodded,

and hugged her.

She relaxed, enjoying the vision, and they chatted. "Can I please remember this when I wake up?" she asked.

"We'll try," he promised.

* * * * *

On a windy island in the Pamlico Sound, Anna O'Neill lay curled up to the man she loved more than anything in the world. He'd fallen asleep—worn out, she giggled—and her head rested on his shoulder. Casey's sister and her friend had rescued McKenna. The Dark Man couldn't hurt her while she was here. Everything was okay.

The first time they'd made love in seventeen years had moved both of them to tears of joy. Neither person could imagine how they'd lived without it.

She thought through the sex, smiling and relishing the memory. Joining with Casey had always been so different than any other experience.

The difference, of course, came from how much he loved her. He used his body to express his devotion, his love, and his intense feelings for her.

From the first moment they came together, she understood the truth. He'd never stopped loving her. No one, she knew, would ever love her as Casey did. She had to concede, also, that she had never ceased loving him.

The love, though, remained flawed until they renewed the physical passion. Anna knew that she had been incomplete without Casey. She'd missed him so much that. . .

She felt something happen deep inside her. Her hand stole down and she laid her palm against her tummy, a few inches below her navel.

My Gosh, she thought. Could it be? But I'm over forty years old. I have a seventeen year old daughter. This didn't happen with McKenna.

Then she understood. McKenna didn't have the Cymreig.

She smiled and snuggled closer to her best friend. Now, at last, she admitted that she lay with the man with whom she wanted to spend the rest of her life. She reached down into her own body with the Cymreig.

"Hello, there," she said aloud. "Welcome." Tears of joy ran onto Casey's chest.

CHAPTER FIFTY FIVE

In the morning Casey discovered Daniel, Cole and Elaine sitting next to the campfire. He and Anna dressed in the sleeping bag, and ate a quick breakfast. The group finished hauling the tools to the graveyard.

The men began to dig. The women hauled sand away and spread it out away from the pit.

The backbreaking work in the soggy heavy sand wore the laborers out in no time. The men took twenty-minute shifts.

By noon they had cleared a substantial area, digging down some five feet. When they found a couple of old coins, the group cheered and applauded.

They decided to stop for lunch. Drenched with sweat, Casey and Anna sat on the edge of the sandy pit, drinking some bottled water.

"If someone put the treasure in that hole, he dug it in deep," said Casey.

"Don't be so discouraged," said a raspy voice behind him.

They stood and turned, startled. Two tall men stood behind them, holding guns. Casey knew one of them.

"Jerry!" Casey said, staring in surprise at the man he knew. "Darn! I forgot to call you. I apologize. We found McKenna yesterday."

"Oh, I know all about that," said Jerry, grinning. He didn't look like an old friend.

Casey hesitated, considering. "Then what brings you here?"

"Why don't we just say I came to encourage you, old pal."

"Well, thanks. I appreciate it." He realized that Anna hadn't spoken a word. "Anna, I want you to meet Jerry LaBonte."

"No," said Anna.

"What?" said Casey.

"Casey," she said. "That's my husband, Alan DiBiasi."

* * * * *

Casey stared at the man he knew as Jerry. He sneered at them. "Hello, Anna," said Alan. His voice turned bitter, edged with sarcasm. His face showed no sign of warmth. "It's been a long time."

Anna's face reflected stunned amazement. "But—"

"I know," he said. "I died in Puerto Rico. How can I be here?" He looked ready to shoot them both on the spot. Casey put his arm around Anna. "How sweet. How cute," sneered Alan. "The two lovers, together again." He took an envelope from his coat pocket and threw it to her. It landed at her feet. She picked it up, opened it, and pulled out a photograph. She sighed and handed it to Casey.

The photo showed a younger Casey and Anna standing next to each other at Westwood High School. The inscription read, "To Anna, All my love." Casey had forgotten about the picture.

"I found that in your old school files when I packed up for our move to our new house," Alan fumed. "I saw how much your daughter resembles this clown. So when your kid had a blood test for her high school physical, I checked her blood type. AB positive. You and I both have type O. I remembered the inscription on your cheap watch and that book."

Anna stared at Alan with contempt as he continued, "So, Dr. Fixx, in just a few moments I intend to give my associate the pleasure of shooting you and your lover."

The other man came forward grinning. Anna saw his face. "Of course. Nick," sighed Anna. "At last, you have a chance for revenge."

"Things look pretty good for you now, Jerry," said Casey, sneering the name. "You can murder five people in cold blood at the same time."

Alan and Nick looked at each other, then stared around.

"Five people?" Alan said.

Casey turned and looked. Daniel and the others had disappeared.

Now he understood. They'd vanished into the trees, hiding and waiting to make a move. He needed to keep Alan talking until their friends could set up a plan.

Alan waved the gun at the shovels. "Enough of this pleasant chit-chat. Jump into the pit. Make that sand fly."

"No," snapped Anna. She put her hand on Casey's arm. He heard the blazing fury in her voice. "No, this has gone far enough." Nick stepped forward, pointing his pistol at her. Anna didn't flinch. "Okay, now you know," said Anna. "Yes, I conceived McKenna with Casey. But she always considered you her father. We're also still married."

"Our marriage ended when he got you pregnant," he snarled.

"We'd separated when it happened and I intended the separation to be permanent. I planned to divorce you," said Anna. "But I came back to you when you lied to me about your family. I didn't know about the pregnancy then. You became the father of a wonderful child."

"To hell with this," snarled Alan. "Into the pit, both of you."

"No," said Anna, now angry, her eyes flashing. She pointed at Nick. "How could you put your daughter in the hands of this psychopath?"

"She's *not* my daughter!" Alan raged, waving his gun.

"Do you have *any* idea how you devastated McKenna with this hideous death charade? You all but destroyed that girl. She had to go through grief counseling for months. How could you betray her love like that?"

"You betrayed me," he bellowed.

"I tried to love you," said Anna, "despite your incessant lies and gambling and affairs." She fixed his eyes with hers. "From the last day of school that year, I never met or even talked to Casey until you forced me to." Alan snorted in contempt.

"McKenna has always been your daughter," Anna went on, calming a little. "She's never even met this man." She nodded to Casey. "Put the guns away. Let Casey go. He's not to blame. I'll stay and work with you to find the treasure. You can have it."

"To hell with this," said Alan. "I'm giving the orders."

"I don't take orders from you, Alan," snapped Anna and the anger returned. "You're being absurd. And stop pretending that you're an outraged husband. You never loved me enough to be jealous of me."

Again Nick threatened with the gun. Anna ignored him.

"I know you," Anna said to Alan. "You're running a money scam of some kind, aren't you?"

"It's life insurance fraud," Casey put in. DiBiasi's eyes narrowed. "Now I remember. It was a famous scam. For a while certain doctors in Puerto Rico would sell a death certificate, a fake grave, coffins and other trappings of death by heart attack."

"I'm impressed, Fixx," smirked Alan.

"Let me take a crack at this, DiBiasi," Casey said. "No need to hurry. No one knows you came here to the island." He turned to Anna. "Alan took out a mammoth policy on himself," said Casey. "Probably several policies. He established himself, under a false name, as a beneficiary for the policy who lived in Puerto Rico. He paid the premiums for a few years. Then he faked a heart attack on the golf course. I'm guessing he collected tons of dollars."

"Brilliant," said Alan, shaking his head in mock admiration.

Casey turned back to Alan. "You got in a jam with your gambling, didn't you? You mortgaged the business and the house, but you were still in big trouble. So you came up with this plan. You've been setting it up for years."

Alan shrugged, still looking amused.

"But his face has changed..." Anna said. Casey nodded.

"You took the money and went to some foreign country for plastic surgery," he said, speaking to DiBiasi. "When they got through, and you grew the beard, no one in the Chicago area would recognize you, except for the two people who knew you best. You can't fake the way you walk, your vocal patterns. Of course Anna and McKenna would know you."

Nod.

"You paid off the bad guys and pocketed the rest of the money. But you ran through the money and needed more."

Shrug.

"Then you decided to go after your life insurance policies on Anna and McKenna by having them murdered. McKenna at the farm. Anna here. Out of the way, no witnesses, no one to identify you."

"Very good," Alan said, looking rather proud.

"That's where Nick came in. You knew what had happened when Anna split with him. You also knew that he had these preposterous fantasies of revenge."

Nick's eyes narrowed.

"I couldn't imagine why you wanted me along," continued Casey. "I think I get it now. I'm guessing you have a large insurance policy on me, too. You hired someone to take the physical for me and name you the beneficiary. Everyone knows you're my good buddy, Jerry LaBonte."

"You've done very well," said Alan. "But I'm tired of this. Get to work, both of you."

"We won't," affirmed Anna, her chin raised in defiance.

Alan shrugged. "Fine. Nick?"

Nick pointed the gun at Anna's knee and shot at her before Casey could get in front of her.

CHAPTER FIFTY SIX

Nick saw Anna's eyes ignite in green flame. He felt them reach down into his mind. Time slowed as he pulled the trigger. In the next moment Nick found himself sitting on a cot in a jail cell. He stood and looked into a smudged mirror above a filthy washstand.

He saw the reflection of a young man, maybe twenty-five instead of forty-five. His head had been shaved. He looked down and saw his right pants leg slit to the knee.

A tired, sad-looking clergyman sat on a folding chair with a Bible open on his knees. "Nick," he said with a tone of weariness. "Please sit down. You only have a few moments."

Nick, horrified, realized where he was. The death cell at the maximum-security Wisconsin State Penitentiary at Green Bay. Fifteen steps down the hall, a large room with many chairs waited.

At the far end of the long room, one chair stood apart. Old Lightnin'. The Wisconsin electric chair.

Nick choked with terror. "How did I get here?"

The priest's face clouded. He frowned and shook his head. "You can't bring her back by pretending you don't know, Son."

Nick swallowed as he remembered everything in grim detail.

Final exams. A case of beer at the fraternity. Dinner with Anna. The apartment. More beer. The struggle. Her sobs of fear. His laughter. Overpowering her. Dragging her to the sofa. Tearing at her clothes. Forcing her legs apart. Thrusting hard. Covering her mouth to stifle her screams of pain. Anna biting his hand. Searing pain. Swinging his fist at her head.

A long exhalation and rattle. Sudden quiet. Complete stillness.

He'd broken her neck.

His roommate found him standing over the body a few moments later. Marty called the police. The arrest. The handcuffs. The arraignment. The trial for murder and rape that cost his parents all they had. The verdict. The death penalty.

"Yes," he said, "I know what I did."

"Then confess it, Son. Give your soul to Jesus. Remember the thief on the cross. Even now, at the last moment—"

Nick's mind cleared for a moment. "Don't talk crazy," Nick interrupted. "Wisconsin doesn't even have the death penalty. How can I. . ."

Nick stopped when he heard the door to the execution chamber open. The footsteps of several people echoed down the hall. Six burly guards stood before the cell as the warden unlocked the door. The cell door opened and they rushed him.

He tried to stand. "Get off me," he yelled. "I can walk." But his legs wouldn't support him. He tried to fight off the guards but they were too strong for him. In seconds they had manacled him and started dragging him down the hall. "No! Stop," he yelled. "Please."

They dragged him through the door. A large group of people sitting on folding chairs glowered in hostility at him. Many yelled insults at him.

"Break his rotten neck, too!"

"Kill the bastard twice!"

"You're letting the creep off too easy!"

He'd never experienced such utter hatred and contempt.

In Nick's tortured mind, he thought that the chair didn't look like a chair. More like a spider web. He imagined a huge spider poised above the chair, waiting for him.

The guards pivoted him to face the audience. They slammed him into the oak chair. They strapped down his arms, legs, and chest.

The chin strap. The saline sponge. The metal skullcap. The

guards performed everything with grim precision of movement.

He pleaded and cried. He begged as the saline solution ran down his face and into his eyes. Derisive laughter and more insults assaulted him from the audience.

The warden read from a scrap of paper. "Nicholas Boyd Wolfe, you have been tried and found guilty. . ."

The warden's voice droned on. Nick looked around the room. He saw his mother and father sitting in the front row, weeping, leaning on each other in despair and terror.". . .murder and assault. . ." he heard the warden say.

He recognized Anna's Aunt Marion and Uncle Claude. Anna's daughter.

In the second row, Nick saw a small woman, her face bruised, holding the hands of two young men.

In the corner an old man and his wife smiled and held up cocktail glasses. ". . .most extreme sanction. . ."

He saw other people staring at him in strange costumes from other centuries. One large man stood in their midst, clad in a brown monk's robe. All of them had copper hair and their green eyes were aglow with anger.

Nick grew even more terrified. *Who were these people?*

"At this time, an electric current will be passed through your body. . ."

Wait. Wait a second. He felt relief surge over him. Anna sat in the front row, her expression stony and cold. She held the hand of a tall blond man. Nick had once fought with that man. He had the strange name of Gareth.

"Do you have any last words?" concluded the warden.

"Stop! No," he screamed. "Anna ain't dead! She's sitting right there! Look in the front row!"

The audience and guards laughed. He heard a phone, its shrill ring as loud as a gunshot. A guard stood next to a large red telephone. Relief coursed through Nick. He'd received a pardon from the governor in the last moment.

"Don't answer it, Mike," said one of the guards.

"Yeah," said another. "Prob'ly just a wrong number." Another ring, louder.

"Or maybe one of them phone solicitors," said another. They laughed, harsh, sarcastic laughter.

The large man clothed in the monk's robe spoke up. "Proceed with the execution," he said. The warden and the guards nodded, and Nick could see that they regarded the large man with great respect.

The warden, still standing in front of Nick, pointed behind him to a sandpit filled with hideous green flame. It hadn't been there a second ago. "Burn in hell, killer," he snarled.

The audience began to chant. "Burn. Burn. Burn..."

"No!" Nick whimpered.

The warden pulled the black hood down over Nick's face. The warden screeched, "Time!" Nick felt a blast of lightning hit him.

* * * * *

Then he jerked back to St. Margaret's, an island in the Pamlico Sound of North Carolina. Nick again found himself standing at the side of a pit in an old graveyard, ablaze with green fire.

He recognized this ghastly pit of green flames. He'd found himself standing in front of it in his dreams for years.

Nick's brain registered that Anna had twisted as he fired. The bullet had slammed into her thigh just above her knee, knocking her backward into the sand pit. She lay on the ground, stunned. A blond guy--named Gareth, Nick remembered--leapt down and knelt over her, shielding her from Nick's gun.

Nick fingered his greasy matted hair.

Anna's eyes opened. "McKenna!" she screamed from where she lay on the sand. "No! Run away!"

"Daddy?" cried a young voice. "Daddy, don't shoot!" Fifty yards away, at the edge of the woods, a teenaged girl began to run toward the pit. Nick registered that this had to be someone related to Cray. She looked familiar.

How did Anna see her? Nick wondered.

A young woman and a burly biker-type tackled the girl. The biker lifted her over his shoulder and they hurried back to the woods.

Nick looked down at the gun in his hand. A man's voice next to Nick shouted, "Shoot them!" He turned toward the voice. A huge bronze snake reared up before him like a cobra. Nick saw himself reflected in the metallic sheen. Still dazed, he shrank back, stupefied with fear and revulsion.

"Shoot the two girls," the snake hissed. "We can have the big man dig up the treasure." When Nick hesitated, it shrieked, "Do it now before they get away and we have to hunt them down!"

Nick stepped back. The gun dropped from his fingers. He looked into the sand pit. "I shot Anna," he mumbled, feeling stupid. He still couldn't figure out where he was or how he'd come here.

He ventured another look at the snake. Now it had transformed into a man who stood at least six and a half feet tall. He had red eyes and a luxuriant black beard spilled onto a massive chest. Nick couldn't see the man's features through the yellow sulfurous smoke surrounding the man's head.

"All right," said the icy hissing voice. "I'll do it."

A voice from behind the pit boomed, "DiBiasi!" Nick saw the huge man turn to look. The man became Alan DiBiasi again. DiBiasi turned ash-white with fear and backed away until he collided with one of the pillars.

Nick followed Alan's gaze. He screeched with fear.

* * * * *

Hearing the two men scream, Casey stood. He saw Daniel, Cole, and Elaine walk out of the woods behind the pit toward the two gunmen. All three wore grim expressions.

Casey couldn't understand what terrified Alan and Nick. His friends weren't even armed. He heard Daniel bellow, "I warned you, DiBiasi. Now I'm going to kill you." Daniel's voice resounded through the clearing as if it was amplified.

Casey saw Alan fire at Daniel. Then Nick retrieved his gun and shot at Cole and Shirley. Both fired again at the three. And again. The three kept coming.

* * * * *

Alan, when he confronted his wife and Casey, had seen an excavation in the graveyard, some ten feet in diameter, perhaps five feet deep. Now he realized it wasn't just a pit.

He comprehended that he stood at the threshold of a gateway to hell. Jagged rocks and cold vicious green flames framed a passageway to eternal torment.

Terrifying people in strange clothing stood around the pit. They glared at him with glowing, acid-green eyes.

Alan's brain, almost numb with terror, yet comprehended that the emerald flames would burn him but he never would be consumed. The fires would sear his flesh like dry ice, slashing at him, gnarling him forever with unspeakable agony.

He recognized at once the same dark figure that had terrified him at his wedding. Alan stood pinned against one of the old, twisted oak trees that marked the entrance to the graveyard. The creature advanced toward him from across the pit.

The specter growled through long hideous fangs. Its hands were eagle talons, long, sharp, and treacherous.

The creature had come for Alan. It would hurl his soul into that pit of infernal green fire, ripping, tearing. Forever.

Alan collapsed to his knees, sniveling with fear. The

creature slapped his face, knocking Alan onto his chest. Alan howled as the claws tore four bloody lacerations on his cheek. The creature sat on Alan's back, pummeling him with its fists. "You shot her, you bastard," it howled.

* * * * *

Nauseous with abhorrence and fear, Nick stared at the other two creatures: flesh rotting away; foul, rotten teeth; matted, tangled hair. But they had wings and claws. He knew that if they touched him, he'd become foul and unclean himself.

Nick swung his fist, but he couldn't connect. One of the creatures seized his arm. Nick yelled with pain and whimpered as the other creature slapped at his gun. It clattered aside.

* * * * *

Casey saw Durango start for Nick at the same moment he did. Durango hit Nick with a vicious cross body block. Nick's breath left him with a *whumpf as* Durango shoved him toward Casey.

Nick threw out his hands to break his fall. Casey whipped a handful of sand into Nick's face. Nick choked on the sand and flung his fists up to try to clear his eyes.

Casey grabbed him by his greasy hair with one hand and jerked him to his feet. His other hand encircled Nick's fat neck and slammed him against the pillar at the entrance of the old graveyard.

Casey kneed Nick in the groin and kicked his knee. He pounded his fist into Nick's face three times. Nick's head banged against the pillar.

Why does this seem familiar? thought Casey.

Casey clouted Nick hard on the temple with his fist while Durango yanked at the fat man's legs. Nick went down hard on his back, dazed and choking from the sand. Casey jumped on him in the next instant, slugging him again and again.

Casey felt two brawny arms encircle him and lift him off

Nick. Durango held Casey's arms. "Okay, Casey," said the biker. "He's through. Calm down."

"He shot Anna!" Casey shrieked, struggling against Durango's iron grip.

"I know. We'll deal with him. But don't become a killer yourself."

Casey breathed deep and regained his sanity. Durango and Cinnamon duct-taped Nick's trembling hands behind him.

Nick wept and pleaded. "Don't let them touch me," he whined. "Keep them away."

Casey heard another struggle and turned back. Daniel held Alan face down, sitting astride the man's back and pummeling him. Daniel grabbed a large rock and raised it over Alan's head.

"No, Grandpa!" Anna cried. She collapsed backwards, the blood from her wound staining the sand.

Daniel paused and glanced at Anna. He nodded and lowered the rock. He gripped Alan's head in his powerful hands and looked into his eyes.

Alan, weeping with fear, stared back at Daniel. After a few seconds Daniel released the blubbering man. He nodded to Durango and Cinnamon, who secured Alan with tape.

Anna's pallor, her clammy skin and weak pulse told Casey that she'd gone into shock. McKenna leapt into the pit and held her mom. Anna's leg wound soaked her jeans with blood. The bullet had passed through the leg.

Elaine jumped into the pit with them. "I'm a nurse," she said. "Let me see."

She went to work on Anna. She directed Casey to slit the leg of Anna's jeans up above her knee with a razor knife.

Oh God, Casey prayed, *Don't let her die. Not when we've come this far. I can't let her go again.*

"Here, Casey," said Elaine. As she directed him, he pulled off his sweatshirt and pressed it against the wound. Then he took off his belt and pulled it tight around Anna's leg.

Casey stood. The wind felt cold on his sweat-soaked t-shirt. His teeth began to chatter. Cole stripped off his coat. "Casey, put this on," he insisted. "You'll catch pneumonia." Casey thanked him as he donned the jacket.

"Casey," Cinnamon said. "I called the Washington police. They'll have a launch out to the island in fifteen minutes. The police called the EastCare medical helicopter at East Carolina University. The paramedics should arrive in less than ten minutes but we need to move Anna to the beach on the East Side where the medivac helicopter can land."

"Okay," said Casey. "Cover them, honey. The other guys will help." He tossed Cinnamon the pistol and picked Anna up.

With Elaine's help, Casey and Durango lifted Anna out of the pit. Casey carried her toward the beach, murmuring comfort to her. Durango and McKenna followed. They hurried down the path through the woods, leaving Cinnamon, Daniel, and Cole to guard the hog-tied prisoners.

Casey slogged through the sand, terrified that Anna would bleed to death before he could get her to the helicopter. Exhaustion from digging in heavy wet sand that morning left him gasping for breath. His arms and back ached. He stumbled several times, but each time he floundered, Durango and McKenna caught him and held him upright.

When they got Anna to the beach, the helicopter sat waiting. The paramedics started her on plasma. As they strapped Anna into a gurney, Casey kissed her and told her he loved her.

McKenna turned to Casey. For the first time father and daughter looked each other in the eye. She returned his smile, put her arms around Casey's neck, and kissed his grimy cheek.

He hugged his daughter. "Go with your mom. We'll meet you at the hospital."

She nodded, her face lined with strain and worry. He held her chin and looked into her sapphire eyes. "She's a real trooper," he said. "She'll be okay."

McKenna smiled and climbed aboard. She held her mother's hand as the helicopter took off.

"All right, Elaine," said Casey, turning to his friend.

Elaine, though, had gone back into the woods. He didn't see her anywhere.

Durango and Casey ran back to the graveyard. They found Cinnamon guarding the two prisoners at gunpoint. Casey looked around. He didn't see Elaine or Cole, nor could he spot Daniel.

"Where did the others go?" he asked Cinnamon in some surprise.

"I don't know," said his sister. "They just disappeared."

Casey called his friend Roger. He dropped everything and sprinted to Bath Harbor for his boat.

Alan struggled against the tape on his wrists, bellowing threats and profanities. Aside from the cuts on his cheek he seemed unhurt. "Casey," Durango said, "why isn't he bruised a lot worse? Daniel gave him the beating of a lifetime."

"I can't imagine," said Casey, squelching a desire to pummel DiBiasi himself.

The police arrived and bundled the two prisoners into their launch. Alan, still cursing, demanded to see a lawyer. Nick babbled about monsters.

They rolled up the camping and digging gear until Roger arrived. Durango, Cinnamon and Casey climbed into his boat and returned to Bath. The three of them retrieved Durango's rental car at the bed-and-breakfast and sped to Pitt Memorial Hospital in Greenville. They found the emergency room entrance, where an orderly directed them to the surgical suite.

They found McKenna standing in the waiting room, clutching her hands to her face. When she saw them, she hurried toward Casey, her arms up.

Casey embraced her. "McKenna," he said. She clutched at

him, weeping with fear and worry and stress.

He caressed her hair. "Don't be scared. I'll stay right here with you." He backed away and looked her over. "My God," he said. "You're so tall and beautiful."

The girl managed a little grin. "Nice to meet you too, Casey Fixx," she said.

"Go clean up, Casey," said Durango. "We'll stay with McKenna."

Casey looked down and saw that he was covered with Anna's blood. "Oh, damn," he said.

"What?" asked his sister.

"I don't remember where I left Cole's jacket."

Cinnamon and Durango exchanged baffled looks. "Cole who?" asked his sister.

"The guy who slapped the gun away from Nick."

"You weren't wearing a jacket, Bro," said Cinnamon.

"No one hit Nick except you and me," said Durango.

Casey sat back, bewildered that they couldn't remember seeing his friends.

Cinnamon found a nurse, who ran to a supply cabinet and pulled out some surgical greens. The nurse led Casey to a shower. After cleaning up, he went back to the waiting area and found Cinnamon and Durango hovering over McKenna.

At last the door to the surgical suite opened. A doctor emerged.

"McKenna?" the doctor asked.

She nodded. The surgeon sat next to her and put his hand on her arm. "Your mom will be okay. She lost a lot of blood but we pulled her through."

McKenna turned into Casey's shoulder and wept. The surgeon turned to Casey. "Who are you, sir?" he asked, smiling.

Before Casey could answer McKenna said, "Doctor, I'd like you to meet my father, Casey Fixx."

"Yes," smiled the doctor, shaking Casey's hand. "I see the resemblance."

Casey stared at his daughter while the doctor gave them some details about the surgery. "We've moved her to recovery. She hasn't come out of anesthetic yet, but she should be able to talk to you in a little while."

After the doctor left, McKenna turned to Cinnamon. "So that makes you my aunt," she said, with tears on her cheeks. The two young women embraced and Cinnamon wiped at McKenna's tears. "Why have I never met you before?" McKenna asked Casey.

"Let's wait for your mom before we talk about that," he said.

Her blue eyes brimmed. "Did you love her?" she asked in a small voice.

"Oh, yes," Casey said. "I've never stopped loving her. No matter what happens that love extends to you from now on. I won't let anything separate us again. I've never had any practice at being a dad, but I promise to try my best."

Her smile reminded him of her mother. "Can I meet the rest of your family?" she asked.

"Of course you can. I can't wait to introduce you to them." He told her about his sister Karen and her husband and their son, Joey; Cheyenne and Derek; Aunt Victoria and Uncle Steve. She giggled. "He looks like a lawn gnome?"

"You'll see," smiled Casey.

CHAPTER FIFTY SEVEN

Casey stood when an orderly brought Anna, still unconscious, into the room. The doctor came in as the orderly and a nurse settled Anna into the bed. The doctor motioned to Casey, and they stepped into the hallway. "She bled a great deal and she's weak but she should be okay. We need to keep her for at least a couple of days." They chatted a moment or two longer.

McKenna insisted that she wanted to stay in the room to wait for her mother to wake up. Casey pulled a chair next to her and put his arm around her. McKenna leaned against his shoulder and dozed off. A few moments later, he fell asleep too.

Durango and Cinnamon tiptoed from the room and left the hospital. They returned with Chinese food. All four ate in silence.

McKenna began to talk about the horror of the last several days. She poured out her heart about the betrayal she felt at learning that the man she considered her father had survived. That DiBiasi had staged his death. That he had arranged for men to kidnap her. That he'd arranged for someone to kill her and his wife, McKenna's mother. That money meant more to him than she or her mother did. The terror of the kidnapping. The hurt. The betrayal.

Casey held her hand, and Cinnamon hugged her shoulder and wiped her tears. McKenna seemed to be comfortable with her new family.

Anna woke up, still groggy. When she saw her daughter she asked Casey, "Am I dreaming?"

"No, it's really McKenna," he smiled.

Anna's smile turned to a pained expression of worry.

"McKenna. Your hand. Did they—"

McKenna held both of her hands up and wiggled her fingers. "I'm okay, Mom. Those creeps just tried to scare you."

Mother and daughter hugged. Casey took Anna's hand. She pulled him to her and kissed him.

She looked at the green surgical scrubs and managed a little giggle. "Nice look," she smiled.

"Oh," he said, relieved that she felt well enough to tease him. "Thanks."

"No, really," she said. "Your taste in clothing keeps improving all the time." Now he chuckled with her.

Then she grew serious. She looked in his eyes and whispered, "You're really here, aren't you? I'm not having a dream of Gareth, am I?"

"It's me, Honey," he smiled. "No dream."

"The last time I was in the hospital you came," she said. "Then you took off and I didn't see you for seventeen years." Tears ran down her cheek at the memory.

He smiled and brushed away the tears. "I'm here," he whispered back. "I always will be."

"Promise you won't leave me this time?"

"I promise," he said, stroking her hair. "We don't have to say goodbye again. I love you."

"I love you too," she said. "I always have." They kissed again.

CHAPTER FIFTY EIGHT

Casey drove with Durango and Cinnamon to the state police station the next morning to press charges. A detective named Dennis Toll talked to them. The detective said that Nick remained obtuse about his role in all this. Nick claimed that he couldn't remember anything of his life since college. He kept claiming he had no memory of anything since one night in college. He couldn't remember anything except for being pummeled by Casey.

Casey understood. His memory had vanished since the night Anna kept him from raping her.

"He may not remember," said Toll, looking grim. "That won't keep the greasy creep's butt out of jail, though." Seeing Nick's size, Casey felt baffled. How did she manage to fight him off? he wondered.

Toll said that Alan DiBiasi's strategy in the interrogation had been to blame everything on Nick and to claim that he had come to protect Anna and McKenna. "But every time he tried to lie, his face would twist with pain," Detective Toll said. "He'd close his eyes, put his head to one side and give it a little shake. Then he'd tell the truth. Almost like he didn't have a choice."

The stories Nick and Alan told in the interrogation left them shaking their heads.

Returning to the hospital, Cinnamon spent a long time talking with Anna. Cinnamon said she'd initiate divorce proceedings when she returned home. "I don't do a lot of matrimonial work, but I do know a judge I can sweet-talk into getting this done in a hurry," she smiled. Casey promised to keep in touch. Durango and Cinnamon flew home later that evening.

McKenna slept on a cot in her mom's hospital room. Casey

took a room in a hotel across from the hospital.

The next day, Casey told Anna and McKenna what he'd learned. "Alan set Nick up to take the fall from the beginning," Casey said. "Alan assumed his new identity of Jerry LaBonte after he staged the heart attack in Puerto Rico. He purchased a private investigator license and returned to the Chicago area. He set up the PI business and then got to know me and the agencies I work with." Anna asked him to crank the bed up a little bit. He did so, and fluffed the pillow behind her head.

"Before you got married, in fact before he even met you, Alan had you investigated," he told Anna. "DiBiasi knew from the beginning that you went through a bad bust-up with Nick in college. He knew how you were run out of Shoal Creek after Nick fell apart. Then, when he came up with this scam, he did some checking. He found out that Nick still blamed you and that Nick's life had been a mess since college. He found Nick in Shoal Creek a month or so ago. DiBiasi didn't have any problem enlisting Nick, who has wanted revenge on you for years."

Anna sighed, shaking her head. "He wanted revenge on me."

"So now he wanted to get Nick involved with the scheme. Nick didn't have any money and had fallen up to his keester in debt. DiBiasi peaked Nick's interest when Alan approached him with a get-rich-quick-and-real-easy scheme."

"From what my aunt and uncle told me, he blew all of his parents' money after they died," Anna said.

"That figures," Casey nodded. "Anyhow, Alan decided that I'd be the perfect stooge. He'd force me to go with you to the island. We'd look for the treasure. When we found the treasure—or even if we didn't—Nick would be crazy enough to shoot you and then me too." Anna motioned with her hand. He brought the styrofoam cup to her and helped her put the straw in her mouth. She sipped, and nodded for him to go on.

"Nick's violent history of bar fights and spousal abuse since he dropped out of college suggested that he had the potential to commit murder. He still hated you with a fury."

"How nice," Anna sighed. "He tries to rape me, and then hates me because I stopped him."

"So, Alan planned to let Nick kill McKenna at the farm in Wisconsin once we found the treasure or had to give up." McKenna shuddered. Casey took her hand and squeezed it. "The plan called for Nick to find you and me on the island and kill us.

"Alan would show up. He'd shoot and kill Nick right after Nick killed us. He'd summon the police and tell them that I hired him to find McKenna. He'd recorded our calls. He would tell the authorities that he had followed Nick across the country and arrived there too late to save us." He took Anna's hand and squeezed it, thinking about how lucky they had been.

Anna shook her head. "Nick never saw a double cross coming, huh?"

Casey said, "I don't think he understands that Alan made him the stooge, even now. Alan and Nick never appeared together after their first meeting. Nick went to North Carolina in a different plane, hired a different rental car, found a different man to haul him over to St. Margaret's. Alan staged it so that Nick always arrived an hour or two ahead of him."

"Ah," said Anna. "So Alan could make it look like you'd hired him as a private detective. You'd put him on the trail of a vicious, revenge-crazed jilted lover."

"That's the idea. He'd say that he managed to kill Nick in self-defense. He made sure no evidence would link them together."

McKenna spoke up. "But wait. Wouldn't Scott—I mean, Dale, the son—be able to identify Dad as the one who hired Nick to kidnap me?"

"No," Casey shook his head. "Dale never saw Alan, never talked to him. Also remember that Nick hated his wife and kids. He planned to kill Dale after he killed you, McKenna."

CHAPTER FIFTY NINE

Anna slept quite a bit as her leg healed. Casey used the time to get to know his daughter. They talked, took long walks together and played board games.

He also did some thinking.

One morning, he visited the university library. Using his research skills, he found information about an automobile accident on Christmas morning, 1928. What he found surprised him at first, but as he thought about it the facts made complete sense. He made some phone calls, then used the internet. At last he spoke to an elderly man in New Jersey.

The old man told a sad story. He asked a grandson to scan an old wedding picture and send it to Casey via e-mail.

Then Casey returned to the hospital to talk with Anna. He explained why he thought he needed to revisit to the island. At first, she stared at him as if he'd lost his mind. Then he showed her the picture and the newspaper stories. Her mouth dropped open. She recovered and agreed with Casey. "I'm sorry I can't go too," she nodded.

"I'll take McKenna," he suggested. Anna said that was a good idea.

Casey and McKenna drove back to the Bed and Breakfast in Bath. Roger and Lesha agreed to loan him a boat with a large outboard motor. Lesha told them not to worry about Anna. She would drive up to Greenville to spend the day with her, talking and catching up.

Roger and Lesha had gone back over to St. Margaret's. They packed up tents and clothing and gear and brought all of it back to the B-and-B. "Someone dug a big hole in the graveyard," Lesha told Casey.

"We don't know what happened to your friends," Roger

added. "We didn't see anyone on the island."

Casey nodded. "I expected that."

He tossed some digging tools into the boat. Father and daughter set out.

They pulled ashore at St. Margaret's and walked back to the graveyard, where they found Cole and Elaine. "How's Anna?" Daniel asked, running over.

"She's getting better," said Casey, grinning. He introduced McKenna to his friends. Daniel appeared delighted to meet Anna's daughter.

"We're too late again," said Cole. "The treasure's gone. Someone beat us to it--"

"Cole," Casey interrupted. "What year is this?"

His two friends stared at him, amazed. "Why, 1928, of course. We've been here for days. We've got to find the treasure and get back to our son on Long Island."

"You won't find him there," Casey said, trying to be gentle.

"What do you mean?" asked Elaine. "Has something happened to him?"

Casey produced that morning's newspaper. Cole and Elaine stared at the date in amazement.

Casey put his arm around Elaine and took Cole's elbow. "Cole and Elaine McClelland lost control of their car in a freak storm on Christmas Day in 1928. They crashed into the side of an ice wagon in Washington, North Carolina. They'd filled their car with digging equipment and luggage and come to Bath to search for the lost treasure of Blackbeard the pirate."

Elaine and Cole stared at Casey open-mouthed. Their faces turned ashen with stunned surprise and disbelief.

Casey pulled out a manila envelope. Inside Elaine and Cole found a Xeroxed copy of an old newspaper article that described the auto accident in 1928. They read it, stunned. Then he handed them the picture.

"That's our wedding photograph," said Elaine.

Casey nodded. "Your son had it sent to me by e-mail."

"By what?" said Cole, mystified. Casey tried to explain.

"Elaine and Cole McClelland died almost 80 years ago," Casey told his friends, tears starting down his cheeks. "Blackbeard claimed two more victims." Elaine put her hands over her mouth. Cole reached for her.

Cole at last shook his head. "Our son?"

"I talked to him on the telephone. He's more than 80 years old and lives in New Jersey. Your mother raised him, Cole. Yes, he remembers you with fondness and love. He's led a happy life. You have several grandchildren and great-grandchildren as well."

Casey related what he'd learned at the library. Their expressions turned from mystification to apprehension.

"How can we be dead and not know it?" Cole asked.

"That accursed treasure has been holding you here for decades," Casey said. "You just don't remember."

"Don't be silly," said Elaine. "Casey, how. . ."

"Look inside yourselves," Casey said. "Listen for the truth."

Husband and wife looked at each other, their faces twisted with fear. Casey embraced them, murmuring comfort.

"You saved my life, Cole," he told his friend. "Elaine, your nursing skills saved Anna's life too. McKenna and my sister Cinnamon and her friend Durango survived that fight because of you. You were willing to die to help us. Our safety came before your own. You redeemed your souls."

"How could you figure all this out?" Elaine asked.

"You never seemed to get hungry and I couldn't remember ever seeing you drink water. Then you vanished at night. I don't know where you went. The men who tried to kill us didn't see you the way Anna and I did. At the hospital, Cinnamon and Durango didn't even remember you."

"Didn't remember us?" said Cole, amazed.

"No. Somehow their memory of the fight didn't include you."

Daniel spoke up in his wise, tranquil voice. "Cole and Shirley," said Daniel. "Let the treasure go and be at peace. You have greater treasure before you."

Casey squeezed their hands. "Let your lives go also," he said. "Flow into the perfect light to a place where no shadows can frighten you and no fear can control you. McKenna, Daniel, and I promise to look for the treasure again today. If we find it we'll send your share to your son and grandchildren."

Daniel took their hands. "I think I can help." He gazed into their eyes, and their expressions changed. Courageous curiosity displaced doubt and fear.

"Look!" McKenna said. She pointed at the gate of the graveyard. A light glowed between the pillars.

Elaine stared at the light for a moment. Her face lit up with joy. "Mother?" she asked the light. "Is it you?" She took Cole's hand. "Look, Cole. Mother is waiting."

"Dad?" said Cole. The light became brighter. Husband and wife walked toward the radiance and began to fade. They put their arms around each other. Cole and Elaine stopped and turned back.

"Thank you, Casey," said Elaine.

"We shall see you soon," said Cole.

They stepped together into the light and disappeared.

The light faded.

CHAPTER SIXTY

After a few moments of stunned silence, Casey and McKenna turned back to Daniel. "What did you do to them?" asked Casey.

Daniel hesitated. "We call it the Cymreig. It's like hypnotism but deeper. Anna inherited the ability. So did I.

"We can Paik people, that is, look into their minds. When we Paik people, they see things. Sometimes the past. Sometimes the future. Sometimes just fantasies." He explained in more detail what he and Anna could do with the Cymreig.

Casey stared at his friend in bewilderment. McKenna smiled and nodded. Daniel looked between the pillars, out over the Pamlico Sound. "I Paiked Cole and Elaine to let them see what happened when they died."

"Did you do something to Alan?" asked Casey.

"I Paiked him too, Daniel nodded. "He won't be capable of lying for quite a while."

"You saved our lives when you attacked DiBiasi," Casey said.

He waved that aside. "You'd have done the same for me. But seeing that Light reminded me. We're supposed to look into the light at ten o'clock. It's about that time now." He pointed toward the gate.

An ornate cast iron arch connected the two stone pillars. The initials WO appeared in the center of the arch. The three walked forward and stood between the pillars.

They saw that the sunlight cast a shadow on the ground, some twenty feet on the other side of the arch. The shadow of the initials fell on a pile of rocks and sand.

Casey, McKenna and Daniel exchanged stares, which turned to huge grins. They seized shovels and picks. They dug where the shadow of the initials fell and pulled the rocks aside. After half an hour they uncovered a sheet of old, badly rotted canvas. Pulling the rotted cloth aside, they found a large cedar chest.

* * * * *

The three expended a great deal of effort in emptying the chest and stuffing the antique gold and silver and jewelry into sacks. They hauled the ancient chest to the beach and loaded the treasure aboard the boat.

"Thank you, Daniel," Casey said, shaking his hand. "We couldn't have done it without you."

He waved a hand, pleased. "The important thing is that Anna will be okay," he grinned. "I'll try to see her soon."

"We'll come to visit you in Arlington Heights," said McKenna.

An uneasy silence ensued. Daniel said, at last, "What do you mean?"

"During the fight, when you were about to bash Alan, Anna called you Grandpa," Casey said.

"You used the Cymreig to come to the island, Grandpa," said McKenna. "You've just forgotten."

"When Nick and his son kidnapped McKenna, you wanted to help," said Casey. "But your broken old body couldn't go to her. So you came here with your mind. Until now, I didn't understand how.

"That day after she came to meet me at the restaurant, Anna stopped off to see you again," said Casey. "You knew that your condition wouldn't allow you to help her the way you wanted. But you love her, so you came here anyhow."

Daniel stared at the ground.

"You also couldn't go to McKenna, of course," said Casey. "But you knew where this place was."

He looked up at them. "No," he murmured.

"When Anna came to see you at the nursing home, she told

you about me, didn't she? That's how you knew my name when we first met."

"You've been away from your body for several days. But now you should go back." McKenna embraced Daniel, who now looked a great deal older.

"I don't want to go back," said Daniel. "Here on the island, I'm not old and decrepit. I'm young and strong and handsome. I—" he couldn't go on.

"Let go, Daniel," Casey said. "We can take it from here."

"But who will take care of Anna?" Daniel asked.

"She's got me," Casey asserted, "as well as McKenna. We both love her. And she knows how much you love her."

A few moments passed. "All right," Daniel said at last. "Gareth, please marry Anna. You can keep her safe from Nehushtan."

Casey took Daniel's outstretched hand, baffled to hear Daniel call him by his boyhood dream name. Then he joined his daughter in hugging his friend who saved Anna's life.

"Do you promise to come to see me at the nursing home when you return?" Daniel asked.

They promised they would, of course they would.

Daniel turned and looked toward Illinois. He took a deep breath, filling his lungs with sea air. Then he licked his lips, tasting the salt. He sighed.

Then, Daniel no longer stood with them on St. Margaret's Island in the Pamlico Sound of North Carolina.

CHAPTER SIXTY ONE

A few days later Casey and McKenna brought Anna home on an early morning flight. She still had some pain, but managed to get around on crutches.

During the flight, McKenna told her mother about Scott's vision of someone joining her in the room at the farmhouse, helping her defeat him. "Could that be true?" she asked her mom.

"I think it is, Honey," said Anna. "I think you'll see a lot of him in your life."

"I see him in dreams, anyhow. I can't quite remember his name. . ."

"Gareth," said her mom. "And he calls you Viviane."

McKenna stared at her mom. Mom hugged her, and told her she'd try to explain another time.

Cheyenne and Derek met them at the airport. McKenna made friends with her aunt Cheyenne in no time. They began giggling together in a matter of moments.

* * * * *

The next day, Casey and Anna took McKenna to the high school. Bernie, McKenna's counselor, arranged a meeting with the administration. The story left the leaders of the high school a little dazed.

That evening Casey drove Anna and McKenna to their house in Lake Forest. Anna and Casey agreed that they wouldn't live together, despite the pain of separation, until the divorce was final. He left about midnight.

At six o'clock the next morning, he heard a loud banging on his door. He opened it and found Anna. "Did you sleep last night?" she asked.

"Not much, no."

"Me, neither. Couldn't get comfortable. Know what?"

"What?"

"This living apart idea stinks."

"I know," he said.

"McKenna told me she had a place where she'd rather live," she said.

"Oh?" said Casey. "Where's that?"

"Wherever you are," said Anna.

"Ah," said Casey, grinning.

"She'll drive over here after school," said Anna.

"Okay," said Casey. "You hungry?"

"More than you can imagine," she smiled. They went in to fix breakfast together. Then they went to bed.

When they woke up in the early afternoon, Casey called a friend who sold real estate. They put the big Lake Forest house on the market.

Cinnamon took Anna with her to meet her judge friend. On returning from North Carolina, Cinnamon had persuaded her friend to expedite the divorce. Anna tried hard not to smile as she saw that he indeed had a dramatic crush on Cinnamon. Then she grew serious as the judge walked her through the divorce proceedings in his office.

Two days after moving into Casey's house, Anna arranged to meet Tom at her Lake Forest house. She told him that she had fallen in love with Casey and intended to marry him. The scene couldn't have been much more unpleasant. He left without saying goodbye.

Anna and Casey met with the staff at the nursing home. The doctor and nurses agreed that Daniel's improvement had been dramatic in the last several days. The nurses told them that recovering his speech and movement as he had bordered on the miraculous.

With Derek's help, Casey began remodeling a portion of his basement to make an apartment for his good friend Daniel.

Anna checked him out of the nursing home. Casey and McKenna picked Daniel up the next morning.

CHAPTER SIXTY TWO

About a week later, Casey and Derek were working on some finishing touches in Daniel's basement apartment. Casey heard the phone ring upstairs. A half hour later, Anna came in. She signaled him to follow her.

They walked upstairs, and sat together on the couch in the living room. "You have to pack," she said. "We leave early in the morning."

"Where are we going?"

"Las Vegas. I just made the arrangements."

"What?"

"We need to get married. It's an emergency."

"An emergency wedding?" he said, chuckling.

"Yes, and I want to bring Grandpa and McKenna. They're up packing now. I told Grandpa he could be your best man. Okay?"

"Yeah, sure, he'd be my choice anyhow. Er...the divorce came through?"

"Yep," she said. "Cinnamon just called. Alan waived his right to appeal. She got the papers today."

"Look, I'm excited about marrying you, of course, but why the sudden rush?"

"You've got a problem with it?"

"Well, no, of course not, but I think my family wants to see us get married, you know?"

"Sure. How about a big wedding and reception when we get home, a couple of weeks maybe?"

"That sounds great. But you didn't answer. What's the hurry?"

She looked out the window for a moment, trying not to laugh. At last: "You know the flu I've had the last few days?"

"Yeah?" he said, mystified.

She handed him a little plastic stick. "I just took a home pregnancy test. See the blue thingy? That means it's positive."

"So. . ."

"So, I'm pregnant, you big dope."

He stared at her.

"The island. The sleeping bag."

He began to grin like a yokel in front of a TV camera. "You're lucky my father died before he could see this," she sniffed.

"Why?"

"Well, of course he would have had no choice but to horsewhip you. Outraged men always do that in Edwardian novels."

"Horsewhip me?"

"On the steps of your club, in fact."

"What club?"

"Don't you have a club?"

"Of course not. Well, I belong to the Screen Actors Guild."

"Perfect."

"But I don't know if they even have steps, though."

"I don't think my father had a horsewhip, either."

"That's a relief. Did he have a horse?"

"No. He liked Chevvies."

* * * * *

The next day, Casey stood at the altar in a Las Vegas chapel. Daniel stood next to him as his best man.

Casey beamed as Anna followed her daughter, the maid of honor, down the short aisle. Anna wore a beautiful ivory-colored suit and looked radiant. She took his arm at the front of the chapel and they faced the minister to say their vows.

Daniel handed Casey the ring with the emeralds and the diamond. Casey slid it onto Anna's finger and it fit as if made for her by magic.

He leaned and kissed her.

The sea breeze whipped his hair and salt air stung his cheek. He looked down at Anna—

But he no longer stood with Anna. He knew this young woman at once and knew his own identity here as well as where they now stood.

"Prudence," he said, beaming.

"Yes," she said, her face radiant.

"You came back."

"I promised I would, Josiah."

"Have we been apart very long?"

"We've never been apart."

Josiah looked down at his clothing. He wore soaking wet cotton duck. His feet were bare. He remembered pulling his shoes off when he was under water. Then he swam to *Emerald*, and saw Prudence on this ship.

The ghastly *Queen Anne's Revenge*.

"Come," Josiah said. Then he remembered. "But what about your chains?"

"I'm free," Prudence said. "Look." She held up her hands. Her fetters had disappeared. The heirloom emerald ring sparkled again on her finger.

"We're both free," she said and pointed out over the water that separated them from a small wrecked ship. *Emerald*.

They had to flee *Queen Anne's Revenge* before the pirates returned.

They hurried to the railing. He leapt first, hit the water and swam a few feet away. He turned back to look. Prudence waved, and leapt. She splashed into the water not far from him and sank for a few moments. Then she broke the surface.

She tugged her copper hair out of her eyes and splashed him, giggling. They swam toward shore.

They didn't feel tired. The salt didn't sting their eyes.

They enjoyed the cool water and laughed as they swam.

Reaching the shore, they joined hands and ran barefoot across the expanse of sand. They climbed a dune and hid in some beach grass. They watched the pirate ship hoist anchor, raise sail and head out to sea. The sails vanished at the horizon.

"We're free," said Prudence.

"Always," Josiah said. They sat there until they could no longer see the sails of the hideous ship.

When they rose and embraced, they noticed that they wore dry clothing, new outfits that seemed to have been tailored for them.

"Look, Josiah," said Prudence. Behind them stood two gigantic old oak trees, hundreds of years old, gnarled, their branches intertwining. A beautiful, pure light glowed between the trees.

"Papa," said Prudence, smiling at the light.

Josiah took her hand. Their fingers laced together as if they had been holding each other's hand for years.

Josiah gazed at the beautiful girl next to him and found her weeping with happiness. He brushed away her tears. The light flowed around them and enfolded them with joyful warmth as they walked toward the trees.

Josiah knew he would never stop smiling. He turned to embrace—

Anna.

Her beautiful green eyes, moist with tears, looked up at him. He knew in that moment that he was no longer Josiah. He'd again become Casey who had just married Anna.

He hugged her and whispered in her ear, "Did you just Paik me?"

Anna shook her head, "No. I went there too. We just witnessed perfect freedom." She looked down at her finger and the antique diamond-and-emerald ring.

The minister cleared his throat to get their attention. "Congratulations," he said. McKenna and Daniel embraced them, laughing and joyous.

"Free," Casey said to his new wife.

"Always," Anna replied.

Far away, in a beautiful Crystal cave, an old man stirred happily in his sleep.

Elsewhere in the dark uncharted depths of the sea, The Snake opened one eye.

They both knew that the woman's pregnancy would produce a child who would have the Cymreig.

They both had the same thought: *Maybe this time.*

Title: ACID

- Author: Jeff Lovell
- Publisher: TotalRecall Publications, Inc.
- HARD COVER ISBN: 978-1-59095-116-3
- PAPERBACK, ISBN: 978-1-59095-117-0
- Nook, Kindle, ISBN: 978-1-59095-118-7
- Number of pages: 352
- Publication Date: 2013

Rick Howell, living in the shadow of two women who have the power to change reality, must risk his life to stop the genocidal exploits of a desperate lunatic who wants to acquire their powers. The discovery of a mind controlling drug opens a pathway to frightening mental abilities for Rachel Farrell, who can move backward and forward in time at will, while Donna Riske, Rachel's best friend, can control the thoughts of others.

Title: The Coven of the Spring

- Author: Jeff Lovell
- Publisher: TotalRecall Publications, Inc.
- HARD COVER ISBN: 978-1-59095-113-2
- PAPERBACK, ISBN: 978-1-59095-114-9
- Nook, Kindle, ISBN: 978-1-59095-115-6
- Number of pages: 336
- Publication Date: 2013

An ancient secret, with frightening new powers, emerges to terrify and destroy.

Grace DeRosa, a gifted research chemist, lives with her husband Jim and their seventeen year old daughter Crissy. Grace finds a hidden spring in the woods near Salem, Massachusetts. She discovers that the consumed water imparts unique and fearful powers that lead to the ability to read minds, create terrifying mental pictures and force the user's will on others.